A Finely Knit Murder

OTHER SEASIDE KNITTERS MYSTERIES
BY SALLY GOLDENBAUM

Death by Cashmere

Patterns in the Sand

Moon Spinners

A Holiday Yarn

The Wedding Shawl

A Fatal Fleece

Angora Alibi

Murder in Merino

A Finely Knit Murder

A SEASIDE KNITTERS MYSTERY

Sally Goldenbaum

AN OBSIDIAN MYSTERY

OBSIDIAN
Published by the Penguin Group
Penguin Group (USA) LLC, 375 Hudson Street,
New York, New York 10014

USA | Canada | UK | Ireland | Australia | New Zealand | India | South Africa | China
penguin.com
A Penguin Random House Company

First published by Obsidian, an imprint of New American Library,
a division of Penguin Group (USA) LLC

First Printing, May 2015

LIBRARY OF CONGRESS CATALOGING-IN-PUBLICATION DATA:

Goldenbaum, Sally.
A finely knit murder: a seaside knitters mystery / Sally Goldenbaum.
pages cm.—(Seaside knitters mystery; 9)
ISBN 978-0-451-47160-4 (hardback)
I. Title.
PS3557.O35937F56 2015
813'.54—dc23   2014048121

Printed in the United States of America
1   3   5   7   9   10   8   6   4   2

Set in Palatino · Designed by Elke Sigal

For these bright and wonderful lights in my life—
Luke Robert, Ruby Jane, and Dax Morgan McElhenny
Atticus Sage, Julian Presley, and Sebastian Jacob Goldenbaum

Acknowledgments

My thanks to readers everywhere, but especially to those who live on or near Cape Ann and allow me to take such great liberties with the towns and places and establishments that make your homeland so unique and wonderful. Rocky Neck Art Colony, Gloucester's Pleasant Street Tea Shop, the Franklin, Sugar Magnolias, the Good Morning Gloucester blog, Ravenswood Park, Bearskin Neck, Toad Hall, and dozens more have provided inspiration and ideas for the Seaside Knitters Mystery series (as well as being terrific places to eat and visit when the Knitters venture out of Sea Harbor). In *A Finely Knit Murder*, in particular, a wonderful Gloucester school—Eastern Point Day School—provided me with the inspiration I needed to create Gabby's Sea Harbor school. Not only is Eastern Point a magnificent structure, but its teachers provide the very warm, nurturing, challenging, and inspiring environment that Dr. Elizabeth Hartley, headmistress, is striving for in her Sea Harbor Community Day School.

This series would never have seen the light of day without my agents, Christina and Andrea, and all those at the Jane Rotrosen Agency who support each book (and each author) in a myriad of wonderful ways. Thanks to my wise, lovely editor, Sandra Harding, and all those at Obsidian/NAL who gently touch the original manuscript and magically make it so much better.

A special thanks to Acia Morley and Cheri LeBlond, co-owners of Mysteryscape Bookstore in Overland Park, Kansas, whose tireless support of authors is matched only by their devotion to readers.

And my forever thanks to Mary Bednarowski, Sr. Rosemary Flanigan, Nancy Pickard, and Don Goldenbaum, who continue to patiently and graciously brainstorm plots and twists and characters with me.

Cast of Characters

THE SEASIDE KNITTERS

Nell Endicott: Former Boston nonprofit director, lives in Sea Harbor with her husband

Izzy (Isabel Chambers Perry): Boston attorney, now owner of the Seaside Knitting Studio; Nell and Ben Endicott's niece; married to Sam Perry

Cass (Catherine Mary Theresa Halloran): A lobster fisherwoman and lifelong Sea Harbor resident

Birdie (Bernadette Favazza): Sea Harbor's wealthy, wise, and generous silver-haired grand dame

THE MEN IN THEIR LIVES

Ben Endicott: Nell's husband

Sam Perry: Award-winning photojournalist, married to Izzy

Danny Brandley: Mystery novelist and son of bookstore owners

Sonny Favazza and Joseph Marietti: Two of Birdie's deceased husbands

CLOSE FRIENDS AND FAMILY

Andy Risso: Drummer in Pete Halloran's band; son of the Gull Tavern owner, Jake Risso

Christopher and Nick Marietti: Gabby's father and her uncle

Don and Rachel Wooten: Don owns the Ocean's Edge restaurant and Rachel Wooten is the city attorney

Ella and Harold Sampson: Birdie's longtime housekeeper and groundsman/driver

Gabrielle Marietti (Gabby): Birdie's granddaughter

Gracie Santos: Owner of Gracie's Lazy Lobster Café

Jane and Ham Brewster: Artists and cofounders of the Canary Cove Art Colony

Mary Halloran: Pete and Cass's mother; secretary of Our Lady of Safe Seas Church

Pete Halloran: Cass's younger brother and lead guitarist in the Fractured Fish band

Willow Adams: Fiber artist and owner of the Fishtail Gallery; Pete Halloran's girlfriend

TOWNSFOLK

Alphonso Santos: Construction company owner

Annabelle Palazola: Owner of the Sweet Petunia Restaurant; Liz and Stella Palazola's mother

Archie and Harriet Brandley: Owners of the Sea Harbor Bookstore

August (Gus) McClucken: Owner of McClucken's Hardware and Dive Shop

Beatrice Scaglia: Mayor of Sea Harbor

Esther Gibson: Police dispatcher (and Mrs. Santa Claus in season)

Father Lawrence Northcutt: Pastor of Our Lady of Safe Seas Church

Harry and Margaret Garozzo: Owners of Garozzo's Deli

Harry Winthrop: Cottage owner

Janie Levin: Nurse practitioner in the Virgilio Clinic; Tommy Porter's girlfriend

Jerry Thompson: Police chief

Laura Danvers: Young socialite and philanthropist, mother of three, married to banker Elliot Danvers

Liz Palazola Santos: Hostess at the yacht club; married to Alphonso Santos; daughter of Annabelle Palazola

Mae Anderson: Izzy's shop manager; twin teenage nieces, Jillian and Rose

Mary Pisano: Middle-aged newspaper columnist; owner of Ravenswood B&B

Merry Jackson: Owner of the Artist's Palate Bar and Grill; keyboard/singer in the Fractured Fish

Polly Farrell: Owner of Polly's Tea Shoppe

Rebecca Early: Lampworks artist in Canary Cove

Stella Palazola: Realtor in Sea Harbor; Annabelle's daughter

Tommy Porter: Policeman

SEA HARBOR COMMUNITY DAY SCHOOL

Angelo Garozzo: School maintenance manager; brother of Harry Garozzo

Anna Mansfield: Student and daughter of Blythe and Barrett

Barrett Mansfield: School board member and Anna's father

Blythe Westerland: School board member

Bob Chadwick: Blythe's cousin

Chelsey Mansfield: Anna's mother; Barrett's wife

Daisy Danvers: Laura and Elliott Danvers's oldest daughter; Gabby's school friend

Elizabeth Hartley, PhD: Headmistress

Josh Babson: Teacher/artist

Teresa Pisano: School secretary; Mary Pisano's cousin

A Finely Knit Murder

Chapter 1

Monday, early autumn

The glass in the headmistress's door rattled, but it was the chilling echo of footsteps on the polished floors that rattled Dr. Elizabeth Hartley's soul. She stood still at the office door and stared through the reception area and into the round entry hall.

Captain Elijah Westerland, the subject of the school hall's gigantic painting, looked in at her, his bushy eyebrows pulled together, his eyes black and small and piercing. Judging eyes.

What had she done now? This woman who held his beloved home in her hands?

But that was foolish. It was a painting, after all, and the captain had been dead for nearly a hundred years. Moreover, his home was no longer a home, but a wonderful school.

She took a deep breath and tried to shake off the unease. Elizabeth hadn't anticipated the volcanic anger or the teacher's abrupt departure. Maybe the captain hadn't, either. But neither of them should have been surprised. Of course he'd be upset. People didn't like it when you messed with their livelihoods—and Josh Babson was soon to be out of a teaching job in a town with few openings.

But the decision had been taken out of her hands. Josh's recent absences were known to the board, his faint excuses not very credible. And although he had a charming manner, he could be prickly.

Elizabeth had attributed it to his artistry. Weren't artists supposed to be temperamental? The few paintings she had seen of his were lovely, and his students liked him. If only he had toed the line a little more precisely.

She'd tried to reason with him as best she could, hoping to help him see that missing work and confronting board members didn't go over well at Sea Harbor Community Day School. She needed the art teacher to be there when the bell rang, when eager students filed into his classroom. And he was getting better, paying closer attention to the artist's clock that sometimes kept him painting at home after the magnificent girls' school on the hill opened its doors, preparing for a new day.

Josh was getting better . . . but once a few of her board members got involved, it was too late. It wasn't within the purview of her position to rehabilitate the teachers or staff, one had pointed out to her.

Controlling his exit, however, was her job.

And that had gone badly.

On the other side of the administrative suite, the door to a smaller office opened and the assistant headmistress stepped into the reception area. Mandy White stood tall and composed. She glanced at Teresa Pisano, who was shuffling papers behind the reception counter, trying to look busy. "What's going on?"

The school secretary lifted her bleached-blond head and shrugged one shoulder. It was an off-putting mannerism, one Teresa had recently developed.

Mandy looked back at the headmistress, still standing in the doorway. "Do you need help, Elizabeth?" she asked.

Elizabeth met Mandy's look and offered a half smile and a slight shake of her head.

I'm fine, the gesture said. Everything was under control.

Before Mandy could pursue the issue, Elizabeth closed her office door and moved back into the safe shadows of the room.

The elegant office seemed tarnished by the anger and harsh words that had filled it moments before. In spite of the faded drapes and worn Oriental carpet, the room seemed to demand quiet and respect, intelligent conversation. Not the hand waving that had scattered the paperwork she had carefully put together to document her decision.

Elizabeth looked down at her computer and checked the next appointment. Ten minutes to collect herself.

And it was just the beginning of the week. If she had had her way, she would have waited until Friday to talk to Josh. Then he would have had the weekend to come to grips with being fired, and he could have come back on Monday to finish up the remaining week in the quarter. Then depart from his students gracefully. She had suggested he tell the students he was moving on to other opportunities. He was talented, she said to him. He shouldn't forget that. There was a life beyond teaching. And she would help him in any way she could.

Sea Harbor was a small town; she owed him some support.

But her plan to wait until Friday was thwarted by the planned Tuesday board meeting, and Elizabeth was asked to tie up this loose end so she could report on it at the monthly meeting the next evening.

Tie up this loose end . . .

Was that what she had done?

Or had she created another loose end, a life left frayed and dangling?

Elizabeth set her glasses on the desk, rubbed her temples, and walked over to the lead glass windows fronting the school. The view beyond the windows was a tonic. She would have given up the ornate desk and elegant bookshelves in a heartbeat. But the view? That she would never give up.

From the day she had arrived in Sea Harbor, the magnificent seaside had soothed her, helped her acclimate to the new headmistress position, helped her through rough days of budget negotiations, decisions to reduce staff and adjust protocols, and dealing with student problems and board disagreements.

She pushed away the sliver of fear that had come with the slamming of the door. The parents and board didn't think of her as fearful. *Audacious. Brave. Intrepid.* Those were the words some of them used—although she sometimes had to stop herself from saying, "No—that's not me. Not really." Fear wasn't a stranger to Dr. Elizabeth Hartley, and it often surrounded the tough decisions she had to make. She was good at this job. Very good.

Her heartbeat slowed as she pushed the heavy windows open and welcomed in the salty breeze. It lifted strands of brown hair from her forehead, cooling her flushed skin.

Just a short distance below the windows, tiers of stone terraces gradually gave way to a wide lawn that rolled down to the sea, its expanse broken only by the granite boulders that seemed to have been tossed haphazardly about the property by some giant prehistoric claw. Beyond the lawn was a narrow road, nearly empty at this time of day save for a jogger or two and an old man walking his dog. And across from it was the old boathouse wedged in among the giant boulders, once filled with the Westerlands' oceangoing sailing vessels, canoes, and motorboats. Another thing on her to-do list. Tear it down? Fix it up? Turn it into a little theater or art studio as students and teachers had suggested?

The thought pushed Josh Babson back into her head. Although the run-down boathouse was used mostly to store odds and ends, there were reports that some—Josh Babson and others—had sometimes used it as a personal hideout to rendezvous with a beer or a woman or a joint.

Or so the rumors went.

But even the boathouse was a part of the view she loved, its history and gray weathered sides merging into the color of the sea.

The view continued on forever, across the boulders, over whitecapped waves—until finally it touched the sky and melted into one single masterpiece.

Peace. She had found it here.

And she would protect it with her life.

. . .

Just a floor below, mixing in with the familiar odors of a science lab and cleaning supplies, the lilting voice of a recently enrolled student filled the wide hallway.

"Angelo, my Angelo—"

The singsong words hung in the dusty air like a hummingbird, fluttering lightly.

Angelo Garozzo looked up from his desk as the long-legged girl with the infectious voice filled the doorframe of his office.

"What was your mom thinking to give you that name?" Gabrielle Marietti asked, a frown teasing the man behind the desk. "Angel? I mean, seriously?"

"Humph." Angelo sneezed. His rimless glasses slipped down to the ball that formed the end of his nose.

Gabby leaned her head to one side, an uncontrolled mass of thick hair falling across her cheek. "But maybe it fits. You're sort of an angel to me. My nonna thinks so, anyway. Even though you're wicked cranky sometimes. I probably should have been more discriminating when I put in my order for a guardian angel."

Angelo laughed at that, his head pressing back into his high-backed chair. Then he leaned forward and glared at his visitor. "Don't you know New Yorkers don't get to use the word *wicked*? You trying to fit in here or somethin'?"

Gabby loved Angelo's accent, the absence of *r*'s. Sometimes she tried to think of questions for Angelo that would require only *r* word answers. "I went to a Sox game with Sam and Ben last weekend," she said, walking into the small room. A slice of sunshine fell from the high casement windows onto her blue-black hair. "So that counts for something, right?"

She brushed a layer of dust from a folding chair and sat down. The small room was crowded with manuals and tools, shoved onto shelves that lined one wall. A single filing cabinet stood beside Angelo's metal desk, a small table holding a coffeepot and lunch box against another wall. The only other furniture were Angelo's high-backed office chair, a heavy table with a printer on it, and a few folding chairs.

But the bright posters lining one gray wall made the office wonderful in Gabby's mind. Broadway shows performed at the local high school, Sea Harbor Community Day School productions, shows performed in a small theater over in Gloucester. Angelo himself had sung a tune or two in his day, he confessed to Gabby one time.

But no matter, he loved them all, and donated generously to keep their doors open.

And Gabby loved that he loved them.

"Whattaya doin' down here, anyway?" Angelo growled. "Shouldn't you be in class somewhere, learning how to behave like a lady?" He waved one fist in the air as he talked, his bushy eyebrows tugging together until they almost touched—a white caterpillar shadowing piercing eyes.

Gabby grinned and flapped a folder in the air. "I'm Miss Patterson's errand girl. I was about to fall asleep in her history class and she took pity on me."

Angelo tsked and shook his head. "You watchit, Marietti. Your nonna holds me responsible for you, God knows why. You get yourself booted out of here and it's all on poor Angelo."

His words were soft, his gruff expression fading into a lopsided smile. He picked up an envelope from the corner of his desk, half rose, and shoved it toward her. "Might as well give you an excuse for coming down here. This gets put directly into Dr. Hartley's hands. And don't lose it, you hear me talkin' to you?"

Gabrielle shoved it under her arm. "Do you doubt me for a second? Of course I'll do your bidding, fair Angelo. Your wish is my command." She stood and bowed elaborately, her arms stretching out and knocking a stack of papers off his desk.

"Outta here, pest." Angelo shooed her off with a wave of his hand.

Truth be told, he loved Gabby Marietti's detours to his office. He loved her sass and her smile. She'd come late to Sea Harbor Community Day School, missing the first few weeks of the quarter after moving up from New York. But no one would have known she was a newbie. In the brief time she'd been there, Gabby had made a place for herself, brought sunshine into the cavernous mansion that housed the old school. Or at least into the office of the chief maintenance engineer, as the black-and-white sign on his door so presumptuously declared. Sunshine was good.

Gabby scooped up the papers and set them back on his desk. She wrinkled her nose at him, the freckles dancing on her fine-boned face. And then as quickly as she'd come, she spun around, arms and legs flying, and disappeared from Angelo's view as she raced down the hall toward the staircase.

The urgent sound of boots on the hardwood stopped Gabby in her tracks just before she reached the bottom step.

"No running in the halls," she imagined the person saying to her. "Decorum, my dear."

But the sound on the steps was loud in the quiet hall, ominous, certainly not an administrator checking lockers or taking someone on a tour—and Gabby instinctively stepped back into the shadow near a utility closet.

The familiar figure that came barreling down the steps was mumbling fiercely, the sound pushing Gabby deeper into the shadows. She wanted to be invisible.

Mostly she didn't want to embarrass Mr. Babson, the slender teacher who was teaching her to paint en plein air and never once considered her ramshackle watercolor of the old boathouse something that belonged in MOBA. Surely it would embarrass him to know a student was privy to the string of obscenities that filled the dusty basement air. Some of the words were ones Gabby had never heard before, even when she hung out at the fishermen's dock, helping Cass and Pete Halloran repair lobster traps. These were unfamiliar, and seemed out of place coming from the mouth of the teacher.

Gabby backed up until she could feel the ridge of the firebox between her shoulder blades, dust motes filling the air in front of her. A sneeze was threatening to break her silence. She pressed one hand over her mouth, the other clutching the papers she was supposed to be delivering. One second before the tickle became utterly painful, Mr. Babson disappeared into the downstairs teachers' lounge, his strangely animated voice trailing after him. Words like *hussy* and *revenge* were mixed in with the curses, until the door finally banged shut behind him, filling the hall with silence.

Gabby released a sigh of relief, pitying the final hour's art class, who would have to face the angry teacher. It wouldn't be pretty.

With a sudden desire to return as quickly as possible to the safety of her class and the trials of colonization, she raced up the steps to drop off the envelopes, pausing more briefly than she usually did in the lobby.

She always skidded to a stop here—even if she only had a minute—planting her feet on the striped hardwood surface and tilting her head back. The portrait demanded it. There was something about the austere expression on the man's face that froze Gabby in her tracks. He'd had something like nine sons, her nonna had said. And they all lived in this house. She gave him her brightest smile. She'd crack that facade. Someday he'd smile back, she told herself.

Sure he would.

And then she rushed into the office suite, startling the secretary to attention.

"Gabrielle, where is the fire?" Teresa leaned over the tall counter and peered at the student, her long face somber.

"Delivering papers to Dr. Hartley."

"I'll take them," Teresa said, reaching out her hand.

Gabby stared at her arm. It was thin, with knobs at her wrist. The kids talked about the secretary sometimes, but Gabby worried about her. She was so skinny, and had recently done something terrible to her light brown hair. It was a dull blond color and seemed to move in odd directions. Maybe it was just a wig, Gabby thought, somehow relieved at the idea.

"It's okay, I told Angelo I'd deliver them—"

"And so you have. To me. You're two seconds too late to see Dr. Hartley. An important board member beat you to it." Teresa reached across the counter and took the papers from Gabby's hand. "Now, off with you, back to class, missy," she said, and motioned toward the door.

Gabby turned back just once. Just long enough to see the back of a woman with platinum hair, standing perfectly still on the other side of the headmistress's glass door.

Teresa had turned and was looking at her, too, in an admiring way as if she wished her bleached blond hair didn't frizzle around her face, but floated back smooth and perfect, every hair in place.

For a second Gabby thought the woman beyond the door was a mannequin, but just then Teresa Pisano turned back in her direction, and her glare prevented Gabby from finding out. She hurried down the hallway to learn more about the founding fathers.

"It's beautiful, isn't it?"

The voice came from behind her, scattering Elizabeth Hartley's thoughts. She hadn't heard the door open. For a brief moment her heart skipped a beat.

How long had she been standing there, watching her from the back, reading her thoughts?

Blythe Westerland never made a sound when she entered a room—and she rarely knocked. "It's a finishing school walk," Birdie Favazza said after a recent board meeting. "One can imagine her with a book on her head, gliding effortlessly and silently on those long, well-exercised legs."

Elizabeth turned toward the familiar voice. It matched Blythe's hair and body perfectly—liquid and smooth. The board member was beautiful in that perfect way magazines managed to accomplish with Photoshop techniques, but in her case, it was real, at least mostly. A few years older than Elizabeth, Blythe always managed to dredge up the same insecurities she had spent her teenage years running from—those years when she watched from the sidelines as others were caught up in social whirlwinds and laughter and fun. The years when she was praised by her teachers for being bright and articulate, when she'd won one academic award after another—but spent most weekends alone in her room with her books and her dog.

But it was different now, she reminded herself. She'd accomplished much since those painful teenage years; even allowing the memory back embarrassed her. It had no place in this office.

She took a deep breath and met Blythe's eyes. "Have I forgotten a meeting with you?"

Beneath the open windows a riding mower started up, pushing the sounds of the sea into the background.

Blythe didn't answer. Instead she walked over and stood next to Elizabeth, resting her long fingers on the sill. Her chest rose as she breathed in the air. "It's truly an incredible view. I never tire of it."

Elizabeth nodded, waiting.

"We used to have our May Day dance right over there, in the middle of that lawn," Blythe said.

Elizabeth watched the memories play across Blythe's face as she looked through the window. The board member was being transported back to a sunny day when the Sea Harbor school was truly a country day school, catering to old New England families. Days when the school's greenhouse was a stable with horses bridled and ready, when limousines climbed the long, hilly drive at the end of a school day to pick up their charges.

May Day. Elizabeth had seen the photographs, some of them framed in the library and in the glass cases outside the auditorium. The Maypole strung with colorful silken ribbons, the girls in white dresses, each one clutching the end of a streamer as she whirled and twirled around on the pole. The beautiful young women surrounding the queen. And surely Blythe would have been one of those queens.

Over the years the May Day practice had become frayed around the edges, just like the school. Other private New England schools had eclipsed Sea Harbor in desirability for the wealthy, and May Day seemed to have diminished in stature, too. It seemed less appropriate, less an event, until Elizabeth had stopped it completely her first year as headmistress. The move didn't settle easily with some of the parents and board members. But in light of declining enrollment and the expense of the ritual, it seemed out of place, elitist, even in its pared-down state. Elizabeth knew the money would be better spent on scholarships and to repair the roof and choir risers. It no longer fit into her vision of Sea Harbor Community Day School.

Today, along with the nation's flag, colorful flaps of sailcloth hung from the top of the metal pole—one a school banner that an art student had designed; another, a Boston Strong flag the students themselves had made in memory of that April marathon day they would never forget.

"Who is that?" Blythe said, pointing to a figure moving across the bucolic scene.

Elizabeth looked down at the flagstone path. It circled the mansion and then serpentined down the lawn toward the flagpole.

The question was rhetorical. Blythe was aware of who it was— and why the man was moving resolutely across the grass, his head held high, tousled hair flying every which way and a lumpy backpack strapped between his shoulders. And she probably knew how angry he was, too. Her voice had been the strongest in determining the teacher's fate. Her determination to have him fired was unusually intense.

Elizabeth watched him casually at first, wondering if someone was taking over his class. Then she looked more closely. Something wasn't normal about the way he was walking. She pressed her palms down on the window frame and leaned forward, shading her eyes. The man's left arm was picking up speed, moving wildly, rotating like a Gloucester wind turbine. At first Elizabeth thought he was waving to someone she couldn't see, perhaps the old man on the lawn mower.

And then the surface of the lawn around him began to change, like a black-and-white film gradually taking on a wash of bright color.

Slowly, deliberately, the well-tended grass became a painting in progress as angry swaths of reckless, canary yellow circles appeared across the grass.

The color of crime scene tape—ugly and intrusive and announcing something evil.

Elizabeth's breath balled up in her chest as she watched the drama unfolding on the lawn. It wasn't so terrible, what he was doing. He was angry, that was all.

What was terrible was having Blythe Westerland standing next to her, watching it.

Then suddenly, as if the music had stopped, the man turned slowly and looked up at the two women, as if he knew they were standing at the windows watching him.

Elizabeth watched carefully, feeling no anger or fear; all she felt was sadness at disrupting a life. She forced a neutral look to her face and started to raise her hand. To do what? To wave at him? To invite him back?

The tall man continued to look, to stare at them, his body perfectly still. She moved slightly, the shadow of the blinds partially blocking her. She watched him with a strange sense of unrest, as if she were listening in on a private conversation. She looked away, concentrating on a spray of paint soaking into the grass.

And then she stared at it again, the random wash of color suddenly transforming into something else. There, in the middle of one of the fuzzy yellow circles, was a stick drawing of a woman, a triangle skirt giving nod to her sex. Slashing through the figure was a straight line—a street sign: NO LEFT TURN. NO TRUCKS ALLOWED. No women . . . No woman . . .

Elizabeth looked at Blythe. Her profile was calm, and little emotion marred her perfect skin. The same half smile, lips just slightly parted, was set in place.

Finally the artist waved, as if happily leaving a festive event. In the next minute he turned and walked resolutely across the lawn toward the old boathouse.

"That's unfortunate," Blythe said quietly.

Elizabeth turned away and walked back to her desk. "Dismissing staff is always unfortunate."

"The dismissal was necessary. I meant his reaction to it."

Elizabeth knew what she meant. She meant the dismissal must have been handled poorly to generate such a reaction. It meant Elizabeth had failed.

"It's unfortunate he was hired in the first place, Elizabeth."

That was the rationale Blythe had brought to the board. He was clearly unsuitable. One had to be careful when hiring artists.

And having a beer down by the dock while he helped Ira Staab paint the school's old boathouse didn't help his case. It didn't matter that it was after the students had gone home. He was on the payroll, Blythe said.

He'd left work early several times, she'd noted. And had spent way too much time at the Artist's Palate Bar over near Canary Cove, no matter that it was on his own time, his own dollar.

Elizabeth knew those things. She had talked with the teacher about mannerisms, school rules, the importance of schedules. She'd been making progress, she thought.

Until she wasn't, because the board had decided differently.

"And also unfortunate that the way he was fired somehow stripped him of his dignity. That's a shame."

Elizabeth chose not to answer. Instead she glanced at the grandfather clock and sat down behind her desk. "I don't mean to rush you, Blythe, but I have an appointment shortly. Is there something you wanted?"

"You're meeting with Chelsey Mansfield."

It wasn't a question.

Elizabeth frowned, wondering when her calendar had become public knowledge. She glanced through the door at Teresa Pisano. Recently the school secretary had become friendly with Blythe Westerland. It was an odd kind of friendship, more an admiration on Teresa's part. Someone had brought it to Elizabeth's attention that Teresa had recently bleached her brown hair and begun straightening it into what vaguely resembled Blythe's perfect bob.

Blythe seemed to like the admiration, even bringing the secretary flowers one day.

Elizabeth pushed away the thoughts that began to crowd her judgment. She put her glasses back on and picked up the Mansfield file. It was a simple progress report on the student, Anna Mansfield, a ten-year-old whom Elizabeth had known for a long time. It was a *good* report. Diagnosed with sensory processing disorder, Anna was sometimes challenged by school and the social world that came with it. But Elizabeth knew that in the right environment and with teachers to help, the student would thrive. And that's exactly what was happening, as slowly but surely Anna was meeting all the goals her teachers had set for her. She was also proving what Elizabeth suspected to be true, that Anna was probably more intellectually gifted than many of her peers. She just needed a little extra help sorting through the stimuli that made up life. And the other students in the school would only benefit from learning that they weren't all cut from the same mold.

That was exactly the kind of environment Elizabeth Hartley was creating. And meeting with the child's mother was the kind of meeting she'd like to have every day—a good student report handed over to a very interested, loving parent.

But of what interest was the meeting to Blythe?

Before she could ask, Blythe stood and brushed an imaginary fleck of dust from her white skirt.

"Actually I came in today to give you support when you met with Josh Babson. To make sure the firing went smoothly."

Elizabeth frowned. If she hadn't changed the time of the appointment at the last minute, moving it up an hour, Blythe would have arrived at her door at the same moment Josh did.

"It seems I was too late," Blythe continued. She offered a sad smile and added, "That's a shame, but what's done is done."

Elizabeth looked down at her desk, collecting herself and holding back words that she knew she would regret if they escaped. She would be gracious. Blythe was a board member, a school benefactor—and related to the man who had donated the building and grounds. Finally Elizabeth looked up. "While I appreciate your offer to help, the board hired me to run this school. It's what I am trained to do. And for better or worse, I cherish this job, *all* of it, even the difficult parts. You and the other board members are wonderfully supportive. But I know you can appreciate that some of the responsibilities are ones I need to handle alone. Especially ones like this. My faculty deserves that kind of respect and privacy."

Blythe picked up her bag and slipped it over her shoulder. Finally, as if Elizabeth hadn't spoken, she smiled and looked at her watch.

"I have a meeting with the women's philanthropic league and a tennis lesson after that. A dinner date in Boston. I need to be on my way." She glanced down at the Mansfield folder. "But please be aware that the Mansfield child does not belong in my—in this school. Keeping her here is terribly unfair to the other students. Not only that, you are doing the child and her parents a huge disservice."

Before Elizabeth could respond, Blythe was gone, a cat in the darkening afternoon. She slowed down for a minute at Teresa Pisano's desk, where she lightly touched the secretary's shoulder and then disappeared through the main school doors.

Chapter 2

"Sea Harbor Community Day School has a fascinating history, my dear," Birdie Favazza said. "And I have it on good authority that you are making it even more fascinating."

Birdie and Gabby sat side by side on the dock just outside Gracie's Lazy Lobster Café, their legs hanging over the edge, shoulders just touching. One body was so filled with youth that it electrified the air around her. The other—her face a deeply lined map of wisdom and grace and kindness—was filled with the vigor of a long life well lived.

Behind the unlikely pair, sitting on the café's outdoor bench, Nell Endicott could feel the joy that filled her friend Birdie's voice. The words were drowned out by the sounds of the harbor—fishing boats coming in for the day, pleasure boats making their way to freshly painted slips, shouts of fishermen and tourists.

"Nick Marietti was a wise man," Ben said. He sat down next to his wife and stretched his legs out in front of him, tilting his head back to catch the day's fading rays.

Nell agreed. Birdie's brother-in-law was definitely that—and Ben was a mind reader, knowing exactly what she was thinking as she watched Birdie and Gabby. Nick Marietti was the mastermind behind the plan to bring Gabby to Sea Harbor to attend school while her father was away. A far better arrangement than living with a nanny and servants in Christopher Marietti's New York penthouse. As Christopher himself admitted to his uncle, "Birdie Favazza will be the teacher. Gabby the winner."

"What's up?" Sam Perry strode down the pier pushing a stroller. He came to a stop in front of Ben and pressed one foot against the baby carriage lock.

Izzy walked around him and gave Nell and Ben hugs.

"We're starving," Sam said. "Isn't that the plan here? What's with the sunbathing?"

Gabby pivoted around at the sound of their voices. In the next instant she was off the dock floor and rushing toward the stroller. She crouched down and began coaxing contagious giggles out of a lively Abigail.

"Gee-Gee," the baby cooed, and Gabby melted right there on the cement dock. Being one of Abby's first words was a huge lottery win in Gabby's eleven-year-old mind.

"They're clearing us a table in the back," Nell said.

As if on cue, Gracie Santos appeared at the door flapping menus in the air. "Your table is cleared and a basket of the world's best calamari is waiting for you. Cass is already in there, so you better hurry if you want any food."

The café owner helped Birdie to her feet before giving hugs all around. Then she held the door open and ushered them into the narrow restaurant.

"Gabby, I hear you're going to my alma mater," she said over her shoulder.

"It's a great school, Gracie. Did you like it there?"

"No." Gracie laughed. "It was too stuffy back then. I wanted to be in the public school with my friend Cass, but my uncle wouldn't hear of it. Santos women went to Sea Harbor Community Day School, he said. So I did."

"The real story, Gabby, is that Cass and Gracie were free spirits," Izzy said. "Not easily controlled."

Gracie laughed. "Well, yes, maybe. But I survived."

"The school is changing. Its focus is different now," Birdie said.

"That's what I hear. I'm glad. Though many of the girls loved it. I was the odd man out."

"The world changes," Birdie said. "Sometimes institutions need to change, too."

Gracie agreed and led them through the restaurant, manipulating the stroller as they made their way to the back of the narrow restaurant. They were all Lazy Lobster VIPs as far as Gracie was concerned and she insisted on treating them that way. If Nell, Birdie, Izzy, and Cass—and any men they could recruit into helping—hadn't spent a large part of one summer painting and sanding and transforming the old fish shack into a clean, bright café, it wouldn't have existed. Plain and simple.

Gracie's place was small and comfortable, the interior filled with wooden tables and chairs, and softened by the woven fiber art of Willow Adams that hung above the fireplace. The seascape, created from knotted yarn in blues and greens and lavender, was made especially for the Lazy Lobster. It swooped and curved against the brick wall, a splash of ocean right there in the restaurant. But what set the small café apart from the T-shirt and bait shops nearby were the tantalizing odors of seafood, lemon butter, and fresh herbs that spilled out into the ocean air. And on Monday nights, especially, the place hummed with a generous cross section of Sea Harbor residents, young and old, all craving Gracie's Monday night family special.

Cass Halloran was standing near a table, her cell phone pressed to one ear. She waved at them and mouthed a hello, then took a step away to finish her call.

Just beyond their table, double doors opened to a small deck that hung directly over the water—the spot where Pete Halloran, Merry Jackson, and drummer Andy Risso were warming up for their version of Monday night karaoke.

Ben pulled out chairs for Birdie and Nell and looked over their heads, waving at familiar faces, mouthing hellos. Nearly every table was full tonight, and Ben knew most of the diners. Practically everyone in Sea Harbor had depended on Ben Endicott for something, sometime, somewhere. Wills, estates, business negotiations. Folks teased him that his retirement to the seaside community had been a simple transition from wearing suits to shorts and tees—not much else changed.

He waved and nodded to a friend a few tables over and sat down next to Nell.

"It's good to see the chief getting out some."

Nell followed his look and smiled. "Well, now. That's good to see."

"You two kids," Izzy teased. "Matchmakers."

Nell laughed. "Sometimes the stars align themselves. Serendipity. We were helping Elizabeth move into that little house she bought on the end of our street a few weeks ago and decided to go to the yacht club for the buffet afterward. Jerry was there, so we invited him to sit with us. He's alone too much—and he and Elizabeth seemed to find a million things in common. Jerry laughed a lot and seemed to enjoy himself enormously. Elizabeth told me later that she never dated much. She was always busy—studying, working on her doctorate, taking on extra jobs to make ends meet. And when she did go out, men didn't seem terribly interested in her."

"But Jerry thinks she's fascinating, and the age difference doesn't seem relevant at all," Ben said. "I guess that's one of those things you can't explain."

"They were completely comfortable together, that's for sure," Nell said.

"Jerry doesn't always find himself at ease with women, maybe because he's been fixed up relentlessly since his wife died. He resists it. This wasn't like that. They were more like old friends, sharing lives."

"Good for them, I say," said Birdie. "Police chiefs need to relax as much as the next person."

Izzy lifted Abby from her stroller and placed her in Nell's outstretched arms. "So . . . are they, well, a couple?"

Sam pulled out a chair for his wife. "Does it matter? They're enjoying each other."

Gabby craned her neck to see who they were talking about, her gaze settling in on her school's headmistress. "You're talking about Dr. Hartley and Chief Thompson." The thought seemed to excite her. She set her lemonade down and, without waiting for an answer, said with some authority, "It's an April-December romance."

"What?" Birdie said.

"That's what the kids call it, Nonna."

"Well, those are both fine months."

"The kids talk about the headmistress dating?" Izzy asked.

Gabby nodded and transferred a tower of calamari from the basket to her plate. She licked her fingers. "It's okay, though. My friend Daisy says the rule of thumb is to never date anyone under half your age plus seven."

"Whose thumb is that? I wonder," Ben said.

"Maybe this is one of those things that doesn't need rules," Nell said. "Besides, no one in Sea Harbor would care if the rule was broken. Jerry is a remarkable man."

Gabby agreed. "And she's cool."

Izzy remained quiet. Her advanced knitters class at the shop had brought up the subject of the chief and the headmistress last week. There had been way too much talk, such as, "What is the woman thinking? He could be her father."

"But rule or no rule, it doesn't matter," Gabby continued, "because if there is a rule, it's not broken. Daisy checked it out. Dr. Hartley is thirty-nine and Chief Thompson is sixty-two. So she's safe, see? Barely, but it still counts."

Cass walked back to the table and caught the end of the conversation. She pulled out a chair next to Gabby. "How do you know all that, hotshot? It makes me wonder what else you know." She motioned for the calamari basket to be passed her way and lightly tugged on a single dark braid falling down between Gabby's shoulders.

Gabby grinned. "I'll never tell. But you better watch your back, Cass. Daisy Danvers can find anything on the Internet. Anything."

Cass slipped off her Halloran Lobster Company cap. "Anything? Okay, consider me warned."

"Like I bet if she were here right now she'd be able to find out who you were talking to on the phone." Gabby lifted her eyebrows and grinned.

Izzy and Nell looked up. Gabby's lack of restraint was refreshing sometimes—and often helpful when they didn't want to ask the question themselves.

But Cass didn't bite. She smiled mysteriously at Gabby. "That's for me to know—and you and cybersleuth Daisy to find out."

The waitress appeared with a pitcher of beer, a menu, and a warmed bottle for Abigail. Without glancing at the menu, Ben and Sam ordered up enough fish tacos, lobster rolls, and sweet potato fries to feed the whole restaurant.

Nell turned toward Birdie and nodded in the direction of the police chief. "Jerry might look relaxed, but Elizabeth looks like the weight of the world is on her shoulders."

"It was a crazy day at school," Gabby said.

Nell had forgotten the acute hearing of preadolescents. Gabby didn't miss a thing.

Gabby continued, telling them about watching the art teacher from the shadows of the lower hall. "I'm pretty sure he came from Dr. Hartley's office—and he wasn't a happy dude."

Birdie looked concerned but tried to cover it over. "Being a headmistress is a difficult job—"

A wave from across the room caught Gabby's attention, and the incident was left lingering on the table as she excused herself and scooted off to greet a classmate.

Birdie waited a moment and then continued, bringing Ben into the conversation. "Something else happened at the school today." She described the painted circles on the lawn that she and Harold, her driver, had spotted when they picked Gabby up that afternoon.

"I phoned Angelo to see what he knew about it, but he wasn't very forthcoming. 'Just a prank,' was how he put it. But there was something in his voice that said it was more than that."

"Angelo is protective of the school. He probably didn't want news of anything out of the ordinary leaving the school grounds," Ben said.

"But it will," Sam said. "News like that travels fast. I was doing a photo shoot down at the boulders and saw the paint, too. My first thought was some art students were painting outside and got carried away, but when I looked through the lens, it looked more like some crazy crop circles."

"So you immediately went over to take pictures," Izzy said, knowing how few things escaped her husband's lens.

Sam laughed. "Okay, sure. I thought about it. But when I got a little closer I saw Elizabeth walking out and motioning to Ira Staab, the old lawn guy. She had her phone out and it looked like she was taking pictures of the paint job. She seemed to focus in on one of the circles. Then she stopped, said a few words to Ira—and in the next few minutes that stretch of lawn was getting a buzz cut like you wouldn't believe."

"It's not wonderful timing, considering the fund-raising gala coming up this weekend," Nell said. "But I suppose kids will be kids."

"You think students did it?" Ben asked.

Nell thought about that for a minute. "I guess . . . I assumed . . ."

"Sure it was the kids," Cass said. "Budding artists showing a little spunk. Sam's first guess was probably what happened."

Izzy looked at her sideways. "Don't even start on Cass Halloran school pranks."

"Well, whatever happened, no doubt we'll hear about it at the board meeting tomorrow," Birdie said.

"Especially if it reflects poorly on Elizabeth," Nell added. "A few members seem to enjoy bringing things like that up. The meddling and criticism can't be easy on her."

"Nell and I are excluded from those who meddle, of course," Birdie said.

"Of course." Ben laughed.

"My money says you're talking about Blythe Westerland," Izzy said.

Nell nodded. She looked over toward the bar where Blythe stood, tall and elegant, talking with Don and Rachel Wooten.

"Do you know she's five years older than I am?"

Sam looked at her. "Okay, Cass," he said carefully. "That clearly requires a response, but I'm not sure what it should be."

Cass slapped his hand and pulled the basket of calamari out of his reach. "She is well kept, as Gramma Halloran used to say. That's all I'm saying. Perfect skin. Perfect figure. Perfect everything. Ageless. But I suppose you could comment on my natural, outdoorsy good looks, Sam? Far more appealing to the masses, right?"

"Far more," Sam said dutifully.

"I get what Cass is saying. Her hair is never messed up," Izzy said. "And she came into the shop the other day after a tennis lesson. A tennis lesson—the kind that leaves sweaty half-moons on my shirt and my hair a tangled mess. Not Blythe. She's picture-perfect. White tennis outfit pressed and pristine." Izzy pushed back in her chair as the waitress filled the table with platters of lobster rolls and fish tacos.

"It helps to live a pampered existence," Cass said. "A quarterly visit to Canyon Ranch would take these wrinkles out of my face, too, I suppose."

"Catherine, you're beautiful," Birdie said. "And if that delightful mop of yours was constrained and perfect, it wouldn't have nearly the character it has."

They all laughed. Cass *was* attractive. And outdoorsy. And even elegant, if she wanted to be, although it didn't happen often. Running a lobster fishing business didn't lend itself to designer clothes.

"Sorry for the attack. I simply don't like the woman, and the fact that she's perfect doesn't help."

And they all knew why. Although Blythe had been spending most of her time in Sea Harbor recently, she had come and gone over the years, usually leaving her mark. The summer Danny Brandley came back to town on an investigative reporting job, Blythe had targeted the unassuming then-journalist as an amusing diversion. Danny had never been forthcoming about Blythe's advances toward him, but his friends were less inclined to be quiet about it and they often teased about how the shy guy with the glasses and huge intellect was stalked by the most beautiful woman in town.

And completely ignored her.

"I had a job to do that summer," was all he'd say. "She wasn't it."

It always brought a laugh, except to Cass. The talk diminished when Blythe began spending more time in Boston than the Sea Harbor, except for the many committees she seemed to frequent, most especially the board of her alma mater, Sea Harbor Community Day School.

But Blythe was now back.

"She's been a regular in the shop. I think she's settling in a bit," Izzy said.

Cass lifted one eyebrow. "At least she has good taste."

"In men?" Izzy asked.

"In yarn shops," Cass said sharply.

"That she does. She loves beautiful yarns—sea silk, cashmere. The other day she stuck around and joined Laura Danvers and a couple of her friends who have kids at Sea Harbor Community Day."

"That must have been an interesting conversation," Birdie said. Her frown explained her words.

"You're right. She listened quietly for a while to PTO talk, our knitting project at the school, various teachers—but before long she casually brought up her displeasure with some of the things happening under Dr. Hartley's administration. It's all said with great gentility, though. She criticizes people in the nicest way. Sometimes you're not even sure it's a jab until you think about it later."

"It's an art," Nell said.

"Right. All done with a lovely smile."

"Why does she care so much about the school?" Cass asked. "She seems to have the world on a string. You'd think she'd have better things to do than bad-mouth the headmistress of a girls' school."

"I can understand why it might be," Birdie said. "She's a great-granddaughter of the captain who originally owned the mansion and a host of other properties. The Westerlands were well known. She has a certain proprietary feeling, I suppose."

"She called the school a safe haven—she loved it. It was home to her," Izzy said.

"There's something sad about that," Nell said. "It makes one wonder about her real home."

Birdie agreed. "But no matter what the reasons are, Blythe takes a very active interest in how the school is run."

"True. And Dr. Hartley wasn't her choice for the headmistress position. She had a cousin or someone she thought would be good for the job. I suspect Blythe is used to getting her way. There was a fuss at the board meetings when it came time for the final selection, and she's never quite forgiven Barrett Mansfield for winning the battle. Or at least that's what I remember." Nell handed Abby a cracker. The toddler immediately sent crumbs flying across the table, which brought an affectionate smile from her great-aunt.

"Blythe is a little like her grandfather. Clarence Westerland, Captain Elijah's son, was on that school's board with my Sonny a million years ago," Birdie said. "Clarence was from the old school and quite contentious. All those Westerland men were. Stuffy and pretentious—that's what Sonny thought about them. Clarence was used to getting his way and he couldn't stand women being on the board, or—for that matter—he couldn't see women doing anything productive other than being in the classroom and having babies, that sort of thing. Men ruled, women obeyed, he seemed to think."

"We know better," Cass said.

Sam humphed.

Nell looked again at Elizabeth sitting with the chief of police. The headmistress was attractive, although in such an understated way she was probably not often described in that manner. Her short brown hair curled softly at the neckline. The cut was efficient, practical, but refusing to be totally ordinary by the soft waves that framed her face and the fact that she didn't seem to have total control over its direction. High cheekbones and intelligent brown eyes gave definition to an otherwise pleasant but ordinary face.

Birdie looked over. "I imagine there are days when Elizabeth would like nothing better than to take two aspirin and go to bed. Today was probably one of them."

"I suspect Jerry Thompson can handle headache duties better than Walgreens," Ben said. "He's more relaxed than I've seen him in a long time."

"Well, let's hope so."

They watched Jerry stand and pull out Elizabeth's chair. She slipped on a sweater and aimed a grateful smile at Jerry. He wrapped one arm around her shoulders as if warding off worries, and led her toward the door.

"An odd couple," Birdie mused. "But both seem completely comfortable with each other."

Blythe Westerland spotted the couple from the bar and walked their way, approaching them just before they reached the door. With a gracious smile and words that no one at the Endicott table could hear, Blythe spoke to the couple, shaking the chief's hand as one would a friend, then turning an equally gracious smile on Elizabeth.

But it was Elizabeth's expression that left a lasting impression on Nell. A weary day seemed to have whipped away the headmistress's defenses, and without a word she stared at Blythe, then turned her back on the board member, tucked her arm in Jerry's, and hurried out of the restaurant.

Blythe stood back and watched them walk away, then turned and walked back to the bar.

Nell turned back to the table, feeling as though she had intruded on a private moment. She knew that the two women weren't friends, but it was the first time she had seen Elizabeth Hartley let her guard down. She had always maintained a gracious facade, even when Nell knew she wasn't feeling that way inside.

Blythe Westerland seemed to have worn it down. And she appeared pleased with herself for having done so.

On the deck, Pete Halloran picked up his guitar, and soon his mellow baritone began singing an old Journey tune. Merry Jackson, the Fractured Fish keyboardist, sang along, her voice blending with Pete's, as Andy Risso moved his feet, tapping to the beat of his drums.

Nell watched for a minute, then turned back to the table, pushing the uncomfortable image out of her mind.

"Looks like we've lost Gabby," Nell said, nodding toward a doe-like figure weaving back and forth in front of the band trio. Daisy Danvers was beside her, her short hair bouncing to the beat. And Shelly, a younger Danvers daughter, stood nearby, a full head shorter but trying desperately to keep up with her two idols.

"Daisy and Gabby are attached at the hip," Birdie said.

"Laura says Gabby is the best thing that's happened to Daisy in a long time," Izzy said. "She'd become a little too bookish, and her mom loves that Gabby draws her out."

Birdie frowned. "Well, let's hope she doesn't lead her *too* far astray." Birdie looked over at the table where Elliot and Laura Danvers sat, proudly watching their girls.

Pete was handing the microphone to Gabby and Daisy now. They latched onto it greedily, their young voices picking up where Pete and Merry left off. "Don't Stop Believin'" traveled through the open doors and wrapped around the restaurant, drawing in more voices as the waiters moved to the beat.

Lobster rolls quickly disappeared from the table as Ben refilled beer and iced tea glasses, and serious talk of school board tensions gave way to more music. Gabby and Daisy had loosened up the crowd, and more people were making their way to the mics, dodging the great round trays delivering key lime pie table to table.

Nell noticed an empty chair. "Where's Cass?"

"She grabbed the last lobster roll and headed off. She said she'd see us later," Sam said. He pointed across the crowded room to where Cass was weaving her way between tables, waving at a dozen people along the way.

"Where's she going?"

It was Danny Brandley's voice, coming from behind Nell's chair. Without waiting for an answer, he sat down in his former girlfriend's vacant chair, greeted the others at the table, and changed the subject. "Sorry I'm late. I had to lock up the bookstore for Mom and Dad."

But then he looked again at Cass's departing figure.

"I dunno, Danny," Izzy said. "I was sort of hoping she was meeting you."

Birdie and Nell watched for an answer, their hopes matching Izzy's word for word.

Danny took several fish tacos from the tray and poured himself a beer. He shook his head. "Nope."

Nell watched his expression, but it was noncommittal. Danny was an expert at keeping his thoughts to himself. Maybe it was the life of a writer that encouraged the skill, living alone with his characters so much of the time.

But in spite of Danny's poker face, no one could convince Nell that Cass and Danny didn't still harbor feelings for each other. She didn't buy their "just friends" description for a minute. Cass didn't talk about it much, not even with Izzy. And Danny didn't, either. But Nell knew.

People continued filing through the front door, heading to the bar and listening to the Fractured Fish musicians turning amateur voices into Paul Simon and Katy Perry. Bodies moved to the music as they waited patiently for empty chairs and tables to appear.

Cass gave a high five to several fishermen she had just hired, but she didn't stop to chat. Instead she continued toward the door, held open to the evening breeze by a large ceramic lobster a Canary Cove artist had given to Gracie.

Izzy stood, taking her daughter from Nell and slipping her into the stroller—an excuse to stand and get a better view of Cass. Just seconds before her friend reached the door, a tall, well-muscled man with a beard and mustache blocked the door. His broad chest and height filled the doorway. Behind him, the lights along the pier created an interesting silhouette.

Cass stopped, her profile revealing a half smile. The smile was returned as the stranger wrapped one arm around her shoulder, leaned down to hear her words, then ushered her out into the night.

Izzy looked at Nell. She was sitting straight in the chair, following Cass's exit with great interest. The men, including Danny, had turned their attention to Jane and Ham Brewster, who had stopped by the table and were recounting an upcoming show at their Canary Cove Art Colony.

Before Nell could ask her niece what they were seeing, Izzy said, "I saw that guy over near Paley's Cove a couple days ago. Gracie said Cass met him in the Gull the other night. Who is he?" The rhetorical question hung in the air between them.

They stared toward the open door, unsure of what was the biggest surprise—that Cass might have a new friend, or that they weren't the first ones to have known about it. Somehow the latter served up the bigger punch.

Nell stood. It wasn't like Cass not to tell them what was going on in her life.

The crowd had thinned and Nell began walking toward the door and a disappearing Cass. There was one easy way to solve the mystery: go meet the man.

She heard Cass laugh. Light. Young.

But when she reached the door and looked out into the night, Cass was nowhere in sight.

Chapter 3

$\mathcal{M}$ary Pisano's "About Town" column in Tuesday's *Sea Harbor Gazette* captured Monday's scene at Gabby's school in all its glory.

Nell spread the paper out on the coffee table in the back room of Izzy's yarn shop. "Mary is a master at elaboration. She describes the scene as 'flying swirls of brilliant color.'"

Running alongside the column was a photo of a grassy lawn faintly stained with yellow paint, not nearly as dramatic as the words Mary strung together to portray it. The photo had clearly been taken after Ira Staab sheared the area with his John Deere.

"Must have been a slow news day," Cass said over Birdie's shoulder.

"Mary attended the school," Birdie said. "Her grandfather Enzo insisted all his children and grandchildren, nephews, nieces—all of them—be enrolled. It was one of his many gestures to buy legitimacy from the town—sending them to an expensive private school and following it up with generous contributions."

"Gracie went there, too." Cass spoke around bites of a giant submarine sandwich Birdie had brought over for lunch. "Her uncle insisted on it. Since her mother wasn't much of a role model back then, Alphonso figured the private school would keep her in line."

"I can't imagine Gracie being out of line," Birdie said.

Cass laughed. "We were both upset that we'd be separated. Me off to the public school and Gracie gobbled up by the elite. She got hold of some handcuffs and we hooked them together so we couldn't be separated. But Gracie's wrists were so skinny that they kept falling off."

"You were, what? Six?" Izzy said.

Nell helped herself to half a sandwich. Birdie had put out a message to the others that she was bringing lunch to Izzy's shop. Only the hungry should come, she texted.

They all knew free food would lure Cass away from her office desk at the Halloran Lobster Company or the dock or wherever she happened to be. And sometimes, but not always, food loosened Cass's tongue.

But so far, Cass held her silence—at least when it came to the bearded man she had gone off with the night before.

"Was Gabby aware of what happened on the lawn?" she asked Birdie.

"She didn't say a word. Not about that. The students were probably not even aware of it."

"So who did it?" Izzy asked. She walked around the large table, picking up spare needles and pieces of yarn as she talked. They'd had a full morning of classes—and there'd be another in an hour.

Nell scanned the paper. "No one's name is mentioned."

"Did Elizabeth call the police?" Cass asked. She helped herself to a handful of fries.

"Ben didn't mention it, and he talked to the chief for a while last night before we left. I tried to engage Elizabeth in chitchat, but she was unusually quiet. She clearly had something on her mind."

"I suppose it's a minor crime. Spraying someone's lawn," Cass said. "But it's not too different from teepeeing trees, which Gracie and I did a lot of a hundred years ago. And never once did I get tossed in jail."

"I don't think Elizabeth is vindictive," Nell said. "She probably wouldn't push the matter—"

"Unless she thought the students or staff were in danger," Izzy said. "We represented a woman once who sprayed WD-40 on the front step of a house, then waited until her husband's lover came out and slid right into a bush where she was waiting with a camera and a can of spray paint. So even yellow paint can be dangerous in the wrong hands."

Nell picked up a pitcher of iced tea and began filling glasses. "I'm so glad you left the world of trials and criminals behind you, Izzy."

"Of course you are." Izzy gave her aunt a quick hug. "Sam said Elizabeth was taking pictures of the vandalism. That was probably smart. Just in case—"

But none of them could imagine what that "just in case" would be. Sea Harbor was a sleepy town, especially in the fall when the tourists had left. It was filled with people who cared about one another and preferred quiet and peaceful to extravagant paint shows.

"I'm sure you take extra precautions when you have young people in your care," Birdie said. "But no matter, I guess we'll find out more about it tonight."

"Tonight?" Izzy asked.

"The school's board meeting," Birdie said.

"I almost forgot you were on that board," Izzy said. "Gabby has somehow transported all of us back to elementary school in one way or another. You know she's signed us up to teach a session of the enhancement program Elizabeth began this semester. We need to come up with some knitting projects—which, by the way, you will all help me figure out at Thursday night knitting."

"Of course we will."

"And don't forget the benefit at the school Friday night," Birdie said quickly. "I've reserved a table and am counting on every one of you. It'll be lovely."

"That's just one of the many things we love about you, Birdie. The glass is always half-full."

"Of course it is," Birdie said. "As it will be Friday night. I'll make sure our glasses are completely full. But you're right about these new commitments, Izzy. Imagine at my age, suddenly attending

PTO meetings and parent-teacher conferences, school concerts, and art fairs."

"And coaxing all your friends into Gabby's world as well," Nell said.

"Coaxing? That's a gentle way of putting it." Cass laughed as she crumpled up the wrapping from her ham sandwich. She tossed it into the wastebasket, her eyebrows lifting at the slam dunk. She stood and collected her backpack from the floor. "My lobsters are calling," she said, and walked toward the steps leading to the main room of the yarn shop. She paused at the bottom step and turned around. "Birdie, is your table at the benefit full?"

"I have your place reserved, Catherine. Don't worry."

"What if I brought a guest?"

Three faces turned toward her.

"A guest?" Birdie said.

"Hey, no problem if the table is full," Cass said quickly. "I know it's better to have a body in every chair. That's all I was thinking. Just trying to help. Stack the deck. That kind of thing."

"As a matter of fact, I do have an empty place." Birdie paused briefly, wondering if she wanted it filled. It was Danny's chair, after all.

Cass noticed the pause and went on, stepping right into the middle of Birdie's thoughts. "I ran into Archie at the bookstore today and he told me his talented son had a book signing in Boston Friday night. I assumed you'd invited Danny to the event at Gabby's school—"

"Yes, that's true. And Danny mentioned he wouldn't be able to make it. So of course, if you know someone who might enjoy it, invite them. Who do you have in mind?"

Cass had already taken the three steps as one, landing at the top of the archway with a kind of plop. She paused and turned around, as if she hadn't heard Birdie's question. "So Laura Danvers is in charge of this thing, right? Shall I let her know I'm bringing someone?"

"I'll take care of it," Birdie said. "She'll have a ticket waiting for you at the event."

A ticket for whom? But they held the question, waiting for Cass to fill in the gap.

Cass frowned at Nell and Izzy. "What's the matter with you two? You're never ever this quiet." She looked down at the shop's calico cat, rubbing against her jeans. "Hey, Purl, did you get their tongues?"

Then she waved and was gone in a flash, black hair flying wildly, looking more eager than usual to leave her trio of friends— even with half a sandwich left on the table.

Ever since Rachel Wooten, Sea Harbor city attorney, had taken over as chair of the Sea Harbor Community Day School board, the meetings were very organized, brief, and well attended. Rachel insisted on sticking to the agenda. Knowing the meetings were set to begin promptly at six thirty, members could usually count on sitting down to dinner in their own homes shortly after eight.

Tonight's meeting fulfilled only one of Rachel's goals—it was well attended.

"But," as Birdie reported to Izzy and Cass later, "at least no one was killed."

Rachel Wooten called the meeting to order in her usual efficient and gracious way, bringing scattered conversations among the dozen or so gathered around the table to a halt. She motioned toward the coffeepot, cups, cream, and sugar, and then brought attention to Harry Garozzo's cannolis, heaped high on a tray in the middle of the library table.

"It's nice to have a deli owner's brother on the staff," she said. "Angelo handed these to me as I walked in. He said he thought it might sweeten us up."

The comment brought smiles to some, but a frown to Blythe

Westerland's face, one that didn't escape Nell, sitting opposite her at the table. Birdie noticed it, too, but ignored it. Instead she lifted up the tray, helped herself to a napkin, paper plate, and pastry, and passed it along to Elliott Danvers, sitting on her left.

"Consider me sweetened," Elliott said, sliding two pastries onto a plate. "But don't tell Laura. My wife has me training for a triathlon or some god awful thing. She'd nix the cannolis in favor of some atrocious green concoction she'd mix up in the blender."

"Your secret's safe with me, Danvers," Barrett Mansfield said in his usual deep and serious voice. He took two for himself. "And mine with you, I hope."

The image of the sedate Chelsey Mansfield and vivacious Laura Danvers sharing gossip about their men brought a smile to Nell's face. It wouldn't happen. They were both lovely, but as different from each other as some of the members of the school board, a fact that Nell appreciated. The Community School board was an odd mixture of Sea Harbor folks—prestigious and plain, young and old, and from different walks of life. She herself was an odd choice at first glance, having no children and not being a native of the small Atlantic coastal town. It wasn't really a mystery, though. Her expertise in discovering grant money in obscure places was legendary. And money, of course, was often the overriding issue small schools faced—public and private—and especially those whose enrollment and endowment had seen a harsh decline over the last decade.

"It will be a short meeting tonight," Rachel promised. "The agenda is on the table in front of you."

Nell Endicott glanced down at the printed sheet. The elegant blue and gold school insignia appeared in the corner and below it, Rachel had carefully detailed the items for discussion.

Nothing unusual, except for the upcoming fall gala that Friday night. Rachel would be encouraging every board member to attend. And if they hadn't done it already, there were still a few tables that could be purchased. There was that, the usual budget report, and a catch-up on repairs being done.

But it was the first item on the list that caught her attention. A single word.

Staff.

She looked around the table, noticing for the first time that Elizabeth Hartley was missing from the meeting. Surely she'd be the one discussing any staff matters.

Birdie noticed the headmistress's absence at the same time, although the others' attention seemed more focused on the cannolis than on who was there or not there.

"Blythe." Rachel looked up from the paper, removing her glasses and looking down the table. "Since this first item was added at your request, I'll let you take the floor."

Nell watched a hint of displeasure flit across Rachel's fine-boned face as she sat back down. She knew Rachel well. When she and Ben had moved permanently to Sea Harbor, Rachel and her husband, Don, were among their first friends. And when Don Wooten proved himself a worthy crew member on Sam and Ben's prized sailboat, that friendship was solidified. Not to mention that he owned the Ocean's Edge, one of their favorite Sea Harbor restaurants.

Rachel was gracious and smart—but never one to let anyone take her for granted. Nell suspected the sudden, undefined agenda item had been a surprise to the board chair—and she didn't like it.

Blythe stood up, looking around the table and meeting each board member's eye. She smiled. "I'm sorry this is sudden, but it was only recently brought to my attention and it's something we should all be aware of. An incident occurred yesterday that is emblematic of school problems, not only on the faculty level but the administration level as well. If we want to be effective as a board, we need to look into these matters and make some pressing decisions, ones that will maintain its fine reputation and ensure the success of Sea Harbor Community Day School."

Birdie lifted her small hand into the air and wiggled her fingers. "Excuse me, Blythe, but is this a discussion Dr. Hartley should be present for? I don't believe she's here yet."

Rachel Wooten looked over at Elizabeth's customary place and interrupted. "Of course, Birdie. I apologize. I hadn't realized—" She looked down at her phone, checking messages, her frown deepening. "She should be here—"

"It's all right, Rachel." Blythe took a breath and began. "Dr. Hartley is one of the items we need to talk about. Specifically her administrative decisions and the way she is handling staff. It's fortunate that she isn't here. I wouldn't want to upset her. One of the pressing matters is Dr. Hartley herself. We need to consider terminating her position as headmistress." Although she addressed Rachel, and spoke to the whole board, her eyes kept traveling back to Barrett Mansfield. He met her eyes, his own dark and angry.

At that moment, the glass in one of the library's heavy double doors rattled and Elizabeth Hartley pushed it open, walking into a silenced room. At first her walk was tentative, as if she wasn't sure why everyone else was already seated. And then she walked more boldly past the display of new books and over to the table, filled now with cannoli crumbs and smudged agenda sheets.

"I'm sorry to be late. I must have misunderstood the message from my secretary. I thought Teresa said the meeting was going to begin later tonight." She paused and looked around at the faces looking expectantly at her. "But a few minutes ago Angelo came by the office and mentioned that everyone was already here. He brought cannolis, he said." A lighter tone came into her voice. But her expression was somber.

Rachel pushed away her own confusion and took charge. "That's no problem, Elizabeth. I apologize for the misunderstanding. We were about to call you. Please sit, and if Elliott and Barrett haven't eaten all the Garozzo pastries, help yourself to one of them."

Elizabeth managed a smile. "Thank you, Rachel."

Her voice was steady, but her hands, holding a brown notebook, were shaking slightly and the tension that had entered the room with the headmistress now hovered over the library table.

Blythe was still standing, her eyes on Elizabeth and her expression unreadable.

"Blythe?" Rachel said.

Nell looked over at Birdie. They read the tone in Rachel's voice instantly, the same authoritative one that made her a successful attorney and advocate of the city. Her diplomacy was masterful and the tone that coated her single word was urging Blythe Westerland to sit down.

But it was Esther Gibson who saved the moment. The ageless police dispatcher put her ever-present knitting down, pushed her ample frame to a standing position, and suggested that Rachel fill them in on details of the weekend gala for the foundation before discussing anything else. She was on the night shift, she said, and might have to leave early if tonight's meeting went too long. She smiled broadly, and the lines fanning out from her clear blue eyes deepened. "Frankly, it's the only thing on the agenda that interests me tonight."

She nodded sweetly to Blythe and then sat back down, folding her hands on the table and waiting for her wish to be granted.

Relief spread across Rachel's face as she thanked Esther for the suggestion, shuffled the papers in front of her, then looked again at Blythe. "It looks like this keeps you standing, Blythe. As the board liaison for the event, you'll want to relate the memo I received today from the organizer, I presume."

Blythe took the sheet Rachel handed her, scanned the report, dropped it on the table, and took in her audience. "Laura Danvers"—she nodded at Laura's husband, Elliott—"has done an excellent job of putting the evening together. It's been my pleasure to help her at every turn." She went on to detail the festivities, music by a student jazz band, and tours of the school and property. But the pièce de résistance of the evening would be the multiple small courses served to the guests, all created by Sea Harbor's finest chefs and accompanied by champagne and fine wine. She added her expectation that each board member take it upon him- or herself to mingle and greet and direct interested donors to one of the foundation's funds. "Laura and I promise the evening will not only be thoroughly entertaining but, most important, will fill the foundation's coffers nicely. Music to all our ears and especially to yours," she said, looking at the headmistress. "Would you like to add anything, Elizabeth?"

Elizabeth didn't meet the look thrown at her, the friendly tone as if she and Blythe were close confidantes, good friends. Instead she spoke to the rest of the board. "It'll be a wonderful evening, and I'm grateful to Laura for the time she has given to this. The whole town seems to have an investment in Sea Harbor Community Day School, wanting it to thrive. And that's quite wonderful."

Birdie sat straight and smiled at the administrator. "You've done a great deal to foster that, Elizabeth. Using foundation money to connect with the community and help other groups has gone a long way in generating the goodwill. You are putting this grand institution back on the map but in a new and interesting way."

"My sentiments exactly," Barrett Mansfield said, his baritone voice filling the room.

Blythe stared at him again, a frown threatening to mar her smooth forehead, then disappearing as she sat back down and picked up the agenda sheet.

There was a shuffling of papers and murmurs of approval as coffee cups were refilled. Rachel glanced at the agenda sheet once more, then began passing out the treasurer's report, ignoring the lead item on the agenda.

Nell felt the emotion before she looked up and saw the clouds gathering in Blythe Westerland's face. Without looking across the table, she could feel Blythe's displeasure. She was being overlooked, her voice silenced, something that she wouldn't accept easily.

Before Nell could get Rachel's attention, Blythe pushed back her chair and stood again, her hands flat on the varnished table and her eyes moving deliberately from one person to the next until the murmurs fell away and a heavy silence filled the library.

"Thank you for your attention," she said. "I have a few things we need to address and I'd like to do it now before anyone else has to leave."

The single agenda item hung in the air. *Staff.* Nell had the peculiar sensation that if she looked up, she'd see the word blinking in neon lights. She looked across the table at Elizabeth. Her face was expressionless. She turned her head and looked at Blythe, waiting, almost as if she knew what was about to occur.

"As most of you know, Josh Babson was fired Monday," Blythe began, then paused for effect as she looked around the table again. "A move *most* of us recommended to Dr. Hartley."

The group was silent, waiting. Esther Gibson thrummed her plump fingers on the table. Birdie took off her glasses and rubbed imaginary smudges from them with the sleeve of her sweater.

Anticipation. Where was Blythe going with this?

They all knew Josh was going to be fired, because Blythe had filled the library table the month before with reason after reason for his dismissal. But it shouldn't be news tonight. Except for the announcement, perhaps, that the artist had, in fact, been fired. An action a few on the board thought unfounded and a few others, those who often missed meetings, didn't know enough about to have an opinion on. But Blythe had a powerful voice. And name.

Blythe took a drink of water, then continued with a dramatic description of the art instructor's dismissal, something she hadn't personally been privy to, but somehow knew several details that made Elizabeth cringe.

She went on to say that proof of the inept firing was in the actions taken by the art teacher after Elizabeth had "let him go." An action she categorized as an act of "violence," obviously motivated by the way the firing was handled.

The last words were said with such vitriol that Elizabeth winced. Members of the board stared at Blythe, some leaning forward in their chairs, waiting for the worst-case scenario: had the firing so badly destroyed Josh Babson that he had hurt himself? Or worse?

"With wanton abandon," Blythe went on, "Mr. Babson sprayed the school's lawn vividly with yellow paint, showing his anguish for the whole town to see." She elaborated on the color, the swirls, and the deadly look Josh had thrown up at Dr. Hartley's office where Elizabeth had been standing in the window. A look she herself had witnessed, she added.

There was a collective sigh of relief. Josh Babson was alive.

Blythe then once again boiled the entire episode down to Dr. Hartley's inefficient handling of the termination, just one of many examples of her inability to be headmistress of the Sea Harbor school.

"I am sorry to discuss this in front of you, Elizabeth," she said in the same gracious tone she might have used to compliment the headmistress on her dress. "But it needs to be said. I had hoped to do it before you arrived, but that didn't happen."

Elizabeth was silent. The message she had received from her secretary was now clear to all of them. Blythe had arranged it.

"My daughter liked Babson," Barrett Mansfield said. "And frankly, if I had my way, he wouldn't have been fired in the first place. So be it. But you can't expect the man to jump up and down with joy at losing his job no matter how it was done. Maybe his reaction was childish, but after all, he was an artist—using paint to show his displeasure might have been better than other options. Clever, actually." He followed his words with a slight smile, an attempt to make a point and lighten the mood at the same time.

"You're missing the point," Blythe said. "We need to pay attention to how the situation was handled. It was handled terribly, which was why the teacher reacted so badly. And it's simply another instance in a long list of things that need to be corrected. We need an administrator here who knows who to hire and how to treat staff once they are hired. We need someone at the helm who isn't pouring money into scholarships for kids who shouldn't be at this school anyway. We need a headmistress who maintains the integrity of not only the school but the home my great-grandfather raised his family in. We need to clean house."

It was the first time Nell had seen Blythe Westerland visibly emotional. It wasn't that they hadn't had contentious discussions at board meetings, but Blythe always managed to hold her emotions intact, arguing calmly—almost too calmly, Birdie had once observed. But not tonight.

Rachel stood and looked at Blythe, then the rest of the board. "This meeting is over," she said. She spoke in the same controlled voice she had probably used in countless court battles. "Please review the treasurer's report, and the last item about repairs to the old boathouse will be discussed at the next meeting. Your concerns will all be considered, Blythe, and discussed once we have something to discuss. Good night, everyone." She managed a smile and began placing her papers in a leather attaché case.

Several others stood and began to gather up the empty cups, relieved to be going home early. Low conversations here and there attempted to cover the unpleasant and awkward silence.

Birdie walked over to Elizabeth. She complimented her on a new social services project Gabby was involved in. "You are teaching students to be kind to others. The greatest learning of all."

Around the table chairs squeaked on the hardwood floor, keys rattled, and good-byes floated on the library air.

Blythe Westerland remained at her place, her bag in her hand. Her composure had returned and she smiled at several people around her, wishing them a good night and a safe drive home.

Finally she walked around the table, toward the spot where Birdie and Elizabeth stood.

Elizabeth opened her mouth to speak, but Blythe walked by as if she hadn't seen her. Instead she followed Barrett Mansfield toward the door, passed him, then spun around, blocking him in his tracks.

The tall business owner was digging in his pocket for car keys with one hand, holding his cell phone to his ear with the other. He looked at her, puzzled. Then he pulled his eyebrows together and slipped his phone into his pocket. "Blythe, if you've a beef with me because of that . . . incident . . . don't take it out on the board or Elizabeth or anyone else. What are you trying to do here?"

"Don't flatter yourself." Blythe's voice was controlled, clear and concise—and audible in the now quiet library. She continued. "This is your fault. You hired her for your own selfish reasons." It was the voice one used to explain an obvious fact to someone who didn't quite understand, a child perhaps. "It's not a kind thing you did in pushing the board to hire her. Not for anyone, and especially not for your daughter. She has learning and social problems, and she should be in a place that specializes in that, not here in my school. You've taken advantage of me, Barrett. People need to know that. You'll regret this, mark my words."

Without allowing time for a response, Blythe turned and walked away from the formidable board member. Her pace was steady and her form graceful, and she never looked back, not once, missing the flush of anger that moved up Barrett Mansfield's neck until it covered his whole face. A vein pulsed in his temple.

Only the three women standing back at the board table—Birdie, Nell, and Elizabeth Hartley—saw his clenched fist. It was squeezed so tightly around a set of car keys that they were sure to leave a permanent imprint in his palm. The anger in his narrowed eyes spoke louder than words.

Blythe is wrong, his eyes said. He wasn't the one who would regret this encounter.

Chapter 4

It was Thursday morning before Nell had a minute to devote to her sweet Abby.

Wednesday had disappeared in the blink of an eye with a trip to the library to help with a grant and then a trip into Boston to meet with a friend. But Thursday was Abby's, without a single meeting or appointment.

"Don't worry, darling," she said to the curly blond toddler. Abby was sitting in her stroller, enjoying the sea breeze, as Nell pushed her stroller through the narrow streets of the Canary Cove Art Gallery. "This won't happen again."

Seeing Abby every day wasn't always possible, but Nell tried hard to make it happen. Sam and Izzy's baby girl had added unforeseen riches to all their lives, and in Nell's mind, being with Abby was the best possible way to make an off-kilter world balanced again.

"So you need balance?" Ben had asked her earlier that morning. They were drinking coffee and sharing their plans for the day, hoping to meet for a quick glass of wine together later that day. A chance to catch up before Nell left for the night reserved for knitting.

"Yes, a little balance would be good. It's Birdie, I think, who has me on edge. She gets this feeling in her bones when things aren't quite right, and it seems to slide inside me easily."

"It's because of the board meeting, I'd guess."

"Probably. Dissension wears on me, especially when I know the people and some are hurt by it. It's even harder on Birdie, now that Gabby is a student at the school."

Ben put down his coffee mug and gave Nell a kiss on the top of her head. "Our Abby will chase those feelings away. She always does."

Ben was right. Abby was the perfect antidote. Nell waved across the street to Rebecca Early, who was unlocking the door to her handblown-glass gallery. The beautiful jewelry born from Rebecca's artistic hands caught stray rays of sunlight and sparkled in the window. Nell vowed to stop back. It was her favorite go-to shop for birthdays and gifts for friends.

But today she was headed toward the Brewster Gallery. Jane and Ham needed a dose of Abby's magic before they began their busy day.

She walked down the street, enjoying the early-morning quiet, soon to be displaced as the area came alive with artists selling their art and preparing for shows. The Brewster Gallery was halfway down the block, right next to Willow Adam's Fishtail Gallery. It was a deceptively narrow shop that fronted a long strip of land that moved inward, back into the hilly grounds behind it. From the street, the garden and cottage that Ham and Jane had lived in for thirty years were invisible, an enchanting surprise to those who made their way farther through the gallery.

Nell pushed open the door, held it with her hip, and maneuvered the stroller inside and around the new display of Jane's pottery. "Jane . . . ," she started to call out, and then she stopped short.

Jane was nowhere in sight. Instead a tall, thin man with heavy-lidded eyes stood behind the cash register. His long fingers were tapping the computer keys and organizing receipts. Blond straggly hair curled around the neckline of his T-shirt, and his paint-stained jeans seemed appropriate for the working gallery.

"Hey," he said, looking up. His smile was slight.

"Is Jane here?" Nell asked.

"She's back there." He pointed a thumb over his shoulder to an adjacent room that Ham and Jane used as an office and sitting area, and then he went back to his work.

The swish of Jane's long skirt told Nell she had heard her name and recognized the voice. She hurried around the door and gave Nell the briefest of hugs, then crouched down to greet and touch baby Abby's cheeks and chin and draw a smile from her favorite toddler. Abby responded immediately with a smile that filled her whole face.

"No one is immune to Jane's charms." Nell laughed.

The man behind the counter nodded. "Yeah. That's a fact," he said quietly, his eyes still on the receipts in his hand.

Jane laughed and pulled Abby out of the stroller, then waltzed her around the room to an old Fleetwood Mac tune playing in the background. She finally circled back to the lean man at the cash register.

He watched Jane with an amused look on his face.

It was then that Nell noticed his eyes—green and deep and as disturbing as the ocean before a storm. Raw, piercing eyes.

Jane looked at him, smiled, and held out the toddler. "This is our secret dose of sunshine. Meet Abigail Kathleen Perry. You'll be happy you did."

The man looked at the child, and his face softened with a kindness that had been hidden a second before. He made a face and winked at Abby, causing an infectious giggle to stir the air.

"I'm here, too," Nell said to Jane. "I'm used to playing second fiddle to Abby. That's okay, but I'd also like to meet this new person working in your gallery."

"Oh, good grief," Jane said. She spun Abby around again, then settled her on her hip, wrapping her arms around a wriggling body. "I thought you knew everyone in town, Nell. Josh, meet my oldest and dearest Sea Harbor friend, Nell Endicott. Nell, Josh Babson."

Josh Babson.

Nell covered her surprise with a smile and a greeting. Of course.

Jane and Ham knew every New England artist from Gloucester's Rocky Neck to Maine. Not only that but the founders of Canary Cove Art Colony had helped many of them get their careers off the ground. He was a teacher, but he was an artist, too. They would know Josh. And know what had happened to him, too. Sea Harbor was a small community, and Canary Cove—even smaller.

"Ham has figured out a way to share our studio with Josh. In exchange, Josh is going to help out in the gallery. He's a wonderful painter. Ben is going to want to start a new collection, trust me." She pointed to a large seascape against a far wall, lit with a tiny spot. "Josh has a special love affair with the sea, and it shows brilliantly in his work."

The man behind the counter cast an unreadable look Nell's way, but a softening in his face showed pleasure in Jane's praise.

He made no move to further the conversation—or officially meet her—so Nell took the initiative and reached over the counter to shake his hand. "I hope we'll be seeing more of your work, Josh," she said.

A half smile appeared, along with a shrug and a reluctant handshake. "Sure. I've seen your husband a couple of times at art shows and around town. Not you, though. Nice to meet you in person."

In person. Josh knew *of* her, knew she was on the board, of course he did. And it was the board that had ripped away his steady, dependable job, the kind that puts food on the table.

"I think I had your granddaughter in class." He looked between Jane and Nell.

"You must mean our friend Birdie Favazza."

"Her granddaughter, Gabby Marietti, goes to Sea Harbor Community," Nell added.

He nodded. "Yeah, that's the one. She was in one of my classes. She was good, not great. She'll never be a Winslow Homer, but she's creative as hell with a personality to match. How it all works out for her will be interesting to watch."

"We've all adopted Gabby," Jane said.

Nell watched Josh as Jane went on about Gabby. His eyes shifted back and forth between the two women and then settled on the papers he'd been shuffling when they walked in. He was handsome in a New England cowboy kind of way—rough at the edges, arty, and not very sociable.

And, according to Gabby and the yellow circles left on the school lawn, he had a temper. That or a strange sense of humor.

But Josh Babson also seemed to be intuitive and caring about his students. And he was talented, according to Jane. So how had he incurred the wrath of Blythe Westerland that had caused him his job? And why?

The question flitted in and out of Nell's mind later that day as she and Abby made their way down the produce aisle at the grocery store and then walked over to the fish market on the harbor. But the thoughts didn't linger long. With Abby at her side and a meal to put together for Thursday night knitting, even Josh Babson was finally brushed aside completely, replaced by fresh crab, potatoes, and a hunk of ginger root.

Chapter 5

"So, where's Cass been?" Izzy took a bag from Nell's arms, holding the yarn shop door open with her back. "Sam saw her at the Gull the other night. She doesn't even like the Gull."

"Who was she with?" Nell followed Izzy through the archway to the back room, where the big wooden worktable was already cleared, plates and wineglasses at the ready.

"A handsome dude. The same one we glimpsed Monday, unless Cass is suddenly seeking out men with facial hair. Sam was meeting a client for a beer, so they didn't talk. But he wouldn't have gone over to them anyway. You know Sam. He takes respecting others' privacy to an absurd level."

Nell laughed and began filling a basket with sourdough rolls. "I suppose we should do the same. She'll be here soon—"

Of course she would. Thursday nights were the closest thing to sacred in the knitters' lives. Other traditions could be shuffled around occasionally—even, on rare occasions, Friday night on the deck. But the place and day that had fostered the four-way friendship over the years was rarely upstaged. They couldn't explain it easily to others. Was it the cozy knitting room with its casement windows that opened to the sea, the comfortable, worn seats around the fireplace? Or Nell's fresh pasta dishes, Birdie's fine pinot gris? The music, the yarn, the intricate patterns that engaged their minds and busied their fingers? All of that. But most of all, it was the friendship that deepened every single week over angora sweaters and finely knit baby hats.

Birdie walked down the stairs, a cloth bag that held her wine looped over one arm, a knitting bag over the other. "Something is going on with our girl Catherine. I've noticed it for a while. I think she's been lonely."

"Her own fault," Izzy said, dipping a carrot stick into a pot of cilantro hummus. "There's Danny waiting in the wings."

"He won't wait forever," Nell said. "Danny is forty. It's not just women who become aware of some clock ticking away in the distance. The breakup with Cass was difficult. Danny sees things in an uncomplicated way—and realizing that the more Cass loved him, the more she felt she was losing something in herself was probably nearly impossible for him to understand."

"Of course it was," Izzy said. "I don't completely get it myself. I kind of do—Cass is complicated. But to push away someone who loves you—and someone you love right back—just because you might feel jealous sometimes or might miss him and need him—or all those other emotions that sometimes get mixed up in a relationship—that's hard to understand."

"I think seeing her own mom be devastated when her father died at sea affected Cass greatly," Birdie said. "It was an awful time for the whole family, and maybe Cass feels pushing Danny away will save her from ever going through that great hurt."

"But it won't work," Izzy said. "I'm sure of it. Cass loves Danny. She'll come around."

Birdie agreed. "But let's allow Cass her privacy, too. She'll be here in a second—her truck pulled into the alley as Harold was dropping me off."

"So stop talking about me," Cass said, her words tumbling down the three steps just seconds before she appeared in the arched opening. In one large leap she was at the bottom.

"What makes you think you're that special?" Izzy said, bringing her iPod to life and turning the music up a little louder than necessary. In seconds Laila Biali's rich vocals filled the air and Izzy floated over to Cass, then twirled her around, joining her own voice to the artist's as she sang out, "Let's go down, down to the river to pray."

Cass laughed. "Now you want me to pray? You're a crazy lady."

Izzy threw back her head and laughed, her thick, streaked hair floating in slow motion. Then she moved away and wrinkled her nose. "And you smell like fish. Were you out on the boats today?"

"Briefly. Someone wanted to see our lobster operation, so I did a little tour thing for the guy." Then her words sped up and she leaned over the table. "Hey, what's in the magic bowl, Nell?"

Before Nell could answer, Cass went on. "No, don't tell me. Crab, a splash of wine, ginger, lemon butter, and . . . uh . . . pasta?"

"Close. It's scooped into potato nests. My mother used to make them. And in case you think we missed it, that was an excellent job of changing the subject."

"It was, wasn't it?" Cass took the glass of wine Birdie offered her and, with the other hand, pushed a handful of hair behind one ear, a nervous gesture they all knew well. "It's no big deal. We're just getting to know each other. I don't mean to seem mysterious."

Izzy set the butter dish down beside the rolls and began rolling the silverware inside napkins. Nell tossed the arugula pecan salad.

Birdie filled the remaining glasses with wine.   ·

As routine and natural as breathing.

In the background the jazz artist was singing an old song Birdie knew well, "The Best Is Yet to Come."

And they waited.

"His name is Harry Winthrop."

"Okay, so, what happened when Harry met Cass . . . ?" Izzy lined the rolled napkins up next to the plates.

"They drank beer," Cass said, ignoring Izzy's tease.

"Another Harry?" Nell said. "We have so many Harrys in our lives."

"He's not in *our* lives," Cass reminded them, "unless you've been in the backseat and I missed seeing you. But he's okay. Smart enough. Great-looking. And he took me to a good restaurant in Boston a couple days ago. Sometimes a change of place is good."

"Boston?"

"He has a house there. It's where he lives in real life."

"Winthrop . . . ," Birdie said, drawing the word from her memory and searching for a connection.

"He sounds rich," Izzy said.

Cass filled her plate and walked over to the fireplace. "He is. A Winthrop. And rich, too. He doesn't seem to be concerned about money, anyway."

"His folks were summer people," Birdie said. "Yes, now I remember."

Cass nodded and sank down beside Purl in the leather chair that had once been at home in Ben's den. "I guess that's what they were. He knows his way around Sea Harbor. I don't remember seeing him before, but then, I probably didn't run in the same circles. Most summers when I was young and free, I worked on my dad's boat."

She bit off a piece of a crusty roll while the others filled their plates and made their way over to the fireplace.

"I knew Margaret and James Winthrop socially. They owned a vacation house over near the lighthouse and had lovely Gatsby-like parties each summer," Birdie said. "I think they were from Boston or New York." She smiled, satisfied with herself for pulling up memories of people she hadn't thought about in decades. "Margaret thought it set the Winthrops apart to buy vacation real estate on Cape Ann instead of the Hamptons."

"That's them," Cass said. "At least I think so. They're long gone. The house hasn't been taken care of in a long time. Harry said he's been back now and then to check on it."

"It looks haunted," Izzy said. "I can't get Red to walk by it—and he's an excellent judge of character." She threw Cass a narrow look.

"So Harry's bad because Red is afraid of his house?" Cass frowned. "Come on, Iz."

"Sorry. I was out of line. It's just that—"

"I know," Cass said quietly.

And they all knew. It was just that they all loved Danny.

"Is he moving to Sea Harbor?" Nell asked.

"I doubt it. He said he had personal things to take care of here. I think he was trying to take care of one of those 'personal things' the night I met him. He was sitting at the bar talking on his cell. I heard bits and pieces. It sounded like he was trying to ask someone out, saying he was back in town, wouldn't it be nice to reconnect, that kind of thing. It was awkward because even though he talked low, I could hear him. Then he hung up, slammed one hand on the bar, and spilled his beer all over my napkin. Anyway, he apologized, mumbled something about an old girlfriend, and then changed the subject."

"So you were his second choice?" Izzy said.

"I was no choice. I was just there—and we started talking. He was embarrassed that I had heard some of his conversation, so he started talking fast about other things—his family vacation house and how he had to fix it up or tear it down or something. He inherited it and had set aside some time to make decisions, come up and figure out what to do with it."

"His parents died some time ago, if I'm remembering right," Birdie said.

"And he waited until now to fix it up?" Nell asked.

Cass shrugged, her mouth full of Nell's savory crab. "Who knows why he waited? Or if it's simply an excuse for him to come back to town and find an old girlfriend. He didn't seem to want to talk about that. He said he had a few weeks in his schedule that he could commit to being away from Boston. He's having his place in Boston renovated, so it's not very livable. Not that the vacation home is, but at least it has heat, he said, and he needs to be here to hire workmen. So it all worked out."

"So those 'personal' reasons you mentioned? Doesn't it bother you that he might have come to reconnect with an old girlfriend?" Izzy passed around a basket of rolls. "Even one who may have hung up on him?"

"Nope. Not at all. I'm not looking for a husband, Iz."

"So he's your date for Friday's party?" Birdie asked.

Cass scoffed. "No, not really a date. Actually he asked if he could come."

"What?" Izzy's voice was incredulous, her feelings about fancy benefits coming to the surface.

Cass slathered butter on a roll. "I know—crazy, huh? He said he remembered the school from summers here and wouldn't mind supporting the event. Make a donation. Be a good citizen, was how he put it."

"That's generous," Birdie said. "We'll be happy to have him at our table."

"What's he like? Do you like him?" Izzy asked.

Cass stood up and brushed bread crumbs off her jeans, which Purl promptly cleaned up.

"Like him?" Cass walked her now-empty plate to the kitchen alcove and returned with a new bottle of pinot gris. "If we're going to explore my love life, I need another glass of Birdie's wine." She refilled all the glasses and sat back down. "I guess that's where you're going with this."

"We don't mean to pry," Nell began.

Cass's robust laugh lightened the lines of her face and brought the old Cass back. "Of course you do. But hey, I love you guys. It's okay. It's just that I don't have much to say. Except lately I've been feeling a little restless—rootless, maybe. Not my usual peppy, Pollyanna self. Premenopausal? Midlife crisis? Who knows? And then this guy shows up at the Gull. I never went to the Gull alone before, but I did that night. And there he was, all alone, with this Tom Selleck mustache, a trimmed beard, and a hot car, and looking kind of sad—I'm a sucker for sad—so I thought, well, why not have a beer? Maybe have some diversion in my life."

"So, are you?" Izzy picked up the rest of the plates and stood next to Cass, waiting for an answer. Her words were soft, not threatening.

"I suppose. He's . . . what? . . . interesting, I guess. I really think he came here looking for a lost love or something and maybe it isn't working out for him. Or, heck, maybe she'll come around. But for now it's surprisingly nice spending time with someone who has few expectations of me. It's safe. It's . . . well—"

She didn't finish the sentence, but all their thoughts turned to Danny Brandley. Cass had fallen in love with him—and she hadn't felt safe. She had felt herself losing her footing. Being dependent, and jealous, even, an emotion she didn't wear well.

"Anyway," Cass said, her voice lifting, "he's nice. He likes boats. I like boats."

"A match made in heaven." Izzy made a face at Cass again and then carried the plates to the table, returning with a stack of wet wipes.

"I'm glad you're getting out, Cass," Nell said. Birdie had been right earlier—Cass hadn't been herself for a while now. She was slightly withdrawn. Her generous laugh had gone down a notch. If Harry Winthrop was responsible for changing all that, it was a good thing. "You work hard. You deserve to have a good time."

Cass didn't answer. Her eyes drifted over to the window that looked out onto the alley—and Danny's parents' bookstore across from it

"Okay, then," Izzy said, clinking Cass's glass with her own and bringing her back. "I'm for good times, too. But mostly tonight I'm for getting Gabby's dagnabbed project off the ground."

"Not Gabby's project, my dear," Birdie said. "It's ours now. And these enrichment sessions are a wonderful addition to the curriculum. Cooking. Organic gardening. And what could be better than teaching knitting? It does marvelous things for developing brains."

"Well, all right, then. You all heard Birdie. We need to get our act together."

With that, the last of the dirty dishes was stashed in the sink, the big wooden table that centered the room wiped off, and chairs pulled out. Izzy carried a pile of bright, colored yarn to the table and spread the skeins out next to a stack of pattern books.

"Gabby and Daisy have done their homework," Izzy said. "Dr. Hartley e-mailed me the paper they'd presented in lobbying for this knitting class."

Birdie took the printed sheet from Izzy, slipped on her glasses, and began to read: "Knitting helps get both sides of the brain going, has a calming effect, and helps students in problem solving." She looked up. "And at the bottom are a list of research references." Her laughter was fluffed up with pride.

"The question, then, is, are we ready for this? Elizabeth said she's having to limit the number of participants because Gabby and Daisy have done such a great job of marketing the sessions."

"So, what do they want to knit?" Cass asked. "And be sure I get the kids who have six thumbs."

"Gabby suggested that each student work on two projects— something for herself and also a warm winter hat for kids in Father Northcutt's community project or that one at the community center," Birdie said. "Or maybe both."

"That's our Gabby," Izzy said, her voice sharing Birdie's pride. "She's a good kid, Birdie."

Good kid. Words that carried so much more meaning when said of Gabby. Not perfect, unusual in some ways, irritatingly precocious sometimes. She hadn't had the most normal life so far, not with a series of stepmothers coming and going, and a father who loved her fiercely but who wasn't around much. And even when he was, Christopher Marietti wasn't always sure what to do with his wild filly of a daughter. But somehow, amazingly, it was working out.

Izzy brought out more yarn, and they all reached for some, exploring the textures with fingers that understood a fiber by touch.

Colors were critiqued and the darkest ones set aside as being too difficult to knit on for beginning knitters. Finally they chose several patterns that they'd present to the class—chic scarfs, and fingerless mittens for the girls—and a wild array of winter hats in brilliant colors for the kids in Father Northcutt's community center program. Happy colors—crimson red, bright yellows, and neon greens—colors they knew would please Daisy and Gabby, who seemed to be calling the shots.

Cass called it a night as they finished storing the yarns and needles in boxes. "This girl needs a good night's sleep," she said.

"Too many late nights?" Birdie asked.

Cass didn't answer. Instead she leaned over and gave Birdie a hug. Then she waved good-bye to Nell and Izzy and slipped out the side door to the alley where she'd parked her pickup truck.

Izzy checked her watch. "It's still early, but I think we've done our duty here tonight." She looked at Nell and Birdie. "Would you two be up for ice cream? I'm yearning for a double-chocolate cherry sundae."

In minutes they had locked up the shop and crossed over Harbor Road to Scoopers Ice Cream Shop. They could see before crossing the street that the line inside was short and the shop nearly empty. "A sure sign the summer people have left us," Nell observed. "We get our ice cream shop back."

Inside they found one table occupied. Chelsey Mansfield and her daughter, Anna, sat close to each other at a table in the window.

"That looks amazing, Anna," Birdie said, gazing at the whipped-cream-topped confection sitting in front of the blond-haired youngster.

Anna blushed and lowered her head, continuing to work on the mountain of ice cream in front of her.

Izzy walked over and greeted Chelsey, then looked at Anna. "Did you know your mother was my teacher in law school? She was a wonderful teacher."

Anna looked at her mother and managed a small smile, then ducked her head away from the attention and back to the ice cream.

"I can hardly remember those years, Isabel," Chelsey said. "But I do remember how you excelled at everything you put your mind to. I must admit that when I later heard you had given up your spot at that law firm, I didn't completely understand it." She was quiet for a moment, her eyes looking over at Anna. When she looked back she smiled slightly. "But in recent years I understand it completely. Totally."

"I've never regretted it. And when I settled in here and opened my little shop, I once again became Izzy—the person I was before tailored suits and fancy offices."

"Izzy it is, then."

"So you don't miss your career? Your life in Boston?" Nell asked Chelsey. She didn't know her well, but thought that she'd like her if given the opportunity. What she did know was that Chelsey Mansfield had been a respected professor at Harvard Law School and a successful partner in a law firm. But since moving to Sea Harbor a few years before, Barrett Mansfield's wife had stayed out of the limelight, devoting herself completely to her daughter and the home Barrett had purchased and remodeled near the water.

"Sometimes I miss teaching," she admitted. "I was close enough in age to the students to understand their problems and career choices a little better than some of the other professors. But I figure I can always pick that up again. And at first, I even missed my practice—although the political posturing was never my thing. Then once we finally had Anna, everything changed, especially our priorities."

"That happens, for sure," Izzy said.

Chelsey nodded and looked at her own daughter, now buried in a book, the ice cream in her bowl melting into a brown sea. She reached over absently and touched Anna's arm.

Anna jumped, surprised, then pulled back and quickly resumed her reading.

"The bustle of Boston no longer suited us. Nor the time our professional lives consumed. But most important, it wasn't the best place to raise and educate Anna. She needed some extra help in school—and we had an amazing tutor there—but as Anna grew, we realized that the quieter, less frantic environment Cape Ann offers might be better for her . . . and for Barrett and me, too. It's a good place for families, as you all know. So here we are. Barrett somehow manages the commute fine and even has time to be involved on the school committee. He's an amazing man. I don't know how he does it, but he says it's worth every mile of the commute to live here—and he'd do anything for Anna. Sea Harbor Community Day School is a godsend. All three of us think so."

"It's a good place. My granddaughter loves it, too."

Anna looked up. "Who's your granddaughter?"

"Her name is Gabby Marietti. This is her first year at the school." Birdie looked over at the young girl. "I think she knows you, Anna."

Anna's eyes lit up. "Oh, sure, I know Gabby. She's, like, a year older . . . but sometimes she eats with me. She doesn't like the cafeteria, just like me. Sometimes we go outside."

"It's probably very noisy," Birdie said, nodding. "If I were there, I'd probably be out on the patio with you."

Nell and Izzy listened, remembering the story Gabby had shared with them about Anna Mansfield. It was during Gabby's second week at the school and she and Daisy Danvers had already found each other. One noon they spotted the younger girl sitting at the end of their cafeteria table. She was holding her ears, and tears ran down her face. So the two of them scooted their trays closer toward her, nearly frightening Anna onto the floor. But they'd finally convinced her that they thought it was really loud that day. And did she want to eat outside with them? The fifth graders were allowed to do that, Gabby said, so they took Anna as their "guest." Once outside, the shy Anna calmed down, wiped her eyes with a napkin, and finished her lunch.

"We got in trouble with the cafeteria lady for bringing Anna with us," Gabby had said. "But the headmistress had walked by, and Dr. Hartley was all over it. She said that since Anna was with two fifth-grade girls, eating outside would be okay now and then."

It was clear Anna's mother had heard the story, too. And that the headmistress knew and understood Anna's difficulty in certain situations. Chelsey smiled at Birdie as if she herself had saved her daughter. Then she added, her voice adopting a lawyerly tone as if arguing a case in court, "There's no one who understands children better than Dr. Hartley. She is that school's savior, and losing her would destroy so much."

"Losing her?" Nell asked.

Chelsey glanced at Anna, and then she lowered her voice. "I know that Dr. Hartley's job is being threatened."

Birdie waved one hand in the air as if brushing away the irrelevant words. "I don't think you should worry about it. I'm not the only one who agrees with you that Dr. Hartley is doing a fine job."

Chelsey listened, but the worry that had come with her words lingered in the fine lines of her forehead. She straightened up, forced a smile, and turned her attention back to Anna as if she might otherwise disappear.

The young man behind the counter hollered that their ice cream was going to melt if they didn't get with it. So they did, with good-byes to the Mansfields and picking up a stash of napkins along with the tray of sundaes.

They moved outside to one of two small tables in the gravel alley that Myrna Sheridan, Scoopers' owner, had designated as her patio. Since it bordered a nail salon, she had little opposition, and Scoopers Patio it became.

"A perfect people-watching place," Izzy said. "We can see the people walking by, but all they see is a dimly lit alley with scary, shadowy figures—"

"Eating ice cream," Birdie added.

They sat in silence for a while, enjoying the breeze and listening to the faint strains of a guitar coming out of a small lounge farther down Harbor Road. The nice weather had brought a larger than usual number of strollers and window shoppers. Across the street, Archie Brandley's bookstore was still lit up and the door held open, something Archie often did when there were still people walking by or he simply wasn't ready to go home and welcomed the company a browser would provide.

"Isn't that Elizabeth?" Nell sat tall in her chair and pointed toward the bookstore.

Beneath the lamplight just outside the shop, the headmistress turned in the doorway and waved good-bye to an unseen Archie. She carried a stack of books and walked to her car, moving around to the driver's side and carefully skirting a string of moving traffic.

Nell raised an arm to wave her over for a bowl of Scoopers' finest, but she was suddenly blocked from view by a small yellow convertible—hip high, as Birdie described it later—that pulled up and stopped, so close to Elizabeth that the three women gasped, wondering for a minute if Elizabeth had been hit. But she seemed to be fine, and turned slowly toward the car that now paralleled her own.

Blythe Westerland rested one arm on the leather seat back and leaned toward Elizabeth, her engine idling. In the moonlight, her platinum hair appeared bright and perfect.

She was saying something other than hello, but from their table in the shadows of the alley, her words were lost.

The expression on Elizabeth's face, however, was clearly visible. The usually calm and gracious administrator was furious.

She started to turn back to her own car, her arms still clutching the books. It was then that Blythe leaned closer and her words brought Elizabeth's face once more into view.

At that precise moment, the breeze softened, the traffic stilled, and the music in the nearby bar was silenced.

But Elizabeth's words were not silent. They traveled at high speed over the hip-high convertible and into the alley where Nell, Izzy, and Birdie leaned forward in their metal chairs.

"You don't know what you're doing," Elizabeth shouted. The words were coated with ice. Her steely voice grew even louder and colder as she glared back at Blythe. "You can't get away with this." She turned, fumbled with the door handle, and finally slid in and sat behind the wheel. In the car next to her, Blythe brushed her hair smoothly back over one shoulder, pushed the gas pedal hard, and sped down Harbor Road, a smile on her face.

Chapter 6

"*L*aura Danvers must have magical powers. This weather is near perfect." Nell rolled the window down a crack as she and Ben drove down the long, winding driveway from Birdie's house. A black sky lit by a harvest moon, a mild breeze that had shifted sometime during the last twelve hours, and enough stars to satisfy the whole town's wishes.

"Maybe the weather is a good omen. I certainly hope so."

"You think we need a good omen for a party, Birdie?" Ben stopped at the Harbor Road stop sign and looked back at his white-haired passenger.

"It wouldn't hurt, now, would it? There's something not quite right, something in the air that makes me a little jittery."

"Any idea what it might be?" Ben asked. He picked up speed and drove down the town's main street, already filling up with Friday night revelers.

"Maybe it's the incident with Josh Babson," Nell suggested. "After all, it's your granddaughter's school."

"Elizabeth handled that paint situation well," Ben said. "I'm sure Jerry Thompson offered advice. It didn't even make the paper."

Birdie was silent for a moment and Nell looked over her shoulder. Their eyes met and she knew they shared the same thought: Blythe Westerland hadn't praised the way Elizabeth handled it. But that was another matter entirely.

"Well, good. It's nice to have Jerry tuned in to things," Birdie said. But she shook her head as she spoke, not convinced that the painting episode was the cause of her unrest. She pulled her silvery eyebrows together, searching for an explanation for her emotions. "I suppose it could be stray emotions from that contentious board meeting. Or simply my overactive imagination. Living with a ten-year-old can do that to one."

Nell thought back to the board meeting. It had left a bad taste in her mouth, too. And then last night's episode on Harbor Road hadn't lessened it any. Blythe was an interesting person, but she certainly wasn't trying to win herself any friends. Not that she seemed to care much about that sort of thing. "Why do you suppose Blythe is so insistent on removing Elizabeth from her job? She has been so vocal at the board meetings."

"She doesn't like the changes that are being made to the school, for one thing. That's her prerogative, I suppose," Birdie said. "But maybe it's something else. Something we haven't been privy to. It does seem a bit extreme. There's nothing the man can say that pleases her."

Ben listened to the conversation quietly. Nell looked over at him. "What do you think?"

"I wasn't there."

"But you know Blythe, maybe better than we do," Nell persisted.

"I know her mostly from the yacht club board. She's a woman of her convictions, opinionated. You have to give her that. And she clearly enjoys being on a board with mostly men, one-upping them when she can. Except—" Ben frowned, remembering something.

"Except?"

"Oh, nothing important. We're on a membership committee for the sailing club. It's more a formality than anything else—if anyone wants to join, great. We welcome them. Add their name. Take their dues." Ben put on his blinker, then turned toward the beach road and the route along the water to the school.

"Your thought seems unfinished," Nell said. She looked at Ben's profile. His window was half-open and a breeze ruffled his hair, blending a few silver strands in with the brown.

"Nope. Not really. I was just remembering that Blythe doesn't always agree with our open-door policy. It makes me wonder if she brings that exclusiveness to the school board."

Nell thought about the words she had hurled at Barrett Mansfield after the meeting. "I suppose she does in a way. I don't know. She's hard to read sometimes."

"Maybe she's just opinionated. That's not always bad. Hey, look up ahead." Ben pulled the wheel to the left and rounded Paley's Cove, bringing the school on the hill into view. "If I didn't know better, I'd think it was the Fourth of July."

To the left, up the gently rising hill, the columned patios, lawn, and lead glass windows of the school glowed against the black sky, shimmering and blinking with hundreds of tiny lights. Lanterns outlined the stone terraces, candles flickered on round white-clothed tables, and soft music floated down the hill, across the winding pathways, all the way down to the edge of the sea. Even the old boathouse was included in the splendid scene, a tiny rope of lights outlining the slanting roof.

Birdie looked over toward the water and laughed. "One might think that old shack was actually attractive."

"Laura Danvers has outdone herself. She's turned this whole place into an extravagant movie set." Nell took it all in as Ben drove slowly up the drive. She waved to several couples walking across the flagstone pathways that crisscrossed the sloping lawn.

"I'd guess some of these folks have never seen the school up close before. It's a smart thing to do, to welcome the town in like this," Ben said.

"Very smart," Birdie agreed. "It's certainly intentional. Elizabeth wants the town to use the facilities when that's appropriate—like the auditorium for community theater productions. She's even thinking of turning the old boathouse into a small theater that groups could use."

"Wise lady," Ben said. He pulled his CRV into a parking place at the end of the row. "She's a capable woman. I like her."

"And Jerry?" Nell lifted her eyebrows.

"I like him, too." Ben laughed.

Nell nudged him in the side until he offered a slight grimace.

"Okay, my romantic wife. Sure. Jerry likes her, too. But you knew that."

Birdie had already gotten out of the car, and Ben leaned over and gave Nell a quick kiss, then reached beyond her and pushed open her door.

Blythe Westerland's yellow Jaguar was parked across from them, the top up tonight. It was shiny and spotless, as perfect as the woman who had almost clipped Elizabeth Hartley the night before. Ben listened to the anecdote, then brushed it off. "Anyone who owns a car like that is very careful not to hit anyone or anything."

They walked on, down the row of cars, and spotted Izzy and Sam waiting at the edge of the parking lot.

Birdie quickened her short-legged pace to keep up with Ben as he headed their way. But Nell pulled back, enjoying the lovely sight of her niece and Sam, and allowing her imagination to add its own flourishes: the glowing school in the background, a cascade of brilliant lights outlining the property, and shafts of moonlight falling down on Izzy and Sam as if it had suddenly discovered this extraordinary couple and wanted to spotlight their presence.

It was an amazing sight, even if she were the only one seeing it in quite this dramatic way.

Izzy's silky blue dress flowed over her body like ocean water. And although Nell couldn't imagine walking upright in the spike heels she wore, she loved the look—with Izzy's long, well-toned legs seemingly endless. Just then a rogue breeze lifted the lacy shawl that covered Izzy's shoulders. It was the shawl Izzy had knit for herself to celebrate the one-year anniversary of the yarn shop. Beautiful hand-dyed sea silk yarn. Designed by Izzy. Knit by Izzy. And now casually thrown across her shoulders with the ease of a model but the abandon of someone who has no idea how lovely she is.

A stirring inside Nell quickened her pace. *Gratefulness.* It hit her at odd times, sometimes unexpected, like this one. The children she'd always dreamed of having hadn't happened for Nell and Ben. But *family* had happened, and in a bountiful way. Izzy. Then Izzy and Sam. And now baby Abigail. And friends. Rich layers of friends.

"What's that look?" Birdie took her arm and smiled up into her face.

Nell smiled back.

Birdie knew.

Ben and Sam left the women standing on the edge of the terrace talking to Father Northcutt, pastor of Our Lady of Safe Seas.

"You're here to give the blessing?" Nell asked, knowing the kindly priest would be the last one to miss a good party, blessing or not.

Father Larry laughed, his chins moving as he tossed his head back. "I'm here to taste that fine Irish whiskey Laura Danvers promised me she'd be pouring." His smile lit up and added dozens of creases to his round face. Thin strands of white hair fell haphazardly across his freckled forehead. "But the blessing, Nell, my darlin'. Sure 'n I'll be doing that, too."

He moved away then to greet Barrett and Chelsey Mansfield. Since the Mansfields had forsaken Boston and moved into their spacious home down the road from Birdie a couple of years before, Our Lady of Safe Seas' annex had been given new air-conditioning and a shiny new kitchen. "A good man," was the priest's grateful assessment. "A blessing."

Nell watched the Mansfields greet the priest, then introduce him to a group of well-dressed guests they had brought to the party. It was a distinguished-looking group who probably had deep pockets when it came to good causes—and the Mansfield daughter's school would fit the category. If he played his cards right, the kindly priest's charity ventures might benefit as well.

"That man has *sex appeal*," Izzy whispered, following Nell's look.

Nell startled. "Father Northcutt?"

Izzy laughed. "Barrett Mansfield. He's often a hot topic in the shop. He's quite the dude."

It was Nell's turn to laugh. It was nice to know a man could still be a hunk in his mid-fifties. She looked over at Barrett and focused on what Izzy saw. He *was* handsome—and happily married. Had Blythe noticed his looks? She didn't seem especially fond of the man, at least not recently.

"Chelsey enjoys the attention in her quiet way," Izzy said. "She knows the man adores her and somehow doesn't even seem to notice the attention he draws. He used to pick her up after her classes in law school and students would practically attack him. Chelsey found it amusing." Izzy looked over Nell's shoulder. "Oh, look—there's Tommy Porter and Janie." She waved at one of Sea Harbor's most popular policemen and the nurse they were all pushing him to propose to.

"All of Sea Harbor turned up tonight," Nell said. Everywhere she looked, she spotted friends and neighbors, fellow board members, students, and parents. She waved to Elizabeth Hartley, walking up from the shore. She looked every bit the headmistress in a tasteful fitted dress. But tonight she'd added a touch of romance—a lacy scarf the color of the sea that was wrapped around her neck, floating in the breeze. The other touch of romance was less visible—a hand tucked securely into that of the chief of police. For reasons that carried little logic, the sight pleased Nell inordinately.

Gabby raced over with Daisy close behind, both carrying a stack of programs in their arms. She hugged Birdie with her free arm, beaming with a pride that said the entire evening was her doing. "Isn't it the most beautiful thing you've ever seen, Nonna? Daisy and I helped Angelo light the lanterns." She pointed to the brass poles planted in the ground. They wound all the way down to the boathouse, each topped with a faceted lamp, the wick inside burning brightly.

"It's beautiful. Amazing," Nell said, looking at the two girls. "As are both of you."

Gabby blushed and tossed her head, sending her blue-black hair flying. Daisy pushed her glasses up her nose.

Gabby turned to Birdie. "Remember I'm spending the night at Daisy's, cool?"

"Very cool." Birdie smiled at Daisy and said, "Your mother said she has a ride to take you both home at nine? If not, I can call my Harold."

The two girls reluctantly said yes, they had a ride. They'd stay until the very end if they could, but the headmistress had decided the students should leave at nine. From then on it was an adult party.

"But," Daisy said with determination, "we have plenty of responsibilities between then and now, so I guess we better get with it." Gabby nodded and the two girls turned, as if on cue, and disappeared into the crowd, pleased with themselves and with life in general as they helped people find their reserved tables—a place to drop shawls or purses—and then directed them to "wander all over the place."

Birdie's eyes followed the sway of the lanterns that were planted in the ground, all the way down to the small dock. "There was a time when that dock was three times as large. In the early days of the school, some of the students who lived in the large sea cliff houses or down the shore would come over in boats. Yachts, actually. A parade of them, with young girls in somber uniforms escorted off their boats for a day of learning. The boathouse was a busy place back in those days—and there was more of a beach. Wind and water have taken that away."

"Did Blythe live in one of those houses?"

Birdie nodded. "I imagine so. The captain had managed to build a whole enclave around here, the school being the largest of his homes. They were passed along to his kin, except for this one."

"A different kind of life, for sure," Izzy said. Then added, "I'd never let Abby take a boat to school." She spotted Cass standing on the lawn near a circle of chairs. She was listening to the student musicians. Izzy waved until she got her attention and motioned her up to the terrace.

"Did you hear them?" Cass asked as she approached. "Those kids are amazing. That's Gracie's cousin on the bass. I used to change her diapers."

"You're alone," Izzy said. "Where's the guy?"

"The guy's name is Harry, Iz. *Harry.*"

"Ah, *Harry*. Got it. As in Harry Houdini. Invisible."

Cass ignored her and spoke to Birdie and Nell. "I had to drop some things off at my ma's, so he drove over by himself. He's here somewhere, swallowed up in the crowd. I swear there are a thousand people here—Harry's probably running into someone he knows from his summers here."

"So he knows his way around," Nell said. "Well, that's good. I'm looking forward to meeting him."

"Students are conducting tours of the grounds and the school. He may have joined one of the groups," Birdie said. The school loomed large and glorious against the sky, its lead glass windows lit from within.

Nell looked down at the program. The evening was planned in an unusual way, designed to keep people moving, talking, enjoying the grounds, the food, and the school. Instead of a regular sit-down dinner, there would be a series of different small courses with a school bell indicating when new plates arrived at the tables, luring people back to their chairs. Then off again to mingle or visit the bar or stroll down to the water.

On the other edge of the terrace, they could see the first course being placed on serving trays. Blythe Westerland was ordering people around, standing out from everyone else in a gorgeous shimmering dress. Gracie Santos stood guard, too, checking the miniature lobster rolls and making sure they were positioned on the plates in curved lines, sprigs of parsley separating one from another, and pots of sauce placed in the center as they were delivered around the terrace, one to each table. "It looks like Gracie has donated the appetizers from the Lazy Lobster," Cass said. "Her donation to her alma mater."

"A very generous one." Birdie waved at Gracie, and she waved back, then added one last sprig of parsley to a tray before heading their way. A breeze blew in from the water and lifted her blond hair from the back of her neck as she approached.

"This is so great," she said. "This whole thing. It makes me want to be back in school again."

"So . . . good memories?" Nell asked.

"Not in the beginning. I missed my Cass." She threw her friend a lopsided grin. "But once I adjusted, I was fine."

"Easy come, easy go," Cass said.

Gracie laughed. "Yeah. Hey, where's the guy?"

Izzy answered for her in a husky Cass voice, "He has a *name*, Gracie. *Harry.*"

Cass dismissed them all with a disdainful wave of her hand and started off in search of Ben and Sam. "At least the guys talk to me about sensible things."

Gracie and Izzy followed her, leaving Nell and Birdie to find a quiet space on a stone bench, out of the mainstream.

People-watching, Birdie said, as well as getting a grip on the lay of the land.

"It looks so different at night, all lit up like this," Birdie said. "It's certainly beautiful—" She shivered and rubbed her arms.

"You still have that feeling of something being off-kilter, don't you?"

"Maybe I'm wrapping myself too tightly in first-time mother garb. Wondering about Gabby's teachers, the homework, the friends she is making. Is she adjusted? Happy?" Birdie reached over and patted Nell's hand. "Nell, dear—remind me every now and then that I am not young, not a mother, but am a woman 'of a certain age' with a million years of experience who knows better than to worry about those things."

"And knows better than to imagine danger on a beautiful autumn night. Consider yourself reminded."

"I suppose being here and reminded of the tensions that have filled this lovely place recently is having some effect." She looked back at the lit school, at the lead glass windows and silhouettes of people as they went through the hallways, touring and chatting and drinking wine.

Fired teachers and disgruntled board members should be the furthest thing from their minds.

Except.

"Oh, good grief," Birdie said. "Now, why would he be here?"

She pointed toward the flagpole, illuminated by several small spots, the three flags at the top waving in the evening breeze. It was not far from the spot that had so recently been mowed clean of its yellow circles.

Nell looked over.

Jane and Ham Brewster stood with a group of Canary Cove artists, soaking in the surroundings with their eyes, as if they all wanted to set up shop with brushes and easels and begin a session en plein air right there in the middle of the party.

Standing out in the group because he rose nearly a head taller than anyone else was Josh Babson.

He had forsaken the paint-stained jeans and torn T-shirt and looked presentable, his hair slicked back and clean jeans and a white shirt fitted over his tall, slender frame.

"He must have come with Jane and Ham," Nell said. "They bought a table or two and probably invited any of the artists who wanted to come. They know most of the fledgling artists can't afford it on their own—"

"Of course, that would be it," Birdie said, but her voice didn't completely disguise her surprise that a recently fired teacher would show up at a school function.

No matter, whatever the true circumstances of Josh's dismissal, both Birdie and Nell were happy he had found a job so quickly. "Jane has good judgment. She trusts him in her gallery," Birdie said.

"I suppose. The curious part, though," Nell said, watching as a hoot of laughter rose like a plume from the group, "is why he would *want* to come to a party at the school. Here, of all places . . ."

Birdie wondered the exact same thing.

Of course, they knew the food would be worth it.

They watched as the lanky artist looked around the grounds while the others were talking. Several students vied for his attention. He grinned and waved, but his look went over their heads as he searched the gathering crowd. He was looking for something, for *someone*, his expression intent as he stepped apart from the group, his head moving back and forth.

The friendly expression they'd noticed earlier was gone as he scanned the crowd, replaced by one you wouldn't expect to bring to a party.

Josh Babson looked determined. And angry. It wasn't the same man Nell had met the day before, someone who crouched down to say hello to a toddler and who had spoken with pleasure about his students. About Gabby.

This Josh Babson looked as if he'd like to kill someone.

Birdie wrapped her shawl around her shoulders tightly.

And this time when she shivered, Nell didn't ask why.

Chapter 7

Birdie tucked her arm through Nell's as they sat quietly, listening to a medley of old Gershwin tunes being played by the student jazz musicians.

But their thoughts remained on Josh Babson. He had abandoned the group of Canary Cove artists and now stood by himself near the musicians. They were clearly happy to see him. But his posture told Nell and Birdie he was still searching for something or someone.

"Tonight is supposed to be an evening of goodwill," Birdie said. "Who's to say Josh Babson isn't capable of the same? That's why he came. Somehow these kinds of messy things work themselves out and the bad feelings go out with the tide."

Nell wasn't so sure, especially since she implicitly respected Birdie's penchant to portend ominous events. She would not describe the look on Josh's face as he searched the crowd as one of forgiveness.

She looked over at Elizabeth Hartley standing on the terrace, greeting a group of guests. She wondered if Josh had spotted her yet. Was she who he was looking for?

Nell looked up at the moon, trying to scatter the disturbing thoughts. She was letting her imagination get the better of her. Elizabeth was fine. And certainly safe in the middle of hundreds of friends and parents and supporters.

And Birdie was right about it being a special night. So she pushed the uncomfortable emotion aside and reminded herself to live in the moment. It was all any of them had, after all.

The image of sweet Harriet and Archie Brandley, holding hands and strolling up from the shore as if they were young lovers, brought a smile and a wave and a settling of her thoughts. Yes, a night of goodwill.

When the Brandleys walked over to chat, Nell left Birdie in charge and excused herself for a quick trip to the ladies' room.

"The teachers' lounge is the one to use," Birdie instructed, pointing toward a set of double doors. "Just go through the library and to your left."

The teachers' lounge was lovely, with desks, chairs, and chaises, places to prepare lesson plans or relax. Fresh flowers, probably for tonight's occasion, graced the tables and soft music came through speakers near the ceiling. She could see Laura Danvers's hand in the details. She had pulled out all the stops to make this evening special. Nell walked through the lounge to the restroom at the far end.

Even that room held flowers, small vases of late-blooming hibiscus and daisies, their reflections glowing in the wall of mirrors above the sinks. Nell leaned forward to pinch off a head, then took a brush from her bag and gave her hair a quick fix.

"You are as quiet as a cat." She spoke to the mirror image of the woman who came up and stood next to her.

Blythe Westerland smiled a hello as she artfully applied a layer of lipstick.

"It's a perfect evening, Blythe," Nell said. "Even the lounge is lovely."

"It's perfect, I agree. And you are wonderful to say so. It's been a labor of love."

Blythe smiled again, then picked up her tiny gold purse and walked back into the lounge area.

Nell gave herself one final appraisal, smoothed down a wrinkle in her black cocktail dress, and walked back through the lounge, greeting Esther Gibson, who was relaxing in one of the chairs, her cell phone to her ear. She put one hand over the mouthpiece and whispered to Nell, "Just checking on my men," then spoke back into the phone to some policeman giving her a report on department goings-on. Mostly likely the report centered on a chess tournament as the officers enjoyed a quiet Friday night at the precinct.

Nell put her hand on the doorknob, then stopped midtwist. The voices coming from the hallway were familiar, and at first listen, one was not cordial.

One voice she recognized instantly because she had just heard it—smooth and melodious. Blythe Westerland. It was the other voice that stopped her from opening the door. It was low and controlled, filled with anger.

"What is the matter with you?" Chelsey Mansfield said. "Barrett and I have done nothing to you. Anna is a child. Leave her alone. Leave *us* alone. And don't you dare play with her life in an effort to punish us. Don't you dare."

There was a moment of silence and Nell could imagine Blythe's expression. Her face would be calm and her smile—her all-purpose, ever-ready, unreadable smile—would accompany whatever came out of her mouth.

"Chelsey, dear"—the words were sweet—"I am encouraging Dr. Hartley to do what is best for this school. Your daughter needs to be somewhere else. It will be better for her, better for the other students, and better for my school."

"The other students? Blythe, your thinking is terribly wrong. Have you ever had a child? Do you understand anything?"

"A child?" Blythe laughed. It had a bitter sound to it. "Of course not." She started to walk away, then paused, just long enough to encourage Chelsey and her husband to enjoy the party.

Nell heard the echoing sound of Jimmy Choo heels fading as Blythe walked away from Chelsey Mansfield.

Chelsey seemed not to move, but her voice was audible, her

words clear and distinct, carrying all the way to where Nell stood behind the closed lounge door.

Her anger was palpable, her voice steely:

"You won't get away with hurting people this way, Blythe. Trust me. You will be stopped."

Nell took a deep breath and waited until she heard Chelsey's footsteps as she walked away.

When she finally walked back outside, neither Chelsey nor Blythe was anywhere in sight. Nell was relieved. They surely would be able to tell from looking at her that she had just eavesdropped on their private conversation, something she didn't make a habit of doing. It was a conversation she wished she hadn't heard. Chelsey's anger was meant to be heard by no one but Blythe.

Elizabeth walked toward her from across the terrace. A beautiful turquoise scarf floated behind her.

"Have you seen Blythe?" Her voice was businesslike and controlled.

Nell nodded. "We spoke in the lounge a few minutes ago. She headed back outside before I came out."

Elizabeth's look was pensive, as if Nell's comment held more meaning than a woman leaving a restroom. Finally she said, "If you see her, would you please tell her I need to talk to her?" Elizabeth managed a smile. "It's difficult to find anyone in this crowd. A nice problem to have, however." She nodded to a teacher waving to her, thanked Nell, and hurried off.

In the distance Nell spotted Josh again, standing alone near a hedge, out of the way of the crowds, watching Elizabeth walk toward the steps. He looked at Nell briefly, then shifted attention back to Elizabeth.

He set his drink down on a tray and walked in her direction, his long strides catching up with her quickly and cutting her off before she was surrounded by a crowd of well-wishers.

Nell took a quick breath, checking around for security guards, for Ben, for anyone.

Josh had put his hand on Elizabeth's arm, and she had turned toward him.

She looked up. Surprised.

A sliver of fear worked its way through Nell and she began to walk in their direction. Then stopped.

Elizabeth had turned, and Nell could see her face and the way she was looking at Josh. There were no traces of fear. She was listening closely, leaning in, nodding. Smiling.

She rested one hand briefly on Josh's arm, looked into his face, and smiled. Then she turned and walked calmly away. She was still smiling as she greeted the next group of guests.

And Josh did the same, walking back to his spot near the hedge.

An evening of goodwill, Nell thought. Maybe Birdie was right.

She made her way back to the bench where she'd left Birdie. She was standing at the stone railing, her blue-veined hands resting on the cool surface, enjoying the sight of so many people milling about the lawn. "It's like Seurat's La Grande Jatte," Birdie said. "Except at night."

"And wouldn't you know who'd be right in the middle of it?" Nell said. She pointed toward Gabby and Daisy, out on the lawn, their arms free of programs as they lifted a brass candle lighter and tried to relight a flame. Gabby, standing on tiptoe, towered over her friend as she clutched the tall pole, all the while trying desperately to control her giggles.

"Oh, dear," Birdie murmured. "Don't burn yourself, dear . . ." She looked away and sat down on the beach.

"What were those words?" Nell asked. She sat down beside her friend, relieved to be thinking of Gabby and Daisy, two beautiful, innocent girls on the cusp of life. "What was it . . . ? Oh, yes. 'You are a woman with a million years of experience who knows better than to worry about such things . . .' ?"

Birdie sighed. It would take practice.

They looked up as Ben's shadow fell across the railing. He car-

ried a tray of drinks and was followed by an entourage of friends—
and one stranger.

Nell started to stand, but the mustached man with the thick
dark hair walked over, his large hands motioning her down. "It's
okay. Don't stand, please." He nodded at each of them, a gracious
gesture that brought a thick lock of hair tumbling across his forehead. "Cass pointed you both out. Birdie and Nell, right?"

"And you must be Harry Winthrop," Birdie said, resting her
hand in his large palm. "See there? We know each other without
having met. If memory serves me, you resemble your father."

Harry lifted one eyebrow. He tugged lightly on his beard.

"I knew him years ago, not well, but from their summers here,"
she said. She watched as he touched his beard again. He was clearly
not comfortable with it yet, and she remembered her Sonny doing
the same when he had decided to sport a beard.

Harry looked a little surprised that anyone would remember
his parents. "Yeah, they liked it up here."

"Do you come back often? Your siblings?"

"No siblings—though I always wanted a dozen or so. And no, I
don't come back much. My folks had a lifetime membership in the
yacht club and I've come up a couple times to sail."

"They loved it here, as I remember. And the house has stayed
in the family all this time, even with no one using it." Birdie
smiled.

Harry looked slightly nonplussed.

The Whitfield place had once been a cottage off the cover of
Coastal Living magazine with sweeping ocean views, white clap-
board siding, and an enviable ambience. Years of disuse had weathered the small home, and now peeling paint, a weedy yard, and
crumbling drive were what people thought of when they mentioned
the Winthrop place.

Birdie filled in the silence and touched his arm. "I didn't mean
that as an insult. The cottage is still one of the best locations in Sea

Harbor and I'm happy that you might bring it back to its healthier days."

"Yeah," he said. "It has good bones. I've never quite got my act together to make a decision about what to do with it but am determined to get that worked out while I'm here." He looked away when he talked, not entirely comfortable. One finger rubbed his mustache. "I stayed in it for breaks when I was at BU, but then life happened."

"Sea Harbor is a perfect escape from college stress," Nell said. "Sometimes I think it's a BU annex, at least if the T-shirts around town are any indication."

"Hey, we Harvard grads spent time here, too," Izzy said.

"And don't forget Holy Cross." Cass waved her hand in the air and began chanting her college fight song.

"I'm with you, Cass." Angelo Garozzo walked up, his short, square frame dressed in a dark suit and tie that made him nearly unrecognizable. He pumped one fist in the air. "Go, Crusaders."

Ben reached over and shook his hand. "Good to see you, Angelo. Great event. Great school. And I hear you have a lot to do with that."

"I try, Ben." He shook his head. "Some days are better than others."

"You know everyone, right?" Ben took in the half circle of people with a wave of his hand.

Angelo looked around the group, his ruddy grin greeting each of them. His greeting stopped at Harry. He frowned and leaned his head to one side, scanning the newcomer's face. Harry shifted from one foot to the other.

"Do I know you?" Angelo asked.

Harry shrugged. "Probably not. Unless from long-ago summers and a guy who sometimes got wild at beach parties. But I didn't have all this hair in those days." He stroked his beard.

"Nah, I don't remember things like that. I'll remember." He snapped his fingers. "Oh, yah. Yacht club. Months ago. I was fixin' something or other in one of the cabins. Yah. That's it. No mustache, though, right?"

He frowned, tugging at the rest of the memory, then shook it off and turned away from Harry and moved on to another matter. He touched Nell's and Birdie's arms, planting his square body in front of them, motioning them away from the rest of the group.

Without preamble he started in, keeping his voice low and private. One finger stabbed the air while he talked. "Whatta we going to do with the board? Can you two help them get their act together? They're crazy, you know that?" His face turned from a weathered tan to a sweaty red as he talked. He looped one finger into his starched shirt collar and tugged at it.

"Take a breath, Angelo. We don't want anyone dying on us at this lovely party." Birdie rested one veined hand on his forearm and silenced his moving finger. "It will work out."

"It hurts Dr. Hartley, you know. She's good folks, that one, and she's doing a good job here. This place is as healthy as I've seen it in years—and it's not only for the students, what she does. She's doing good things for Sea Harbor. But—"

His words cut off as he looked off in the distance, his angry face landing on his prey.

Birdie and Nell followed the darts that seemed to visibly leave his eyes.

On the lawn a few steps below, Laura and Elliott Danvers stood with the mayor and a group of important-looking guests from out of town. In the middle of the group, her hair pulled back into a low, elegant bun and her shiny dress highlighting every curve of her body, Blythe Westerland held court. She held a champagne glass in one hand, and the other was tucked through the arm of a gentleman Nell recognized as owning a vacation home up on the cliff.

Angelo shook his head. "The goddess wants Elizabeth gone. I think it's a power thing. I don't quite know what to do about it." His voice was angry and sad and determined, all at once. "I knew a couple of the Westerland men, y' know. Used to do some work for them, fixing things up. Her granddad—he was a powerful man. And her father, too, always trying to one-up his brothers. Power-hungry. That's what they were.

"They're all gone now, except for her—she's the last of the Westerlands. Ha. Someone should write a book about it. She needs to be gone, too, like the rest of them, before she does more damage to the good folks around this place." The last words were mumbled, intended for himself. Then he turned away without ceremony or a good-bye and stomped over to talk to a discreet clump of security guards, hired by the school to monitor parking lot traffic and keep the grounds safe and secure.

Before Nell and Birdie had a chance to react to Angelo's outburst, a school bell announced that the first course was being delivered to tables. The jazz combo picked up its beat, and guests moved to the rhythm and found their places.

Father Northcutt moved to the wide fan of steps and Laura handed him the microphone. He hushed the crowd with arms spread wide, then offered up a thank-you to the Almighty "for the finest, tastiest food known to man." He smiled in his inimitable way and suggested a toast to the fine evening they were about to enjoy.

Glasses were lifted, cheers filled the air, and trays of tiny lobster rolls were passed around the tables.

"This whole evening is magical," Birdie said as she settled down next to Ben and accepted the glass of wine he offered her. She looked at the tray of Gracie's rolls. "Father Larry got it right—the finest food on the Cape. Not only is Laura making sure everyone eats well and sees every inch of this magnificent property, but she's giving us a chance to walk off our calories in between. Such a wise young woman."

In addition to Gracie's rolls, baskets of calamari, with the Ocean's Edge restaurant special buttermilk coating—were eagerly emptied. A medley of sauces dotted the table.

Nell glanced over at Cass, sitting next to Sam. "Did we scare

Harry off?" she asked, glancing at the empty seat between her and Cass.

"Yes, you are plenty scary, Nell." She looked over her shoulder, then swiveled in the other direction. "He was around here not too long ago. He probably spotted some guy he knew or something. He's been stopped a couple times by some of his parents' old friends, though most of them don't connect him with the fresh-faced kid he used to be—not with all that hair on his face. Anyway, he'll be back."

Cass was right. Harry returned a short while later and sat next to Nell, his eyes going immediately to the baskets of calamari and lobster rolls.

Nell suggested he take his fill before Cass noticed that there were some left.

On his other side, Cass was talking to Sam about some photos he'd taken of her new lobster boat, and Harry seemed content to not be talking at all. Instead he sat back, enjoying the food. He shifted in the chair, watching the crowd, his eyes moving from group to group. One foot tapped the stone floor, a slight nervous movement that Nell could feel.

"Are you running into people you know?" Nell asked, leaning closer to be heard over the crowd noise.

Startled out of his reverie, Harry jerked his head toward her. "Know?" he stammered.

"Cass mentioned you might know some people here. Old friends?"

The question seemed to confuse Harry, and Nell briefly regretted her attempt at drawing him out. She tried again, turning the attention away from him. "Many people come back here—like homing pigeons, I guess. It's addictive. Ben and I are perfect examples. His family had a vacation place here for more years than any of us remember. I fell in love with it the first time Ben brought me up. Sea Harbor summers are memorable.

"And when circumstances allowed, we moved up here permanently. My niece is the same way. Izzy used to spend every summer here, from the time she was a teenager. It's how she and Cass became friends for life. It's where she learned to sail. Experienced her first kiss."

She was talking too much, she knew. But there was something about Harry that made her nervous, perhaps because he seemed distracted. Or nervous. Or at least that was what the tapping foot said to her. She slowed down her chatter. Smiled. "I don't mean to sound like I work for the Chamber of Commerce. I simply like it here."

Harry had recovered. "Sure, I get that," he said. "I didn't spend too many summers here. But I kinda remember hanging out on those boulders down near the boathouse. It was a good fishing spot."

Cass turned from Ben and leaned into the conversation. "Want to go revisit it? See if it's changed? Catch a fish or two?"

"The boathouse?" Harry asked.

"Sure. The calamari is gone. I think I ate half a basket by myself. I need to walk it off."

Harry shrugged and pushed out his chair, nearly colliding with Laura Danvers.

Laura laughed it off, excusing herself for sneaking up on him. She greeted everyone at the table with her hostess charm, urged them to visit the bar, thanked them profusely for coming, and moved on to the next table.

Blythe Westerland was just steps behind her, not wanting to be outdone in the hostess category. Her shimmering dress caught the table's candlelight. She moved to Ben's side and greeted him with a warm hug, then repeated Laura's gracious welcome, moving around the table, trying with difficulty to keep her champagne from sloshing out of the glass.

Nell remembered Elizabeth's request and mentioned to Blythe that the headmistress had been looking for her. "It's a great crowd, but it's difficult to find people."

Blythe seemed to toss off Nell's message and instead laughed and chatted on about the enormous turnout, the money raised, and her plans to suggest some changes to the board about how the money was spent. Travel was one idea, she said. "Maybe trips to Paris for the older girls."

Nell held her silence, imagining the board discussions looming in the future. Travels to France would definitely not be how Elizabeth wanted the foundation money spent. It wasn't at all what she had in mind when she proposed additional scholarships or more community involvement.

But Blythe had already turned her attention to greeting Cass, touching her arm for attention, nodding a hello.

Harry stepped away from the table. "Ready, Cass?" he said.

Blythe stepped back in surprise. "Well, now. I thought for a minute you were Danny Brandley," she said. Her head leaned to one side, a curious smile on her lips. Her fingers touched her chin as if she, too, had a carefully trimmed beard. "Hmm. Nice beard."

Cass put her hand on Harry's arm and began to move away. "Sorry, Blythe. He's not Danny," she said, edging backward toward the terrace steps. Harry rested one hand on her lower back.

Nell half expected his foot to start tapping.

Blythe stayed still but watched the couple with an amused look, as if assessing the combination. She sipped her champagne, her eyes steady over the rim. As they moved away, she lifted one hand and wiggled her fingers in a wave. "Be good, you two," she said.

Cass didn't answer.

Blythe smiled. "Later," she called out. Several people turned to look, wondering to whom the shimmering Blythe was talking.

Cass adeptly ignored her and quickened her step.

Nell held back a smile. *Later* for Cass would most certainly mean *never*.

Harry turned back once, then lowered his head to listen to Cass as they started to disappear in the crowd.

Nell felt the brief wave of tension. There wasn't any love lost between Blythe and Cass.

But Blythe seemed impervious to it. She watched Cass walk away, an amused expression on her face. "I must need glasses. How could I have confused him with Danny Brandley? There are no similarities whatsoever between those two. Nada." She chuckled, then said, "So . . . exactly where *is* our Danny boy?" The question was meant for no one. A random thought that found its way into words.

Nell watched the expression linger on her face. Was she surprised that Danny Brandley wasn't there next to Cass? Blythe Westerland was impossible to read. Nell wondered if she played poker. She would be good at it.

Blythe seemed to feel Nell and Izzy watching her and pulled her attention back to the table. "Silly," she said matter-of-factly. "The man looks good in a mustache, doesn't he?" And then she turned toward Ben and engaged him in yacht club talk.

"She left just in time," Izzy said. "I was ready to bop her. Cass would curse us all if she thought we were talking about her personal life with Blythe Westerland."

Nell agreed. She looked over Izzy's shoulder and caught a glimpse of Cass and Harry, stopping near the flagpole to talk to Jane and Ham Brewster.

She didn't know what to make of Harry. Blythe was right—he looked good in a mustache, and he seemed nice enough. A little nervous, maybe. He was good-looking, in a movie star way. But there was something about him that she couldn't quite put her finger on. He seemed to treat Cass fine. So perhaps that was all that mattered. And the fact that he intended to turn the old and weathered beach home into something pleasant was also a good thing for Sea Harbor. No one liked seeing run-down cottages along the shore.

Blythe began walking away, then turned back. "Cass looks good tonight, don't you think? Her boyfriend, too. Is that what he is?"

Izzy's radar pulled her around and her thoughts merged with Nell's. They didn't like Blythe talking about Cass, but on the other hand, they couldn't quite decide if it would be good or bad to have Blythe show an interest in Harry Winthrop.

"He's nothing like Danny, do you agree?" Blythe said. "Not with all that facial hair, anyway." She held out her glass as a waiter passed by and waited for a refill.

It was a curious comment, but both Nell and Izzy chose to ignore it. Nothing Blythe said could really surprise them.

Then Sam joined in, "Well, his name *is* Harry—"

Blythe smiled. She looked out again, scanning the groups of partygoers filling the lawn. "We certainly have our share of interesting guests tonight."

Before Ben or Izzy could respond, the society editor and photographer from the *Boston Globe* beckoned to Blythe. Also waiting for the photo shoot was a well-known senior partner in Elliott Danvers's Boston law firm, his infatuation with Blythe visible in his waiting smile. Blythe returned it, and was soon standing before the camera, comfortable and happy.

The evening moved on in unending samplings of Sea Harbor restaurants' most delicious entrées: skewered pork and apples, cucumber soup, roasted fall vegetables, and chunks of succulent sautéed crabmeat.

Blythe Westerland was everywhere, greeting each group of guests as if the school were her elegant home and she were Pearl Mesta, a hostess everyone would remember. Always, it seemed, there was an elegant man at her beck and call. *Hovering*, Cass called it, and suggested that she wore some potent perfume that was probably illegal.

As they reached the last course—generous slices of key lime pie that were being passed around the terrace—Laura Danvers stood on the fan of steps overlooking the partygoers, beaming. Just a year or two younger than Izzy, Laura handled such affairs with the ease and aplomb of someone twice her age. Gracious and smart, she was the go-to person for nearly every charitable event in town—and as she had done tonight, they were all successful.

She tapped her handheld microphone for attention, gathering people to the terrace area. Many were already at their assigned tables, but others were scattered in happy groups everywhere. "I think the crowd has grown with each course," Nell murmured to Ben as they sat down next to Izzy and Sam. "I don't know if we'll ever see Birdie again—she claims everyone she has ever met in her life is here."

Cass waved from the bar that she was bringing over a fresh carafe of coffee.

Another tap of the microphone hushed the crowd, and Laura looked out at the crowd, asking for quiet while she thanked the school staff and the myriad of other generous people who had made the evening possible.

First came the restaurateurs who had donated the innovative tapaslike courses they had all enjoyed. The applause was rousing.

"And next, for those of you who don't know her, Dr. Elizabeth Hartley has pulled our school together and given it new life. If you haven't met her yet, make sure you do before leaving tonight. You'll be glad you did." She looked blindly into the crowd, motioning for Elizabeth to come up to the microphone.

Necks swiveled, seeking out the headmistress. An awkward silence followed, people shifted, and those still standing moved, in case they were blocking her way. At the edge of the terrace, Jerry Thompson stood with a puzzled expression on his face, looking around the crowd.

Laura held her smile and waited patiently.

A door opened, and Elizabeth appeared, hurrying across the flagstone terrace, her face flushed and the sound of her heels magnified in the silence that had fallen over the crowd.

Nell felt her embarrassment.

"It's like the Academy Awards," Izzy whispered next to her. "Caught in the bathroom when your name is called."

At the steps, Laura hugged Elizabeth warmly and thanked her for all she had done—and was doing—for the school and for the whole community. Her words brought great applause from the crowd.

Elizabeth took the microphone and spoke a few words, enough to express her deep love for Sea Harbor Community Day School, for her job, and for the people who had made it all possible. And then she handed the mic back to Laura and wound her way through the crowd until she stood safely at Jerry Thompson's side.

Next Laura asked all the board members to stand. "These folks are giving enormous amounts of time and energy—not to mention fund-raising—to this school and to the community projects it supports and fosters. Frankly, they're great," she said, "and not just because my charming husband is one of them." She blew a kiss in Elliott's direction and the crowd laughed. Again necks craned in the direction of shuffling chairs as Nell and Birdie, Barrett Mansfield, Elliott, and half a dozen others stood, nodded, and quickly resumed their seats.

"One of you needs to remain standing and accept your own round of much-deserved applause," Laura said graciously, peering out into the crowd.

Nell looked at Birdie. "That's generous of her."

Birdie nodded. "Our Laura knows people. And she knows how much Blythe covets attention. It will put her in good stead."

How true. And how wise of Laura. Surely Elliott kept her attuned to some of the more dramatic meetings of the board. This might be one good way to calm Blythe down.

"Blythe Westerland, please come up and take a well-deserved bow." Laura looked out over the sea of heads toward the mayor's table, where Blythe had been sitting. Mayor Beatrice Scaglia shrugged and nodded toward an empty seat.

"Blythe hasn't been off her feet all night," someone murmured from a table near Laura. "She's everywhere."

Laura picked up on the remark. "That's true—Blythe hasn't stopped for a minute. She's probably helping with the dishes." The image brought a wave of laughter, waving off the awkward moment. "Be sure you seek her out before you leave tonight and let her know what a superb hostess she's been. Now let's get on with a wonderful wind-down to the evening. Please enjoy the rest of your pie, help yourself to the coffee bar, and drive home safely."

Within an hour the crowd had thinned to just a few dozen folks, some helping Laura collect stray programs and others simply reluctant to call it an evening while the wine was still flowing. Ben noticed the tired lines on Birdie's face and the slowness of her step. "It's time to go," he said.

Birdie gratefully agreed and gave a farewell wave to Angelo, who was bending over to pick up stray napkins, the pants of his neat dark suit straining against his girth. "You never rest, do you, Angelo?" she called out as he straightened up and called back, "Keeps me outta trouble, Birdie. You know that."

He laughed, waved, and then began barking orders to the crew to take down the tables, clean the lawns, make sure stray sweaters and glasses and scarves were collected with care, and snuff out every single hurricane lamp, all the way down to the water, so the place wouldn't burn down.

The parking lot was a jumble of good-byes, hugs, and brief conversations about the evening.

A *perfect* party, Harriet Brandley said.

Esther Gibson agreed as she ushered her husband over to their truck, waving good-bye to Ben and Nell. "Not a single emergency call," the alert dispatcher called out to Ben. "The guys spent the evening playing chess at the station. Now, how perfect a night is that?"

Ben and Nell laughed, knowing that, of course, Esther would have called in not once, but many times during the evening. Whether she was on duty or not, the dispatcher's thoughts were with the Sea Harbor men in blue and keeping the town safe, even though if there *had* been a disruption, it most likely would have been something as severe as a fight in Jake Risso's Gull Tavern over a baseball score, or a rowdy party down on one of boats. Or maybe a firework or two being set off in a quiet neighborhood.

Disruptions were mild in Sea Harbor. Almost always.

Ben dropped Birdie at her home and he and Nell drove through the quiet night to their house, their bodies weary, but with the contented slowness that an enjoyable evening brought about. Along Harbor Road, shops were closed and lamplights lit the way for late-night diners and revelers meandering out of Jake Risso's bar or the Ocean's Edge restaurant.

Ben had almost reached the corner of Sandswept Lane when the sudden sound of sirens pierced the stillness. Startled, Nell pressed forward against the seat restraint as Ben pulled the car over to the side of the road.

They looked around, unsure of where the alarms were coming from or in which direction the ambulance would be speeding.

Suddenly the night was filled with what seemed like hundreds of sirens—although there weren't that many police cars on all of Cape Ann.

In the distance, spinning lights lit up the dark sky.

And in that single instant, a perfect evening was shattered.

Chapter 8

The ringing of the doorbell at two a.m. would have paralyzed Nell on a normal night, jarring her out of a deep sleep and causing her heart to skip a beat.

But neither she nor Ben had slept much. They'd stood on the back deck, watching the sky light up as police cars and emergency vehicles headed north along the shore road.

And then they had gone back inside and up the back stairs to get ready for bed because at that late hour there was no one to call for information, no one to assure them that everything was fine. No one to say that it was a minor car accident, but no one was hurt. A slow night for the police, so they sent out the whole crew. It was just a bad scare. Everyone—everywhere—was fine.

Sleep came reluctantly, and when it did, it was a slight, light sleep, dipping just beneath that thin layer that separates sleep from wakefulness.

Ben was out of bed in an instant at the first ring.

Pulling on sweatpants, he took the back stairs two at a time. Nell was seconds behind him, grabbing the sash of her robe where it hung loose, flapping against her leg.

Stars still lingered in the black sky, but not enough to distinguish the figure on the front step. Ben clicked on the porch light and opened the door.

Chief Jerry Thompson stood in front of him, disheveled, the

light catching his badge. Behind him, nearly hidden by his frame, was Elizabeth Hartley.

"Ben, Nell," the chief began, his deep voice catching in his throat. He took a deep breath, moving slightly, and it was then that Nell saw Elizabeth's face. It was pasty white, and filled with something unreadable. Something beyond fear.

Without a word, Ben pushed the door open wider, stepped aside, and ushered them in. Nell led the way to the kitchen, where she automatically filled glasses with water and pulled out the island stools.

"An accident . . . ," Nell began, the question not really forming. But at least her friends standing on the doorstep were both safe. Able to walk away from whatever it was that had happened. Except for Elizabeth's shock—that was the expression, she recognized it now, *shock*—they were unhurt.

Elizabeth still wore the dress she had had on for the party—a dark silky dress, a splash of turquoise at the neck. She had looked so pretty at the party. But that prettiness had been replaced by the circles beneath her eyes and the pasty look on her face.

She looked over at the chief. He, too, still wore the suit he'd gone to the party in. But instead of a handkerchief in the front pocket, it was covered over with a Sea Harbor police badge.

"You're on duty, Jerry," Ben said.

He nodded. "I have to go back to the school, but I didn't want to leave Elizabeth at her dark house. It just seemed . . . well, since she lives just down the street—"

"Of course," Nell said quickly, not knowing why they were there, but it suddenly didn't matter. Elizabeth looked as though she needed comfort—and she and Ben could certainly supply that.

Ben took a bottle of whiskey from the cupboard and poured Elizabeth a shot. She looked fragile, as if she needed something to bolster her up or she might crumble.

"The boathouse," Elizabeth managed to say. She took a sip of the whiskey and swallowed it with a grimace as if it were medicine. "I knew we should have taken it down. It was such a wreck, but teachers had ideas for it . . ." Her voice drifted off. It was a faraway voice, as if she were alone in the room and her thoughts had unintentionally taken the shape of words.

Jerry reached out and covered her hand. "Shh," he said gently, then explained to Ben and Nell how the boathouse played a role in the middle-of-the-night visit. "The cleanup guys went down to extinguish the gaslights lighting the paths to the water. They were clear around the boathouse—people had wanted to see the old place, so the path around it had been lit, too, to keep folks from falling on the gravelly path and boulders. It's a rocky shore in that spot." He paused and took a drink of whiskey, and then went on.

"One of the hurricane lamps on the far side of the boathouse had been knocked down and the glass was smashed against the rocks. When they went to pick it up, they spotted a chasm between two boulders, less than two feet wide. The first thought was an animal, maybe a young sea lion, had been tossed against the boulders by the waves and was wedged into the space, buried there. But then the light from the moon hit the shadowy form and it sparkled, almost as if it were alive. When they got closer they saw immediately it was a body."

"A body?" Nell said. She pulled out a stool and sat down, feeling suddenly weak. Had a swimmer been swept in by the tide? Someone none of them knew, caught in some dangerous undertow and pushed between the boulders while they partied up on the hill, oblivious of nature's treacherous tricks.

Elizabeth had been staring down at Nell's kitchen island as if gathering strength from the butcher-block top. When she looked up and spoke, her voice was steady. And very sad.

"It was Blythe Westerland, Nell. She's dead."

Jerry left soon after. He had to get back to the scene where his second-in-command, Tommy Porter, was winding things up. Ben walked him to the door.

"Most of the guests were gone when they found her," Jerry said. He and Angelo were helping Elizabeth straighten up some things, making sure the cleanup crew had finished with their tasks.

"The scene?" he said. "You called it the scene—"

"I didn't say *crime* scene. But we have to treat it that way. Right now all we know is that Blythe is dead. She had a nasty blow to her head. Either she somehow got in the water, lost her footing, and the waves smashed her into the boulder—or something else caused the blow that killed her. That's what needs to be figured out."

Ben stood on the step and watched his friend walk away.

The chief reached his car, then turned back toward Ben, one hand resting on the car handle. His voice was weary.

"But face it, Ben," he said. "It was a hell of a time for Blythe to go swimming."

Chapter 9

A s was the way of small towns, the news spread like flood-waters, rolling down the hills and valleys of the sleepy seaside town, waking up its residents to a brilliant fall day that would quickly lose its color.

"Gabby is still at the Danverses'. Laura called me before I had had coffee," Birdie said, talking without pause as she walked through the family room and into Nell and Ben's kitchen. She dropped her bag on the floor near the island. "Ben, coffee, please."

It was clear from her face why Birdie was there.

Nell quickly filled her in on the little they knew.

"Elizabeth stayed here with Ben and me for a very short while, but she thought she'd have a better chance of sleeping in her own bed, so Ben walked her home."

She and Ben had gone back to bed after that, the windows open and curtains fluttering in the breeze as slowly the sky turned into day. They lay together, finding comfort in the touch of each other's body, and talked quietly, hearts heavy, as they remembered the party minute by minute. *When they had seen Blythe.* And then *when they hadn't.*

It was a conversation that would circulate around breakfast tables all over Sea Harbor that Saturday morning.

Birdie's thoughts were on the same page, repeating it aloud. "Blythe wasn't around when Laura went to introduce her," she said, pouring a hefty stream of cream into her coffee.

"Was Laura still at the school when they found . . ." Nell stopped. *Found the body* was too difficult to say. Too impersonal when talking about someone who was flesh and blood and beautiful, greeting guests, not twenty-four hours before.

"No. She had already left. Almost everyone had." Birdie paused, then went on talking as if words would somehow make sense of it all.

"She called first thing this morning because of Gabby, thinking I'd be worried about her, but of course I didn't know what she was talking about. Why would I be worried? I asked her, suddenly afraid something had happened to the girls." Birdie stirred her coffee, the awfulness slowly settling in.

"And then she told me. But first she assured me that the girls were making pancakes and didn't know anything about what had happened—there would be time for that. She hadn't known, either, she said, until Elliott came back from his early-morning run along the water. He'd gone the long way around the shore because the weather was so perfect, and then came home past the school. That's where yellow tape and flashing cameras made him stop. Tommy Porter was pulling out of the parking lot at the same time and told Elliott what had already been released to the press."

A death. A terrible tragedy. Blythe Westerland.

Nell took a bowl of yogurt and blueberries from the refrigerator. "Blythe seemed happy last night. Playful, almost."

"I'm not sure that's what Angelo thought when he looked at her."

Birdie looked over at Ben. "You're unusually quiet, Ben."

He was leaning against the counter, a pensive look on his face as he thumbed through messages on his phone. "Just checking with the outside world. Sam and I had a sailing date with Jerry this morning."

"He couldn't have gotten any sleep last night. I doubt if sailing is on his mind."

"Probably not," Ben murmured, his mind elsewhere as the messages passed quickly across the screen.

Nell absently scooped the yogurt into three bowls and sprinkled each with granola, her mind trying to put the evening into focus. When had Blythe gone down to the water? And why? Had they seen her before they left the party? She was difficult to miss in that beautiful, glittering sheath. But already, in this short a time, the order of events, the conversations, the waves and hugs, had all started to merge together. She handed Birdie and Ben each a bowl. "Eat," she said.

Nell ignored the frown on Birdie's face—yogurt wasn't her first choice for breakfast. She'd much prefer the buttery blueberry kolaches her housekeeper had probably made that morning. "It's good for you," she added.

"Of course it is," Birdie said.

Ben was checking his watch, a spoonful of yogurt already on its way to his mouth. "Jerry left a message. He didn't say much except to remind us to check in on Elizabeth. He was going to try to get over there later."

"Of course. Birdie and I will walk up."

"Poor Elizabeth," Birdie said. "This will be so difficult for her. It's as if it happened at her 'house,' at her party."

Ben rinsed his bowl in the sink and headed toward his den. "Sam is picking me up. We have to file some registration papers for the boat and may drop in to check on Jerry, see if we can help."

"How?" Nell asked. "How could you help?"

Ben shrugged. "Tackle an irritating reporter maybe? Sam'd be good at that." He half smiled and when the horn honked in the driveway, gave Nell a hug that was tighter and lasted longer than the usual "see you later, dear" embrace. In the next second he was gone.

No sooner had the door swung shut than it opened again.

Izzy came in carrying Abby. Like Birdie's, her voice announced her presence as she walked through the house and into the kitchen.

"Blythe Westerland wasn't swimming," she said. "That's the craziest thing I've ever heard. Not with that four-thousand-dollar Julien Macdonald dress on."

"Did you stop at the coffee shop?" Nell asked. As wonderful as the coffee was—and the shaded patio—Coffee's was a hotbed for rumors, sometimes spun by night workers, those grabbing early cups of coffee, practically before the sun was up, as they dragged themselves home after the night shift on the newspaper or hospital or some security job. People with access to overnight news.

"Sam did. He went out for doughnuts and coffee and came back with the awful news, sprinkled with some of the guesses being tossed around. It doesn't take long—" She handed a giggling Abby to Nell and set a bag of bagels on the counter. Smothered in thick cream cheese, it was fast becoming Abby's favorite snack.

"I agree. The swimming story is hogwash. It was just something to say. Blythe was taking her hostess responsibilities very seriously. I think she spoke to every single person at that party. Taking a dip in the ocean would not have been on her mind. That rumor will be pulled apart like strands of seaweed in no time. Even if she had enjoyed an ample share of champagne—which, from what I saw, was probably the case—she wouldn't have embarrassed herself like that."

"So, if it wasn't the waves or the tide that threw her against those rocks, then what was it?" Izzy sat Abby on the floor along with a collection of Nell's Tupperware containers.

Nell and Birdie were silent, letting Abby's joyful squeals fill the air and block out the unease that floated around the room.

An easy explanation was that she slipped on the rocks. The boulders were perfect for climbing, for sitting on top and looking all the way to Boston. And they were slippery when wet. An unfortunate accident. That was what they wanted it to be. Tragic. Understandable. Nell herself had slipped on the back-shore boulders not long ago. She had lost some skin on her knee. But not her life.

How?

The answer came sooner than expected.

In the time it took for Nell to make another pot of coffee and to move Abby out to the deck to chew on a cream-cheese-covered bagel, Sam and Ben were back to pick up their sailing gear.

But their somber expressions as they walked out on the deck spoke less of sailing than of their recent visit to the county offices just off Harbor Road—and the adjacent police station.

"Blythe was killed by a blow to the head. But she didn't fall on the boulders or slip. Someone crushed her head with a rock. The coroner said the blow probably killed her instantly," Ben said.

Sam picked up Abby and kissed the top of her head. His baby daughter was his equalizer.

"And there are two hundred and fifty-seven suspects," Ben said.

"There are . . . what?" Birdie frowned.

"The number of people on the property when Blythe Westerland was murdered."

Chapter 10

Ben didn't mean it of course, not literally. But as Jerry Thompson put it, each one of the guests and staff who attended the amazing party that Friday night could have, might have, seen something that might help them figure out how—and why—Blythe Westerland's life ended in such an inglorious and tragic way.

Far more sobering was the thought that the person responsible for the tragedy could have been strolling around on the lawn under that perfect moon, drinking champagne, eating Gracie's lobster rolls, laughing, and having a good time.

"But it could have been someone who came along the shore, not a guest at all," said Ben. "People climb on those boulders all the time—and the boathouse shielded the spot from people on the lawn."

"So it could have been anyone. Anyone in the whole universe," Izzy said. Her voice was edged with fear and anger that her baby daughter could be exposed to horrible things, no matter how hard she tried to protect her and hold her close.

She stood and picked up Abby, whose face was covered with cream cheese. She pressed her sweet face into her blouse, ignoring the white smudges that would still be there when she put her down. "I have to get to the yarn shop. Mae's nieces are helping out today, but it'll be crazy."

"Do you want me to keep Abby?" Nell asked.

Izzy shook her head. She wanted Abby with her. Nell understood. And Abby loved the commotion and attention the shop provided, especially the Magic Room, a small room in the shop that Izzy had filled with toys for children whose mothers were shopping. Today Izzy needed her close, around the corner hugging a rag doll or knocking over blocks.

"One thing, though—" Izzy looked at her aunt. She paused, but only for a minute.

"I'm thinking dinner together would be nice. Is seven okay? Your house?"

Nell smiled. Of course it was okay. And the thought had already taken root before Izzy ever mentioned it. They had missed their Friday on the deck, after all.

Dinner would be better than okay.

After the others left, Birdie and Nell rinsed the coffee cups and put them in the dishwasher. They were quiet, their thoughts fragmented, unable to find a focus.

Finally Birdie said, "It's Gabby's school. That makes it seem so close, so personal." Her voice was soft, her eyes on the towel she was using to wipe out a cup. "A woman . . . was murdered there. I don't know what to do with it."

Nell nodded. And she knew there wasn't anything Birdie could do with it. Not today. Not yet. And maybe not at all. Gabby wasn't in danger. She'd be safer now than ever before with the eyes of Sea Harbor on the community day school. Any other alternative didn't make sense.

She hung the towel on a rack and reached for a sweater. "Let's check on Elizabeth. Imagine what her thoughts must be."

"This is an awful thing, no matter the circumstances," Nell said as they walked up the shady street to Elizabeth's bungalow just a few houses up. "No one deserves to die in such a horrible way and we all feel sadness over her death. But there's an extra layer of emotion, I think, when the person was someone you might have disagreed with."

"You feel even worse?"

"Maybe. A friend in college had a horrible fight with her boyfriend just an hour before he stopped at a QuikTrip for gas. He was killed there in a random accident. We all felt awful about his death. But Charlotte was inconsolable, as if somehow the breakup was the cause for his death. If only she had done this or that."

"So Elizabeth may feel worse because . . . because of what?"

Nell was quiet. It was a fair question. Where was her thought going with all this? *Because of what?*

"I know what you're thinking, Nell, but I think you're imposing our feelings on Elizabeth. We didn't like the way Blythe treated her. We didn't appreciate the things she said at the board meeting. But we don't know how Elizabeth feels or how she was handling it. Maybe it was just a little problem along with many others that you deal with when you're the administrator of a school. It's business. Who knows, maybe she had no feelings about Blythe whatsoever. Neutral. We all know someone we feel that way about, especially when it relates to business—which is what her relationship with Blythe was—board business, school business."

It was business . . . until it was murder.

But Birdie was right. Elizabeth guarded her feelings closely. Except that night at the Lazy Lobster. She looked whipped that night. And although Nell didn't know it for a fact, she strongly suspected it was Blythe who had contributed to the whipping. They had seen it in action at the board meeting.

They walked up the short walkway to the plain bungalow that Elizabeth had turned into a bright harbinger of autumn. Huge pots of mums and Gerbera daisies welcomed them, and turned the plain gray-shingled home into a reflection of autumn.

Before they had a chance to ring the bell, Elizabeth opened the door.

It was the first time Nell had seen Elizabeth dressed so casually.

It startled her for a moment—the Harvard T-shirt and jeans stripped the headmistress of her usual formality. With her face free of makeup and her hair slightly disheveled, she looked even younger than her almost forty years. And vulnerable.

"We came by to make sure you're all right. It's been a terrible few hours for you. What can we do? Do you need anything?"

"I don't think so." Elizabeth took a deep breath and released it slowly, then pushed a stray curl behind her ear and admitted ruefully, "Actually I've been standing in the middle of my kitchen for fifteen minutes, debating about getting coffee somewhere—I'm completely out. Jerry told me not to go over to the school today, which is what I usually do on Saturdays.

"So I considered getting out in the fresh air to get a cup of coffee. It seemed like a good idea. I thought it might clear the fuzziness from my head. But seeing people—students, parents, maybe—kept me from going very far."

"Coffee and nourishment," Birdie said briskly. "That's an excellent idea and one we can help you with very nicely. If you'd like company, we'll walk with you. It'll be good for all of us. Come—let's go." Birdie's arm motioned toward the door.

The tension in Elizabeth's face lessened a little as Birdie took charge. She needed a minute to get her purse, she said, then reappeared from the side door and met them on the sidewalk.

"A good idea, yes?" Birdie said, and without waiting for an answer, began walking briskly down Sandswept Lane.

Nell waved at several neighbors raking leaves and some bikers heading toward the beach. As they neared Harbor Road, Birdie suggested a change in direction. "I think we should head to Canary Cove instead of the Harbor Road haunts. There's a wonderful little place there—Polly Farrell's Tea Shoppe. Polly makes the best soup on the East Coast. And she has great coffee, too, in spite of the name. It's just a slight detour, but it might cure all our ills."

Birdie's reasoning was crystal clear to Nell—and wise. Canary Cove was a longer walk but a way to avoid the more crowded lunch places on Harbor Road. Crowds were something Elizabeth didn't need to tackle today. Whether or not Birdie was right about it curing all their ills was a little optimistic. Nell suspected it was going to take more than soup and coffee to do that.

They moved close to the side of the road as a biker headed their way. Then they smiled and waved as they recognized Harry Winthrop, helmet in place. He waved back, slowed slightly, then stopped, balancing the bike with one foot and taking off his helmet. "Found this old thing in the garage," he said to Nell and Birdie. Then he turned to Elizabeth, assessing her for a minute. He nodded slightly as if surprised to see her, then slipped his helmet back on, waved a good-bye. In the next minute he picked up speed and disappeared around a curve in the road.

"Who was that?" Elizabeth asked. "He looks familiar."

"I'm sorry—I should have refreshed your memory," Birdie said. "You met him at the party—he was a guest at our table."

"I'm afraid it's all a blur," Elizabeth said. "But I vaguely remember meeting him or someone pointing him out." She turned around to look again, but both the bike and rider had disappeared from sight. "The more I try to bring clarity to last night, the more the evening escapes me, turning into a hazy surreal event."

Nell nodded. "I think we all suffer from some of that. A beautiful evening with such a tragic ending—it's difficult to separate it all out."

They crossed the street and walked briskly along the narrow road toward the art colony, talking about mundane things like the weather and the increasing number of sea lions basking on the harbor rocks. It would be easier to talk at Polly's place—and the soup and sandwiches might bring the color back into Elizabeth's face.

The two tables out in front of the Tea Shoppe were empty, and Nell suggested Birdie and Elizabeth grab one while she went inside and ordered.

Polly waved to Nell and mouthed that she'd be with her in a minute, giving Nell time to read the blackboard menu, even though in the end, she would order whatever Polly told her to order. She loved the tiny restaurant, from the hand-painted teapots lining the shelf on the wall, to the old, uneven tables and chairs that often tipped to one side or another. She never brought Ben here, fearful a chair might collapse beneath his over six-foot heft. But take-home soup was always greeted with delight.

There was a scattering of people at the half dozen tables inside. She waved at Margaret Garozzo and Harriet Brandley, two Sea Harbor natives who had known each other for fifty-plus years and never run out of things to talk about together. Their heads nearly touched as they chatted and gossiped. The cheerful expressions on their faces indicated they hadn't heard the news of the murder yet. A cherished state, Nell thought. Harriet and Margaret were still living in a town that felt safe and relaxed. They were probably talking about a trip north to catch the early leaves, or Harriet's son's new book, or Izzy's latest shipment of merino wool.

But not murder. Not yet.

A few artists Nell knew slightly looked up, waved, then went back to bowls of Polly's cucumber dill soup and flaky rolls.

At a window table she spotted Mary Pisano and started over to say hello. Then she stopped abruptly. Mary was sitting with her cousin Teresa, whose eyes were damp, her expression distraught.

The realization hit Nell when she noticed the tears: Teresa worked at Sea Harbor Community Day School. She tried to remember her position. She wasn't a teacher—maybe a librarian? Or an administrative assistant? She knew she'd gotten e-mail notices about board business from her occasionally.

Her oblong, frowning face—so opposite her lively cousin Mary's round, always expressive, one—was drawn and immeasurably sad. She was younger than Mary by at least a dozen years, probably close to Izzy's age—but her face today looked prematurely aged, as if the tragedy at the boathouse was a personal one. Her unnaturally blond hair was drab, a few strands clinging to her damp cheeks. Across from her, Mary listened, nodded, and occasionally gave her cousin's hand a sympathetic pat.

It would be a difficult day for anyone connected to the school. Blythe was well known to the teachers and staff. And probably some of the students, too, since she seemed to be more involved there than most of the board members. And she was a colorful figure, a beautiful woman, not someone you met and forgot easily. Teresa would surely know her.

Nell turned away just as Polly called out to her from the counter—three bowls of today's soup were ready to go. She motioned for Nell to get the door for her and she carried the tray of soup and warm rolls to the table.

Nell introduced Polly to Elizabeth. Polly wiped her hands on her apron, then shook Elizabeth's hand. "My niece Karina is a student at your school. Look her up. Karina Farrell. She's a wonderful girl, smart as the dickens, and she loves school. Loves it. Every single minute of it." She spotted a customer walking through the door and flapped her hands in the air. "No rest for the wicked, now, is there?" She smiled broadly and hurried back inside.

"This place is a hidden gem," Birdie said. "Lots of folks think it's just a place to get tea and crumpets and we don't tell them anything different."

The soup was creamy, spicy, and delicious, the coffee strong and fragrant, and the conversation purposefully mellow. In a short time, the combination had brought color to Elizabeth's cheeks and a wakefulness to her eyes.

"You two are just what I needed today. I know Jerry wants to be a help to me—but he can't right now. It's . . . it's so complicated with his job, and my role at the school. The whole thing is a nightmare."

"But Jerry is a wonderful man," Nell said. "He'll make this go away—for all of us." The words were hopeful, but held little meaning.

Elizabeth breathed deeply. "I hope so, Nell. I don't even know which way to turn or how to prioritize. I have to make some decisions—how to deal with the staff and the students, not to mention the board members. Jerry wants to separate the . . . the murder . . . from the school as much as we can. It was something that happened down at the shore. Not in the school. Not even on the terraces or the lawn. Take it away from the students and their learning here at the school as much as possible."

It made sense, but it would be difficult to do. They knew that. Blythe was closely connected to the school. It had happened during a school event. The deceased was at the party.

And quite likely the murderer was, too.

The look in Elizabeth's eyes told them that no matter how wise the plan was, she was more than acutely aware of the difficulty of the task.

Nell pushed back her chair and began reaching for her purse as Birdie and Elizabeth gathered napkins into a pile.

It was when Nell stood up that she noticed the man watching them from across the street, a cigarette hanging from his lips.

Josh Babson leaned lazily against the Brewster Gallery. His tall figure, nearly reaching the top of the window frame, was clearly identifiable. His eyes were focused intently on the diners in front of the teashop.

Nell turned away, slightly discomforted by his stare. She turned her attention with some relief to Mary Pisano, who was walking out the Tea Shoppe door.

Mary greeted them all warmly and began a prolonged commentary on the amazing soup she had just eaten—even though her silly cousin had barely touched hers.

A minute later, Teresa Pisano came out. At first she didn't notice the others standing with Mary. With one hand, she was rummaging in an overstuffed shoulder bag. The other hand gripped a white take-out container of uneaten soup.

Teresa was thin to the point of being worrisome. Mary had commented recently that her cousin naively thought it made her look beautiful and had been intentionally shedding pounds. Instead she looked gaunt, and her nose seemed a little too big for her face, her shoulders too narrow, and her skinny jeans slightly loose.

Mary frowned at her cousin, nudging her to say hello. "It's your boss, Teresa."

Teresa looked up with a start. Her eyes flitted from Nell to Birdie, then zeroed in sharply on Elizabeth Hartley.

"Hello, Teresa," Elizabeth said gently.

But social pleasantries seemed to be the furthest thing from Teresa Pisano's mind. Her dark eyes lit up with sudden, unexpected anger.

For a minute they thought the younger woman was going to attack Elizabeth, but in the next second she took a step back and began to yell—her voice so shrill and harsh that Polly appeared in the doorway and a car slowed down as it passed.

Her words came out in a torrent of rage. "This is your fault, Elizabeth Hartley. You hated her—I know you did. Everyone knew it. You killed my Blythe!"

And then, before anyone could stop her, she hurled the small container of cucumber soup at Elizabeth Hartley, spun around, and ran down the street as if she were going to be the next one to meet an untimely demise.

Chapter 11

For a moment, no one moved. The shock of Teresa's words trailed behind her like bad fumes.

In the next instant, there was a flurry of action.

Mary, her face red with shame, uttered an apology and set out after her cousin.

Polly grabbed a towel from her apron band, tsking at the waste of her delicious soup, but happy none of it had landed on Elizabeth.

Birdie handed a glass of water to a shaken Elizabeth.

Nell wiped the table clean, and Polly disappeared inside with the rags and tray of dishes.

In all, the fuss lasted less than a few minutes.

The look on Elizabeth's face, however, told them the aftermath of Teresa Pisano's words would last much longer.

Nell picked her bag up from the chair and handed it to her.

She looked around to be sure they hadn't forgotten anything, and then, almost as an afterthought, she glanced across the street.

She had nearly forgotten about him, but he was still there, standing as still as the wooden statue that guarded the gallery next door.

Josh Babson hadn't moved, his eyes fixed on the scene playing out in front of Polly Farrell's Tea Shoppe.

Nell narrowed her eyes, straining to bring his face into focus, looking for acknowledgment of what he had seen. Their eyes met—

and a careless smile seemed to curl his lip just seconds before he leaned forward, letting his cigarette drop to the sidewalk where he snubbed it out with the toe of his shoe.

He looked over once more, a brief glance, then turned and pushed open the door to the Brewster Gallery.

And then he disappeared from sight.

Birdie and Nell walked on either side of a quiet, shaken Elizabeth. They headed away from the art colony and onto a quiet street that wound its way back to Sandswept Lane and to home.

For several blocks, they walked in silence, each wrapped up in her own thoughts and emotion.

The pain in Elizabeth's face was raw.

Finally, as they neared Elizabeth's house, Birdie said, "People express their sadness in different ways. I suppose that is what Teresa was doing. Was she close to Blythe?"

"Close?" Elizabeth repeated the word as if examining it carefully. "Teresa knew Blythe because she came into the office often. Teresa didn't seem to have many friends among the staff, though I couldn't be sure of that, but Blythe was nice to her. She brought her small gifts sometimes. I suppose you could say they were friends. They spoke often."

"That surprises me," Nell said. "Though I have no reason to think they shouldn't be. Except . . ."

"I know. Except they were so unlike each other. I thought that, too. I don't know. I wondered about it. Maybe it was just . . ." Elizabeth's words trailed off, as if there was more there, but she wasn't sure how to address it—or if she should.

They had reached Elizabeth's house and stopped near the front door. "Thank you for giving me part of your day," she began. She took a step toward the door and dug her keys out of her purse.

But when she went to use it, the door opened on its own.

Nell and Birdie stared.

Elizabeth looked down at her keys as if they had failed her, then managed a short laugh. "I must have forgotten to lock it. Sometimes I do that. It upset Jerry when he noticed it one day. I wouldn't have dreamed of leaving my place in Boston unlocked, but somehow Sea Harbor seems to be the kind of place where it would be okay." She stopped, listening to her own words and thinking about them.

Sea Harbor was a place where you didn't have to lock your doors . . . but where a woman could be killed with a rock during a festive school event.

"Let's just be sure . . . ," Nell said, and moved past Elizabeth and into the small entryway before she could object. She wasn't sure what they were being sure of, but today wasn't the same as yesterday or the day before. Today—and maybe all the tomorrows for a while—were days for locking doors, and for checking to see what was behind ones that weren't.

Elizabeth tried to object, but it was too late—Nell was already inside with Birdie close behind her. Reluctantly she followed them through the door.

The bungalow was small and neat and light, with magazines stacked on the coffee table, books lined up on polished shelves, and a beautiful knit afghan in every color of the sea draped over the couch. Framed paintings of seascapes created bright spots of color against the white walls.

Elizabeth went in and checked her bedroom. She came back, announcing that it was fine. "There's no little bear sleeping in my bed," she said, attempting to lighten the mood, but Nell and Birdie didn't smile. "I've no jewels to steal."

"Caution isn't a bad thing, Elizabeth," Birdie said. "Not when someone has been murdered."

"Of course not. I appreciate your concern, but I'm fine. Honestly I've left the door unlocked before, many times. But I won't anymore. I won't be foolish about this."

"You're anything but foolish," Birdie said. "But these are unusual times."

"I understand. And please know that I appreciate what you've done for me today—the soup and walk were truly the therapy I needed. I can't thank you enough."

"Maybe you can get some rest now. You can't have had more than a couple hours' sleep last night—"

She nodded, weariness returning to her face, as if she'd somehow been given permission to let it seep in. "There will be a lot of questions. Jerry warned me of that. I know I will need a clear head. Last night is all a blur right now."

"There'll be questions for all of us, no doubt."

The questions would go on and on. The hope was that there would be answers.

Nell and Birdie headed for the door.

There would be endless questions for all of them—friends and neighbors, staff and teachers and board members.

Board members. The thought hit Nell with some force. How would the board members' interviews play out to the Sea Harbor police? A board fraught with dissension. And much of it centering on—and created by—Blythe Westerland. If they wanted to look for people with motive and opportunity, questioning the Sea Harbor Community Day School board might be hitting the mother lode.

Chapter 12

Saturday night dinner began as a somber hodgepodge.

A hodgepodge of people and a hodgepodge of food. A hodge-podge of emotion.

A gathering of people who simply wanted the warmth of food and Ben's martinis. And the comfort of old friends.

The night was cool—sweater weather, a knitter's dream—and the warmth from Ben's grill and the stone fire pit that he and Sam had built was welcome.

Cass and Birdie were the first to arrive, bringing Ella's apple crisp and fresh loaves of bread. Sam had picked up ribs that Ben would warm on the grill. The Brewsters showed up, too—with daisies from Jane's garden and her famous peanut slaw. Probably more food than any of them could eat. But that would be all right, too.

"Is Harry coming?" Izzy asked Cass.

"Nope." She rummaged around in the small deck refrigerator for a beer. "I thought about inviting him. I needed to be with all of you tonight, and I thought maybe he would need company, too, you know? But he doesn't know us all that well, and so, I don't know, I opted to come alone. He was okay with it. He totally got it. He said he was going to work on the house a little, figure out exactly what needs to be done. Originally he thought he'd stick around and supervise, but now he thinks maybe he'll just hire the right guys and head back to Boston."

"I suppose a lot of people who don't live here might feel that way. The town's charm loses its luster in the face of a murder," Birdie said.

"But you do know he'd be welcome here, Cass," Ben said, poking the coals.

"Sure, I know. Thanks. You guys would welcome a circus clown if I picked one up along the way."

"No, no, no circus clowns," Izzy said. "They scare Abby." She looked over at the sleeping blond baby, curled up next to Sam on the chaise and oblivious of everything around her but the safe warmth of her daddy.

Cass laughed. "Okay. For Abby I'll take clowns off the pickup list. Anyway, it was a selfish decision but hey, I'm selfish."

Birdie set a plate of crackers and cheese on the low deck table. "We didn't talk long, but he seems like an interesting man."

Cass didn't reply. Instead she smeared a cracker with Brie and popped it into her mouth.

A familiar voice rumbled up the back deck steps. "Hey, guys. Anyone home?" Danny Brandley appeared, coming from around the side of the house and taking the deck steps two at a time. "I figured I'd find at least two friends here. I got a bunch. Must be friend karma."

"You're back." Nell walked over and hugged him. "I'm glad. And I'm glad you found us."

He greeted everyone on the deck with his signature slow smile, his glasses reflecting the dozens of candles Nell had lit around the deck. When he got to Cass, his look lingered and his eyebrows lifted, as if he was checking to be sure she was okay. Cass met his look and allowed a smile. *I'm fine,* it said. And his nod told her that was good.

Danny walked around the group and sat down next to Nell. "Not good news to come home to. Especially for all of you who were there at the party—" There was a bit of apology in his tone, as if he somehow should have been there, too.

"It's pretty awful for everyone. But especially Elizabeth Hartley," Nell said.

She had only repeated the awful incident at the Tea Shoppe to Ben—but the memory of Teresa's harsh accusations was still raw in her head. Elizabeth had been visibly shaken, then very quiet on the walk home. She had tried to get Elizabeth to come for dinner, but she had graciously declined.

Nell suspected—or hoped—that Jerry would get over to see her.

"I can't quite get my arms around this whole thing," Danny said. "Maybe because I wasn't there like you were, but it's also because some people seem invincible. Blythe was one of them."

"There's that," Jane said. "But didn't Orwell address invincibility? Something about the person who's winning at a particular moment always seems invincible. Maybe in some other part of her life, she wasn't winning . . ."

Jane's words settled around them as they sipped Ben's martinis and thought about Blythe Westerland. She was on top of the world. In charge. At least that was what they'd thought. But maybe she wasn't?

"My mom and dad were really disturbed about the whole thing," Danny said. "Mom said they had walked down to the shore at the party. It was romantic, she said. A perfect evening. And then they heard the news this afternoon, what little there was of it. And it all fell apart. Memories of the party would no longer hold anything romantic. The perfect party wasn't perfect anymore."

"None of us has a clear idea of what happened," Birdie said, "other than that Blythe died from a blow to the head. But what time, exactly? And wouldn't someone have heard a tussle? Lots of people were going back and forth to the shore that night."

Ben nodded. "*That* night. It seems like we've been living with it for a while, that it has had time to fester and ferment—but it hasn't even been a full day."

"Most of what I found on the Internet focused on Blythe's life," Birdie said. "Her civic involvement, her townhome in Boston, and here, her beauty."

There had been no marriages, no children, and the friends quoted in the reports seemed somehow remote, Nell added.

Ben mixed a new shaker of martinis and strained the cocktail into glasses. "Jerry is a good chief. Smart and careful. He keeps things close to his chest until he's sure what's going on. And it'll take a couple days just to sort out what really happened. Even finding the murder weapon will be a challenge. There are hundreds of rocks around those boulders near the boathouse. Ones that could be picked up and held in a hand—or two hands. And if the rock that had been used by the killer was then tossed or rolled down into the water on its own, the tide could have taken it to God knows where by now."

"So they may never find it," Nell said.

"Probably not."

"So, then, where does one even begin?" Jane asked.

"With Blythe," Izzy said. "That's where you start. She's the only one who knows what happened. Her life needs to be picked apart, piece by piece."

Danny was listening carefully to Izzy. He leaned toward her, his elbows resting on his knees, nodding in agreement. The former lawyer and the mystery writer—their brains traveling along the same road. "That might take some work," he said. He took off his glasses and rubbed the bridge of his nose. "Even though she's been spending most of her time here for the last couple of years, I'm not sure any of us knew her very well."

"Well, someone did. Someone knew her well enough to want her dead," Izzy said.

The thought sobered them into silence, and for a few minutes the only sounds were the wind whistling through the giant elms and the pounding of the surf against the shore. Gulls, foraging above the water, squawked as they dove for their dinner.

Birdie shivered and pulled her sweater tightly around her. "There's such cruelty in all this. *Hatred.* How can it become so severe that it propels one to kill?"

Nell sat quietly in the chaise, her head back and her eyes nearly closed, thinking about Birdie's idle comment. How did hate evolve into the need to kill? Did it develop slowly—a slow-growing cancer that eventually reached an unbearable level, propelling action? She supposed there was that kind . . . but she couldn't for the life of her come up with an example. Or the opposite, a hatred that springs forth suddenly, maybe out of love, even—or fear. Or maybe it wasn't hatred at all that killed Blythe Westerland.

"Danny has a point. I see Blythe often, but I couldn't name one friend of hers," Izzy was saying. "She was usually alone—"

"I disagree, Iz. More often than not she had a man on her arm," Cass said.

Cass was trying with difficulty not to look at Danny. Nell could feel it, and Danny could, too. She could feel his body tense beside her. Danny *could* have known Blythe better, but he had resisted her blatant attention—and everyone knew it. At the time, Cass had, at first, been worried, and then relieved, her interest in Danny just begining to blossom. Nell wondered how she felt about that now.

Nell got up and began bringing out the salads and breads, filling the long outdoor table with their dinner and keeping one ear on the conversation moving at odd angles around the circle of friends. Then she refreshed the cheese platter and settled back next to Danny. Ben followed suit and took the ribs off the grill, piling them on a platter and adding them to the mix. Sam took over at the bar and refreshed drinks.

Izzy was exploring Cass's comment. "Okay. Sure—she seemed to attract men. But were those men her *friends*? Sometimes I got the feeling they were *blings*—accoutrements, you know what I mean? I was thinking of 'friends' in the way you and I are friends. Blythe was almost always alone when she came into the yarn shop, even when she stayed for a while in the back room. I have to say, though, that she was always pleasant—knitting seemed to bring out the best in her."

"As it does with many of us," Birdie said sweetly. She reached into her bag and pulled out a partially finished hat of soft merino wool—a sample for next week's class at the school. She stroked the yarn as if it were Purl the calico cat, and then began rhythmically knitting the vibrant colors into a round. It was difficult to think about hatred with yarn in your lap and your blood pressure being lowered with each stitch. The process stoked her memory and she looked up. "I do know of one friend she had."

Nell turned from the table. *Of course.* How had they forgotten the recent encounter at the Tea Shoppe? And it wasn't a handsome man once seen on Blythe's arm, but a nondescript woman who had raged in pain, flinging out hurtful accusations.

Attention turned to Birdie. "Teresa Pisano," she said. "You all know her, Mary's cousin. She's been secretary in the administrative office at the school for several years. That's probably where she and Blythe met."

Cass scoffed and dismissed it. "Teresa? No. I went to school with her. Blythe wouldn't have been her friend." What she didn't say spoke louder than her words. Mousy, sad Teresa Pisano was the most unlikely choice of friend imaginable for the glamorous Blythe.

"We don't know how long they had been friends or if it was even a friendship, but Teresa is clearly devastated by Blythe's death. Mary was trying to console her today in Polly's Tea Shoppe," Nell said.

Nell and Birdie both sat quietly, hesitant, wondering if repeating the episode that had happened outside the Tea Shoppe would be gossip or helpful. Nell looked at Jane Brewster. She looked as though she was wondering the same thing.

"Were you at your gallery this morning?" Nell asked her.

Jane nodded. "The door was open. And what I didn't hear, Josh Babson repeated for me."

"Oh, yes, Josh," Nell said. Josh had bothered her inordinately by his stance, his presence, and what she still imagined was a slight grin before he disappeared back into the gallery.

Birdie went on to relate the brief but awkward encounter

between Elizabeth and Teresa. "Elizabeth was shaken but composed, as is her way," Birdie said.

"And Mary was chagrined by her cousin's actions. I imagine Teresa got an earful, grieving or not."

"That's the kind of incident that'll find its way back to the police," Danny said.

"No. It was said out of grief," Nell said, but her words came back to her, sounding hollow—just as she knew they did to everyone on the deck. Danny was right. The police would need to hear about the accusation, as outlandish as it was.

She met Birdie's look. The two of them, more than the others gathered on the deck, would know where Teresa's outburst would lead.

The accusation would lead to other things, to more questions—and eventually would wind its way to a recent board meeting.

The board meeting in which Blythe Westerland had tried to get Elizabeth Hartley fired from the job she dearly loved.

Chapter 13

For reasons she couldn't explain to herself, Nell hadn't talked more about Josh Babson with Jane and Ham during dinner or later in the evening, when the drop in temperature had brought them all inside, where they'd made themselves comfortable in the Endicotts' open living space. Maybe it was because she didn't know what to ask or to say.

Would she say that Josh had stared at them from outside the street, outside Jane's Gallery? But Jane already knew that and she didn't think it odd. The startling, unusual thing was Teresa's screaming. It was the hurling of awful accusations. And Josh had nothing to do with that.

Was it that she didn't trust him or that he made her wary or that he had a puzzling smile? That made little to no sense, not without reasons for her feelings. And she had none. Jane and Ham would have thought her a bit daft. Not to mention that she didn't know Josh Babson well enough to feel any particular way about it—or him—at all. Even Birdie hadn't totally shared her feelings when they talked about it on the way home. He was friendly to Birdie, and she had bought one of his seascapes for Harold because he loved the stormy colors Josh had used in the painting.

So she'd held her silence and didn't mention his name until after the last car had driven away after midnight, and she and Ben coaxed their weary bodies up the back steps and to bed.

Ben listened in the dark, his arms folded behind his head.

"It's a feeling," she said.

"Your feelings have always been worth listening to."

"Maybe not this time. I'm not even sure what my feeling is about him. He's a talented artist. He said nice things about Gabby—and she likes him, too. Jane and Ham don't seem to have reservations about him. They trust him in their gallery."

Ben was quiet, knowing that Nell's thoughts sometimes became clearer to her as she spoke them aloud to a trusted ear.

"On the other hand, he vandalized the yard. Blythe obviously had strong reasons for wanting him fired. Some, I suspect, she didn't even tell us about. And he showed up at the party—less than a week after being fired and having shown his displeasure in a very graphic way. What does that say about a person? That he is arrogant and wants to prove a point? That he has a grudge that needs to be satisfied?" Nell listened intently to the night sounds as if they had the answer.

Ben was right. Saying it out loud helped, but the words didn't put a period on anything. It was nothing but a feeling. But one that she couldn't shake loose, even as she pulled the down comforter up to her chin and pressed herself into the welcoming curve of Ben's side, his arm around her, his heartbeat right beneath her fingertips.

Even then.

Chapter 14

Sunday's paper featured the murder at the school, as everyone knew it would. Many Sea Harbor residents didn't read news online, and their first grasp of the tragic happening—beyond that of rumor—would be the Sunday *Sea Harbor Gazette.*

Nell and Ben followed Annabelle Palazola out to the deck of the Sweet Petunia Restaurant, listening to the restaurant owner's litany of rumors and comments and theories about what really had happened that Friday night.

"No one really knows, that's the only thing that is clear," was the restaurant owner's conclusion as she ushered them over to their usual Sunday table—the one at the end of the narrow deck that allowed for expansion, depending on who joined them that particular day. "You already have company, by the way," she said, then disappeared back into the kitchen through an outside door.

Cass was already at the table, the Sunday paper spread out in front of her and a half-empty cup of coffee next to it. Harry Winthrop sat across from her, his mustache perfectly trimmed and his large sunglasses reflecting the trees that towered above the edge of the deck. He seemed in another world entirely, his gaze on the sailboats just visible in the distant harbor.

Nell held back her surprise at seeing him. Birdie often showed up with a nonregular, as she called them. Why shouldn't Cass?

Why, indeed? He was certainly welcome, as Ben had made clear the night before.

They both looked up as shadows fell across the table.

"You're late," said Cass.

Nell laughed. If Cass came at all, she usually dragged in last for Sunday brunch. Sleep, she claimed, sometimes trumped food. Not often, but sometimes. "You might be a good influence on our Cass," she said to Harry.

Harry partially stood and shook hands, then sat back down. "She's the one with influence," he said. "She pounded on my door early today, telling me it was time for breakfast and I'd like this place." He glanced around. "It's nice. I don't remember it being here when I was a kid."

"Annabelle opened it after her husband, Joe, died at sea. She had five children to raise, a great talent for cooking, and lots of friends. This place was an old shack, up on this hill overlooking Canary Cove, and she literally transformed it."

Ben filled their cups from the carafe on the table. "With the help of Joe's friends—all fellow fishermen determined to help Annabelle through those rough days. They practically built this place with their own hands."

"But we don't normally let tourists know about it," Cass said. "So you're lucky, Winthrop."

"You calling me a tourist?" he asked.

Cass just laughed, then turned her attention back to the newspaper. Across from her, Harry leaned one arm on the railing and sat back in his chair, quiet.

Nell watched him as he looked at something beyond the deck and the art colony at the bottom of the hill, beyond the harbor. He glanced over at Cass now and then, a look that said little to Nell— affection? Friendship? He seemed to like being there with her. Having a friend, being included. But he made little attempt to know anyone.

Every now and then Cass looked up, smiled at him. She was

comfortable. Relaxed. And she seemed to have taken a little more time with makeup and clothes than she usually did for breakfast with her friends. Her T-shirt was gone, replaced by a vibrant yellow blouse and colorful lace scarf that Nell had knit for her last birthday. Her thick black hair was loose, the waves dark and dramatic against her tan skin.

"Your omelet's getting cold," Ben said gently, tugging her out of her thoughts. He turned to Cass. "Is there anything new in the paper?"

"No. It's all hearsay. And irritating, that's all," Cass said. She pointed to the largest photo accompanying the article about the murder, the one of the school. "The school doesn't need this kind of attention. The murder probably had nothing to do with the school. Why focus on it?"

Beneath a full photo of the school was the caption S.H. COUNTRY DAY SCHOOL: A SEA HARBOR LANDMARK MIRED IN MURDER.

"They used the old name of the school in the headline," Nell said with her own touch of irritation. It was almost a silent protest. Elizabeth, with the approval of most board members, had changed the school's name to indicate the emphasis on community involvement—and Blythe Westerland had led the charge in objecting to the change, but she had lost that fight. And now some reporter, although he mentioned the new name later in the article, had put it back out there in large print, almost as if giving Blythe the last word. What must it be like for Elizabeth to wake up to this and find the school she loved so clearly advertised in such a tragic way?

Birdie walked over to the table. Gabby was a step behind, comfortable and smiling in her customary jeans and T-shirt.

"I finally got my granddaughter back," Birdie said as Ben added two chairs to the long table. "I thought the Danverses weren't going to let her go, but Harold and I went over and claimed her this morning. He and Ella were falling into a depressed state without Gabby in the house. 'It's a tomb,' Ella told me, and we certainly can't have that."

Gabby's laugh was full and contagious, unrestrained. And as it always did, it drew smiles from everyone.

"It's awful about Ms. Westerland," she said, taking a fried apple biscuit from the basket. She dug a spoon into a jug of Annabelle's homemade apple butter and spread it on the warm yeast roll.

Birdie watched her devour the pastry. "How will you ever leave Sea Harbor? You're addicted to those biscuits."

"Annabelle promised to teach me how to make them. She's doing a cooking class at school as part of our enrichment program, and these are what we're making." She wiped the flakes of fried dough from her mouth and looked over at Cass's newspaper. The old boathouse was pictured front and center.

"Dr. Hartley sent us all e-mails," Gabby said, her eyes on the newspaper photo. "Every person in the whole school."

A wise thing to do, they all agreed. The students would get their information one way or another, and it was best coming from the woman who was at the helm of their school—and who cared deeply about the girls under her roof.

"That old boathouse is such a cool place," Gabby went on, pointing to the photo. "Daisy and I wrote a proposal that it be an art place and we gave it to Dr. Hartley."

"Art place?" Cass asked.

"Yeah, like a studio, sort of. Mr. Babson took us down there sometimes to paint. It was very cool. He kept some easels there for us and sometimes we'd climb on the rocks to paint the ocean. Daisy liked to paint the boathouse and he told her maybe it would become a famous Sea Harbor motif, like that red shack—the Motif #1 over in Rockport. He told Daisy maybe she'd be famous for starting the trend."

Ben laughed. "Maybe so. You're talking about the art teacher, right?"

"Uh-huh. He used to be, anyway. He was way cool. Did you know he was at the party Friday? Daisy and I walked down to the boathouse with him that night and talked about how great it would be to fix it up. He still thinks it's a good idea even though I guess he doesn't have much say about it now. Unless . . . unless maybe they'll hire him back."

"Did he say that he might get hired back?" Birdie asked.

"Not exactly. But sort of. Like maybe Dr. Hartley would reconsider. But anyway, we gave our idea to Teresa to give to Dr. Hartley."

"Dr. Hartley pays attention to her students' ideas," Nell said. "She mentioned some of them at a board meeting." She managed a smile, keeping to herself her surprise at Josh Babson's thinking he'd be rehired *now*.

"You're right, Aunt Nell. She's nice. She listens to us. To everyone. Usually."

"Usually?" Cass asked.

"Well, yeah. Daisy and I talk to her a lot. She likes us. But some other people, not so much."

A waitress appeared with the Sunday special: roasted fall vegetables picked from Annabelle's garden—spinach and tiny peppers, thin slices of radishes, and late-blooming heirloom tomatoes—blended with cream, basil, eggs, and Gruyère cheese.

Ben beamed at his Sunday indulgence, one Nell allowed him but only with the firm warning that he'd be eating grilled fish and roasted vegetables for the rest of the week. She was not about to contribute to another heart attack, like the one years before that had convinced them to move to Sea Harbor and slow down their lives.

"Harry, you're quiet," Nell said. She picked up her fork and looked over at him.

Cass answered for him. "Harry's contractor on the old house says it needs some structural repairs or it'll fall off the cliff. He's bummed. One more thing to be fixed before he can sell it."

"Sell it?" Birdie asked.

"Yeah. Seems silly to keep paying taxes on it," Harry said, looking up from his omelet.

"Oh."

The fact that anyone would forsake a cottage in Sea Harbor

with such an amazing view of the water was unfathomable to every person sitting at the table.

Harry seemed not to notice.

"Are you staying there?"

He nodded. "In a bedroom filled with paint and plaster buckets. But it's okay. It works."

Nell looked at Cass to read her expression, but it was neutral. She had brought Harry to the party—and today to breakfast—but for the life of her she could not read Cass's feelings about the man. Perhaps Ben would have some insight later. He was a good mind reader on occasion.

They all concentrated on the perfectly cooked omelet, enhanced by a gentle curve of melon slices and blueberries. Ben engaged Harry in stories about his and Sam's sailing adventures, once he discovered something he had in common with the younger man. Cass went back to the newspaper, and Gabby and Birdie gabbed back and forth about Gabby's weekend at the Danverses', Gabby happily enthusing about Daisy's sisters, her built-in bunk beds, and Mr. Danvers's yacht.

And Nell listened.

In between, Gabby would answer Birdie's well-placed questions meant to tease out feelings about the Friday night murder. Laura and Elliott had talked to the girls after the headmistress's e-mail arrived. Whatever they'd said had satisfied the girls, although the thought of someone dying on "their" rocks was still an issue. Daisy had checked the statistics, and most people killed on rocks fell off them or onto them. Murder wasn't as common, especially using one of the boulders as the murder weapon.

"We were right there, Nonna. Can you believe it?" Gabby said, her expression a mixture of awe, excitement, and utter horror. "What if we'd handed the murderer a program, what if we were so close to him we could touch him? What if we'd been down there, putting out the hurricane lamps, when . . . when he did it?"

Nell looked closely to see if there was another emotion on Gabby's face, one that might mitigate somewhat the concern she saw growing on Birdie's face. *Fear.* Fear could be a deterrent in seeking adventure. In exploring places that might not be safe.

The excitement and awe and even horror were there, dwindling only when Birdie insisted on asking Gabby what she would like for dinner.

Fear never entered the picture.

And that worried Birdie and Nell in equal measure.

Cass and Harry left the restaurant soon after, but not before Ben promised Harry a turn at the controls of his and Sam's forty-two-foot Hinckley. They set a time and it seemed to bring some life to Harry—at least the man was speaking now and then. Nell tried to analyze his mood in her mind, but finally gave up, realizing that she would have to know him better to determine if he was sad, depressed over his cottage, or simply someone who didn't talk a lot. The strong and silent type.

Birdie and Gabby left next. Harold texted them from the restaurant's parking lot. He was sitting in Birdie's Lincoln and wouldn't be the slightest bit disappointed if they were to bring him and Ella a sack of Annabelle's fried apple biscuits and a jug of apple butter.

Warm, if possible.

Nell and Ben sat alone for a while after everyone else left, enjoying the breeze, the Sunday *Times*, and being alone with each other. It hadn't happened often in recent days.

Nell's eyes and soul were filling up with the picture-perfect scene in the distance—the sky and sea nearly seamless and a fleet of Sunday sailors heading out to open sea. The whale watching boats had already left the harbor, while small fishing vessels still tugged their way out around the shinier, fancier, bigger boats.

Ben finally put down the opinion page of the paper and looked over at her. "It's just beginning," he said.

A quiet voice at his elbow confirmed that to be true.

They both looked up into Jerry Thompson's concerned face. He stood alone, dressed uncharacteristically in jeans and a knit shirt, his thick hair brushed back with streaks of silver serving as attractive highlights. The Silver Fox, some of the girls at the station called him, Esther Gibson had told Nell, but he didn't have quite enough gray for that yet.

"It's going to be a mess," Jerry said, and sat in the chair Ben pulled out.

Ben poured coffee. "Food?"

Jerry shook his head. "I'm here for breakfast takeout. I thought I'd take something over to Elizabeth Hartley's—a peaceful meal away from crowds." He glanced out toward the parking lot. "I didn't intend to come farther than the kitchen door, but I spotted your car in the lot and Annabelle let me sneak out here through the kitchen."

"It's a rough time," Ben said. "Everyone wants answers."

"Yep. And when I can't give any, folks make them up. Or put things together that really don't fit."

There wasn't much to say. Jerry was right. Nell felt a slight twinge of guilt that they had done the same thing. In less than two days the facts and nonfacts of Blythe Westerland's murder had been stacked up and scattered about haphazardly. Attempts to sort it out before there was enough there to create a pile.

"I understand it," Jerry said. "Everyone wants the town to go back to the way it was a week ago, to make this thing go away. The problem is you have to be so careful. We can't destroy more lives because we're desperate for a semblance of peace."

The words seem to make his wide shoulders sag, his eyes lose their clarity as he focused on his strong, blunt fingers on the tabletop. The chief of the Sea Harbor police looked more haggard than Ben and Nell had seen him look in a long time—and maybe ever.

Finally he looked up. There was genuine sadness in his eyes. "We don't want the wrong person to be hurt in all this," he said.

Chapter 15

Ben and Nell walked with Jerry out to the parking lot, exiting the restaurant the way Jerry had come in—through the fragrant aroma of Annabelle's kitchen.

Annabelle handed Jerry a white bag filled with fried biscuits along with his order. "Elizabeth likes these," she said. She gave him a quick hug, then attempted to lighten the mood. "And who knows, Chief, it might make you sweeter."

Jerry hugged her back, a quick display of uncharacteristic affection. They walked over to his pickup truck, parked in the shade of a maple tree near the Endicotts' CRV.

"Traveling incognito, I see," Ben said.

He shrugged. "I'm not on duty. It makes it a little easier not to be spotted. It's a helluva situation we have on our hands." He pulled out his keys. "I didn't know Blythe Westerland very well. For a while she seemed to be in and out of town a lot—sitting on some boards here but had a life in Boston, too. But her life seemed pretty ordinary, as far as I know. Not the kind that would breed enemies. She was always friendly. Sometimes overly so, I guess you'd say."

"That happens to handsome eligible bachelors, Jerry," Nell said.

But Jerry knew that. In the fifteen years since his wife, Fran, had died, he had been on many single women's radar. The number-one choice to fix up with a friend for a dinner party. He dated some of the women he was matched with. But it had never felt right. His Frances was still too much a presence to allow another woman in.

Jerry seemed to give Nell's words undue thought. "Yeah, okay, there was that," he said, dismissing it. "Who knows, I'm so rusty— she was probably just friendly or wanted me to fix a parking ticket for her. Not to speak ill of the dead, but she was an odd one, Blythe Westerland was." He looked off, as if remembering things that were not entirely pleasant and that he shouldn't have expressed in the first place. He gave a shake of his head and had started to climb inside the cab of his truck when fingers grasped his arm tightly.

Ben and Nell looked over, startled.

Teresa Pisano had come out of nowhere, climbing off a bike and letting it fall to the ground.

"Arrest Dr. Hartley, Chief. Right now before she hurts someone else. She only wants the money. That's all. We can't let her get away with this."

The pain on Jerry's face was palpable. But his voice was calm, controlled, professional. "Teresa, I told you yesterday when you came into the station that we are talking to everyone. We will do everything in our power to find the person who killed Blythe."

Teresa Pisano began to cry, large tears running down her long, homely face. Nell went over and touched her arm. "Teresa, would you like a ride home?"

Nell saw Jerry's look of thanks as he climbed into the cab of his truck and immediately brought the engine to life, then slowly backed up and made his way out of the parking lot.

"I was out riding," Teresa said, glancing over at her bike. "And I saw the chief head up here. I just wanted to talk to him, to make him understand."

"Jerry is a good police chief, Teresa," Ben said.

"He's a good man, I know that."

"You look tired," Nell said.

She nodded. "I haven't been sleeping well."

Ben picked the bike up and hooked it to the rack at the back of his CRV. "Nell and I can give you a lift home."

Teresa climbed into the back of the car without protest. "To

Ravenswood," she said. Then added with a feeble attempt at a smile, "Please."

Nell looked over the seat. "To your cousin's bed-and-breakfast?"

She nodded. "I moved over there to help Mary out. I'm staying in the suite that used to be Grandpa Enzo's. I do night desk sometimes and help out on weekends."

Mary Pisano was a good woman, Nell thought. Her cousin Teresa wasn't like the rest of the Pisanos—friendly and motivated and assured of their place in the world because of the newspaper empire their grandfather had built. Teresa was a loner, moved slower than the others. Nell knew from board discussions that Teresa's secretarial job at the school had been "encouraged" by an uncle's contributions to the school.

And now she was living in the lovely expansive bed-and-breakfast that her cousin Mary had inherited from old Grandpa Enzo.

And she was probably a help to Mary, since Mary stayed at the home she shared with her husband when he wasn't out at sea. "What a wonderful place to live," Nell said.

Teresa didn't answer and when Nell looked back, her eyes were closed, her head back against the seat.

That was a good thing. Nell didn't want to hear a word about Elizabeth Hartley.

They drove the rest of the way through town in silence—along Harbor Road and up to the historic Ravenswood neighborhood, once home to shipping magnates, wealthy quarry owners, captains of the sea—and Enzo Pisano, owner of a dozen newspapers.

Ben slowed and drove up the wide drive, past the neat white and gold sign that read RAVENSWOOD-BY-THE-SEA. And below it, WELCOME.

Teresa seemed to have recovered somewhat and looked less disheveled than when she had nearly attacked the police chief.

She helped Ben take her bike off the car rack and thanked them for their help. "I'm sorry for acting the way I did. I just don't think the police are looking in the right places. They make mistakes sometimes. I wanted to help, that's all."

"Of course," Nell said.

She thanked them for the ride and walked around to the back of the inn.

"Let's see if Mary is here," Ben said. "A chance to say hello."

But his message was clear. *Let's make sure Teresa is all right.* And maybe Mary could fill them in on Teresa's vendetta against Elizabeth Hartley.

Mary ushered them into the large kitchen of the B and B, where there was always coffee brewing and usually a basket of scones on the large center island.

Ben filled her in on the encounter at Annabelle's restaurant.

Mary grimaced. "She's come a little unhinged over all this," she said.

"How long has she been living here?" Nell asked.

"It's been a while. I just don't talk about it, because the other cousins think I'm a little daft for doing it. Teresa is simply not a family favorite. She isn't savvy and successful and filled with self-importance." Mary laughed. "But she helps me out in exchange for the room. It works."

"Do you know why she has this thing against Elizabeth?" Ben asked. "It's almost an obsession."

"I'm just beginning to hear about it," Mary said. "Maybe I didn't pay attention before. I'd noticed that Teresa was trying to change her looks, bleached her hair, lost some weight—way too much weight, in my opinion."

"But why?" Nell asked.

"It took me a while to figure it out because frankly, I don't see Teresa much. She takes the desk when I'm not here, and since I don't live here, our paths usually cross over business things. But I realized recently that she was talking more and more about Blythe Westerland and then it dawned on me that she was trying to look like her. She wanted to be pretty."

"How old is she?"

"She's the baby of the clan. Thirty-eight, I think—and never been kissed."

"So—" Ben wrinkled his forehead. "So this thing Teresa had with Blythe might have been like a schoolgirl crush on a teacher?"

"I think so. Something like that," Mary said. She looked down at the stainless steel surface of the island and drew a lazy line with her finger. "But honestly, Ben, I don't know what to think about her animosity toward Elizabeth. She said Elizabeth was terrible at her job—an opinion I'm sure she got from Blythe, so who knows how legit it is? I suspect not much at all. She said Blythe was going to save the school by getting Elizabeth fired—and she was helping her."

"Helping her?"

"I'm not sure, but I suspect that Teresa relayed things to Blythe that were going on in the administrative offices. Making herself into a little mole. She practically said as much one night, telling me how she had changed a board meeting time so Elizabeth would be late for the meeting. She seemed inordinately proud of being complicit in Blythe's little plan, as if she were collecting Brownie points or something. And then she showed me some cheap necklace Blythe had given her. I said she was going to get herself fired, but she just laughed. It seemed she'd do anything for Blythe."

That explained the last board meeting. It was Teresa's doing. And now Teresa was without her anchor, adrift in the head office. And furious about it. That explained a lot of things.

"Teresa thought she was protected against any and all evils because Blythe was her friend. And Blythe's goal was to get rid of Elizabeth. So that was Teresa's, too."

Elizabeth knew about Blythe's goal, of course. The whole board did. Elizabeth loved her job passionately. Which in Nell's mind was why she was such an excellent administrator. But if she thought she was going to lose that job . . .

No. She refused to go there.

But the police would.

They wouldn't have any choice.

he beginning of the week didn't bring an arrest in the Blythe Westerland case, but it did bring some normality back to Sea Harbor.

"School is in session today. Elizabeth is trying to keep everything as normal as usual," Birdie reported. "I stopped in to see her when we dropped Gabby off, just to be sure she was all right and to see if there was anything we could do. She was busy, as you'd expect, not only with the normal run of things, but fending off a pesky reporter."

"It's too bad she has to deal with things like that," Izzy said. "Geesh, what a mess."

They were walking along the beach—Izzy, Birdie, and Nell taking turns pushing Abigail's thick-wheeled stroller and taking advantage of Izzy's day off. She had refused to take time off for years, but finally caved in when Mae Anderson, the store manager, threatened to quit if Izzy didn't spend more time with Abigail. Putting it like that was genius—and of course Izzy started taking a day off now and then. This Monday seemed like a good day.

"Angelo was practicing his bouncer skills and did a nice job of removing the man from the premises. But there was a line of parents outside the office door, all jittery, with fear in their eyes. The police have talked to a lot of them, especially those who stayed late at the party. And that only makes it worse because everyone imagines they might have been standing next to a murderer, or talking with one, or might have seen something. And that only adds to the fear, of course."

"I can imagine," Nell said. "Everyone is nervous—but it must be worse for parents whose children are there at the school, so close to the crime scene. It isn't logical but it's certainly emotional." She looked at Birdie.

"Of course," Birdie said, feeling Nell's question. "I worry, too. But I know that the school is probably the safest place in town."

"Was Teresa Pisano in the office?" Nell asked.

"No. And that was making things more difficult for Elizabeth. Dear Mandy White was trying to juggle Teresa's job and her own assistant headmistress responsibilities all at the same time."

"And doing a better job than Teresa would have done, at least today," Nell said. She filled them in on Sunday's incident in the parking lot. "She seems convinced Elizabeth had something to do with Blythe's death."

"How awful for Elizabeth," Birdie said.

Nell agreed. It *was* awful for Elizabeth. They all liked her—and suspected things were going to get more difficult for the headmistress before they hopefully got better.

Birdie and Izzy were quiet, too—processing the thought and the accusations.

Izzy bent over and tucked a blanket around Abigail. The breeze was chilly enough for thick sweaters today but too early for hats, although she'd put one on Abby anyway—a floppy green hat with a huge crocheted flower on the side. It was exactly like one Gabby wore—her signature hat, she called it—and she had knit it up for Abby in three different sizes so she'd never be without.

As they started up toward the road, they spotted an easel set up near a pile of boulders at the end of the beach. In front of it stood a tall man swinging a brush across the canvas, his mouth moving along with his strokes.

He spotted the women walking along the beach and nodded in

their direction, then waved his brush briefly in the air. It wasn't clear if it was a wave to them or the air or to a gull hovering overhead.

"Josh Babson," Nell murmured. They waved back, but rather than disturb an artist at work, they continued toward the road that led back to Nell's.

"You don't like him, do you, Aunt Nell?" Izzy said softly.

Nell frowned. The comment made her uncomfortable. "I don't know him well enough to not like him."

"But I can tell from your voice that he isn't someone you'd want to invite to Friday night dinner," Izzy said. "I don't know the man from Adam, but Gabby likes him. She told me he was a good art teacher and she was sad he got fired."

Nell knew that—and Gabby had proven herself to be a good judge of character. So what was it about the man that bothered her?

"He acted odd at the party," Birdie said. "There was an unpleasantness about him. He was clearly looking for someone—and he didn't look happy about it."

"So, do you think he was looking for Blythe?" Izzy asked. "Why?"

Nell looked at Birdie, who shrugged. "I don't know. But he was attending a party at the school that had just fired him. Blythe was a part of all that."

"But he should have been looking for Elizabeth," Izzy said, bringing logic to the guesswork. "She was the one who fired him. He probably was furious, especially if he was as good a teacher as Gabby thinks he is. Maybe he wanted to confront her, embarrass her in front of everyone. Just like he did with the yellow paint."

Nell's frown deepened. She looked at Birdie, then back to Izzy. "Actually it wasn't Elizabeth who wanted him fired," she said. "It was Blythe Westerland. She wanted him gone because he didn't conform to what she thought the school's teachers should look like, or act like."

Izzy was surprised. "Blythe? I saw her with Josh one night at the Gull. I think they had come in together and they didn't look like enemies."

"That's a surprise."

"Well, it was months ago. Or weeks, maybe. Not recently."

"Well, no matter. The point is," Birdie said, "Josh wouldn't have known who was behind his firing. Elizabeth Hartley is the consummate professional. She would have assumed the responsibility for it. I don't think she would even have hinted that Blythe pushed for it."

They all thought about that as they walked up the winding street, listening to Abby's delightful new sounds.

Elizabeth was the headmistress. She was the one who had fired him. That was a fact.

She was the one Josh Babson would hold responsible. "That's an assumption, though," Izzy said. "We don't know that."

But what they did know was another fact: although Elizabeth fired him, it was Blythe Westerland who had forced her hand.

"Maybe I've been wrong about Josh Babson," Nell said to Ben that evening. "Elizabeth fired him. She would be his target if he was seeking revenge. I go back and forth. My logical, rational mind tells me I'm misjudging him. Yet I can't shake this feeling I have about him. It refuses to let go of me."

They were driving over to the yacht club. Ben had to pick up some things he had left on the boat, and the club was having a seafood special that Ben found difficult to miss. But mostly they both craved quiet time together to try to make sense of the turbulence in their town.

"I don't think I've spoken two words to Josh Babson. Ham seems to think he's an okay guy. He wouldn't have hired him if he didn't."

Nell had had the same thought. But it didn't seem as simple when mixed with other thoughts. "Jane thinks you'll like his paintings. She said he paints beautiful seascapes."

She told Ben about seeing him that morning at the beach, working on one.

"Maybe I'll stop by the Brewster Gallery one of these days. Meet the guy."

"But not to buy any paintings, Ben. We don't have any walls left."

"Where there's a beautiful painting, there's always a wall, Nellie, dear."

The yacht club parking lot was nearly full, a tribute to the chef who had recently moved over from the Ocean's Edge and was now giving the Edge some healthy competition.

Ben parked beneath a lamplight and they walked through the early-evening light to the clubhouse.

Liz Palazola Santos, the club manager, met them just inside the dining room door.

She hugged Ben and Nell. Annabelle Palazola's oldest daughter was as competent and gracious as she was beautiful—and everyone connected with the Sea Harbor Yacht Club was grateful that her marriage to wealthy contractor Alphonso Santos hadn't taken her away from them.

"What a sad week," she said. "I can't quite get my arms around it all. It's so awful. Blythe had just been in here that very day. She's been a regular for the past few months. There were certain nights we could set the clock by her. But before that, too, when she was in town. Actually even before I was manager—back in my hostess days. I can't believe anyone would want to kill her."

"Were you two friends?" Nell asked.

Liz considered the question, then answered carefully, "No. I certainly make an effort to be friendly to everyone who comes here. I try to learn people's names, a little bit about their families. But Blythe was very self-contained. It was almost as if she didn't need friends. From what I know of the family—the Westerland men— they were that way, too. Strong, powerful men who had a habit of getting their way."

"Except Blythe was a woman. But the other description seems appropriate," Nell said.

"Yes," Liz said. "But she played with power quite adeptly herself." The manager started to say more, then held back. "Never speak ill of the dead, my mother always said." She turned to Ben. "Anyway, I noticed you got out on the water today. A good sail?"

"Short but good."

"Saw Sam. But who was the other man? He looked vaguely familiar and I'm trying to get better at keeping everyone straight around here. It makes my job a lot easier."

"He was a friend of Cass. His family used to vacation up here, but that was before your time."

"Good." She laughed. "One less face to remember."

"Is there a lot of talk around here?" Nell asked. "Of Blythe, I mean."

"What you'd expect, I guess. I talked to the staff this morning, encouraging everyone to keep things as normal as possible. And to avoid discussions about it."

"The best remedy—the only one—is to find out who did this. It's the only thing that will get the town back to normal," Ben said. "The only thing."

"But in the meantime there's this awful tension. I feel it everywhere, no matter what I tell the staff to do or not do."

Ben looked over to the bar and the small patio that opened off it. "Liz, I don't have my glasses on. Is that Chief Thompson on the patio?"

Liz nodded. "He was waiting for someone. Dr. Hartley, I suspect. He had a dinner reservation for two, but he told me a few minutes ago to cancel it. He decided to have a fish sandwich in the bar and then get back to work. The poor guy—he looks like he has the weight of the world on his shoulders."

"The weight of Sea Harbor, for sure," Ben said.

They thanked Liz and walked through the bar and out the open sliding doors. Jerry was sitting alone at a high-top table on the small

bar patio, his back to the bar and any customers who might be inclined to join him.

"Jerry," Ben said, coming up behind him.

Jerry turned around and looked at them, then smiled a greeting.

Nell gave him an unaccustomed hug. "You look like you need
that," she whispered in his ear.

Jerry managed a small smile. A half-eaten sandwich sat on the
plate in front of him, a half-drunk bottle of beer beside it. "You're
both a welcome sight. I was going to give you a call. Can you sit for
a minute?"

"Sure," Ben said, and ordered two glasses of wine from the
waitress.

Jerry was quiet for a moment, his eyes intent on his blunt fingers tapping the table. Finally he looked up. "I have a favor to ask.
Both of you, really."

"Sure. Anything."

"It's about Elizabeth," he said.

Nell felt a small stab of worry. The look on Jerry's face was haggard and sad.

She and Ben waited while Jerry seemed to play with a jumble of
words in his head, searching for those that would make the most
sense.

"This was a difficult day for her. No, worse than that. It was
hellish. For me, too . . . and I need, hell, I don't know what I need.
I've never been faced with this before."

The conversation lapsed while the waitress set the wineglasses
on the table and brought a fresh beer out for Jerry.

He continued. "You were there yesterday when Teresa Pisano
had her outburst in the parking lot—so you know that she's causing some trouble. She's in the station every day. She's a little goofy,
she overreacts, says things that don't make sense, then refuses to
explain them. She's sure Elizabeth is in it for the 'money,' whatever
that means.

"But it's more than Teresa, really. It's the whole investigation.

It's what happened that night and why. The whole thing is thorny and touching people we know." He coughed slightly, a gesture to clear the sadness in his voice.

"It's . . . it's hovering over Elizabeth. Blythe very much wanted her out of that job. People have come in, told us Blythe was talking to people, waging her own private campaign to get rid of Elizabeth. It was a power thing, I think. But I don't know why. Not yet, anyway. You're on the board, Nell. You know some of this."

Nell nodded. "But Elizabeth has far more supporters on that board than detractors."

"Sure she does. She's a good woman. A wonderful woman. But she has landed smack dab in the middle of this. She . . ."

"She can't be a suspect," Nell said, but her words fell off as she realized that of course Elizabeth was a suspect. Not the only suspect, but one that the police would have to pay attention to. Not to be arrested now, but certainly to be questioned. And maybe questioned again and again. And she was Chief Jerry Thompson's close friend— his "lady" friend, as Esther Gibson would gently put it in the days to come. Gabby and Daisy's April-December romance couple.

The chief continued. "I've put Tommy Porter in charge of large chunks of the investigation. I need to step back a little. I know how people talk, how they think. Even good people, and I can't let the force suffer because of what people might see as signs of impropriety— though I'd quit my job in a New York minute to be able to stand by her side. But it's Elizabeth who's taking the lead on this."

He leaned back and swilled down half a bottle of beer. Ben and Nell sipped their wine, the table weighted down with thought.

Jerry's smile was sad. "She doesn't think we ought to see each other for a while until this thing evens out a little. Tommy had to go to her house and talk to her, *question* her. And he's probably going to have to bring her in to the station. It's awful for her. I tried to tell her we would be discreet, but she is convinced we can't be seen together, and she's adamant. A stubborn woman. She needs me right now— and I can't help."

Whose need was greater? Nell wondered. It was a trying time for both of them. And they were two fine people who clearly cared deeply about each other.

But Elizabeth was a wise woman. And a selfless one. She cared more about Jerry and his career than her own comfort level right now.

"I never thought there'd be room in my life for anyone after my wife died. But in spite of our age difference, Elizabeth and I have connected in a way neither of us ever expected. I can't define it. She fills this gaping hole in me that I didn't even know was there."

Jerry took a deep breath, then slowly released the air in his lungs and dropped his napkin beside the remains of his dinner. He stood and lifted a jacket from the back of his chair, then looked into the darkness beyond the lounge patio.

The waves were close, hidden in the darkness beyond the tennis courts. They crashed with abandon against the shore, a fitting backdrop for the night.

Finally Jerry looked back at Nell and Ben. "So here's my favor. What I'm asking is—for right now at least—will you two watch out for her? Be there if I can't?"

It was the kind of request only a good friend would make of other good friends.

Nell and Ben embraced the favor wholly.

Then they got up from their chairs and embraced Jerry Thompson as well.

Chapter 17

The man was walking toward the deli door at the same time that Nell and Cass walked out, carrying two large bags of Garozzo's famous pastrami sandwiches.

He was of medium height, about Danny and Sam's age, dressed in khakis and a knit shirt. He took his sunglasses off and looked at them intently.

On a normal day, they would have smiled, greeted the stranger, and gone on their way. But Blythe Westerland's murder less than five days before had changed things. And suddenly a normal Tuesday didn't seem normal—or safe—anymore. In fact, the woman's murder had changed nearly everything in the lazy seaside town.

Strangers now appeared suspicious, sinister even. Because surely it was a stranger who brought this awful curse to their town.

So they stopped, looked back at him carefully, and then recognized what he really looked like wasn't sinister.

He looked lost.

"May we help you?" Nell asked.

"Hell, I don't know," the man said, then tried to smile away his brash answer. "Sorry. I'm a little frustrated, that's all. There was a pileup on 128 and then once I got here I realized that as small as this place is, I didn't know where to go. And I said I'd be here at ten, not noon. Believe it or not, I've never been to Sea Harbor before."

That was certainly believable, Nell thought. Many people

hadn't been to Sea Harbor. But if he thought he should have visited earlier, he probably should have. It was a magical place. At least it once was, and it would be again.

Cass shifted her bag to the other arm. "So you're looking for a place? A person? Maybe we can help."

Nell checked her watch. They were headed down the street to the small park across from the historical museum—a quick lunch meeting. Izzy and Birdie were there waiting, probably already poring over the final details for the week's sewing class at Gabby's school.

The man looked around, then back at Cass. "The courthouse or police station. I'm really not sure. I was going to ask in the deli." He thumbed the door behind him. "I just got back in the country, and jet lag has my head doing strange things." He pulled out his phone and flicked to a message. "Courthouse, it says."

"It doesn't matter. They're next to each other. We're headed that way if you'd like to walk with us," Nell said. "The courthouse is just a couple blocks off Harbor Road."

The man looked grateful and held out his hand. "Thanks. I'm Bob Chadwick. And please, the least I can do is carry those for you."

Nell and Cass relinquished their bags without protest. They were heavy and Bob Chadwick's broad chest and muscled arms would do a better job of carrying them down Harbor Road. And if he was sinister after all, he'd have his hands full.

"Smells good," Bob said as the aroma of Harry Garozzo's pastrami and garlicky sauce rose from the bag.

"It is," Cass said. "Best pastrami sandwiches on the north shore. Where're you from?"

"Boston," he said.

"And you've never been to Cape Ann? Shame on you," Nell said.

He laughed. A nice friendly laugh and the two women relaxed a little. "It is a shame, actually. I like sailing. Mostly up in Maine. But don't know why I never explored this place—I've been invited often enough." Between the shops he spotted dozens of white sails, heading out to catch the breeze.

"If you decide to give it a try, we know some mighty nice sailors," Nell said.

"Over there." Cass directed as they passed Izzy's yarn shop. She pointed across the street and to the end of the block, just across from the museum, where a small square of green was crisscrossed with paths. A small gazebo and benches invited picnickers and others to stop and rest.

Izzy and Birdie waved as Cass and Nell walked around the stone statue of a lobster to where they sat in a circle of benches, papers spread out on the ground in front of them.

"About time," Izzy said. "We're starving." She looked again, startled. "Oops. Sorry. I thought you were Jake—the guy who works at the deli. Except you're not wearing his greasy apron."

Bob looked down at his khakis. "Nope, he refused to give it up."

Nell took one of the bags and set it down, then introduced Bob Chadwick to Birdie and Izzy, who greeted him curiously, wondering, no doubt, why some stranger was carrying their bags for them.

"These nice ladies are helping me find my way around town," Bob said, and set the other bag down. "I have a meeting that I'm two hours late for. But I'll definitely stop back at that deli before I leave town tomorrow morning. These sandwiches smell terrific."

He shoved his hands in his pockets and looked around the park. Then across the street to the old brick museum. And in the other direction where he looked again at the white tips of sailboats waving back and forth. "This place looks like Mayberry, U.S.A. with an ocean," he murmured, more to himself than to the three women looking at him with restrained curiosity. He shook his head, still talking to himself. "Not what I was expecting . . ."

He looked back at the women. "This sure doesn't look like a place where someone would bash someone's head in."

"So you know about the awful week we've had," Nell said, watching his face change from pleasure to something else—not concern, exactly. Surprise, maybe. With a touch of sadness and disbelief.

He nodded. "I don't know much. I guess I'll know more soon."

"Are you here to help with the case?" Nell asked. He didn't look like a policeman. And Ben hadn't mentioned that they'd be bringing people in. But who knew how these things were handled? He could be a detective.

"No," he said.

"Do you have relatives here?" Izzy asked.

The man was giving answers in a perfunctory way. He had mentioned jet lag earlier. Nell wondered if that explained it. Or it could be that they were pummeling him with questions.

"Yes," he answered. "Well . . . no. I did have relatives here. A relative."

For a moment they were all quiet. Then Birdie lifted one hand to her mouth, realization dawning on her. "Oh, my," she said, and instinctively reached out to touch his arm.

His head moved slightly, a nod. "She was my cousin—the woman who was killed," Bob said. "Blythe Westerland."

Things moved quickly after that.

Birdie had pulled a bottle of water from the deli bag and practically ordered Bob to sit on the empty bench. "Drink the water," she said.

"Everyone in the courthouse will be out of their offices until one," Nell said. "They won't be missing you."

Cass pulled the sandwiches out of the bag and passed them around. "The deli owner is a friend. He always gives us extras."

Later they would talk about how instinctual their actions had been. It was what you did when someone died. You brought food. Offered drink. Company.

But usually you knew the grieving person you sought to console. Bob seemed completely surprised by the attention swarming around him. But he followed instructions and seemed relieved to be putting off for a while longer the reason he was there. He sat, took a drink of water, unwrapped the pastrami sandwich from the waxed paper, and took his first bite, closing his eyes as his taste buds woke up to Harry Garozzo's amazing sauce. "This is fantastic," he murmured. "I didn't realize how hungry I was. It's been a long night."

"We're terribly sorry for your loss," Birdie said. "Were you and Blythe close?"

Bob took a few more bites before responding. He pushed his sunglasses into a thatch of thick brown hair, took a drink of water, and spoke slowly, answering their question with one of his own.

"Did you know my cousin?"

"It's a small town, Bob," Birdie said. "Everyone is connected in one way or another. We all knew Blythe."

But did they? Nell wondered. Birdie was being comforting to someone who had just lost a relative in a horrific way. And yes, they knew her. But not in the way you knew those close to you—or even neighbors and shopkeepers, who shared illnesses and births and children losing first teeth, who accepted help when plumbing gave out or knew when your first grandbaby was about to be born. She knew Blythe by observing her, but no, she didn't really know her.

"Blythe had a difficult time letting people into her life. I guess I knew her as well as anyone did," Bob said. "Our mothers were twins, and we were both only children. So there was that."

"Her mother? Does she know?" *A mother—losing her daughter.* The thought brought a sudden pain that burrowed deep inside her. She looked at Izzy and saw a flash of pain in her eyes, the same sad thought settling in.

But Bob shook his head. "I'm her only living relative. I didn't see her much when we were growing up, but we inherited a double brownstone together in the Back Bay when my mother died. Blythe lived there sometimes. Recently she'd been spending most of her time up here, but she was always back and forth. Doctors, dentists, dinners, a couple boards she was on, things like that always brought her back. She had her share of men no matter where she was."

"Where did the brownstone come from?" Izzy asked.

"I grew up in one of them, one side, actually, and my mother bought the other side as an investment. She died a while ago and left it to both of us. I think she somehow wanted Blythe and me to be closer, and that was her way of doing it. And it worked. That's when Blythe and I got to know each other. For two independent people, we actually became dependent on each other in odd ways. Rides to the airport and doctors' appointments, talk about relationship crises. We took care of each other's places if one was traveling, paid bills. It was good for both of us. Every now and then, we even confided in each other. Not often. But when it mattered.

"Blythe was the kind of person who seemed to have everything, but she never wanted the things most people think about—she was adamant she'd never marry, never have kids. And she was true to her convictions, even when it meant . . . making difficult decisions." Bob stopped, his forehead furrowed, as if he'd brought up a memory he hadn't intended to let enter the conversation. He coughed slightly, then went on.

"But I think she knew herself well and those decisions were probably good ones. I don't think she could have handled that kind of life. She certainly didn't have any role models who could have helped her."

"What about her mother?"

"She died early, at least as best we can figure out."

"You don't know for sure?" Birdie asked.

"My aunt Sandra—Blythe's mother—married Clarence Westerland when she was young. He was a dozen years older. He was taken by her beauty. And she was impressed with his money and prestige, or at least that's what my mother thought. Sandra had one child—Blythe. But according to my mother, Sandra—who was gorgeous, as you might have guessed Blythe's mother would be—was never an emotionally strong person, and living as a Westerland wife was unbearable for her. When Blythe was two or three, her mother took off—and no one ever saw her again. Not even my mother. I don't remember her at all. Blythe doesn't—didn't—either."

"Abandoned her own daughter?" Izzy's mouth had dropped open. Another inconceivable thought to try to digest.

They sat in silence, the screech of the gulls and the light traffic on Harbor Road the backdrop as they tried to wrap their thoughts around a mother abandoning her daughter. A daughter now dead. Suddenly Blythe Westerland was changing before their eyes.

"Who raised Blythe? Your mother?" Birdie asked. But that didn't fit the little she knew about Blythe's upbringing. She had attended Sea Harbor Community Day School. And Bob said he hadn't known her until they were adults.

"No," Bob said confirming her thoughts. "My mother wanted to raise her, but she didn't have a say in the matter. Blythe's father was a Westerland. That made Blythe a Westerland. My mom became estranged from Sandra when she married into the Westerland family. Mom thought the estrangement was encouraged, maybe demanded by the Westerlands.

"The family had money and servants and lots of power in Boston and Cape Ann, too. Homes all over the place. Blythe was raised by the Westerlands—a family of men with numbers after their names—Elijah the second, Clarence the third or fourth, or whatever."

He crumpled the sandwich wrapping and tossed it into a nearby container. "Her own father—the grandfather, too, and a couple uncles—had absolutely no use for Blythe from what my mother was able to piece together."

"What? Why?" Izzy looked as if she was going to attack someone. Nell put a hand on her arm.

"Because she was a woman—and even worse than that, she was her mother's daughter and looked exactly like her—a constant reminder of someone they considered a weak, useless woman who ran away. Someone clearly beneath them. But you don't give away kids. It doesn't look good. So they kept her."

Bob checked his watch and got up, brushing crumbs off his tan slacks. He thanked them, got directions from Cass, and said he'd be in touch.

They watched him walk off.

They kept her. "How awful for Blythe," Nell murmured. *"Kept her,* like a piece of furniture."

She thought about the Blythe who had sat on a school board with her, the woman of taste and means who had a gorgeous condominium near the water, who was involved in civic affairs. A woman who always seemed to have a man at her side. A woman seeking power, like the men who had raised her . . .

Nell tried to put the odd and mismatched pieces in a puzzle frame that made sense. But they resisted and fell to the ground, mixing with crumbs from their pastrami sandwiches.

In the end, all her thoughts produced was lunch for a hungry gull.

Chapter 18

The school was quiet, the students gone for the day. A crisp breeze sent a sprinkling of leaves falling to the ground, the colors just beginning to change. It was tranquil. Peaceful. One would never have imagined that days before a murder had sullied the grounds.

It had been a busy day. An hour after meeting Bob Chadwick, Nell and Birdie had received e-mails that sent them following in his footsteps. Could they please come to the station to meet with one of the men working on the case? When Nell called back and mentioned she was with Cass and Izzy, they were included in the meeting. It's routine. Just to touch base, the policeman said.

The meeting had indeed been routine, a series of who was where and when at the party. Who talked to whom? They were also checking on any out-of-town guests, especially ones who might not have been invited. Cass mentioned Harry, but only because he was an out-of-towner. "He had a paid ticket," she said, and the officer dutifully recorded it.

Although it had been so recent, memories of the party seemed far away, and conversations a blur. But they all promised to think about them, write things down, and send on anything they remembered.

Two hours after that found Izzy and Nell each carrying a box of supplies up the fan of steps leading to the school's main entrance.

Before they reached the door, Angelo appeared out of nowhere, his arms stretched wide.

"Ladies, ladies, ladies, that is Angelo's job." He piled the boxes on top of one another, his head barely visible above them.

"Yarn and needles and doodads," Izzy said. "Nothing contraband, Angelo." She held open the door and followed him into the foyer.

Angelo chuckled, then sobered quickly. "Not a time to joke about anything criminal, Izzy. Sad times we have here." He set the bags down and nodded toward the administrative suite. "How she does it, I don't know. But she is holding it together."

"We were concerned about her. This is a difficult time." They told Angelo about their hour at the police station that day. "I don't see how they are going to question everyone at the party. It will be impossible."

Angelo agreed. He'd spoken to an officer himself earlier that day. "And I expect I'll be back. They're desperate for some glimpse of something off, something that might lead them from the party to the rocks. But the truth of it is," he said, "it was probably someone who was coming along the shore. A diver, someone in a boat, or even someone climbing that rocky shore on foot. And just waiting for Blythe to make an appearance."

"But how would he or she know Blythe would walk down there?"

Angelo shrugged. That was a sticking point. But she could have gotten a message from someone. She was in demand that night, he said.

It didn't hold together, though. Not completely. A far more rational explanation was that Blythe and a guest at the party were having a private conversation down behind the boathouse. And that person had killed her.

Someone at the party. And though Angelo knew that made sense, Izzy and Nell could both see that he wouldn't yet let himself go there. Not yet. He had lived in Sea Harbor all his life, and he probably knew almost all the people there that night, except for the occasional out-of-town groups.

"Dr. Hartley is racking her brain," he said instead. "She talked to nearly everyone that night, working at cementing relationships, doing all those things administrators are supposed to do."

Nell and Izzy agreed. "We saw her that night, so gracious and hospitable. Everyone felt her warmth."

"She's a good boss. Dr. Hartley doesn't think about herself. Ever. It's all about the school. The girls. The teachers." His frown deepened as he glanced again toward the glass windows of the suite.

His head moved from side to side and his eyes narrowed. "But that other one—" He lowered his voice so that Izzy and Nell had to lean in to hear. "Even in death she is trying to destroy our school. She was evil."

A hand lay gently on his arm as Elizabeth Hartley appeared at his side from across the entrance foyer. She smiled at Izzy and Nell, then spoke gently to Angelo. "Let it go, please, Angelo. I need you to hold it together."

But the expression on Angelo's face only became more pronounced, the furrows in his brow growing deeper, the look in his piercing blue eyes so intense that Nell turned briefly away.

When she turned back, it was still there. A look of hate so strong she rubbed her arms, willing the uncomfortable feeling away.

Angelo turned away, as if trying to shake off the power Blythe Westerland seemed to hold over him from the grave.

From one of the hallways that stemmed like an octopus arm off the round lobby, a teacher called to him. Trouble with a riser in the auditorium. Would he help?

He took a deep breath, the old familiar Angelo reappearing as he said good-bye and hurried off after the choral director, his mind moving on to things more manageable.

Elizabeth watched him disappear. Once he was out of earshot, she apologized. "Angelo tries to protect me. I couldn't do my job without him—but he needs to take care of himself, not me." There was a note of regret mixed with her apology, as if she wished they hadn't seen his anger.

Nell watched the stocky man disappear down the hallway. Elizabeth was right. Angelo needed to look after himself but maybe not in the way the headmistress meant. Emotions were running high along the streets of Sea Harbor. Neighbors looking at neighbors. And everyone wanting one thing: the murderer, whoever that might be, behind bars. There was a "someone" who might be walking too close to their children, someone who had wanted someone they knew dead—and someone who had made it happen. Allegiances sometimes fell away in the face of fear. Angelo needed to hold his anger in, lest it be snatched up, magnified, and used against him.

Elizabeth glanced at the boxes on the floor.

"Supplies for the knitting class," Izzy explained.

"Of course," Elizabeth said. "Just leave them right here. I'll have someone take them to the supply room."

She sent a quick text to security, then brought her attention back to Nell and Izzy.

"Elizabeth," Nell said, "it's almost silly to ask you how you are. An empty question. Except you need to know that you have plenty of friends ready to help you through this time. We'll do whatever we can for the school, for you. Somehow this school has worked its way into many hearts."

Elizabeth seemed to deflate slightly from the kindness, her professional smile and demeanor slipping away with each of Nell's words. What remained was an ordinary woman with tired eyes. A sad woman.

"Would you join me for a cup of coffee?" she asked.

Her voice told them the coffee didn't matter a bit, but a few minutes with friends did.

Yes, they could help, at least by being present, if nothing else.

They walked through the empty outer office and Nell glanced

at the tall counter and the small receptionist's desk behind it. A white plastic rectangle read TERESA PISANO.

Elizabeth followed her look. "Teresa didn't come in yesterday. She showed up today but spent most of the time cleaning her desk and was clearly too upset to concentrate. I had the assistant headmistress suggest she take a few days off. She's having a difficult time handling this."

Her sigh was resigned. "I think she came back because she was afraid I might look at her things or do something." Her voice trailed off and she looked again at the empty desk as if it might have some answers for her. "Do something? I don't know what I would do . . ."

She moved on into her own office, her words trailing behind her.

Nell glanced at the desk again and wondered briefly what motivated Teresa Pisano to hurl such awful accusations at her boss. Was it simply grief—or something more?

The memory of Teresa's rant rattled around in Nell's head, and she imagined how clearly it must appear in Elizabeth's. Had Teresa repeated those same words to others? To people who would cast them off as meaningless rants from a young woman grieving a friend, but would remember them later, wonder about them? Maybe even pass them along to others until they took on a life of their own?

Nell and Izzy settled into the comfortable seating area at one end of the tasteful room. A coffee table held a pot of coffee and tray of mugs, some used, some clean.

Elizabeth glanced at the table. "Please excuse this mess. I've had a parade of parents in today and haven't had time to straighten up."

"Parents?" Izzy said.

"They want to be assured their daughters are safe here."

"The police don't think there's a random crazy man out there," Izzy said. "Why are they afraid?"

"Because they are parents," Elizabeth said, "I don't blame them. Can you?"

"No," Izzy admitted. "You're right. A part of me is logical, rational, and knows this was a targeted action. It had to have been a personal thing between Blythe and whoever did it and it doesn't spill over into our lives. And yet I'm holding my Abby as close as I can. There's no rationale behind or beyond my hugs. Just an umbrella kind of fear, I guess, until this person is behind bars."

Elizabeth nodded. "That's the only thing that will end this nightmare."

"Blythe spent so much time around here," Nell said. "I've been going over board meetings she attended, conversations I had with her. Anything that might point to someone or something that was bothering her."

"And you've come up empty, just as I have. Many of us had problems with her. That's the hard part."

Nell thought about the recent firing of Josh Babson, and how Blythe had publicly blamed Elizabeth for it at the board meeting. It hadn't made sense then, not entirely. Aloud she said, "She seemed concerned about Josh's firing."

Elizabeth looked toward the lead glass windows. "Yes. She showed up in my office that day, wanting to be here when I fired the poor man. To help me, to make sure I did it right, whatever that meant. But I had moved the meeting up at the last minute and she missed it. What she didn't miss was his dramatic departure. She had a ringside seat for that."

"The painting on the lawn?" Izzy said.

She nodded. "We watched him, Blythe and me, from the windows over there. We could see the intense anger in his very posture as he walked across the lawn. Blythe assumed I had done it wrong— the firing, I mean. Somehow he should have been able to walk away with dignity, and instead he was filled with anger. I had messed up again, was her message."

"Anyone would have been upset," Nell said. Blythe treated Elizabeth like a child, she thought. How utterly degrading. And yet . . . and yet there was a strength in the headmistress, despite how mild-mannered she sometimes seemed. Elizabeth Hartley had a kind of grit. The kind that would help her weather all kinds of Blythe Westerlands.

"Sure. And he was upset. But he was a gentleman underneath it all. He sought me out at the Friday night party and apologized for slamming the door when he left."

"And the circles on the lawn?"

Elizabeth managed a small smile. "No, he didn't apologize for those. They weren't meant for me, and Josh knew I knew that. Somehow he was aware that Blythe was up here watching. He probably saw her car in the lot or maybe saw her come in. I would never have mentioned her role in his firing, but somehow he knew without being told. I don't know how, but I think those two had some bad blood between them."

She reached for her cell phone and turned to the film roll, found what she was looking for, and looked up. "Once Josh painted the yard and left, I went down to see the damage. I wasn't sure at the time what we were dealing with, and both Blythe and I had seen something peculiar in one of the circles. It was more of a drawing, like a traffic sign, with a stick figure in the middle. So I went down to look, and when I saw what it was, I took a photo of it before Ira mowed it down." She watched Izzy flipping through the photos of the yard. "I'm not sure what I was going to do with any of them. You get used to documenting things at a school—some for insurance reasons. Anyway, it seemed like something I should photograph. I knew Blythe blamed me for things, and—well, I'm not proud of it, but I suppose I thought maybe I should collect things that might protect me down the road." She handed the phone to Nell and Izzy.

Izzy used one finger to swipe through the photos of the bright yellow circles on the grass. She stopped at the last one, the circle Elizabeth—and Blythe—had seen from the window. The one that stood apart from the others.

The yellow circle with a stick figure of a woman in the center, the bigger-than-life traffic sign in the middle of the school lawn. What they hadn't seen from the window were the initials painted directly below the figure: *BW*. And slashed through the whole thing—a diagonal line, stretching like a threat from one edge to the other.

The sign was clear. It wasn't deer or trucks or skateboarders that weren't allowed down that road.

It was Blythe Westerland.

Chapter 19

$\mathcal{N}$ ell's and Izzy's phones both pinged at the same time as they left the school. Different message alert tones, but the same messages.

Since the noontime meeting had been devoted not to teaching a knitting class, but to Bob Chadwick, Cass was calling for another session. There was no way she was going to face kids as precocious as Gabby Marietti and not have a better idea of what they were doing.

Izzy called home. Sam was happy being home alone with Abby. They'd hang out, watch a Patriots game maybe, he said. Abby was suggesting pizza and beer. Baby food was for the birds.

Ben was equally accommodating. He had some business to take care of and was taking Jerry Thompson out on the boat for a couple of hours to get him away from an increasingly frustrated force, not to mention the town. They weren't making much headway, lots of dead ends, though each day they heard about someone new whose life was easier without Blythe Westerland in it.

Izzy knew the back room in the yarn shop was already booked—Mae's twin nieces were teaching a class to a Brownie troop to earn some kind of badge. Mae would oversee it all—and the shop—with her usual eagle eye.

But it didn't matter—no one wanted to cook, so Birdie arranged for Merry Jackson to save them a corner table on the Artist's Palate deck in Canary Cove. It was a nice night and the Palate grill was a little more out of the mainstream than the Harbor Road restaurants. Privacy—at least a semblance of it.

And she hadn't had a perfect burger in at least a year.

Merry had already set out her towering heaters, though they were on the lowest setting tonight because the breeze off the water was gentle, the air brisk but pleasant.

"It's a perfect evening to be outdoors." Merry greeted them at the deck steps, flapping a handful of menus in the air. With her long blond braid bouncing between her shoulder blades, she led them through a maze of tables to one at the very edge of the deck. It was separated from the water by a sharp decline and a thick line of mis-shapen pine trees, the sea just visible in silvery streaks as the wind parted the heavy boughs.

"I call this my 'creative table,'" Merry said. "Danny Brandley has written all four of his bestselling mysteries right here, on this very picnic table. All four." She tapped it with her fingernail, as if the words were still there, engraved in the wood. "So sit, eat, and think deep thoughts." She grinned and disappeared, her energy palpable in the pine-scented air.

Izzy lifted one leg over the bench on one side of the table. Cass joined her while Birdie and Nell pulled out chairs on the other side.

"Merry's wrong, you know," Cass said, looking down at the ta-bletop as if the young restaurant owner had punctured it with her finger.

"Wrong?" Izzy looked sideways at her friend, a lock of streaked hair falling down her cheek. She pushed it back behind her ear.

"Danny wrote two of those books at my house," Cass said. "He proofed them here." She followed up her words with a smug look that said, *So there,* before picking up a menu that she knew by heart and scanning the type, effectively dismissing the topic.

Nell slipped on her reading glasses and looked over at Cass. Well, that was interesting. It sounded to her as if Cass had Danny on her mind.

"Where's Harry tonight?" Birdie asked.

"He was thinking of coming by. I said I had plans. He's going to get a beer somewhere. I'll see him later."

That was healthy, Nell thought—that Cass was making her own plans. It didn't sound like a committed relationship. But the relationship still mystified her. And Cass said little to demystify it. Ben said it wasn't up to them to figure it out, his gentle way of telling his wife to back off. Nell was trying.

Merry had sent a waitress back with a pitcher of pale ale. "Merry says this will help the process."

"Is it what Danny drinks?" Izzy asked innocently, but wrinkling her nose at Cass.

The waitress looked confused, but Izzy quickly agreed they'd love the pitcher of ale. And some glasses, too, please.

Rather than spend time on the menu, they stacked them up and let Birdie order for all of them. Grilled steak burgers on Merry's homemade toasted buns, sweet potato fries, and arugula with goat cheese salads to mask the cholesterol surge.

It was a slow night, but Merry's deck never went without its regulars, mostly Canary Cove artists and gallery owners who considered the restaurant their own kitchen. Rebecca Marks waved from across the way, mouthing a hello as she lifted a large lobster roll in the air. She was joined a minute later by her roommate, Jules Ainsley, the Brewsters, Josh Babson, and Polly Farrell from the Tea Shoppe. Nell watched the odd mix of friends and shopkeepers and artists, all of whom were at home on Merry's deck whether they knew each other or not. There was no such thing as a stranger at the Artist's Palate. There was always someone to talk to, someone to listen. It was a community all its own—and she loved it.

Izzy reached down into her bag and pulled out a few sheets of paper. Her nod to the reason why they were there—the knitting class. But it was an excuse; they all knew that. The real reason they wanted to be together was different. It was a reason, but more of a need. The need to share the cloud they'd been walking under and through and around for four days. The one that was beginning to hover with threatening darkness over people they cared about.

"I printed out some knitting information so Cass won't be intimidated," Izzy said. "It's simple. It's mostly about being patient so they don't get nervous. And hey, we're all good at that."

"Gabby will be in the class," Birdie said.

"Gabby? She could teach it," Nell said.

"Which she shall," Izzy said. "She'll help, especially with the kids who are more experienced like herself."

The waitress brought their order and they pushed the papers aside, allowing the table to be filled with piles of fries and burgers nearly as big as the plates they were served on.

Cass dug into her sandwich almost before the waitress had left the table. "I'm worried about Angelo," she said, around a bite of meat. "And so is Ma." The Garozzo family had been friends with the Hallorans for generations, the two families proving to all of Sea Harbor that chianti and Guinness could live together in perfect harmony—not to mention deep friendship.

Drips of butter escaped Cass's bun and she caught them with the edge of her napkin. "His brother came into the office today to order lobsters for the deli. He's worried. He said Angelo hated Blythe Westerland, talked about her all the time—"

Nell nibbled on a fry and listened. *Hated* was an awful word—so harsh and somehow irrevocable. It was difficult to take back once you had hurled it out there. And yet what she had seen in Angelo's eyes that afternoon fit the description.

"Why do you think he felt that way?" Birdie asked. She wasn't really aiming for an answer, but rather a discussion. "I sensed it, too, Friday night at the party. And even Gabby talked about it. She loves Angelo, but she sensed his anger. Blythe irritated him something awful, she said."

"I think he hated what Blythe was doing. She demeaned Elizabeth, objected to her plans for the school, made her life difficult," Nell said. "He's very protective of the headmistress."

"The police are sure to talk to him," Nell said. "He's a good man. But he wears his feelings on his sleeve, just like his brother. Big noisy Italians, both of them. And I saw him staring at Blythe that night. If looks could have done the deed, Angelo would have been responsible."

"But Angelo isn't capable of killing anyone." Izzy spoke definitively, but they all knew there was little meaning in her words.

No one knew what another was capable of. Not until it happened. And then it was too late.

"Gabby brought home some information today about a choir concert that the administrators and choir director are planning," Birdie said. "They're calling it a festival of some sort. It's not completely defined yet, but Gabby is in the group and thrilled, of course."

Nell smiled. "It's Elizabeth's effort to erase the images people still hold about that night, about the school, and to replace them with something wonderful. Music is the perfect medium. Music and children. She's a wise woman."

"According to Gabby, that's what it will be. Wonderful. Joyful."

"But not unless we can drive away this fear before then," Izzy said. "I doubt if anyone will want to gather on the front lawn of Sea Harbor Community Day School as long as Blythe's murderer is still walking our streets. He was there, for heaven's sake. Right there, on that lawn, or close by." Her voice had slipped into the one Nell imagined her using in the courtroom, sensibly addressing a crime, the steps to a solution. Logical. Persuasive.

But Izzy was right. The town was cowering, hesitant. Even though people went about their daily lives, they were looking over their shoulders, imagining evil in places where it didn't have any right to be.

Izzy went on. "It's affecting Elizabeth Hartley in a terrible way. Aunt Nell and I saw it today." She looked over at Nell, then repeated the talk they had had with the administrator that afternoon. "She's a private person, but she's in pain. You can see it in her eyes."

"I think it's going to get worse for her," Cass said. "Pete says there's talk down at the dock today that she's going to be questioned again."

"Where do they get their information?" Nell asked with a touch of annoyance. But it didn't really matter where. People listened, people talked. And people filled in the gaps with what might be.

Izzy glanced across the room at Josh Babson, then told Birdie and Cass about the pictures Elizabeth had taken with her phone.

"She needs to show those to the police," Birdie said.

"I thought the same thing," Nell said. She followed Izzy's glance to where Josh sat comfortably with his friends, draining a bottle of beer. His elbows were on the table, his head propped up by the heels of his palms. He looked serious, but calm. Certainly not guilt-ridden.

She had gotten an e-mail from Jane the day before, or rather from the gallery itself, that the Brewster Gallery was going to be featuring some of Josh's works. Ben wanted to go. Maybe that was a good idea.

"I think Elizabeth has mixed feelings about saying anything," she said. "I think she believes in Josh. And in a way she blames herself for his anger. If she had refused to fire him, things might be different."

"Do you mean Blythe wouldn't be dead?" Cass asked.

They were all quiet for a moment, the burgers taking center stage. What had she meant? Cass's interpretation meant she was indicting the man. If he hadn't been fired, he wouldn't have killed Blythe? Picking the thought apart brought a realization of something that had been bothering her. "How would Josh have known so fast that Blythe was a powerful force behind his firing? He didn't blame Elizabeth—he even apologized to her for showing some emotion that day. Elizabeth would never have told him about Blythe's influence. She'd have taken full responsibility for it herself. Our board is also discreet."

"Maybe it was something else, not the firing at all." Izzy took a bite of her burger. "Maybe there was something about Josh besides his teaching techniques that Blythe didn't like. Maybe she was getting back at him for something."

On the table in front of them lay the tips for teaching knitting, and an educator's theory of putting complicated pieces together. That was certainly needed here.

"Revenge? That's a good point, Izzy," Birdie said. "We're looking at surface facts. And we know so little about Blythe and what made her tick. Revenge sounds like something she wouldn't be averse to."

"Even her cousin doesn't seem to be able to offer anything concrete about Blythe," Cass said.

"I'm not sure about that," Nell said. "I think we were all a bit stunned when we met him, unsure of his feelings, unsure of what to say. I talked to Ben this afternoon and he was at the courthouse when Bob came in. He liked him—and they all found him cooperative."

"Is he going to stay around?"

"He's staying at Ravenswood tonight. Ben said he was going back to Boston tomorrow morning for a meeting. But he'll be back. Father Northcutt wants to meet with him, and the police will have more questions. Ben is trying to find a will. So there's a lot going on."

"Does Bob know anyone here?" Cass asked.

"Us," Izzy said.

Music began playing in the background, pumped from speakers above the bar and on the deck posts. People came and went as waitresses lit the hurricane lamps on the table. Nell waved at Andy Risso and Pete Halloran, lumbering up the steps and heading over to the bar. And then she looked again. Bob Chadwick was a step behind them, still in his khaki pants and knit shirt, following them to the bar and to the display of thirty-six brands of beer that Merry proudly advertised as being the most extensive selection in town.

"Look," Nell said. "Pete and Andy just walked in with Blythe's cousin."

Cass looked over at her brother and his drummer friend Andy

Risso. "Good for Pete. Sometimes he shows he has a soul. I told him about Bob and that he probably didn't know anyone here. It had to be a rough day for him, and the only one working at the bed-and-breakfast tonight is Teresa Pisano. Somehow I wasn't sure she'd want to go out for a beer with Bob."

"Or vice versa." Izzy laughed, finishing her own glass and asking the waitress to bring coffee. "They probably figured the same thing we did, that Merry's place would be a little out of the mainstream and they wouldn't have to introduce Bob to curious people."

Pete spotted them, waved, then turned back to the bar and his old—and new—friend.

"Cass," Birdie said a minute later, her glasses perched on her nose. "Look over there. Another friend is joining them."

It wasn't that no one else in Sea Harbor had ever grown a mustache or beard. Maybe it was his Clark Gable looks. But heads turned as Harry Winthop walked across the deck to the bar, greeted Sam and Andy, and accepted the bar stool they scooted over to him.

But it was when Bob Chadwick turned around and was about to be introduced to Harry that the Knitters' attention was piqued.

Bob stood, shook his head in surprise, then man-hugged Harry like an old friend.

Chapter 20

They'd left the Artist's Palate a short while after, intending to say hello to Pete and his friends, but the men were nowhere in sight.

When they met the next day to teach knitting to a group of exuberant girls, Cass filled them in.

"They decided to show Bob the town. Pete says he's a nice guy."

"And what did Harry say?" Izzy asked.

"He doesn't say much. Maybe that's why I like him."

"Why was he with them?"

"He wasn't. He stopped in to get a beer. He didn't see us sitting at the side or he'd have come over. Or maybe he wouldn't have. Like I said, he doesn't like to talk much."

"It looked like he knew Bob," Nell prompted. She dug into a box and pulled out a supply of wooden knitting needles. They were on the school's veranda, grateful for the mild day, and pulling chairs and tables together before the girls arrived.

"I asked him. He was kind of noncommittal, but he did offer that they belonged to the same tennis club in the Back Bay for a while. He didn't stick around. He drank his beer and went back to his place to do some painting."

"Did Bob talk about his cousin?" Birdie asked.

"Not much. The guys let him take the lead and he didn't seem to want to go there. He seemed sad, Pete said. Blythe had been dealt a rough hand in life. She had a heap of neuroses generously given to her and nurtured by being raised a Westerland. In Bob's mind, that excused a lot of her behavior toward people."

How little they knew about this woman. There were probably layers and layers to peel off before the Blythe they had known—and the things she had done—would make sense.

And only then would they know why someone killed her.

Izzy put out several baskets of yarn on the supply table, along with the needles and a pile of printed patterns. Each of the knitters had knit up a sample—Cass, a winter hat that she had perfected over the years. She knit one for not only every member of the Halloran lobster fleet, but any fishermen she spotted around town who had a bare head in cold weather. Birdie knit a top-down poncho in soft wool that required no seaming, and Nell and Izzy were adding a collection of dramatic scarves that would make the girls feel like accomplished knitters in no time. And to go along with the scarves, a pattern for fingerless gloves.

"You're here!" Gabby came out a side door and flew across the veranda, her pleated uniform skirt flapping in the breeze. Daisy was in close pursuit, her shorter legs working overtime to keep up with Gabby.

"Of course we are." Birdie beamed, embracing her granddaughter.

"Daisy, this will be old hat to you," Izzy said. "I remember when you took your first knitting class at the shop."

"It was a cool class," she said, pushing her glasses up her nose. "My mom says I can knit as well as she does because I had such a great teacher." She grinned.

"Well, that expertise makes you and Gabby our helpers today. And I promise some time for your own project."

The two friends had already picked out what they wanted to knit—fingerless gloves for Daisy, and a fringed poncho that Gabby would wear with great flair.

Elizabeth Hartley was the next to arrive. She carried a class list and handed it over to Izzy while Daisy and Gabby took over arranging the supplies.

"A couple of students won't be here, so the class today will be smaller," Elizabeth said.

"Just for today?" Birdie asked.

"No, permanently. They're leaving."

"The school?" Nell asked. The concerned tone in Elizabeth's voice was telling.

"Yes," Elizabeth said, then forced a smile to her face and added, "The good news is we have a waiting list for this class, so we'll fill the spots by next week's class. It will make a couple of girls very happy. You're in demand." Her smile attempted to cover up concern, but her brown eyes betrayed her, even when she slipped on her glasses to read the agenda items Izzy had printed out.

Nell looked over at Birdie. Parents were taking their children out of the school.

Birdie's concerned expression mirrored her own.

But Nell tried—as Ben often urged—to put a stop on her emotions until she knew all the facts. Often things weren't as they seemed. Families moved away sometimes. Circumstances changed—Gabby herself was proof of that, starting school a bit after the semester began. But from the look on Elizabeth's face, it wasn't as simple as that.

Elizabeth looked at her watch. "I have an appointment downtown shortly. But Mandy White is in her office and can help with anything you need." She took a deep breath, as if bracing herself for something unpleasant, then turned and disappeared into the cavernous school.

A dentist appointment might explain the headmistress's expression, Nell thought. But Elizabeth didn't seem like the kind of person to schedule dentist or doctor appointments during a busy school day. An appointment downtown at one in the afternoon could mean only one thing.

Elizabeth was going to be questioned by the police—again.

The class sped by, a roller-coaster ride with energetic fingers tangling and untangling yarn, pulling out stitches, laughing and giggling and gossiping, girls seemingly untouched by the more serious events going on around them.

"It's refreshing," Nell said to Izzy as they watched the girls from a few feet away. "A brief interlude."

"I heard two of the girls talking about their parents' new house rules, and the fact that they can barely step out the door without armed guards—I guess those are parents—a few feet behind them."

"Ten- and eleven-year-olds think they're invincible," Birdie said.

Cass walked over. "The kids are stoked about that fall music event. The school must be playing it up. Gabby says they might even let Pete and the Fractured Fish open for them."

They laughed. It was a lovely diversion, something to look forward to, which most certainly was why the administrators had come up with it. Lighten the mood, bring families together under the magical spell of music.

And by then, absolutely by then, there'd be a murderer behind bars.

Cass walked back to several girls needing help with pulling out stitches. "My specialty," she claimed.

Nell spotted Angelo Garozzo at the far end of the terrace, talking with some teachers. He saw the knitters and walked in their direction, his gait slow.

"Ladies," he said, lifting a hand in greeting.

"Your step is heavy, my friend," Birdie said, walking over.

"And I have a heart to match."

"It must be difficult for you to be watching this play out," Nell said.

"Worse."

"Has something happened?"

Angelo looked off toward the sea. He shrugged. "I spent three hours today down at the police station, surrounded by guys I've known my whole life. Or their whole lives, I s'pose, since some are like that Tommy Porter, just young whippersnappers. But they're good guys, fair men. And they're trying every blasted angle they can think of, mapping out that school party like I don't know what."

"Mapping it?"

"Drawing lines on a huge blackboard. Who was where when, who talked to whom. It's a tangled mess. We were all there, and plenty of us had the evil eye for Blythe Westerland that night. Plenty of us."

"Angelo," Birdie said quietly, holding his gaze. "I have two questions for you."

Angelo nodded. He wasn't the only man in town to stand up straight when confronted by Birdie Favazza. Nor was he the only man who would protect the small silver-haired octogenarian with his life. He leaned in slightly, listening carefully, his hands shoved in the pockets of his pants.

"First, why did you dislike Blythe?"

They all listened carefully for his answer. Although they hadn't talked about it, Angelo's feelings toward the woman seemed excessive sometimes, propelled by something they couldn't quite put their finger on.

At first Angelo didn't answer. They watched a range of expressions flash across his face as he pondered the question. It was almost as if they could read his thoughts as emotion lit his eyes and clenched his round jaw.

"Okay, you're right. I never liked her, even before Elizabeth. She needed a life, is how I see it. She was livin' her life to prove to a bunch of dead men that she was a woman, she was beautiful, and she was every damn bit as powerful as they ever were. Sometimes I'd see her looking up at old Elijah Westerland's portrait in the school as if to say, 'See? Who's the best of them now?'

"Anyway, right or wrong, that's how I see it. But why did I dislike her? I don't have nothin' against powerful women. My wife Hildie's one of 'em.

"What got my undies in a bunch was the way she treated other people. And especially someone like Elizabeth Hartley, who was spending her life doing good things for the school and this town. Trying to get her fired. Saying bad things about her."

Nell listened. They all knew that, board members, even townspeople. "Who else didn't she like?"

"Is that the second question?"

Birdie smiled sweetly. "No. Nell asked that one, not me. I'm still holding on to mine."

"There was Anna Mansfield," he said slowly. The crevice in his forehead deepened, as if he was unsure of how far to go with his own opinion.

"Anna," Izzy said. "She's a child. How could she dislike Anna?"

"Right," Angelo said. "Maybe she didn't dislike her personally—though I don't think she liked kids much. I asked her once if she wanted any kids and she looked at me like I'd asked her to eat rotten meat."

"But Anna . . . ?" Nell asked, pulling him back.

"Blythe wanted the school to be perfect. She didn't think Anna was perfect. It wasn't so blunt. She just didn't think the school should have to spend time on kids who weren't status quo and smart. But between you and me and the bedpost, I think . . . I don't think that's what's going on here at all . . ."

He looked up, the frown disappearing as if the real answer had come to him as he talked. "I think it was Anna's father she disliked—and targeting Anna was the best way to get to him. It wasn't Anna at all."

The thought settled in with a thud.

Izzy looked over at the girls, worried that one of them might have heard. But they were happily knitting and purling with determination in their fingers and sitting as straight as only ten-year-olds can sit. Izzy walked back to them, a shepherd protecting her flock from all cruel thoughts—and from grown-ups who do cruel things.

"Just my opinion, you know," Angelo said, watching her walk away.

Several of the girls now looked as though they could use an accomplished knitter nearby and Cass followed Izzy, knowing "accomplished knitter" was a relative term when coming from a ten-year-old.

"I need to move along, too," Angelo said. "You nice ladies are going to get me fired for all this lollygagging." He turned to leave.

"There's still that last question, Angelo," Birdie said, pulling him back.

"One more. Okay. One. Throw it at me, Birdie."

"Why do you think Blythe Westerland was killed?"

Angelo stared at Birdie as if she'd asked him if he loved his wife. Or his job. Or Sea Harbor. It was as clear to him as the sun or moon or the stars he and Hildie watched through his telescope. Finally he answered, "Blythe hurt lots of people. But that night, the night of that party, she must have caused in someone a pain so awful that it killed something in that person. A pain so great, it drove that person to retaliate. To take a life.

"Hers."

Chapter 21

I t was the only free night they had all week, Ben was quick to remind her. And he needed some fresh air. Art, fresh air. Who could say no to that?

Nell was tired, bone-weary. Maybe it was trying to keep up with the frenetic energy of young girls in the knitting class. Or maybe the strain of the worrisome days. Her head was full of frizzled, dried-out thoughts.

What she wanted to do was curl up on the couch with Ben's comforting arm around her, a glass of wine nearby. And let the quiet of their home seep in and soothe her body and spirit.

But mostly she wanted to be with Ben. So she said, "Sure. Fresh air is good," and slipped on a sweater to ward off the evening chill. "I've been wanting to see Jane anyway."

"But not Josh Babson," Ben said, grabbing his keys.

Nell smiled, following him out to the car. "Oh, sure. Why not?"

Ben backed out of the drive and they headed down Sandswept Lane. "I left Elizabeth Hartley a message early this afternoon saying we'd stop by later tonight with sandwiches. She texted back, saying she'd be home. This couldn't have been a good day for her."

Nell was silent, feeling a wave of guilt. Between the knitting class, the girls, and the uncomfortable talk she had had with Angelo, she hadn't given Elizabeth another thought. Until now.

Elizabeth had left school in the middle of the afternoon. Off to an appointment, she had told them. And they all knew—or thought they knew—with whom she was meeting. Of course she hadn't had a good day. How could being questioned by the police be good?

"Did she say how she was doing . . . ?" Nell began.

Ben was quick to answer and change the conversation. He'd only be guessing, he said. "Let's wait and see for ourselves."

They drove in silence for a block or two, trying to do as Ben suggested. Wait and see.

Finally Nell said, "Have you had any luck finding Blythe's will?" Facts, mundane tasks, were easier to deal with than emotions and a woman's spirit being slowly eroded.

Ben nodded that he had. "Bob looked through her things and found the lawyer she used. Apparently she switched her entire inheritance away from the Westerland financial advisers just as soon as she could. I talked to someone in one of the Boston firms that represented the family. He said that before the dirt had settled on her father's grave, she effectively took every cent, every investment, and moved it as far away from Westerland lawyers as possible."

"Was she the only heir?"

"There were a couple families that broke away a long time ago and never lived up here. But Blythe is the only one from the Boston branch. The rich branch, as one of the lawyers so delicately put it. She was the only woman and the sole heir, something the lawyers thought would turn old Elijah and his progeny over in their graves."

"Why?"

"They didn't like women, except to cook and bear children, preferably male ones."

"How awful."

Ben agreed. "The man I talked to was new enough with the Westerlands' firm that he didn't know any of the Westerlands, but their reputation echoed in the hallowed halls, he said. The Westerland men ruled everything and anyone they could get their hands on. One banker compared them to the Koch brothers—those guys in Kansas. Rich and powerful and controlling."

"But how does that explain Blythe?"

Ben glanced over, then back to the road. "What do you mean?"

"She's a puzzle, a contradiction. You're insinuating that she wanted to separate herself from the Westerlands, which—if her cousin's account is correct—is understandable. But sometimes she seemed proud to be a Westerland. And she loved the building that her great-grandfather once raised a family in and then turned into a legendary school. She loved it; I honestly believe that. And I think she was sincere in her efforts—as ill-founded as they were—to restore it to the way it was twenty-five or thirty years ago: a pristine institution for young women of means."

Ben listened, nodded slowly. "You're right. It's difficult to figure out how—in that bundle of contradictions—anyone will be able to pull out a reason why someone might want to kill her."

They played with the jumbled, confusing facts as they knew them, the complicated woman they knew—and didn't know—finding little in them that brought logic or sense to her murder.

Then Nell remembered her original question. "So, where is her will?"

"It's with the firm she transferred her affairs to. We'll get it in the next day or two."

"Has Bob seen it?"

"He will. He's coming back up tomorrow or Friday. We'll set up some meetings. Jerry needs to talk to him again. More questions, along with the hope that some answers he gives might lead somewhere. Father Northcutt talked to him today before he left. He suggested they put together some kind of memorial for her. Bob thought that was a good idea. They're going to finalize those details when he comes back."

"What did you think of him?"

"I like him." Ben brought the car to a stop, allowing several joggers to cross the road. "At first I was put off a little. Maybe it's because I expected to see more sadness in him."

Yes, there was that. "Izzy mentioned that, too. He was friendly, but she couldn't figure out what was beneath that top layer."

"Izzy is very observant when she gets in her lawyer mode." Ben pulled into the parking lot at the edge of the artists' colony. "Some people don't wear their emotions on their sleeves, and I think he's one of those people. And Blythe was complicated. By the end of our meeting, I figured he cared. And he's a sailor. If there's time, Sam and I will take him out. He'd love to meet the Hinckley, he said. That's in his favor, too."

They walked together beneath the clear sky, lamplight guiding their way down Canary Cove Road to the Brewster Gallery. The pleasant weather had brought out more people than usual on a Wednesday night. Maybe they weren't the only ones who heeded the e-mail about Josh's paintings and decided to take a peek before the weekend traffic.

Or maybe they were all trying to act as if things were normal in Sea Harbor. It was a safe seaside town. And whoever had ended Blythe Westerland's life in such a tragic way was long gone from the town and, hopefully, even the earth. Nell waved at Don and Rachel Wooten, walking across the street to the gallery.

They could hope.

Josh didn't have enough paintings yet to have an official show, Jane had said, but she wanted people to get a taste of what he could do, so she was highlighting a few oil paintings in the small room off the main gallery area. Whet people's appetites, she said.

Nell knew Jane well. She was always thinking of the artists' colony she and Ham had founded all those years ago, but even more, she was thinking of the artists who lived and worked there. Another motivation in staging a middle-of-the week invitation would be to help the other galleries, to fill them with visitors if she could, to help the artists now, before the long months when winter closed the galleries weeknights—and some during the day.

They spotted Cass a block ahead, heading in the same direction. Beside her, Harry Winthrop lowered his head, leaning in to catch whatever Cass was saying.

"Looks like we won't be the only ones there," Ben said.

"Mary Halloran's birthday is coming up. Cass wanted to get her mother a painting of a fisherman."

Ben laughed. "Mary has even more of those than I do." He took Nell's hand, wrapped it in his larger one. "So, what do we think of this Harry fellow?"

Nell could see Cass's hands moving as she talked, explaining, directing. "I don't know. He's handsome. He takes Cass to nice restaurants. His place in Boston has a plumbing problem or something, so he's stuck here for a while. And none of us can get a good reading on him from Cass. Her feelings are safely hidden beneath that stubborn Irish facade of hers."

Ben listened, more amused than concerned.

Ham Brewster met them at the gallery door, a cup of coffee cradled in his large hands. He clapped Ben on the back. "Glad you're here. I think you'll like this guy's work."

"He can't like it too much, Ham," Nell warned.

"You can always build an addition." Ham lifted one bushy eyebrow and stroked his beard.

Nell glowered at the gallery owner, then followed it up with a hug. "Let's go see what I've heard Jane rave about."

They walked toward the adjoining room, its center wall displaying several paintings, all by Josh Babson. Small strategically placed lamps highlighted each painting.

Several people were grouped around them, quietly admiring the new artist in town.

Nell looked around. Harry and Cass were standing near a refreshment table talking to Jane. Others milled around the gallery, in and out of the three rooms, admiring the eclectic art Jane and Ham represented. The Brewsters' own paintings and pottery were in their usual niches and cubbyholes, always changing and always coveted and quickly purchased.

"Where's the artist?" Nell asked Ham.

"He'll be back. He went out to grab a sandwich. Josh isn't the most sociable artist in the Cove, but he promised to show up."

"But you like him?" she asked quietly.

"Well, look for yourself." He pointed toward the exhibit.

It wasn't what Nell was asking, and both she and Ham knew it. But it was a better answer for now. She moved through the wide archway into the space that had been arranged for Josh's paintings.

The space in front of the paintings had cleared, and Ben and Nell stood several feet apart looking at a series of small seascapes, all oil paintings, and all showing a breadth of color and light and unexpected emotion. From painting to painting, the vibrant sea changed in personality, from a golden, pink-streaked dawn with the silhouettes of two fishermen on the side; to another focusing on a still sailboat, the light seeming to come from the sails themselves; to dark, foreboding swirls at night, softened only so slightly by a sliver of moonlight.

Nell looked at Ben. He was concentrating on the smaller paintings with a familiar glint in his eye. He was becoming immersed in the sea he loved. It was the look that most often led to having to clear space on an Endicott wall.

Nell sighed and moved a few steps over to a larger painting at the end of the row, framed simply in a polished maple frame.

It was stunning. A majestic, fierce sea with a brilliant burst of light above the swells, so bright it caused one to squint or blink, blurring the images around it.

Nell took a step back and looked again, her eyes adjusting to the light. The images at the edge of the sea slowly came into focus: a mound of gray, rugged rocks—romantic and sinister at once.

Familiar boulders, familiar angles, flat and sharp, with just a faint shadow of an old boathouse at the edge of the painting.

A scene that she knew only too well. One she might not have recognized, had it not so recently turned her dreams into terror.

Chapter 22

*N*ell felt his presence before he spoke.

"You recognized it." Josh Babson stood near her, just a step behind, out of her vision.

It was clear, undisguised. Magnificent in the color and contrast. Of course she recognized it. It was the same spot that had been photographed and splashed around Sea Harbor for days, fuzzy newspaper photos, iPhone shots on social media sites. Live television shots.

But this painting was beautiful, mesmerizing.

"You're talented," Nell said. Her thoughts were muddled. Did he paint this last weekend? Before Blythe was barely a statistic? She wondered if he could read her thoughts and sense the emotion that caused her arms to chill beneath the cotton sweater.

"Jane chose this painting," he said, but without the touch of apology Nell half expected. "She wanted it included in the exhibit."

"You've put much feeling into your art," Nell said.

"What was it Picasso said? 'Art brushes away the soul's dust.'"

Nell considered his words. "Is your soul dusty, Josh?" she asked. Their voices were low, almost intimate, and Nell kept her eyes on the painting as she talked and listened, waiting. Like a priest in a confessional, she thought. Protected in that dark private space, not seeing each other's face, where honesty wasn't as difficult as it was face-to-face. She could feel Josh's smile and she heard his short, humorless laugh.

"I suppose we all have a bit of dust on us," he said.

The crowd around them grew, and Nell stepped back to allow others to stand in her space. Josh was soon swallowed up by well-wishers and possible collectors, many asking when there'd be a bigger show.

Nell watched as the artist shoved his hands in his pockets, smiled politely, and as soon as he could, slipped into a quiet spot where he stood against a wall, watching reactions to his art silently, without the annoyance of chatter.

"What do you think?" Cass asked, coming up beside Ben.

"He's talented. I like them."

"Me, too. I'm buying the *Sea at Dawn* painting for Ma. She'll see all sorts of spiritual things in the light, like the Mystical Body and all that. I'm not sure what she'll do with the two fishermen on the side, but for sure one is my pa."

Ben chuckled and looked over at the painting. "Good for Mary Halloran. She's my choice for an art critic any day."

"Harry, do you like art?" Nell asked the mustached man standing near Cass. He was positioned with his back to the exhibit, looking uncomfortable, moving from one foot to another.

Harry seemed to consider the question, then said, "No, not the way people who go to galleries like this do. I guess Babson's paintings are good, at least from the look on people's faces. But I can't really tell the difference between them and something I'd buy at Target. They're all pretty pictures."

"He's here under protest," Cass said. "I couldn't even get him to look at the paintings. He wanted to watch the game at the Gull. So we compromised. First the exhibit, then the last four innings of the Sox game."

"How's the house coming?" Ben asked.

"Okay, I guess. Lots of work. Lots of decisions. I hoped to hurry it up, but no luck. I'm stuck for a while."

"Sea Harbor isn't a bad place to be stranded," Nell said.

"No, I suppose not." He slipped an arm around Cass.

Cass looked surprised at the gesture, then glanced at her watch. "Time to go. We don't want to miss the eighth-inning singing of 'Sweet Caroline.'"

Nell watched them leave.

Ben saw her watching them through the gallery windows and came up beside her. "Ours is not to wonder why . . ."

"I guess not." Nell continued to watch them walk down the road. "What do you think? Does Cass like him?"

"I haven't a clue," said Ben.

The gallery door opened again a minute later, and Barrett and Chelsey Mansfield walked through, Barrett in his three-piece suit and Chelsey in tailored slacks and a cashmere sweater. She looked relaxed and without the worried lines so noticeable when Nell had last seen her.

Jane had greeted the newcomers and Nell watched as they chatted pleasantly near the door about the weather, the exhibit, a new gallery opening up. Barrett, as was his way, stood at his wife's side, unaware of any glances, any attention his formidable presence brought, simply being there for his wife. He looked content. Happy, even, without the no-nonsense business manner that was often evident at board meetings.

He was valuable to the board, often bringing astute business advice at needed moments, the same kind of expertise Nell presumed made him so successful in his businesses. It was simple and unpretentious, and always helpful. He was generous, too, a trait board members sometimes lacked. She suspected his donations were considerable, and he and Chelsey had brought a whole entourage to the school party.

Nell's thoughts wandered back to that night, to watching Barrett graciously attend to their guests and the crowd and the introductions. Chelsey had been the quiet one that night, standing back, watching the crowd, but not joining it.

Until she collided with Blythe in the school hallway.

The scene came back to Nell with such force that it startled her.

It had been buried somewhere in the confusion of the days and the fear in the town as people looked over their shoulders, searching for someone, anyone, who looked or acted suspiciously. For a murderer walking among them.

The Chelsey she had listened to from behind the school's lounge door that night was not the woman standing beside her husband in the Brewster Gallery. That Chelsey had been strident, her voice harsh and filled with anger. That Chelsey had hurtled a threat through the quiet hallway of Sea Harbor Community Day School—one aimed directly at Blythe Westerland.

The couple spotted Ben and Nell and walked over to them, greeting them cordially.

Nell took the glass of wine Ben handed her and concentrated on the amber liquid, as if hiding her thoughts from Chelsey Mansfield.

Tonight's Chelsey was intelligent, pleasant, a good wife and nurturing mother. Not the woman who had threatened Blythe Westerland with words made of steel and coated in anger—and hatred.

"Have you seen Josh's work before?" Ben asked.

"No," Barrett admitted.

"We're fans, though, sight unseen," Chelsey said. "Our daughter likes Josh very much. He's a good teacher, good to the children. I'm sure Anna wasn't the only one that Josh bolstered up and made feel good about herself."

Beside her, Barrett's somber nods showed agreement. "He seemed to know, as we do, that Anna is an amazing child with unique needs," he said.

Nell looked up at the emotion in his voice. A slight catch as he mentioned his daughter's name.

"Maybe more rational decisions will be made going forth," Chelsey said beside him. Her manner was gracious, but her message was clear. "Good teachers need to be valued, not cast aside for personal reasons."

Barrett looked slightly uncomfortable with the conversation. He sipped his wine in silence, and seemed relieved when Ben switched the talk to more neutral topics—the upcoming concert at the school, a sailing class for adults at the yacht club that Chelsey wanted to take. Nell listened with half an ear, focusing on Barrett watching his wife. His look was guarded, but she saw something else in his deep, intelligent eyes. A look of devotion—a look of clear, unadulterated love for this woman and, she had no doubt, for his child. Having that child be played like a pawn—if Angelo was correct—would be an unbearable hurt.

Minutes later Barrett suggested they wander over to the exhibit. "We need to relieve Anna's sitter soon, and we promised our daughter a full report on Josh's paintings when we get home."

Nell sipped her wine, watching them move across the room. From his shadowy post on the other side of the room, Josh spotted the couple, too, and came toward them. He greeted them with a handshake, a few words, and not much else. His usual way, Nell was beginning to realize, and she felt some relief that she wasn't the only one who brought out the artist's laconic nature.

"People are enjoying his work," Ham said, coming up beside them. He gave Nell a bear hug.

She laughed. "Thanks, dear Ham. I needed that hug."

"Anytime, no charge." Ham Brewster was a teddy bear—big and sometimes boisterous, his gray-streaked beard bushy and his clothes usually smudged with some palette of whatever paint colors he was using. "An artist's badge of honor," he'd say.

Nell loved him dearly, paint smudges and all. "What's your assessment?" she asked, nodding toward the exhibit.

Ham scratched his beard, looking from Nell to the paintings and back. "That depends, Nellie. Are you asking about the artist or the paintings?"

Ben laughed. "You know her well, Ham."

Nell smiled. "Okay. Paintings first."

"He's good. I think most of those who came tonight think so, too."

They all looked over, scanning the looks on people's faces. The crowd had ebbed and flowed, but right now most people had moved to the refreshment table. Barrett and Chelsey stood side by side, not speaking, carefully taking in each painting. Now and then one would murmur a word or two to the other, then move on to the next.

Finally they stood as one in front of the large painting at the far end of the wall. Jane's pick. The painting that had caused Nell to close her eyes, to catch her breath, and to come back to it more slowly.

She couldn't see their faces, but she saw Barrett's arm wrap slowly around Chelsey's waist, his suit sleeve a dark band against the soft golden cashmere of her sweater.

Chelsey leaned slightly into her husband, her head inclined as if to view the painting from a different angle.

"Hey, you two, we're coming to dinner Friday night," Jane said, motioning to Ham to stay at the desk in case someone had questions.

Nell nodded, trying to pull her attention back to Jane. She glanced once more at the exhibit, but Chelsey and Barrett had turned away from the paintings and were walking over to Ham. She looked back at Jane and smiled brightly. "Of course you're coming. Where else would you be on Friday night? Besides, you've nicely ignored us tonight and I need to catch up with my friend."

Jane grew serious. "Me, too," she said. "We need to help each other make sense of the world, dear Nell."

If that was at all possible, Nell thought.

She looked at Chelsey Mansfield, standing at the door, waiting for her husband. Chelsey was looking around at the art displayed in the room—Jane's beautiful ceramics and some of Ham's watercolors. Her face expressed appreciation of what she saw.

She noticed Nell just as Barrett walked up to her. Waved, then tucked her arm in her husband's. And then they were gone.

"Hey, good news," Ham said as he and Ben walked toward them from the order desk.

He waved a check in his hand. "Who would have thought?" he said.

Nell glared at Ben. He put up two hands and proclaimed innocence. "Not me. I'm waiting for the bigger exhibit. Ham promised me my own preview."

"So, if not you . . ." Jane moved toward her husband and the flapping check.

"Josh sold his first painting tonight. It will pay several months' rent for the guy, maybe more. He's a happy camper."

"Which painting?" Jane asked.

But Nell knew which one before Ham confirmed it.

He handed the check to Jane. "The big one," he said.

Nell looked over her shoulder at the check.

In the left-hand corner, just above the enormous sum, she read the address:

Chelsey and Barrett Mansfield
22 Seacliff Road
Sea Harbor, MA 01930

Chapter 23

Ben called ahead from his cell, then double-parked in front of Harry Garozzo's deli and ran in to pick up their order.

Nell rolled down the window to let in the evening breeze. Instead Tommy Porter leaned in, his forearms resting on the door. He was dressed in jeans and a T-shirt.

"Hi there. What's up, Tommy?"

"Just wanted to say hello. I've seen Ben off and on this week but have had hardly a glimpse of you."

Nell smiled. She had known the young policeman since he was a kid fishing off the pier. She had watched him grow from delivering papers to lawn jobs, including the Endicotts'. One of several children in a fishing family, Tommy had strayed off course by attending the police academy, and his family was inordinately proud of him. "A cop in the family can't hurt," his dad joked to anyone who asked, his chest puffing up.

"It's good you're getting a night off now and then," Nell said.

Tommy glanced down at his jeans, and his smile melted away. "Nah, not really. None of us will really be off duty, ever, not until we catch this guy. We're all on alert, always looking, all the time, no matter where we are. You can't shake it, you know? You just never know, some overhead conversation in a bar or a stray piece of gossip—maybe it'll lead somewhere. It's hard on all of us, but especially on the chief. The guy isn't sleeping much."

"It hasn't even been a week, Tom—" But Nell knew, just as they all did, that every day without new leads diminished the chance of catching him.

Tommy was quiet for a minute, as if he wanted to ask something, then thought better of it and held it back.

"Are there theories?"

Tommy nodded. "Yah. A couple."

"And suspects?"

Tommy sighed. "Yah. And motive. Lots of people aren't sad that Ms. Westerland's not around. But . . . but the people the investigation keeps pointing at, well . . ." Again he looked as though he wanted to say something else, ask a question, but then fell silent, his head lowered and his eyes staring sadly down at nothing.

Nell tried to give the conversation a twist. "Blythe was never married, was she?"

He shook his head. "From what I hear, she wasn't the marrying kind, even though men were attracted to her something crazy. You have to admit, she was quite the looker. One summer a couple years ago my older brother, Eddie, seemed to be the object of her affections. It didn't last long. In a couple weeks she tossed him overboard like a bad fish. She liked conquests, Eddie said, and control. There was this guy, a friend of Eddie's, whom she came on to. He went out with her a couple times, but he was kind of traditional, and was uncomfortable with all the flash. Eddie convinced him his days were probably numbered anyway, so he cut it off himself. That didn't sit well with her. It was her job to conquer and discard, not his, I guess."

"What happened?"

"The guy worked at the yacht club. Blythe had him fired."

"What?"

"I know. She had this weird power. But I should zip it. I know it's not good to speak ill of the dead and all that—my mom would be ashamed of me. But this woman has gotten in my head. I don't like her there. But—"

"But until the murderer is caught . . . ?"

Tommy nodded. "Right. Until then, she's going to be front and center—and giving me migraines." He looked up as Ben walked around the car to the driver's side. Tommy waved a hello. "Looks like a first-class feast," he said, eyeing the white sack.

"Nothing but the best for my bride." Ben smiled and waved good-bye as Tommy headed down the road.

Ben slid behind the wheel, bringing with him smells of garlic, ham, tomatoes, and cheese. And freshly baked bread. He handed Nell a bottle of wine to hold and started the engine.

"What if Elizabeth's already eaten?" Nell asked, positioning the bag of sandwiches between her feet.

"Then I'll eat the leftovers." He shifted into drive and headed toward their neighborhood.

They pulled into Elizabeth's drive. The house was dark.

"I wonder if we're too late," Nell said. "Maybe she's gone to bed."

"At seven thirty? It's just beginning to get dark." Ben got out and checked the front door, then peered in the front window and a small one in the garage. He got back into the car beside Nell. "Her car's gone. Something must have come up."

They both pulled out their phones and checked for messages. There were none.

"This isn't like Elizabeth," Ben said. "I wonder if something kept her at school."

"It's a nice night for a ride. Let's drive over there. If she's still working, we can at least give her something to eat—"

Unsaid was a sudden worry that worked its way inside Nell. Undefined, irrational. And real.

She looked at Ben. He felt it, too.

The school parking lot was lit with security lights and Ben drove around it, past several golf carts the maintenance staff used and a pickup truck near a storage shed. At the side closest to the school, they spotted Elizabeth's small green Prius, parked near the lit walkway that wound around to the entrance.

Nell smiled in the dark car, relief settling in.

But when they reached the entrance, the door was locked. Ben took a few steps back and looked over to the windows that surrounded the headmistress's office. Dark. The only lights visible anywhere were the security spots strategically placed around the building and yard. He walked around to the side, and only the corner security lights added light to the stone school.

Nell walked to the terrace, looking out toward the water. The boathouse was silhouetted against the darkening sky. "I know this is silly," she said, "but let's walk down to the dock. Just to make sure . . ." *Make sure of what?* Nell wasn't sure. But somehow knowing that Elizabeth wasn't alone, down near the rocky shore, seemed suddenly all-important.

Ben took Nell's hand and squeezed it as they walked across the terrace and down the winding flagstone path. The hurricane lamps used for the party were gone, but small spots shone up into trees, and low solar lights were turning on as darkness set in, lighting the walkway. A light breeze lifted Nell's hair from her neck. It could have been romantic, lovely, a peaceful walk at day's end.

But Ben's squeeze of her hand was hard—there was nothing romantic about it. And there was nothing romantic about the determination that propelled their footsteps across the yard to the ocean beyond.

They crossed the narrow beach road and approached the rocky shore, slowing down, as if intruding on a private space. The dock was old, but a good place to sit, to think. Something Elizabeth might be in need of.

But there was no one around, no fisherman out for a final catch, no strollers or joggers.

No Elizabeth Hartley.

They stood still, scanning the shore, then beyond the boulders, out toward the spit of land that housed Canary Cove. The sound of the waves crashing against the shore was deafening, blocking out traffic and town noises, breathing and heartbeats.

It was Ben who finally looked over at the boathouse. Its angles were haunting in the diminishing light, the slight lean of the roof, the broken shingles along the side. Gone was the yellow tape, along with any sign of danger or crime or tragedy. As if the boathouse and majestic granite boulders that separated it from the sea were simply there for painters to capture in beautiful strokes on stretched canvas.

"She's not here, Ben," Nell whispered. Her voice wobbled uncertainly, and Ben didn't answer. Instead he walked over to the boathouse.

The windows were dirty, but the small flashlight on Ben's key chain showed the inside to be as empty as the beach.

"I think we need to call Jerry Thompson," Ben said, pulling out his phone.

It was then that the sound of the waves diminished briefly, their punishing crash falling off in the distance, as if controlled by Sirens reclining on the rocky edifice.

Another sound took its place, making its way into the night.

Soft, like the mew of a kitten.

Nell looked around, then over to the boulders that separated the boathouse from the water.

Ben was a footstep behind her as they walked quickly toward the sound, the waves picking up again as the power of the wind pulled and tugged.

Elizabeth sat on a smooth outcropping of the largest boulder, nearly hidden from view by the closer pile of rocks. Her knees were pulled up to her chin, her face a shadow in the receding light.

"Elizabeth," Ben said softly, not wanting to frighten her.

She turned slowly, the tears streaming down her face visible now.

Nell climbed over several boulders and sat near her, a crevice filled with seawater between them.

"We were concerned . . . ," she began.

Elizabeth wiped her face with the back of her hand and tried to push a smile into place. She was still dressed for work, dark slacks, now damp and rumpled, and a silky blouse, its ends loosened from the waistband. "I'm so sorry. I lost track of time—" She turned toward Ben. "You were so kind—and look at me. A mess."

"I hope we're not intruding." Nell looked off in the direction Elizabeth had been facing, seeing what she was seeing—endless ocean, and a sky beginning to come alive with stars. "I find strength and peace at the ocean's edge," she said.

Elizabeth nodded. "Maybe that's what I thought I'd find here. I don't know . . ." She pressed one hand against the cold rock. "I had hoped that coming down here, to this spot, might help me make sense of this nightmare. Maybe I could feel what had happened that night."

She didn't look at either of them as she talked, but rather at the boulders and the sea.

"This isn't like me. I don't do things like this. I've always been able to weather storms, keep calm, think rationally. My mother died when I was young and my father raised me to be strong and resilient. He loved me fiercely but always made me stand up to problems, solve them, move on. He taught me how to make thoughtful and wise decisions. But I'm floundering with all this. It's a treacherous awful storm, and it's pulling people I care about into its waters."

"What decisions are you talking about, Elizabeth?" Ben asked. His voice was as soothing as a confessor's.

"I'm deciding if I should resign from the school."

It wasn't what Nell was expecting, nor Ben from the look on his face. Elizabeth loved her job.

"We've had some parents pull their children out of school, and there are a dozen rumors going around. People like Angelo and Jerry—they're forced into terrible positions trying to protect me. Angelo knows better than anyone what Blythe Westerland and I thought about each other. Jerry knew, too."

She turned slightly, looking in the other direction across the wide lawn, toward the school, spread out over the land like a fortress.

"Many people knew Blythe wanted me fired—and a few knew that I wanted more than anything to stop her from doing it."

"All of that could be true, but it doesn't mean anything," Ben said.

Elizabeth looked sadly at Ben. "I wish you were right, Ben. But right now it means that unless someone else steps forward and confesses to the crime, a good many people in Sea Harbor will be looking at me. I feel it. I'm sure Jerry feels it. The teachers are loyal—and most of the students, blessedly, have escaped some of the buzz. And people like you have been wonderful. But it's there, a swarm of bees surrounding me, ready to sting."

Nell watched her face closely and saw the hollows beneath her eyes. A look of utter weariness. "Did something happen today when you went to the police station? Something new in the case?"

Elizabeth looked at her, then Ben, then pushed herself off the rock and climbed over the boulders to solid ground. Nell followed.

"They found something back here." She pointed back to the deep crevices in the rock formation. "It was a small piece of a scarf, ragged and torn, tangled in seaweed."

"A scarf . . . ?"

"My scarf. Or at least one like mine."

Ben and Nell were silent. Finally Nell asked, "Who found it?"

Elizabeth sighed. "Angelo," she said.

Hours later, they wrapped up the remains of the sandwiches Ben had retrieved from the car and watched the dying embers in Elizabeth's office fireplace. Ben had built the fire, not necessarily to ward off the early autumn chill, but to bring some kind of warmth into the sadness that was invading their lives.

Ben refilled their wineglasses and sat back down, thinking as he looked into the flickering logs.

Angelo wasn't by himself when he'd found the scarf, Elizabeth said. "And that was fortunate. He might have been tempted to destroy it if he remembered I had a similar scarf. He's a sweet man, and has become a dear, loyal friend. It would have been awful for him to put himself at risk because of me."

She'd asked Angelo to look at the boathouse, and he had taken several workmen with him, she explained. "We need to do something with the building, something to erase the image that is becoming embedded in people's minds. They went down to take pictures and consider the feasibility of some of the teachers' and students' ideas. Angelo didn't realize what the scarf was when he pulled it out of the crevice."

"Did he show it to you?"

She nodded. "I knew immediately what it was. It was a small piece of a scarf, one that looked identical to the lacy scarf I wore the night of the party."

Nell remembered it. Turquoise and elegant, knit from sea silk yarn. Chelsey Mansfield had knit it for her, she'd told Nell that night. A graduation gift when she finally received her PhD.

Nell didn't want to ask, but a simple answer could clear it all up: the scarf was in her drawer, safe, sound, and in one piece. "Do you have your scarf?" she asked.

Elizabeth set her wineglass down on the table and stared into the fire. "I searched everywhere last night. I don't know where it is. I never missed it. I was so tired that night, I could have dropped it anywhere—in my office or on the lawn. Or dropped it on a chair when I got home. I could have left it on the terrace when we were cleaning up. Police, ambulances—the shock of seeing Blythe Westerland dead. That's what has taken over whatever memory I have left."

"It's definitely not in your home?" Ben asked gently.

"No. It's gone. Except maybe for the small piece now in the hands of the Sea Harbor police."

Chapter 24

It was Nell's day with Abigail Kathleen Perry—a sacred time, something not even a night of little sleep would keep her from.

She welcomed the baby with open arms as Izzy rushed in and out of the kitchen in a flurry of words: "Sam will pick her up later." "She'll need a nap." "Stroller's in the driveway." "And it's Thursday, Aunt Nell! Finally. I thought it would never come. See you tonight for knitting."

Lunch with Danny Brandley was on the day's agenda—he'd been in and out of town on book tours, and Nell was looking forward to catching up. And a trip to the market to find something for the knitters' dinner that night. Maybe an hour or two working on a grant proposal for the community center while Abby napped.

And Elizabeth Hartley would be with her the whole way. At least in her thoughts.

She had seemed broken last night. A strong, intelligent woman weighted down with more than any woman should have to shoulder.

Ben had wanted to call Jerry from her office, but Elizabeth said no. He had enough on his plate, enough worry about her. The last thing he needed was to add to it. But they'd accomplished one thing: more talk and several cups of coffee had convinced Elizabeth that resigning from her position at the school would be a bad decision—not only for her but also for the school. At least for now.

Elizabeth had almost looked relieved, as if she had been needing someone to play devil's advocate, to keep her from doing something she desperately didn't want to do. Ben and Nell's opinion had saved her from dooming herself—even though she knew there were major hurdles to overcome before her position was secure.

They'd followed her home, making sure she got in safely, then gone on down the block to their own bed and a restless night.

Nell looked down at Izzy's baby, sitting in the center of an activity toy, vigorously batting a rotating wheel. Peaceful and playful and beautiful.

Exactly what she needed.

"Come, my sweet Abby," she said. "We have a day to live."

By noontime, Abby and Nell had charmed the owner of the Cheese Closet, collected some books Nell had reserved at the library, then strolled their way down Harbor Road, in and out of shops, as Nell checked off things on her list. The fat wheels of the stroller glided smoothly through the door of McClucken's hardware store.

Gus, the owner, bent down on two creaky knees to entertain Abby while Nell picked up a teak wax Ben needed for the boat. As she walked back to Abby and the checkout counter, she came face-to-face with Harry Winthrop, his hands full with a bag of nails and a can of paint. He greeted her, then placed the items on the table for Gus to ring up.

"You got that place nearly finished?" Gus asked him.

"Close. That crew you recommended is doing a good job. I'll be out of your hair soon." Harry spotted Abby and crouched down, his blue eyes engaging her. Abby responded immediately, reaching out to touch his mustache. He laughed, then continued to speak to her in soft playful tones that brought giggles—and then the contagious full-blown laughter that caused everyone within earshot to smile.

"Beautiful," he said, standing up but keeping his eyes on the blond toddler in the stroller.

"She is certainly that," Nell said. "A blessing for all of us." She handed her credit card to Gus. "Do you have children, Harry?"

Nell immediately regretted her question. She didn't know this man. For all she knew he had a wife hidden away, a houseful of children somewhere. But there was something about the way he looked at Abby that spoke to a love of children.

Harry didn't answer, but his face turned pale, as if Nell had brought him devastating news. In the next instant the shock gave way to anger, red, moist anger. And then finally, profound sadness. It was as if she were watching a movie that was being fast-forwarded.

"Harry, I'm sorry. That was indelicate of me. I shouldn't have—"

He held up one hand to stop her words, then took a deep breath as he regained his composure. "No, it's okay. I apologize." He looked down at Abby, then finally met Nell's eyes. "I lost a baby . . . before he or she was born." He looked off, as if visualizing the baby, giving it life in his mind.

"That can be a shattering experience," Nell said. She waited for him to say more, but he was silent, his eyes filled with anguish.

Finally he looked up. "It was devastating. Especially when you have no control over it." He looked at Abby again, and his eyes warmed to her sweet sounds. "The baby would have been like Abby, special, amazing. You dream about it, you know? It's all I ever wanted. Friends wondered about it—I even saw a therapist once who assured me such an overwhelming desire is more common in women, but some men have it, too. Maybe being an only child has something to do with it, I don't know. My parents were only children, all up and down the line. I'm what's left, no siblings, no cousins. I'd give everything I own in the world to have a child." He paused, took another deep breath, then said, "Izzy and Sam are very fortunate. I hope they never forget that."

He looked once more at Abby, shoved his receipt in his pocket, and left the store.

Nell pushed Abby's stroller down Harbor Road, her head filled with thoughts of Harry Winthrop. She tried to sort through the conversation, unsure what to make of it. He appeared raw, vulnerable, almost naked in his emotion—this man who had barely spoken a dozen words to her. She hoped he wouldn't regret that she had seen him that way.

Still waters run deep, perhaps.

She knew women whose deep-seated need and desire to bear a child dominated their life. This was the other side of it, what it was like for a man. So difficult. She wondered about the mother, and hoped she hadn't suffered as grievously as Harry had. Nell had several friends whose marriages had been pulled apart by such a loss.

Her thoughts circled around to Cass, who had rarely talked about having children, although Mary Halloran lit vigil lights every day to that end. It had never entered her mind that Cass wouldn't want children. She loved Abby, that was clear. But what Nell had heard in Harry's voice was a desperate kind of need, one she wasn't sure Cass would share.

And then she looked up into the face of the man standing in the door of Garozzo's deli, and her face lit up, thoughts of Harry Winthrop disappearing in an instant.

"There she is, lovely Nell," Danny said, his arms wrapping around her.

"You are a sight for sore eyes," she said.

But Danny was already crouched down, and Nell was all but forgotten as he played a finger game with his goddaughter, one that made her giggle and laugh and tug on his arm to be lifted out of the stroller and cuddled in the writer's arms.

Another man who loves babies. It seemed to be in the air today. Nell pushed a now-empty stroller after Danny as he carried Abby into the deli.

Margaret Garozzo, the restaurant owner's wife and business partner, ushered them to a choice booth—one in the back with a window that opened out to the Harbor. Danny held Abby on his lap for a short while so she could watch the fishing boats move in and out of their slips, unloading an early morning catch. She waved her chubby hand to anything that looked as if it might move, gulls included. When she tired of their nonresponses, she squealed and Nell settled her with a tray full of musical toys in the stroller.

Margaret appeared with two heaping bowls of clam chowder. "We're worried about Angelo," she said without preamble, moving the salt and pepper shakers and placing a basket of warm rolls in the center of the table.

"This murder has taken a toll on him," Nell said.

Margaret nodded. "Angelo and my Harry fight like a cat and a dog, but when it comes to protecting each other, there's no better brother either of them could have or want."

"Has he talked much about how this is affecting the school?" Danny asked. "Murder anywhere is awful, but at a school it seems more dangerous somehow."

Margaret looked over her shoulder to be sure customers were happy—and not listening. She leaned closer. "Angelo talks mostly about his guilt."

"Guilt?" Nell frowned. "Why?"

"Guilt because he's not sad she's dead. She had been pushing Angelo to the edge. He did not like that lady, not one bit." One finger shook in the air.

"How did she push Angelo? He's a pretty tough guy." Danny took a spoonful of creamy soup.

"Well, here's the thing. It was that headmistress. Angelo was obsessed with her, with helping her, protecting her. My Harry wanted him to quit the job. He didn't think it was healthy."

Nell was confused. "Not healthy? Did he think Angelo—" She wasn't sure how to word it. *Did he think he had a crush on Elizabeth?* The incongruity of the thought brought an unintended smile to her lips.

Margaret's cheeks reddened. "Well, you know those Garozzos and their Italian imaginations. They're romantics, the whole bunch of them. But there was something going on that bothered Angelo. The problems Blythe Westerland was causing for the school. And for the headmistress. It worried all of us that Angelo would get too involved. He gets crazy sometimes when he thinks people are treating him or people he cares about poorly."

"I understand," Nell said, though she wasn't sure she did. She was sure Angelo had been questioned by the police early on, but she wondered if his sister-in-law, Margaret, had been. If so, she hoped she wasn't sharing her thoughts with the police in so subjective a way. Before Nell could comment, Margaret spotted an empty table cluttered with dirty plates and glasses and hurried over to clean up the mess.

Danny seemed intent on enjoying what the sign in the deli claimed was the best clam chowder in New England, but Nell could tell from the look in his eyes and the deep line between his eyebrows that he had listened carefully to Margaret Garozzo and was trying to order things in his head.

Finally he looked up. "This thing is consuming the town," he said. "My dad said he's sold more books on self-defense techniques and making your home secure in the last week than he has since he opened the store. It's not a healthy vibe, that's for sure."

"No." Nell looked down at Abby's curls, moving to whatever music she was hearing in that precious head of hers. Innocence—it was soul-stirring. And that was what the town had lost.

"I had breakfast with Jerry Thompson today," Danny said.

Nell looked up.

"We meet now and then to talk about police things. He's been a big help in keeping my mystery novel facts accurate. And over time, we've become friends."

"Does he talk about cases when you're together?"

"You know Jerry. He's discreet and professional, always. What he says about the case is kind of what Ben knows, I'd guess. We might hear something new a few hours before, but what he would say is pretty much public knowledge. He does share some personal things now and then. It's clear to me that nearly every person the police have interviewed who had a reason to kill Blythe Westerland—and who had opportunity—is someone Jerry knows. And that's killing him. He's says it's the hardest case he's ever had."

"Especially because of Elizabeth."

Danny nodded. "He cares a lot about her. They have something good together. And sure, he's thinks she couldn't possibly have done this . . ."

"But?"

Danny didn't answer right away. He buttered a roll and broke off a tiny piece, putting it down on Abby's tray. Finally he said, "The thing is, Nell, you and I both know what love does. It blinds us."

Chapter 25

*N*ell carried Danny's comment with her to the market and then back home, where Abby happily settled down for a nap and she sat in front of her computer, pretending to write a grant proposal. But all she saw on the blank screen were Danny's words.

Love blinds us.

How personal was Danny's comment? Was he truly analyzing the murder—or was it something else? They'd talked little about Cass, although it was clear from a few things he said that he knew Harry was still in town and that he was at least a semiregular presence in Cass's life.

And that he didn't care for the guy.

And as Ben said when he arrived home that afternoon, that was about as much as the two of them knew about the whole situation, too.

He sat at the kitchen island nursing a beer, listening to her talk about her day and watching her chop a pile of fresh vegetables for a quick and easy seafood salad. She knew the knitting group would be happy with something light—as long as there was plenty of it.

"So Harry Winthrop loves kids. I guess that kind of surprises me, but it shouldn't," Ben said, cutting into a block of aged cheddar that Nell had picked up at the Cheese Closet.

"I had the same reaction. Danny loves kids, and that doesn't surprise me one bit."

"But we know Danny."

Nell handed him a whisk and a bowl of sauce. "Speaking of Danny, he said he had breakfast with Jerry—"

"So I hear. Jerry thinks Danny's top-notch—and not only because he mentions him in the acknowledgments page in his mysteries."

Nell laughed. They teased Jerry about it, his obvious pleasure in seeing his name in a *New York Times* bestseller. Something sincere and well deserved, according to Danny.

"You saw Jerry today?"

"For lunch. He just wanted to talk through some logistical things—like Blythe's will and the body. It can be released and somebody needs to claim it."

"Bob Chadwick, right?"

"Yes. He's coming in to talk to the chief again and staying for the weekend. I suggested he bring back any legal papers I might be able to help him with. Also Blythe's papers, bills, that kind of thing—anything that might trigger a thought or two. Things that probably will tell us nothing, but who knows? I'm not sure Bob can be of much help, but the guy is trying. He's also going to meet with Father Northcutt to put together a memorial for Blythe."

"And the will?"

"Sure, he'll be interested in that, too. He's her only relative and from all accounts, it's a sizable estate. I haven't seen it yet but will soon." Ben whisked the sauce ingredients together, the scent of cilantro and lime wafting up into the air.

Nell settled back against the counter, watching him. "How is Jerry doing? Finding that scrap of scarf must have set things back."

"That wasn't a welcome find, for sure. Although it might not mean much."

"But it's probably Elizabeth's. She said so herself, and it's causing such heartache. Tommy Porter called her in again today for more questioning. That's, what, three times? And not that she would, but this time they told her not to leave town."

Ben handed Nell the bowl. "They have to look into it, sure. How many people saw Elizabeth wearing that scarf Friday night? And not only that, but the woman is brutally honest. She volunteered that someone made it for her. It was unique."

"That kind of honesty isn't exactly what you'd expect from a guilty person." There was a slight edge to Nell's words. A touch of anger. It wasn't rational, but it was there.

"You're upset Elizabeth has to go through all this." He moved over to the sink and wiped his hands on a dish towel. "Me, too."

Nell poured the sauce over the grilled shrimp and spooned in the vegetables. She mixed it together with deft, swift sweeps, finding relief in the movement.

"I'm going to a meeting at the club tonight, then having a sandwich and beer with Danny and Ham. Jerry may come. Or not. He's noncommittal these days."

Nell barely heard the rattle of his keys or felt the kiss to her cheek as Ben headed out.

Instead it was Danny's words that came back with a force, rattling around in her head and blocking out all other sounds.

"The thing is, Nell, you and I both know what love does. It blinds us."

But from what?

Mae Anderson was at the cash register organizing the day's receipts and talking to one last customer before flipping around the closed sign. Nell walked in carrying dinner. She'd made up a small container for Mae, as she often did, and walked it over to the counter.

Chelsey Mansfield turned around, a smile filling her face when she saw it was Nell.

She pulled open a bag to reveal several luxurious skeins of deep green cashmere yarn. "A cashmere sweater is about to be born."

Nell handed Mae her dinner and looked admiringly at the yarn. "This is absolutely beautiful. Is it for you?"

"For Anna. Dr. Hartley suggested that she participate in one of the choir groups. Her small ensemble will be a part of the fall music program. The girls were told to dress in autumn colors."

"It'll be perfect. She's a lucky songstress," Nell said, moving toward the back room. "It's nice to have something happy to look forward to."

Chelsey didn't answer, but Nell could feel her watching her as she walked away. She stopped at the alcove to the back room and turned back. Chelsey's smile was gone and her long, angular face bore the look of a lawyer about to argue a case. Her voice matched. "I know it's only been a week since Blythe was murdered," she said slowly, "but Elizabeth is already helping bring the school back to life again. The school, the students. Things are alive again."

"Alive?" Nell frowned, unsure of where Chelsey was going.

"Yes. The unity, the respect for each child's uniqueness, the spirit of goodwill that Elizabeth was trying to instill in our school is moving ahead without the roadblocks Blythe was creating. The school's soul is intact." She took a breath, then added, almost as an afterthought, "No matter what happened a week ago—or how, or why, or who—I know it was tragic and I should feel bad about it. But you know what I feel? Relief."

She waved good-bye to Mae. Then she tucked her coveted yarn under her arm and walked out of the shop.

Nell watched her leave the shop, the discomfiting words hanging in the air. She looked over at Mae.

Mae simply shrugged, dismissing Chelsey's comments. To the store manager, Chelsey was simply a happy customer, one pleased at the thought of knitting a lovely cashmere sweater. None of the rest of it made much sense.

But she's a little dramatic, don't you think? was what Mae's body language said.

Dramatic wasn't exactly how Nell would describe it. She shifted the food bags and walked down the steps, wondering if she was beginning to blow things out of proportion. Perhaps Mae had the right approach. Keep things simple.

But simple wasn't helping them find a murderer.

Birdie was already in the knitting room, getting out glasses and approving of Izzy's choice of music. Her foil-wrapped glass dish was on the counter. Once again Ella, the Favazza housekeeper, had come through with a perfect dessert for a nippy autumn night— apple cobbler, with apples handpicked by Gabby and Daisy from Russell Orchards.

"Where's Cass?" Nell asked. Although it was rare that one of the foursome was missing on Thursday night, Nell wanted to be sure.

"She's on her way." Izzy turned up the iPod and began swaying to the smoky voice of Madeleine Peyroux singing an old Ray Charles song.

A horn blasting in the alley announced that Izzy was right.

Nell emptied her bags on the old library table and began tossing the seafood salad, spooning up the dressing that had collected at the bottom. Birdie warmed the rolls in the shop's small oven, and Cass breezed through the side door.

She took the opener from the counter and began uncorking Birdie's wine.

"Long day?" Birdie asked, handing Cass a fat slice of aged cheddar cheese.

Cass nodded. "But it's over. So let's eat and drink and be merry."

"Be merry. A large order," Nell said.

"We can do it," Cass said.

The routine on Thursday nights was so ingrained in each of them that words weren't needed to start the dance. Once the food was ready, they filled their plates with Nell's grilled shrimp salad and added slices of cheese, gherkins, and olives to the side. The basket of rolls and the butter plate went on the low coffee table, and in minutes they were cozily settled around the idle fireplace, the harbor lights slanting in through the open casement windows, warming the hardwood floor.

Cass poured four glasses of wine before flopping down in the old leather chair taken from Ben's den years before. Cass claimed it still smelled of his Old Spice aftershave and it brought her great comfort, she said. Purl waited until Cass tucked one leg up beneath her before jumping off the chair arm and taking her place beside her.

The knitting would wait until plates were empty and hands clean, but conversation would start before the last person sat down.

"Is Harry around?" Nell asked. She'd struggled with what to say or ask or bring up with Cass, unsure if her conversation with him had been a private one, though usually things discussed at Gus McClucken's checkout counter didn't fall into that category. She was still baffled by the unexpected emotion Harry had shown.

"Around?" Cass asked innocently, biting into a warm roll. "Like 'around tonight'?"

"I guess that's as good a place as any to start," Izzy said. She stabbed a shrimp with her fork.

"He's around. He doesn't understand routines—or knitting—so he actually thought I might be free for a beer tonight. 'Thursdays?' I asked him. 'Are you insane?' I think he's going to grab a bite at the yacht club, drool over a few boats, and go back to work on the cottage. It's looking good."

"I ran into him at McClucken's getting some paint." Nell paused, waiting for Cass to fill in the silence. Had Harry told her he saw her? Replayed the conversation?

But Cass had moved on to another forkful of salad. She bit into a shrimp and closed her eyes. "Nell, whatever you marinated this shrimp in is amazing."

Nell smiled and passed around the basket of rolls. "I had lunch with Danny today," she said.

Cass looked over at Nell, then into her glass of wine. She swirled it slowly. "You know, whatever you think, I do miss Danny," she said. "He's . . . he's a great guy."

Nell nodded and Birdie smiled. They didn't push, just kept their thoughts quiet and tried hard not to let their feelings spread across their faces. They knew Cass well, and knew that getting too close would shut her down. So they took what she offered, held their silence, and moved on.

"Elizabeth Hartley came into the shop late today," Izzy said, sensing it was time to change the topic. "She's aged ten years in this horrible week. Frankly if the murderer isn't found soon I worry that we're going to lose an outstanding headmistress. It's like her spirit is slowly eroding. She puts on a good front, but it's clear what this is doing to her. And it's simply not fair."

It was clear where Izzy was coming from. In her former lawyer life, she had seen innocent people destroyed, proven innocent or not. The longer that cases went unsolved or the longer trials dragged on, the more severe the damage to innocent people.

"The more I talk with her, the more I like her," she went on. "And she's a very fine knitter, on top of it all."

The latter was attempted to lighten the mood, but Izzy's message echoed in the cozy room. They all liked Elizabeth. And they all hated to see people they cared about suffer, whatever the reason.

"Jerry Thompson isn't in such great shape, either," Nell said. She bit into a warm roll, then wiped a trace of butter from the corner of her mouth. "I can't imagine how difficult it must be to be so close to an investigation that keeps digging up things incriminating someone close to you."

"What kind of incriminating things?" Cass refilled her plate and walked back to her chair.

Nell filled them in on what had happened the evening before: finding Elizabeth down near the boathouse, and then learning that a scrap of scarf, similar to the one Elizabeth had worn the night of the party, was now in the hands of the police.

Izzy was crestfallen. "That was a gorgeous scarf. Unique and so finely knit—tiny little stiches for the main section, and the romantic, lacy edge. Chelsey Mansfield told me she knit it for Elizabeth when she got her doctorate."

"She knew Elizabeth before moving here?" Cass asked.

Birdie nodded. "I think so. Back in Boston."

"Are the police sure the scarf was hers? After a week tangled in water and seaweed, it would be difficult to tell," Cass said.

"Elizabeth is sure. She can't find her own—and she identified the scrap, regardless of the wear and tear. But she has absolutely no idea how it ended up in the sea and then caught in the boulders."

"She may not, but I think I have an idea," Birdie said suddenly. She pushed aside her plate and sat up on the couch, her back as straight as a bamboo knitting needle.

"Clearly we need to pull some things together here," she said. "If we were able to figure out that complicated anniversary shawl with all those panels and stitches that we made for you and Ben, Nell, then surely we can figure out this mess. Or at least come up with feasible possibilities to hasten this awful plodding investigation."

The fact that it had been only a week didn't escape any of them, but in light of the lives it was affecting, it had been an interminable week.

Birdie went on. "We are expert at ripping things apart and putting them back together. We are expert at knitting fine things. No matter how finely knit this murder is, surely we can help figure it out. So let's do it."

They were all sitting up straighter now, except for Izzy, who had cleared all their dishes while Birdie talked, scooped the warmed apple cobbler onto plates, put on a pot of coffee, and returned to the group with a tray of dessert plates. She passed them out without fanfare and sat down next to Birdie.

"Birdie, you said you had an idea about what happened to the scarf." It was Cass, feeling that somehow she had missed something. "What was it?"

"It was last Saturday, the day after the murder." They all knew about Teresa's explosion at the Tea Shoppe, but Nell and Birdie hadn't talked about the rest of it—the possibility that someone might have gone into Elizabeth's house while she wasn't there that morning.

"She said she had forgotten to lock the door. That was probably true. There were no signs of someone breaking in. She also didn't find anything missing. But she looked around all of two minutes. Would she really have noticed if the scarf was missing? She hadn't slept. Someone could easily have gone in the side door, looked around for something of hers, and taken it."

"To incriminate her," Cass said.

"Only one person would have reason to do that," Birdie said.

"The real murderer . . . ," Izzy said. Then she pushed the thought further. "Or Teresa Pisano. Sam and Ben said she's at the police station constantly, giving them reasons to arrest Elizabeth. She is convinced Elizabeth killed Blythe. Maybe she was trying to nail the coffin shut."

"I was thinking the same thing," Nell said. "Except for one thing."

Birdie nodded, reading Nell's thought. "Teresa was at the Tea Shoppe while we were there with Elizabeth. And when she left, Mary was right on her tail."

"So if Mary stayed with her for at least the next hour, it couldn't have been Teresa," Nell finished.

"An easy thing to check," Birdie said, mentally planning a meeting with Mary Pisano.

Nell fell silent. Listening to the conversation, reliving the day, the walk, and trying to tug something to the forefront that she was missing. She half listened as the others continued the discussion, pushing her memory. She was missing something. And it was refusing to reveal itself.

"So that takes us back to the murderer," Cass said. "Elizabeth—no matter how sure we are that she couldn't have done it, she had plenty of motive. And she had opportunity. She needs to be considered."

"Cass is right," Izzy said reluctantly. "But as Birdie said, we need to explore everyone we know who might have wanted Blythe gone . . . or dead."

"Josh Babson." Nell spoke quietly, still wondering about her own feelings about the artist. He managed to pull her emotions one way and then the other with a sleight of hand.

They talked about the painting exhibited at the Brewster Gallery. "It was the scene of the crime—the same boulders, a tiny slice of the boathouse."

Cass was surprised. "I looked at it, too, but I didn't even make the connection. There are so many spots on Cape Ann that are similar."

"But without an old boathouse," Nell said.

"Sure. Okay, but more than that, it wasn't a painting that spoke to murder in any way. It was a beautiful oil painting. Kind of romantic."

Nell agreed. "And that was strange, I thought. That he'd romanticize a murder scene."

"But back to his motivation. He was angry at Blythe. He knew she was behind the firing," Nell said. She explained the photo they had seen on Elizabeth's phone. The giant circle with a line slashed through Blythe's initials.

"Do the police have the photo?" Izzy asked.

"Yes. Ben talked to Elizabeth about it, and she agreed to give it to them—reluctantly. She was worried about incriminating Josh. I think she figured he'd been through enough—and some of what he'd been through she felt responsible for."

"Eat," Birdie said, reminding them all that research showed food was good for creative thinking.

No one dared to mention that copious amounts of sugar might not be what the studies had in mind. Instead they happily dug into Ella's sweet, addictive apple cobbler, the fresh apples offering a welcome burst of energy.

"I think there's more to Josh's role in this than the fact that he was fired," Nell said.

"Why is that?"

"I'm not sure. There's just something about him that makes me think there's more to the story. He doesn't seem to be the kind of guy who would let being fired devastate him. Or even make him that angry. Unless . . ."

"You mean maybe there's more to why he was fired?" Cass asked.

"Maybe. Why did Blythe want him fired? The things she brought up to the board didn't always add up. Josh was a good teacher, apparently, and I think Elizabeth was against the firing."

"Barrett Mansfield had reservations, too," Birdie said. "That's an interesting point."

"Speaking of Barrett, both he and Chelsey had problems with Blythe." Nell repeated the exchange she'd overheard between Chelsey and Blythe the night of the party. "Chelsey came close to threatening her if she didn't stop trying to get Elizabeth fired."

"Chelsey admires Elizabeth. She thinks she is a wonderful head-mistress," Izzy said. "She talked about it in the shop with other moms, praising the way she treated individual kids."

Nell was quiet, wondering again if she tended to read too much into things. But if she was doing that, the best people to call her on it were sitting right here in front of her.

"Chelsey was buying yarn tonight when I walked in the shop," she began.

And then she repeated the strange conversation. "Mae didn't think it was strange. She thought Chelsey was simply dramatic."

"Chelsey Mansfield isn't dramatic," Izzy said. "She was an amazing lawyer, confident, calm, logical . . ." *Not dramatic.*

"Basically she said she was relieved that Blythe was murdered," Cass said. "That's what I'm hearing."

"That's awful," Izzy murmured.

"But honest, I guess." Cass scooped up the last bite of apple cob-bler, then got up and began collecting the bowls. "People often sanctify even bad people when they die. Chelsey was calling a spade a spade—at least in her opinion, anyway."

Nell nodded. "Yes—and there are probably others who share that opinion. And being relieved isn't exactly the same as being glad. But you're right, it's certainly honest. And it tells the world what she thought of Blythe. Combine that with the conversation I overheard—that Blythe would be stopped in her efforts to fire Elizabeth. It was close to a threat."

"And once again, they both had opportunity." Izzy wiped her hands on a napkin and pulled the beginnings of a sweater out of her knitting bag. It was a simple shrug in bright colors that two of the girls in the school class wanted to make—a simple knit that started at one cuff, then worked all the way across to the other. Her sample, she hoped, would help keep the newbie knitters from getting lost along the way. She stroked the soft crimson yarn. "But no matter what she said, I can't imagine my former instructor killing anyone. I just can't."

Birdie had begun knitting Gabby a pair of fingerless mittens. She checked the cable row and said quietly, "I can't imagine anyone killing anyone. But they do."

They fingered their knitting and counted stitches, thoughts floating along on Madeleine Peyroux singing the slow lyrics of "Don't Take Too Long."

And they all hoped that would be true.

Nell finally pulled out the sweater she was knitting for Ben. The thick cotton would keep him warm when the wind and the *Dream Weaver* sailboat beckoned to him and Sam on cold fall days. Cass took out wool skeins in red and navy and began casting on for her specialty—warm winter hats, this one with stripes in the New England Patriots colors.

"Another hat?" Izzy said. *For whom?* hung in the air, unasked.

"For whomever," Cass said, reading her friend's face. "This soft wool makes me feel loved."

"Hmm," Izzy said, pouring herself a glass of wine. "Well, now we know that. When Cass is friendless, give her wool."

Birdie shushed her with a wave of her hand. "My dear Angelo is next on our list," she said. It was the first name on the mental list that everyone in the room would like to immediately scratch off.

"He was there, he found the scarf, he wanted desperately to protect his boss's job."

"His brother was worried about his zeal," Nell added. She told them about her and Danny's conversation with Margaret earlier that day.

They were silent, knowing Birdie was right to keep him on the list. Angelo was devoted to the school, to the students, and to Elizabeth Hartley. And his recent tirades indicated he'd do anything to stop Blythe Westerland from damaging the people and things he cared about.

Their knitting needles clicked away while four minds used to solving complicated knitting patterns tried to work their magic on a different kind of pattern. Pulling apart one that didn't make sense so they could put it back together in a way that did.

A terrible kind of pattern. The complicated pattern of murder.

Finally Izzy said, "The thing that keeps us from stitching any of this together is that we're still trying to figure out who Blythe Westerland was. Birdie, what is it you said about finding the person who commits a crime? You have to ask the victim. She's the only one who can tell us."

Nell took a sip of wine. "We know some things. We're learning, I think. And we've seen Blythe in action."

"But what really made her tick? Why was she so nasty to some people—like Josh Babson?" Izzy asked.

And other people, too. Nell remembered the conversation she'd had with Tommy Porter—his brother who had been thrown overboard by Blythe. She repeated the story aloud.

"Poor Eddie," Cass said. "He always went for the glam. And it never worked for him. He finally realized that if he forgot about the glitz, he might find someone he could make happy—and who would love him, too."

They laughed. Eddie had finally settled down with a waitress from the Sweet Petunia, had three little kids—boom, boom, boom.

And was one of the happiest guys on the Halloran Lobster Company payroll.

"Tommy mentioned another guy his brother knew—good-looking but really quiet, easy prey—who hung out with Blythe for a short while," Nell said. "The fellow finally broke it off himself."

"Good for him. What happened?" Izzy asked.

"Blythe had him fired from his job."

"Geesh," Cass said. "I'm glad she didn't come on to me."

"Maybe it was the loss of power that pushed her to action. Eddie wasn't punished, but he didn't end the relationship. Blythe did. Breaking up seemed to be exclusively her prerogative."

"I'm glad Danny had the sense not to get involved," Cass said.

Izzy thought about the picture emerging about Blythe and relationships. "When you're as beautiful as Blythe, it's probably not difficult to get men to respond to you."

"And Blythe enjoyed men, we know that. Ben said she liked being on boards that were mostly men."

"Maybe it was to show them up," Cass said.

"She liked men, but never married," Izzy said. "I wonder why."

"Maybe growing up in that male-dominated family had something to do with it," Cass said.

"I think it had everything to do with it. Living with men who disliked her. Who kept her in her place. Blythe made sure those days were behind her. "

Of course it did. A young girl without a mother. Raised in a household of powerful men—all of whom had little or no use for the female in their midst.

The thought was a sobering one, one that had somehow been pushed to the back of their minds because it was too uncomfortable to think about. A child being deprived of love—while probably being showered with all that money could buy. A murder in its own right, but with no visible body.

Izzy shivered, rubbing her arms and sending invisible hugs to Abby, asleep in her bed and surrounded by love.

"That's why she never married," Cass said.

"And maybe why she had to exert her own power over her life. Over people in her life. It's all she knew."

"Perhaps she was proving something to her own father. Or grandfather. She was the one with power now, no matter that they weren't alive to see it," Birdie said.

Their opinion of Blythe Westerland shifted slightly as they talked. Not focusing on the cruel things she did, but on a young girl raised in a household with every imaginable material advantage, surrounded by people who wished she hadn't been born.

"Izzy's point about getting to know Blythe is the key. We're getting there, inch by inch, but we need to dig deeper. And then Blythe herself will tell us who murdered her in this awful way and why."

Their thoughts were all on the same page, their convictions ripe and firm. Nell looked at the skeins of yarn in front of each of them, the needles in their laps and their fingers. The colors and textures strong and enticing. Birdie was right. They had already begun pulling apart the stitches, trying to make sense out of the event that was shaking their lives. And getting ready to stitch them back together.

Birdie looked over at Nell. "I can read your thoughts, my dear friend. We all can."

Nell laughed. "It's what we do, isn't it? Read thoughts, join hands. Piece together stitches until they make a whole, until they make sense. And I think we've already figured out more than we think we have."

"We know Blythe used men. And we know why," Izzy added. "It makes perfect sense that she wanted to tip the scales—to be the one with the power. It's an odd kind of revenge."

"Yes. She exerted the power, but when someone crossed over that line and tried to have an equal role in the relationship or was so bold as to break up with her, she had them fired or tossed them aside, or tried to tarnish their reputation, or whatever tricks she had to pull into play," Birdie said.

"What we don't know is what kind of hurt was so overwhelming, so awful, that she was killed because of it," Nell said.

Saying it out loud, watching their words fall into some kind of logical order, brought satisfaction. And it also brought a clearer picture of where they needed to go.

"Yes," Birdie said, her eyes lighting up with the wisdom of her years. "It's right here in front of us. The pieces. A pattern we need to put together. And I'd say the best time to start stitching in earnest is right now."

$\mathcal{N}$ ell filled Ben in on the Thursday night knitting discussion the next morning. She watched a slight cringe shadow his face as she mentioned Birdie's determined plan.

"Stop with that look, Ben." She poured a cup of coffee and joined him at the island. "It's not really a plan. It's something all of us, you included, have been doing since the moment we heard about Blythe's murder—trying to find the guilty person. Being observant as we walk through the day isn't putting us in any danger. But maybe it's helping Elizabeth. And Angelo. And anyone else who might be harmed by this."

"Someone was killed," Ben said, his words heavy. *There is a murderer out there.*

"You said yourself that the police think it was a targeted killing. Not random."

"But the murderer doesn't want anyone figuring out that he killed Blythe. Asking questions can put you in danger, Nellie. The police are trained to handle things like that. You're not. Birdie, Izzy, and Cass aren't, either."

But Ben knew Nell better than he knew anyone on earth. He knew she'd listen politely. And he knew she and her friends would do what they needed to do to help a friend. It was still worth saying. Just maybe his warnings would linger for a while, and, at the least, he had to make them. It was as ingrained in him as his own mother's warning—never letting him leave the house without telling him to "drive safely."

"If anyone wants this person caught and off the streets, it's Jerry Thompson," Ben continued. "I know you like Elizabeth, but imagine what he's going through and how hard it's making him work to find the true killer."

Nell was quiet as Ben talked, listening as she always did. Everything Ben said made sense. But so many things went unsaid. Like the fact that the police didn't have the same access to a town, to neighbors and friends, to fishermen and shopkeepers, as the ordinary person walking through an ordinary day did.

That was all any of them were saying last night. *Listen. Look. Follow the patterns.* It was second nature to the women who met in the back room every Thursday night. And they were very good at it. And although she would never say it out loud to Ben, Nell sincerely thought they were inching their way to the finish line.

Blythe Westerland was becoming more real to them in death than she ever had been in life—and she was about to speak.

"Ben," she began.

But Ben changed the subject, hoping a shorter message might have a longer shelf life in Nell's memory. And convincing himself that these women so integral to his life would never knowingly put themselves in danger.

The problem was that danger sometimes came to them.

"Jerry joined Ham, Danny, and me for a beer last night," he said. "I was surprised he came, but glad to see him."

"I'd rather see him with Elizabeth than with you."

Ben managed a smile. "Me, too. And I've no doubt that would be his choice, too. I know he's calling her, keeping in touch that way at least. But Elizabeth is doing him a favor in the long run by keeping her distance, especially now that the piece of scarf caught on the rocks is getting so much attention."

"I think someone took that from her house, Ben," she said. It wasn't until she said it out loud that she realized she believed it completely. It was the only thing that made sense. Elizabeth was so upset the night of the murder she probably tossed that scarf on a chair, the floor even. If someone was looking for something personal, it would be so easy to spot: the color was vibrant. Easy to fold up and slip into a pocket and be out of the house in an instant.

She and Birdie had very conveniently taken Elizabeth out of the house, allowing the person easy entry. She retraced their steps that day and said out loud, "We were gone at least a couple hours." She frowned, remembering the walk, the Tea Shoppe, the walk home—and she remembered something else. The thought surprised her. Her eyes widened.

Ben was watching her face. "What?"

"Nothing," she said quickly. "Random thought." One to bury in the shadows for now. But not to forget.

"Tommy Porter should know about the possible break-in. It's at least something, though the whole scarf thing is perplexing. It's weak, I think, which is good. And the break-in possibility makes it even weaker. If it had come loose when Elizabeth was supposedly down on the boulders, why didn't someone see it sooner? The police canvassed that whole area. Sure, smaller boulders can shift with the force of the water, hiding something between them, maybe, but it seems awfully convenient."

"There's also the matter of the rest of the scarf." Nell reached over and took a bagel out of the toaster. "It'd be wonderful if they found it."

"Or not, I suppose, depending on where they find it and what it tells them."

Maybe. It was exceedingly odd that a small piece of the scarf ended up in the crevice of the boulder while the rest of it—yards of elegant hand-knit silk—had disappeared. It had been planted there; Nell was sure of it, but she held it in, knowing Ben would want more than his wife's emotions to agree.

But even after forty years of marriage, Ben sometimes surprised her. "I think you're right, Nell. It could have been put there by someone wanting there to be no doubt that Elizabeth was down at the boathouse that night and murdered Blythe. Someone determined not to be a suspect."

"So you'll talk to the police?"

"Sure. This morning."

"I don't suppose Jerry mentioned anything else last night . . ."

"No, nothing we don't already know. Bob filled him in on her upbringing. Being raised by the Westerlands was unfortunate."

"It wasn't unfortunate. It was terrible," Nell said, more emotion than she anticipated carrying her words.

Ben took a swallow of coffee. "You're right. It softens one's view of Blythe Westerland. Not an easy way to grow up."

Izzy found Blythe's upbringing almost unbearable to talk about. Lonely and sad.

She climbed out of Nell's car in the Canary Cove parking lot, the utter horror of a baby like Abby being left with people who didn't want her weighing down her thoughts. She tried to shake it off as she lifted Abby's stroller out of the back of the car and snapped it into position. Suddenly she stopped and looked up. "That's it, Aunt Nell. That's why she had such affection—such an investment in the school. She probably felt more at home there than anywhere else in the world when she was a child."

Of course, Nell thought. That made all the sense in the world. It was a safe haven for the young Blythe.

She carried a happy Abby over to the stroller and strapped her into the seat. Then she kissed the top of her blond curls and placed a small Red Sox hat on her head. She and Izzy stood there for a minute, watching the bouncing movement of her head and the small plump hands cuddling a bunny blanket.

Loving her.

And thinking of a child who never had that kind of love.

It was a sunny day, and the excuse for being in Canary Cove

was to drop off an old painting of a ship that had once belonged to Ben's father. Ham Brewster had offered to clean it up. Friday at noon would be a good time, he said.

Izzy wanted to tag along. She hadn't yet seen Josh Babson's paintings and her curiosity couldn't wait any longer.

They picked up take-out coffee at Polly's Tea Shoppe. Nell promised Polly there'd be no throwing of soup.

Polly laughed. "Teresa was acting crazy that day," she said, her wide smile never leaving her face. "She's usually shy and quiet. She simply has a bee in her bonnet that needs to get out; it's just a shame she picked the headmistress as her target. Elizabeth Hartley is a very nice lady. My grandchild is thriving at her school. The woman could no more murder anyone than I could."

They left the Tea Shoppe, sipping Polly's strong coffee and trying to imagine a shy and quiet Teresa Pisano flinging a container of soup across the patio.

"Iz," Nell began. Then stopped. Then she started again. The thought needed a home. Someone to attend to it with her. "There was something else that happened that Saturday when Birdie, Elizabeth, and I were walking." She talked slowly. It was unformed. And made little sense. But it was something to think about. Perhaps to look into. To see if there were any legs there to stand on, ones that might have been hidden behind more obvious people in Blythe's life.

Izzy listened carefully, her face expressing concern. And then she tucked it away, too, knowing it needed to be brought up later. And hoping no one would be hurt in the process.

They made their way down the road to the Brewster Gallery in silence. Even Abby had settled down, her hand playing with a tiny bell attached to her stroller and her eyes watching the gulls and the clouds and leaves falling in her path—the things in life that others sometimes missed.

Nell had called ahead to see if Josh was working Friday morning. He was.

Nell still was ambivalent about the artist, but wanted to see him again, to figure him out. It was becoming a challenge.

Izzy thought he was "cute"—a descriptive Nell didn't especially like. Birdie didn't know him, and Cass thought he was a typical artist, whatever that meant. Ben thought he was talented. And he was working in her close friend's store. She supposed the biggest plus on his side was that Gabby and Daisy were clearly fans. That weighed heavily in his favor.

The shop was empty of customers when they pushed the stroller through the door, jingling the brass bell above it. Josh stood behind the counter, fiddling with the computer. The bell brought Jane out from the back room.

"My Abby is here," she said, her long skirt swishing against her legs as she hurried to the stroller's side. She leaned over and let Abby tug on the long beaded necklace that looped and swayed in front of the baby.

Nell laughed and asked if Ham was in the back, then took her painting from beneath the stroller and disappeared to find her friend.

Josh looked up briefly, then went back to work.

Izzy left Jane with the baby and walked over to the artist. She stretched one hand across the counter. "Hi. I think we met a couple times but always in crowds. I'm Izzy Perry and hear by the grapevine that you have some paintings worth seeing."

"Sam's wife," Josh said. He hesitated at first, but then reached out and shook her hand.

"You know Sam?"

"He and I were chasing the same colors one day."

Izzy laughed.

"It was a couple months back, after a nor'easter. I was out early and spotted a wicked rainbow over some schooners. I headed down to the harbor to paint it. He was there taking pictures."

"I think I remember that. Sam's an early riser. He says the light then is good for photo shoots. You have to move fast to catch the rainbows before they disappear behind the horizon," Izzy said. "Painting one has to be even more of a challenge."

"Yeah. For sure. I was late for my job that day because of that rainbow—not at all appreciated by the powers that be. But hey, rainbows wait for no man. Or woman, I s'pose. It was worth it."

"Right."

"So you came to see my paintings?"

His voice had changed as they talked, warming slightly.

Izzy nodded, and he pointed through the archway to the exhibit wall.

Izzy walked over and Josh followed her, leaving enough distance not to intrude.

"They all have Sold signs on them," Izzy said.

"Yah. Rent money."

"And then some," Jane Brewster said, coming up behind them.

"Well, I think I can see why." Izzy began on the left with the first small painting of sailboats, smiling when she saw her uncle's initials beneath the sold sign.

"Josh is good with light, just like Sam," Jane said. "His paintings remind me of Fitz Hugh Lane's. Ben liked that, too, and the way the light reflected off the white sails."

"It's beautiful. Does Aunt Nell know she has to find a space on a wall?"

"Or build another room?" Jane said. "She'll make it work."

Josh had moved into a shadowy corner and leaned against the wall, a mug of coffee cradled in his hands, enjoying the women's reactions.

"I need another dose of Abby," Jane said to Izzy, excusing herself and moving back to the stroller.

Nell came out of Ham's studio and stood near Izzy, watching her face as she moved from painting to painting. Her niece was very creative, and she wondered what she would glean from the largest painting. Light? Shadow? Life? Or would she see an enormous boulder, one on which a woman tragically died?

They had talked about the painting at knitting group, the mystery of why he would paint it. And display it. Izzy knew before she stood in front of the large painting what she would see: a murder scene.

But that wasn't what she saw.

Nell saw the awe in Izzy's eyes almost before it lifted her face.

Josh saw it, too.

Nell tried to read Josh's expression, but he was a master at remaining unreadable. She wondered what *he* saw in the painting: murder or beauty or . . .

And she wondered again why he had chosen to perpetuate a tragic scene in a masterful painting.

"It's romantic. Breathtaking," Izzy said softly.

She looked around and saw Josh watching her. "I see romance and moonlight. Glorious light."

Josh was quiet, waiting for more.

"But it's the scene of a murder," Nell said.

"No," Josh said. "It's not."

Nell looked at him.

"I painted it a couple months ago."

Nell and Izzy looked back at the painting.

When they didn't speak, Josh went on. "I don't like the painting much, though I suppose I did at the time I painted it. For sure I experienced some artistic pleasure in painting it. And hopefully that's what anyone who looks at it sees. They shouldn't see murder. There was none."

"But you don't like it?" Nell looked back and forth between Josh and the lovely oil painting. "Is it because someone was murdered there?" A reminder of a night he wanted to forget?

Josh was surprised by Nell's reply. His laugh was more a scoff. "Blythe Westerland's death? No. I don't think about that when I look at this painting. But there was romance in the painting when I did it—and that's been dead longer than Blythe."

"But it was there when you painted it?" Izzy said.

He shrugged and looked back at the painting, as if maybe the answer was there in the light and shadow. Finally he said, "I felt romantic when I painted it, sort of. It wasn't exactly a romance, more a fling—but sure, there was that kind of explosion that comes when a man and woman are together. When a beautiful woman pursues you."

He stopped, looking more closely at the painting as if remembering the spot in an intimate way. When he looked back to Nell and Izzy, there was a play of amusement in his green eyes. "It's kind of fun for a while, having a woman take charge, the flirting, arranging dangerous rendezvous spots like that boathouse." His chin lifted, nodding toward the painting. "But it was crazy from the start. What reputable teacher fools around at his school? Damn foolish. I wasn't running on full batteries, and definitely not thinking with my head."

"You met a woman in the boathouse?" Izzy asked.

"It was her choice, not mine. I just followed orders."

"Blythe Westerland," Nell said slowly, the name coming out on a long breath as the pieces fit together.

"She was the wicked witch of the west." He stared at the painting. "Ironic, isn't it, that the witch in *The Wizard of Oz* melted when water was poured on her? This one died covered with water and weeds."

"What was it with you and Blythe? A relationship?"

He took a deep breath, then released it slowly. "No, not really. She was dangerous, Blythe was. She'd come by when I had kids painting down at the shore. She always had a reason for being around, a meeting or whatever. She'd make me uncomfortable with sly flirts that I was always afraid the kids would see, but I couldn't stop her. She was a master at it. Did just enough to send me into a spin, but always keeping her own cool. She was like a femme fatale. Like a black widow spider. Snaring things. No one's going to talk about it now that she's murdered, but she was a force of nature. I think she loved the danger and the fact that she held all the power.

She was in command. It's like she wanted to dominate men. And she did a damn good job of it. I wasn't her only prey, believe me."

"Why . . . how . . . did it end with her? What went wrong?" Izzy asked.

"Me, that's what went wrong . . . or right, as the case may be. I started to think with my head instead of body parts and I broke it off with her. I liked my students. I liked my job. And I didn't like being a toy. I told her I'd go to Dr. Hartley if she didn't leave me alone."

Nell looked back at the painting. There was a lifetime between the origin of the painting and what had happened in that spot a week ago. "So you broke it off. And she was fine with that?"

"Fine? Not exactly. I made one big mistake. I should have let her think it was her idea—then she would have been fine. No man hath seen such fury as that day." His laugh was short, humorless. "It wasn't because she wanted me. I had no illusions there. It was because she had lost control. I'd taken over and she hated that." He scratched his head, staring back at the painting. "I knew she'd have the last say. I just didn't know how or when the shoe would drop. All I knew for sure was that it would."

And it did. The day Josh Babson was fired.

Chapter 27

Somehow the fact that it was Friday and that she'd probably have a houseful of hungry people on her deck that night hadn't registered with Nell in any meaningful way. Instead it was the Friday that she and Izzy had a revealing discussion with Josh Babson, artist. They were burrowing closer to Blythe Westerland's soul.

And maybe her killer.

When they left the gallery, Jane walked with them down to the parking lot, pushing Abby while Nell and Izzy talked about Josh Babson.

Jane was mostly silent, listening.

"I suppose this doesn't mean he didn't kill Blythe," Izzy said. "In fact, his story gives him even more motivation for doing it."

"But . . . ?" Nell said.

Jane spoke up. "I don't think he did it. He wouldn't have been so brutally honest with both of you if he had. He didn't have to tell anyone about his connection to Blythe. No one would have known."

"That's true. But he *could* have done it, no matter what we think," Nell said. "He's a suspect—at least until we find out he couldn't have done it. Just like a whole group of other people that we like and want to believe they couldn't have done it."

"The police have talked to Josh already," Jane said. "Twice, I think. They had a photo of the yellow circles he painted on the lawn—and the one with Blythe's initials in the middle, so elegantly slashed out. They didn't arrest him, of course—but they told him to stick around. He thought that was funny. 'Where do they think I'd go?' was his response to Ham and me. He seemed complacent about the whole thing. Certainly not worried."

"How did he get to the party that night?" Nell asked.

"Josh rode over with us that night. He doesn't have a car. Ham laid out that fact for Tommy Porter loud and clear. And, more important, he rode home with us. We left a little early, and sure, he could have hopped on his bike and gone back to murder Blythe, but somehow I don't think so."

"Birdie and I watched him for a while the night of the party," Nell said. "He looked like he was looking for someone, and he was clearly angry."

"He probably wanted to give Blythe a piece of his mind. Maybe even embarrass her. Can you blame him? He lost a job he liked because of her," Jane said. "Though I'm not sure if given the chance he would have done even that. The guy looks defensive and antisocial, angry, even—but it's a front, I think. He's like a lot of artists Ham and I know. He protects himself and his work, and sometimes that comes across as defensive. But I've watched him around the studio. I think he's shy."

"I think you're right," Izzy said. "He struck me that way, too— reluctant to talk to me at first. But he warmed up when I didn't step away. A little, anyway."

"Nell?" Jane said. "How about you?"

"I don't know. The biggest thing he has going for him in my mind is that he was sweet with Abby. I watched him go over to her stroller before we left and make funny faces at her, getting her to laugh. In my mind, that goes a long way."

"Of course it does," Izzy said. "But then, who could resist Abby?"

She pushed the stroller across the street to the parking lot and opened the trunk to Nell's car. Izzy lifted Abby from the stroller and collapsed it with a tap of her foot.

Jane took Abby from her mother and fastened her in her car seat. "I agree, no one could resist this darling baby."

Nell opened the driver's door and climbed in. Jane leaned down, her elbows on the window edge. "Nell, in addition to being nice to babies, Josh works right next to me in our gallery. He closed up the other night, and has opened the shop for us all week, giving us two more blessed hours of sleep. Sometimes it's just the two of us working there alone, cataloging prints, tallying receipts, checking inventory. He's been dependable, on time. So here's what I think and don't think.

"I don't think he murdered Blythe Westerland—but I think the thought might have crossed his mind once or twice. And I, for one, can't say I blame him."

She gave Nell a quick peck on the cheek and headed back toward the Brewster Gallery.

Nell and Izzy dropped Abby back home, where the nanny was waiting. "That was an interesting lunch break," Izzy said. "Though we forgot about lunch."

"If you have time, I'll treat you to a salad at the Edge."

Nell knew Izzy couldn't refuse the lobster salad at the Ocean's Edge. It was the best on Cape Ann, lemony and spiced with just the right amount of homemade mayonnaise. And she wanted more time with her niece to help her sort through some conflicting thoughts.

The restaurant's hostess showed them to a quiet table at the back of the restaurant near the bar. It was past the lunch hour rush and the normally busy restaurant had relaxed to a welcome lull. Iced tea and lobster salads appeared in record time.

"You like Josh, don't you?" Nell asked.

"Like? Not sure. I don't know him well enough, but I think he's interesting. And I wouldn't mind getting to know him better."

"That answers my next question. You agree with Jane. You don't think he could have murdered Blythe."

Izzy stopped eating, giving the question some thought. "No, I don't think he did it. But my gut feeling wouldn't pass Birdie's test of having proof."

"So that means we have to find proof that someone *did* it instead of didn't do it."

"Is this a private conversation?"

They looked up. Chelsey Mansfield stood a few feet away, her face hesitant. "I don't want to interrupt—"

"Of course you're not. Would you like to join us?" Nell asked. The lines of worry on Chelsey's forehead couldn't be denied. She hadn't come over just to say hello.

"Maybe for a moment. Barrett and I were having a rare lunch together today—" She sat and nodded beyond the bar, where they saw the broad back of Barrett Mansfield leaving the restaurant. "He usually leaves for Boston at the crack of dawn, but Chief Thompson wanted to see him at the station this morning."

"About the Westerland case?"

Chelsey nodded. "It's so consuming. So intrusive into all our lives. The questions don't stop. I hope the police close the case soon. Barrett wasn't sure they were getting anywhere with the investigation, though they've questioned all of us. Certainly me and him."

"Was Barrett able to help?" Izzy asked.

Chelsey looked back across the room, but Barrett was gone. She looked down at her purse as if wondering if she should leave. Then she sat back in her chair, looked at Nell and Izzy, and decided to stay. "I don't think they were asking for his help. I think they were asking if he could have murdered her."

Nell and Izzy were silent.

Chelsey continued. "The police are interested in people who had problems with Blythe. That's no surprise. It makes sense. When they looked through the school's board notes, they discovered that

Barrett and Blythe locked horns often. Almost from the beginning when Elizabeth was interviewing for the position." She looked at Nell. "You're surely aware of this."

Nell was aware of it, having been privy to some of the heated arguments, but she wondered exactly where Chelsey was going with it.

Chelsey took a deep breath. "We knew Elizabeth Hartley before we moved here and long before she was headmistress. She took a class I taught on law and education when she was getting her doctorate at Harvard. I recognized her potential right away—and the need for what she was interested in. She was specializing in improving learning for children with conditions that make it difficult. Like Anna."

The waitress appeared with another iced tea. Chelsey wrapped her fingers around the chilled glass as if to steady her hands.

"So that's how Barrett knew about Elizabeth as a possible candidate," Nell said. "I remember him saying that he could personally vouch for her expertise. His opinion has always been solid and well respected and it added to her recommendations."

"Yes. We hired her to work with Anna when our daughter was younger. Elizabeth performed miracles with her. She knows so much about learning and psychology, about calming children or stimulating them when they need it, about how to create a solid learning environment for all kinds of children so they can learn and socialize together, and not be segmented and labeled with Asperger's syndrome or ADHD or sensory processing disorder—or a myriad of other things. Every child is unique—and with good teachers, children can all learn and not only that, they can learn from each other. That's what Elizabeth believes. That's what she makes happen." Her eyes were alive with conviction and passion. She finally paused to take a breath.

Nell spoke. "The board saw that—her range of expertise and her passion." Her voice was calm, soothing. "And I understand now how important hiring her was to you and your husband."

"But not just to us. To all children."

The three women sat in silence for a moment, the only sound that of ice cubes clinking against glasses—and Chelsey's breathing.

Finally Izzy broke the silence. "You moved here a couple years before Elizabeth was hired, right?" She remembered her surprise when her old law professor became a regular customer in the yarn shop.

Chelsey nodded. "We knew Sea Harbor would be a good place to raise Anna. Large, noisy environments, even the traffic in Boston, can all be difficult for kids who have trouble with sensory processing, which was Anna's problem. We fell in love with this town, but we kept in touch with Elizabeth. And then, when she was looking for a job and this one opened up, it seemed like some kind of karma."

"It sounds like it was perfect timing for Elizabeth. Perhaps it was exactly that—karma."

"Maybe. Or maybe it was Barrett's determination to do everything in his power to give Anna what she needed—and me, too. He's always wanted the very best for his family and has done everything possible to create a wonderful life for us. He's an amazing man. I am so fortunate." Her voice cracked slightly.

"That kind of thing usually goes both ways," Nell said.

Izzy took a forkful of salad, stabbing a juicy chunk of lobster. She chewed it thoughtfully, trying to organize the conversation in her head. "What happened when Elizabeth applied for the position at the school?" she finally asked. She looked at both Nell and Chelsey.

Chelsey said, "Barrett said people were impressed. She was imminently qualified. After she got her degree she worked at a private school for a couple years and received sterling reviews. She was young, but so talented."

"Blythe Westerland put up a fuss," Nell said. She picked at her salad as she tried to remember what arguments surfaced over the interviews and hiring. Elizabeth was too young, some of the board members had said. But it seemed rather an old-fashioned criticism in light of female CEOs of the same age. She remembered Birdie speaking up, wondering if the board was getting lost in the Brontë version of headmistresses and not moving ahead with the times. As always when Birdie spoke, people listened.

"Yes, Blythe made an awful fuss," Chelsey said.

Nell watched her carefully. Chelsey seemed nervous, fidgety when she talked about Blythe. Perhaps it related to her admission that Blythe's death brought relief.

Nell handed her a bowl of lemon slices.

She squeezed a bit into her tea. "Blythe was unfair. Quite awful, really, and Barrett came home so angry after those meetings."

"Were the other applicants less qualified?" Izzy asked.

Nell knew where Izzy was going with the question. Perhaps the Mansfields were thinking too much of their own child and not considering who was the best candidate for the whole school. But thinking back, she didn't remember it that way. She remembered considering Elizabeth's qualification carefully. And she had been impressed. She couldn't remember the other candidates at all. "What I remember is that Elizabeth was truly the best applicant for the job. In fact, I don't think the others came close."

But it was absolutely true that Blythe Westerland put up roadblocks every inch of the way, none of which convinced the rest of the board, although she gained a few allies with some of her comments, including her support for a distant relative for the post.

"Blythe tried to discredit Elizabeth, and she used Barrett as her weapon," Chelsey said softly.

Nell and Izzy leaned in to hear. Her voice was quiet, but coated with distaste for the woman so recently murdered.

"Barrett missed one of the monthly meetings around that time—I had the flu and he was reluctant to leave Anna and me. Blythe jumped at the opportunity and used that night to make a scurrilous attack on his integrity."

The meeting came back to Nell suddenly, perhaps because of Chelsey's strained voice and the pain reflected in her eyes. Blythe had insinuated that Barrett's reasons for hiring someone he knew so intimately had little to do with the betterment of the school. He wanted to keep his "mistress" close at hand. It was a horrendous accusation.

Nell had almost forgotten about the incident, though with Chelsey sitting there in front of her, it came back in bold relief. Blythe's unfounded accusation had upset the board, but not in the way Blythe intended. People were angry at the tawdry element she had insinuated into their serious discussion. She had nothing to back her claims, and the board hired Elizabeth soon after that. Blythe went off to Boston or Europe or somewhere for a couple of months while things cooled off, and when she came back, she slipped back into her emeritus position on the board and back into her usual posturing, now focusing on the terrible job that Elizabeth was doing. The event was nearly forgotten—but certainly not by Chelsey Mansfield.

The waitress refilled their drinks and brought the check.

"This was presumptuous of me. I didn't intend to take up your whole lunch with my woes." Chelsey leaned down and picked her bag up from the floor. "I'm not sure why I unloaded like this on you both. It's not like me, but I don't have many friends in Sea Harbor, and you've always been warm and accepting. I guess that's what I needed—someone to listen, and not to judge. All of this has put so much stress on Barrett, all the questioning by the police, dissecting rumors and innuendoes, and some of the things Blythe tried to destroy in her wake . . ."

Chelsey stood up, though it was clear there was more she wanted to say.

Chelsey wasn't finished unburdening her soul. But she also wasn't sure she wanted to.

"We're glad you stopped by. And we're good at listening—it's what knitters do." Nell smiled, then added, "Well, we talk, too, but in confidence when it's called for. But you know that, don't you?"

Chelsey responded with a half smile.

"Is there something else Blythe tried to destroy?" Nell asked gently.

Chelsey breathed deeply, her face weary. She nodded.

"My marriage," she said.

Chapter 28

"**I**t happened before Elizabeth was even a candidate for the headmistress position," Nell told Ben later that day.

Once the words were out of her mouth, Chelsey had sat back down at the table and ordered a glass of wine. And then she had peeled away another layer of Blythe Westerland for them, although one that fit into the pattern without even adding extra stitches.

Nell took a package of cod from the refrigerator and handed it to her grill chef. She glanced at the clock. Friday night—deck night—and running late. Fortunately they never had much of a schedule for these nights. Late meant more cheese and crackers and sipping martinis more slowly. More time to talk. No one would complain.

"Why do you think Chelsey talked to you about all this?" Ben asked, unwrapping the fish and placing each fillet in a pan. He sprinkled each piece with Cajun seasoning.

"Izzy wondered that, too. I think she just needed support, needed to talk with someone—and we were there."

"Do the police know?"

"That's the thing. Yes. They brought it up while questioning Barrett this morning. I think that's why Chelsey needed to talk. Her private life was being picked apart in a way that both she and Barrett find extremely difficult."

"How did they find out?"

"Barrett had rented one of the yacht club's guesthouses while their house here was being readied. It was several years ago. He wanted to be able to come and go when he could get away from work to supervise the remodeling. On weekends, he'd bring Chelsey and Anna up."

"I remember that," Ben said. "Barrett bought a small Sunfish so he could introduce Anna to the water. He's usually a serious fellow, but get him out of that suit and on a boat and he's a different man. So that's when it happened?"

Nell nodded and reached for the cheese slicer. "The police naturally questioned people at the club since Blythe spent a lot of time there. I suppose they were looking for odd behavior, people she talked to, met with. Anything that might help the investigation. There's been a lot of staff turnover through the years, as you'd expect, but a couple old-timers remembered some things from a few years ago and mentioned Barrett's name. Details were kind of sketchy except that Blythe had seemed interested in making the handsome businessman feel at home in his little guesthouse."

"Knowing Barrett, I'd guess it didn't amount to much." Ben took a bottle of olives from the refrigerator.

"You're right. Barrett said it was nothing, which was essentially what the bartender had said, although he added that Blythe didn't take *no* lightly and it wasn't a one-time-only brush-off. She was persistent. Barrett didn't even tell Chelsey about it until today—and only then because he was concerned the story might end up in a rumor mill and he didn't want her reading about it in the paper."

"Did it bother her that he hadn't told her?"

"I don't think so. She doesn't seem to worry about Barrett in that way."

"What was her main concern today?"

"That Barrett might become a more viable suspect. At least that's what Izzy and I surmised."

But somehow they both suspected there might have been more

to the story. Probably something Chelsey herself wasn't even aware of. But they knew someone who might be able to help.

Only it would have to wait.

Before she could say anything else, there was a banging of the front door and a parade of footsteps. The Perry clan appeared in the family room. Sam was carrying a sleeping baby Abby and motioned silently that he was taking her up to her Endicott crib. Red, their aging golden retriever, followed Sam dutifully up the back stairs.

"Red guards over Abby like he's her very own angel," Izzy said.

"We all need a Red." Nell watched his waving tail disappearing around the stairs.

"You two look serious," Izzy said. She carried an arugula and pecan salad over to the island. "Aunt Nell must be telling you about our talk with Chelsey."

Ben nodded. But before he could speak, Birdie came in with Cass right behind her, carrying a bag of French bread and a bowl of fruit.

"No Harry?" Izzy asked. She took the bags from Cass.

"He mentioned checking on his Boston place. Or getting a beer with someone. Or something. I can't remember." She looked over at Ben. "You and Sam have done some damage with that guy. He's talking sailboats nonstop."

"Oh?" Ben looked over from his martini making.

"He liked being on the boat—he used to sail with friends."

Nell was silent, listening more carefully than she usually did to sailboat banter. Mostly she was trying to figure out Harry Winthrop. He was an enigma. And she wasn't sure enigmas made good boyfriends. The protective bear in Nell was working its way to the surface.

She buried her thoughts and concentrated instead on finding a basket for the bread.

"He talked about that, said he'd always wanted a boat," Ben

said. "He's a little rusty at the helm, but it always comes back, like riding a bike."

"He says sailing always helped him clear his head."

"Not a bad way to clear the head," Sam said, coming down the stairs with a soiled diaper in hand. "That's why mine is empty most of the time."

"So that's what does it," Izzy said. She laughed and tugged at a loose lock of his sandy hair. "You need a haircut, unless it's your attempt to cover up the empty head."

"Hey, photographers are artists. Straggly hair, Birkenstocks." He lifted one foot. "It's all part of our mystique."

The Brewsters and Danny arrived in time to look at the bottom of Sam's sandals and claim the last three martinis.

Danny balanced his and Jane's glasses between his fingers while Jane carried her cheese pâté out to the deck.

"Anyone else coming that you know of?" Nell asked Ben.

"I invited Bob Chadwick—he came back to town this morning. But he declined. Some business he had to take care of, he said. Meeting someone. He sounded preoccupied and I got the feeling he wasn't looking forward to the meeting. He planned to take care of whatever it was, down a beer and burger, and hit the sack. He has plenty on his plate tomorrow."

"Not a bad plan," Nell said. "The beds at the Ravenswood are the best medicine in the world. It's been a long week for him. Sometimes I forget that." She turned up the music, picked up a pitcher of iced tea, and joined the crowd on the deck.

The mood was light. A pleasant change from the week's heaviness. It was a feeling they all wanted to bottle up and bring out at will. In the background, Nikki Yanofsky was belting out "On the Sunny Side of the Street."

Nell wondered if the song was a good omen. She was certainly ready to cross to that side. She felt more optimistic somehow. The pieces were piling up. Finding the pattern in their angles was the challenge that lay ahead.

Pete surprised them as Ben took the lemony cod off the grill. He walked up the back deck steps with Willow at his side. "My gig was canceled for tonight," he said. "Can you imagine anyone canceling the Fractured Fish? Wicked, evil folks."

Willow, who even in her highest boots didn't reach Pete's shoulder, punched him playfully, then explained the canceled gig to the rest of them. "They were supposed to play for a rehearsal dinner over in Rockport," she explained. "The bride changed her mind and didn't show up. The best man suggested they party anyway, but no one seemed to be in the mood."

Pete rubbed his arm with a touch of drama. "People are nuts sometimes."

"So, what's new out here?" Willow asked, giving Nell a hug. "Are there any developments on the Westerland case?"

"Blythe's will arrived today," Ben said. "Much to his surprise, Father Northcutt is stated in the will as the executor. He's asked me to sit in to explain some of the jargon and procedures, though he's done this before."

Of course, they all remembered it. It was Finnegan's will. The old Sea Harbor fisherman had fully entrusted the priest to his soul, his Irish whiskey, and to handling his estate. And then handling the biggest surprise of all—notifying Cass Halloran that Finnegan had left his entire estate to her, saving a struggling Halloran Lobster Company from closing its doors.

"I saw Blythe with Father Larry several times at the yacht club," Nell said. "They seemed to have a nice relationship."

"Blythe told Father Larry once that making her go to church was the only good thing her father ever did for her," Ben said. "She found peace there, along with some powerful women, albeit dead ones. She was especially fond of Mary Magdalene, he said."

Birdie smiled. "Well, now. Who would have guessed?"

"Has Father Larry read the will?" Izzy asked.

Ben nodded. "There were only four beneficiaries. Blythe's

cousin Bob, whom you've all met by now. She gave him all her property—the townhome in Boston and her property here. There are also some real estate investments that go to him. In addition, she left sizable sums to a church she sometimes attended in Boston and a hefty bequest to Our Lady of Safe Seas."

Ben paused to take a forkful of cod while Nell refilled water glasses. Sam came back from checking on Abby and refreshed everyone's wine. It had been a rather haphazard meal, people helping themselves to fish and salad, rolls and Jane's pâté, crackers, and cheese, in any order they chose. It seemed to reflect the turmoil in their town, Nell thought. But at least no one had begun with the rhubarb pie she'd picked up at the bakery.

She looked over at Ben. "Didn't you say four beneficiaries? That's only three—"

"Ah, yes," Ben said. "And here's where this gets interesting. *Ironic* is a better word."

Izzy stopped collecting empty plates. The others looked at Ben.

"Blythe's will stipulates that the rest of her very sizable estate will go to her alma mater, the Sea Harbor Community Day School— though the name in the will is, as you might expect, the old one, the Country Day School."

There was silence.

Then Birdie's small face broke into a wide smile. "Oh, my. What a lovely, lovely gift. Elizabeth will put it to very good use. Everyone will benefit, I suspect the whole town in one way or another."

"The interesting thing is that Blythe didn't intend to die when she did. I'm sure she thought Elizabeth would be long gone by the time her money went to the school," Ben said.

Birdie only smiled wider. "Perhaps there's a bit of justice or retribution or some such thing inherent in all this. Maybe Blythe herself is smiling at the twist, wherever she might be."

Izzy continued clearing plates and Ben lit logs in the stone fire pit while thoughts of Blythe Westerland glowed with the embers.

The irony was somehow a pleasing epilogue to what had been a tragic week.

Nell maneuvered a tray of pie slices onto the low round table and passed out napkins and forks. "From the market to the bakery to your mouths," she said, and settled down beside Ben.

Ben looped one arm around her shoulder, pulling her into the warmth of his side.

"Bob Chadwick was saddened by the will. Two churches, a school, and himself. No children, no great friends or people who had touched her life. It painted a solitary existence. And it didn't have to be that way, he said. It might have been different."

"Different?" Izzy asked.

"It was rather cryptic, the way he said it—something about a decision she'd made not too long ago. So maybe he meant nothing more than she could have lived her life differently, no matter how it started out."

Danny had talked with Bob that morning, he said, and came away thinking Blythe's death had affected him in ways he never anticipated.

"Basically he said her death was a damn shame. He blamed it partly on a family of powerful men. They certainly had a hand in her death, he said."

Something everyone on the deck would agree to.

But her family was gone.

And the person who picked up a rock and ended her life wasn't.

Nell waited until Ben had brushed his teeth and crawled into bed beside her. The window was open and cool, almost cold air ruffled the curtains. Nell pulled the down comforter up to her chin, welcoming its warmth.

And then she turned to Ben.

"Ben, about the will . . ."

Ben rolled onto his side, one arm curved behind his head on the pillow. As happened so often, he knew what was coming before Nell spoke.

Nell touched his chest and looked into his eyes. "Elizabeth Hartley didn't know about the will, did she? Please tell me she didn't."

Chapter 29

Birdie and Cass were in the kitchen with Ben when Nell came down the next morning. Izzy would meet them at the outdoor market on Harbor Road a little later, Cass said. The season was coming to an end and none of them wanted to miss the last of the tomatoes and spinach and squash.

Birdie had walked in with the same question about the will, and Ben was answering it patiently. They had nearly forgotten about Teresa Pisano's rants. Once the will was revealed, it was remembered with startling clarity. "She just wants the money," the school secretary had told the police and anyone else who would listen to her. But few did. Mary Pisano had tossed it aside as meaningless, that Teresa probably thought Elizabeth was dipping into the foundation moneys or some such ridiculous thing.

But it all came down to a will.

"As a beneficiary of the will, Elizabeth was given a copy the other day. But she had heard about it before, and had no hesitation in telling the police yesterday when they asked. Apparently Blythe had shared the information with Teresa, just another way to gain her confidence so she would keep Blythe apprised of school business. She probably hadn't counted on Teresa becoming angry at Elizabeth one day and screaming at her that Blythe loved the school so much she was leaving it most of her money."

Elizabeth hadn't given it another thought. Teresa said many

things to her that went in one ear and out the other and carried little truth. That was one of the many.

"So Elizabeth now has yet another motive for killing Blythe Westerland," Birdie said, shaking her head.

"The worst part of it is that the focus will be more on the will, and less on finding the real murderer," Nell said.

"Maybe it's the police focus," Birdie said. "But that's not our focus."

Ben looked up.

"Don't worry, dear Ben." Birdie patted his hand. "The police have to do what they have to do, but they're walking down the wrong road."

Ben left soon after. He was meeting with Bob Chadwick, Father Northcutt, and the amiable priest's right-hand person, Cass's mother, Mary Halloran, who kept the whole parish on an even keel. Mary and Father Larry had called the meeting to plan a memorial Mass for Blythe. Bob thought it was a good idea, even if he was the only one who might attend.

Izzy was waiting at the entrance to the market. Esther Gibson's husband stood at the back of his pickup truck, twisting balloons into lobsters and dogs and kittens, and Abby's giggles were helping him attract a crowd.

Birdie, Nell, and Cass surrounded the stroller, and with Cass at the helm and two lobster balloons bobbing above the stroller, they pushed their way down the narrow paths, filling their bags with produce along the way. At the opposite end of the market, the harbor came into full view, sunlight reflecting off the water in glorious streams. Pete, Merry, and Andy Risso had set up in the small gazebo and were playing catchy tunes to a gathering crowd of kids. Gabby and Daisy were in the center, twirling in circles and bellowing out the lyrics to "It's Going to be a Great Day."

The women dropped their bags on a picnic table and sat far enough away from the gazebo to hear each other, close enough to feel the positive vibe the young bodies gave off. And each of them knew that, although the produce was a draw, the real need that morning was to figure out a murder before an innocent woman lost her spirit, her livelihood—and anything else she held dear.

"The murder doesn't have a thing to do with the will or money or maybe even the school," Izzy began. "I thought about it all night and we were almost on the right road before we started to get distracted with things like wills and a ranting Teresa Pisano." She reached down and handed Abby a slice of apple.

"Money has a way of doing that."

Birdie put on her glasses as if they were needed not only to read, but to think. "Izzy's right. We need to turn all our attention back to Blythe. We need to listen to her and let her guide us."

A shadow fell across the table and they looked up into Danny Brandley's dark-rimmed glasses. He carried a cup of coffee in one hand and a white Dunkin' Donuts bag in the other. His ever-present computer backpack was slung over one shoulder. "Is this a closed group?" he asked. "I think I know what you're talking about—it's on my mind, too. I'd like to join you."

Cass tilted her head to one side, looking him over. "You have donut holes?" Her dark eyebrows lifted and her gaze zeroed in on the white bag with telltale stains on the side.

He nodded once, holding the bag closer to his side, his face deadpan.

"Glazed?"

"What? I need to bribe my way onto this bench? You're going to take away my donut holes?"

Cass nodded, reached up, and took the bag away, pulling open the top. The first one went to Abby and the rest were quickly passed around the table.

Danny feigned resignation and lifted one long leg over the bench, squeezing in next to Cass.

The casual, teasing exchange meant nothing—but it managed to give inordinate pleasure to Cass's group of best friends.

Danny leaned in, his elbows on the table. "I was in Boston the other day on business and had some free time, so I invited Bob Chadwick to a late lunch."

He had their attention. They all turned toward him, a huddled group of listeners.

"Why?" Cass asked.

"I like him. And I think he holds a key to this whole mess and doesn't even know he has it."

"Go on," Nell said.

"I saw the dual townhomes—his and Blythe's. It's a shared brownstone with a home on each side. It's a really great place in a high-end neighborhood. Bob said he took care of Blythe's place often, since she'd be gone for weeks without checking in sometimes. They depended on each other for practical things, paying bills when the other was gone, trips to doctors when they were both there, that kind of thing. Things you'd ask a friend to do."

"Doctors?"

"If one of them needed a ride or support or whatever. Which, apparently, Blythe did a few months ago—see a doctor, I mean. He was evasive about it when I asked. A little mysterious. I tried to push it, but he wasn't going there. He said he needed time to think.

"But I did suggest he pull together any records, bills, paperwork and bring it with him this week. He thought that was a good idea and said Ben had suggested it, too. You never know where a lead might take you."

"Did he know her friends? People she dated in Boston?"

"Not many, but a few. He said Blythe's relationships were usually short-lived, so he tried not to get involved. He seemed like he wanted to say more about that, but then changed his mind, as if somehow he was breaching a confidence or needed permission or something. But I could tell there was something needling him, something he was trying to sort out in his own mind. We're going to have dinner tonight and I hope we can talk more about—"

The ringing of Nell's cell phone interrupted. It was Ben. And the fact that it was a call, not a text, made Nell think it might be important.

"Go ahead, Aunt Nell," Izzy said.

Nell stepped away and listened while the others tried not to listen. But it didn't matter because Nell said little. A comment here and there, then more listening. She frowned through most of it, then told Ben she'd get back to him and hung up.

"Now, that's odd," she said, sitting down on the bench. "They can't find Bob Chadwick. Ben wondered if any of us had heard from him."

"Bob's lost?" Izzy asked.

"Well, he didn't show up." Nell explained the planned meeting at the church. "Ben said there was another meeting lined up after the one at the church—they were going to go over some provisions in the will. And Bob had asked that Jerry Thompson be available."

"Did they check Ravenswood-by-the-Sea? Mary told me yesterday Bob was coming back for a few days. She was happy about it; she likes having him around," Birdie said.

"Yes, they checked. Bob had mentioned to Ben he hadn't slept well the night before, so they figured he overslept. Mary double-checked the room because his Subaru was in the parking lot, but there was no sign of him."

"What about last night?"

"Ben invited him to dinner, but he was busy. Mary saw him leave late afternoon. He told her the same thing. She offered to find something in the kitchen, but he said no. He was meeting a friend. And he was off, walking—to help him think, he said. She didn't see him come back last night, but he had his gold Ravenswood key, so it wasn't that unusual that no one saw him return."

"That's strange," Danny said. He thought about his conversation with Bob. "He's a pretty dependable guy. Levelheaded. I don't think he'd miss a meeting without a good excuse. He mentioned the will briefly to me—he's going to donate her place here to something or other. He was looking for suggestions. I don't think the money was important to him."

"Any ideas?" Izzy asked. "Do you think he just wants to escape this whole mess?"

Danny shook his head. "No, I think he wants to solve a murder."

That sobered them, and the donuts went unattended as they considered Bob Chadwick.

And his search for his cousin's killer.

Izzy left soon after, needing to return to the yarn shop. She was taking Abby with her to play in the shop's Magic Room. Daisy and Gabby would be in shortly to provide watchful eyes and caring hands in the kiddy room—and mostly dote on Abby, which was fine with her mother.

The others talked a little longer with Danny, tugging and playing with ideas. Not being able to define exactly what they were looking for—but knowing it was there in the pile of relationships they were dissecting. Something in one of them that was devastating. Irreparable.

"Angelo summarized it well," Birdie said.

"The killing?" Danny asked.

"The reason. He said Blythe hurt someone so badly that the agony of it, the irreparable pain, killed something inside that person. And it caused him or her to kill her."

"I think that's right," Danny said. "Nothing else makes logical sense, even though I know the police have to follow all kinds of things: the will, the money, the job."

"Instead of the more intimate life Blythe led," Nell said. "Feelings. Intuitions."

"And lots of relationships," Cass said, speaking up for the first time. "We have a whole lineup."

They repeated them to Danny, hesitating slightly when his own name came up on the list.

"Hey," he said. "I never got far enough to get dumped. Or even to dump her."

"Neither did Barrett," Nell said. "At least we don't think so. But I think anyone she touched—or who touched her—was in danger of being hurt. And if not them, then someone close to them. I think Blythe absolutely couldn't stand anyone taking power away from her. You're right that you probably don't factor in, Danny—"

"It's because I saved you," Cass said.

Danny looked at her. He frowned.

"I kind of liked you back then. I told her I'd dump live lobsters on her platinum head if she made another move."

Nell and Birdie laughed out loud.

"You didn't," Birdie said.

"Maybe I did. Maybe I didn't." She got up from the table and picked up her bag. "Blythe needed to know she wasn't the only powerful woman on Cape Ann. Not by a long shot."

Danny just shook his head, trying to hide the small smile that lifted the corners of his mouth. "Okay, then," he said, clearing his throat. "The key is to peel away all the layers. I suppose some people might kill because they were dumped by a beautiful woman, but somehow I don't think that's what happened here. Frankly Blythe wasn't all that lovable—and I would bet a lot of guys, even ones having a good time, were fine moving on when Blythe was ready to do the same."

"The person who seemed to have the biggest infatuation with Blythe was Teresa Pisano," Nell said. "And she would have had nothing to gain."

"She wasn't cast aside like the others, either," Cass said. "As far as Teresa was concerned, Blythe was her best friend."

"Right," Danny said. "So I think the hurt or pain or whatever she did to whoever killed her had to be a lot deeper. The murderer wasn't just losing a girlfriend. It was something bigger, something enormous—to him or her, at least.

"A pain so enormous it took a life."

Chapter 30

A short while later, Danny left. He pulled the heavy backpack over his shoulder and brushed hair off his forehead. "I'm going to find Ben and see what's up with Bob Chadwick. Maybe I can help find the guy."

They promised to keep one another in the loop and watched Danny walk toward his car, concern shadowing his face.

Danny was a surprise bedfellow, but in the realm of things, it couldn't hurt to have a mystery writer to consult with.

Even Cass agreed. "But now I'm starving," she said. "How about you two?"

Nell was planning on exactly that. Cass's appetite never failed them. "I think we need to have a chat with Liz Santos over at the yacht club. How about a sandwich on their deck?"

It was a nice enough day to sit on the club's terrace, provided one had a sweater on. The hostess found them a table just outside the open French doors with a view of the sea and sailboats.

Liz was in her office, the waitress told them, trying to straighten out some kind of mess. She'd have her stop by their table to say hello.

Cass began drawing lines on the tabletop with the tip of her finger. She looked up from her doodling. "What pain is that big?"

"I was thinking about the same thing," Nell said, moving aside while the waitress set down a plate of pickles, olives, and slender bread sticks. "What could someone do to you that would make you kill them?"

"If someone were going to hurt Gabby, or one of you," Birdie said, "I think I'd be capable of almost anything."

They all sat silently, applying that to themselves, and to people they loved who might suffer at the hands of another. They'd do anything to stop it.

Just as Barrett and Chelsey Mansfield would do for their daughter, Anna . . .

"You are certainly a silent group." Liz stood at their table, smiling. "Betty said you wanted to see me?"

"We always want to see you, dear," Birdie said. "You brighten our day."

The waitress returned with tea and water. They ordered the lobster rolls and salad, then turned their attention back to Liz.

"It's busy out there on the water. You need a traffic patrol to keep the sailboats from colliding," Nell said. "And in here. Everywhere." She looked across the terrace and down to the water. The well-maintained yards were filled with strollers walking along tree-shaded paths that wound all the way down to the marina, the beach, and the yacht club dock and slips.

"It's such a glorious time of year," Liz said. "We're getting the first of the leaf watchers and also the sailors trying to get in every gust of wind before the cold weather freezes them out. There's a whole fleet going out today—it's a parade of white."

"That's all good, right?" Birdie asked, catching a worried look that passed across the manager's face.

Liz brought back her smile. "Yes, of course. We're growing. That's good. But sometimes growth brings glitches." She looked at Nell. "We had a problem with keys to the boats this morning. Somehow the keys got messed up. We thought a set was missing; then it reappeared this morning. I'm going to call Ben and Sam and get their committee together to figure it out. Those two guys never fail me."

"What kind of keys?" Cass asked.

"Keys to the sailboats. It isn't really that big a thing. I just don't like confusion—and it was confusing this morning. Most of the owners keep a set of keys to their boats on a big board in the equipment building down near the slips. It's helpful in case someone calls in and needs us to check something on a boat, move it for some reason or repair something. They got messed up, that's all. But in answer to your comment, yes, it's really busy around here right now. Weekends are crazy. In fact, our guesthouses are completely booked for the next few weeks."

"That's wonderful. Speaking of those little cottages, do you have time to sit for a few minutes?" Birdie asked. She held up her glass. "The mint tea is delicious. Have one."

Liz laughed and pulled out a chair. "Sure. I'm headed home from here but always have time for this group. What's up? Don't tell me you have need to rent a guesthouse, Birdie?"

Birdie laughed, used to being teased about her eight-bedroom home. "Not just now. But Nell has many a question about the cottages."

"Two, in fact," Nell said. "Chelsey Mansfield was telling us how nice it was when they were in the process of moving to have one of the little cottages at their disposal. And it was especially nice for Barrett when he'd come check on the remodeling."

"Sure. I remember that because the cottages were new and the club was trying to get the word out. I was a hostess, not a manager, back then, so I saw Barrett often," Liz said. She was hesitant, unsure of what was coming next.

"You also mentioned that Blythe Westerland spent a lot of time here—" Nell purposely left the comment hanging. She didn't want to push Liz into areas she didn't want to go.

"Yes, Blythe has always spent time here." She hesitated just for a minute. "And I think I probably mentioned to you about her attraction to Barrett. The police know that, too."

"Could you tell us exactly what happened? I don't want to put you on the spot, but here's why I'm asking. Blythe clearly didn't like Barrett Mansfield. She seemed to be against anything he was for, including having his daughter in 'her' school, as she called it. And objecting to his choice for headmistress. I suspect it's because Barrett refused her advances, because we know she had a problem with that and often managed to make people sorry if they made the unfortunate decision to move out of the relationship. But her grudge with Barrett seemed somehow extreme."

Liz looked out to sea, thinking about the comment, formulating an answer. Finally she said, "You're right. It was more than that. Her grudge was most likely because of what happened that night—and I'm sure it was intense. The whole incident is still clear in my head. For one thing, I was the hostess, so was ultimately responsible for smoothing it out. But also because I think everyone involved felt awful about what happened. Blythe seemed almost lonely that night, and she was determined that Barrett pay attention to her. Somehow she needed affirmation. But I think in her zeal, she had a few too many glasses of champagne.

"Barrett is always such a gentleman, but that night he had had it. When she refused to leave his table and began putting her hands on him, he said a few choice words to her, then got up to leave and go back to his guesthouse. She jumped up, but her dress caught on the table leg and she stumbled, then fell. She ended up flat on the floor, champagne covering her dress and her hair. She was a mess.

"The bar was crowded. Everyone was staring at her. And for someone who is always perfect, it was completely, totally humiliating. Awful. I felt terrible for her."

"Geesh," Cass said.

Liz nodded. "I know. You can imagine how she felt. Barrett, being the all-time wonderful gentleman that he is, tried to help her up. He felt bad, too, though he had nothing to do with her falling. But she slapped his hand away, said something to the effect that she'd get even with him even if it took the rest of her life, and then somehow pulled herself up. We helped her clean herself up, called her a cab. And that was the end of that."

"And the beginning of the poor man's struggles," Birdie said. "No wonder she was determined to get even, even though he didn't cause it."

"At least that explains her anger," Nell said. "It makes it less mysterious. Sometimes the easiest way to get rid of embarrassment is to blame the other person. Not exactly admirable, but I suppose it's a way to save face, if that's the most important thing to you. And clearly it was to Blythe."

"It also helps me understand Barrett's patience with her, even when she was less than cordial to him," Birdie said. "I'm sure he regretted her humiliation."

"She bounced back, though," Liz said. "The next time she came in, she looked perfectly gorgeous, every hair in place, and acted like nothing had ever happened."

"It's an admirable trait, I suppose," Birdie said.

"Is there any update on finding the person who killed her? I've noticed the skittishness in our neighborhood. No one is jogging these days, at least not once the sun sets. It's even getting hard to find babysitters. Moms want their kids home. Or they want to be with them—something I completely understand. Our nanny lives with us, and we consider ourselves fortunate."

"I think it'll soon be behind us," Birdie said, almost without thought.

Nell looked at her with surprise, then realized that she felt the same way. It would be solved soon.

"That brings me to one more question. Liz," she said. "You mentioned that Barrett wasn't the only man that Blythe met here at the club. I don't want to put you on the spot, but I got the feeling when we talked the other day that there was something or someone in particular you thought of mentioning, but then held back—"

"You don't miss much, do you, Nell?" She smiled. "Yes. She was still coming here regularly, but often it was for meetings with the mayor's group or planning meetings for one event or another. The episode with Barrett was the last really aggressive flirting I saw Blythe do publicly—here, anyway. She didn't really have to. Men liked her, if for no other reason than they looked better with Blythe on their arm. So recently it was more business related than anything else. In some ways she was quieting down a little.

"But last spring I saw her here several times with a man. It wasn't a flirtatious kind of thing. It was almost as if they were a couple, though with Blythe it was hard to tell. But they came as a couple, if you know what I mean? It was during a really busy time, but they stayed in a guesthouse here a couple times."

"Do you know who the man was?"

Liz pulled her eyebrows together, trying to think back. "I'm sorry, I don't."

"What did he look like?"

"That's tough. It was a busy time with lots of people coming and going. And now that I have all these management duties, I spend more time in my office than doing the fun things, like talking to people. I suppose the reason I even noticed them was that . . . well, it was Blythe. It was always hard not to notice her. And I remember that together they made a very striking pair."

"Was he from around here?"

"I don't think so. He was handsome in a kind of all-American way. Dark hair—with that sexy five o'clock shadow, sort of like the guy in *Mad Men*? He didn't keep a boat here, at least I don't think so. Though they may have rented one a few times." She furrowed her brow, trying to come up with something more helpful. "There are so many people who come and go," she said apologetically.

"Of course. We understand."

"I might be able to re-create it in my head, just give me a little time. I can also check the guesthouse log when I'm back in my office. I think they were here a couple weekends. I'll be in touch."

"That would be helpful. Thanks, Liz. It might be important."

Cass listened to the conversation, then looked at Birdie, who was doing the same. Listening. Processing. Trying to slip another piece of information into an already crowded picture.

Nell thanked Liz and watched her walk away, a sudden heaviness weighing her down. And in her head she thought she heard a noise, like a large thump, something falling into place. And she wasn't at all sure if it made her happy or sad.

Liz left and they ate their lobster rolls in silence, the gentle waves a deceptive background as they thought about Blythe Westerland, about the men in her life, and about the reason why one of them might have killed her.

Chapter 31

*N*ell dropped Cass at the dock where she was meeting Pete to check something out on one of the lobster boats.

Pete was in the parking lot talking to Willow when they pulled up. He walked over to the car and leaned in through the open window.

"Hey, if you're free and easy tonight, come on over to the Gull. Merry, Andy, and I are jamming. It's for a good cause."

"What is the cause?" Birdie asked.

"Us," Pete said. "Jake Risso is getting dotty—or maybe it's because his son is the drummer—but no matter, he pays us nicely."

They laughed. Jake had owned the Gull for longer than anyone could remember, and in spite of his gruffness, he was a generous soul.

"Seriously, though, we'll be passing a hat for that Big Brother sailing thing that Ben and Sam are doing next spring. You'll feel like losers if you don't come."

"Of course we'll come." Somewhere along the way, Ben had mentioned it, and then they had both promptly forgotten about it. But they'd show up, even though a noisy bar might not be the way to end the week they had had.

"Hey, hairy Harry stopped by the dock, wondering if you'd moved," he said to Cass. "Seems you're elusive."

"And you said . . ."

"That you'd be around. He said you had plans together tonight, but I told him you were coming to the Gull."

Willow pulled him out of the window. "Sorry, Cass. I don't know when your baby brother decided he'd make a good social secretary, but Harry was okay with it. He'd come, too, he said, and could you pick him up? His Bimmer is being checked."

Cass shook her head as if dismissing her brother from her life forever. She slid out of the backseat. "It's so nice to have guardians," she mumbled in fake annoyance, and then she waved good-bye to Nell and Birdie.

Nell drove up Harbor Road toward Birdie's neighborhood, maneuvering the twists and turns in the forested road as she wondered about Cass. She was so difficult to read sometimes. She had bantered with Danny, and seemed happy about seeing Harry. She seemed oddly content for reasons neither of them could fathom. But Cass was Cass. And they loved her.

Content would suffice for now. It was the only choice they had.

"Before you drop me off, let's check to see if Mary is at the B and B," Birdie said. "Perhaps Bob is back by now and we can relieve Danny's mind. He seemed genuinely worried."

Nell agreed and drove up the long driveway. She pulled into the small parking lot beside the sprawling bed-and-breakfast.

Mary's car was there, along with several others with out-of-state licenses. And at the far end, Bob Chadwick's Subaru sat in the shade of a gnarled old elm tree.

They parked and started walking across the lot when a back door slammed and Mary came out of the inn, meeting them on the back porch.

"No, he's not back," she said, before anyone could ask. "Are we to be worried about this?"

The diminutive inn owner wore jeans and a plaid shirt, looking as though she'd been cleaning. "Ben has called, then Father Larry, then Danny, and now here you two are. This means 'worry' in my mind. She tapped her head, her short hair flying. She motioned for them to follow her through the back door.

"It's simply odd, don't you think?" Birdie said to her back.

Mary didn't answer. They walked into the large kitchen that anchored a portion of the back half of the bed-and-breakfast. Mary kept coffee, muffins, tea, and whatever else had sounded good to her that day at the guests' disposal. She poured three cups of coffee and pulled stools up to the long stainless steel counter that ran through the middle of the room.

"Bob got in yesterday, and he wasn't his usual, friendly self. Nice, gracious, but he clearly had something on his mind. I asked if he was okay and he said he hadn't slept well, so at first I left well enough alone. I try not to intrude on my guests' personal business— or otherwise—but Bob is slowly becoming more than a guest. Maybe because of the reason bringing him here. It is difficult for him; I can tell."

Nell poured a stream of half-and-half into her coffee and stirred it slowly. "We all desperately need closure. And Bob needs it in an even more personal way."

Mary agreed. "I could tell he wasn't quite himself the minute he walked through the door. He put his things up in his room and came back down for something to drink, so I made him some chamomile tea and sat down with him. We talked about Blythe—he hadn't expressed much emotion before, but yesterday I could tell that he did care about her in his own way—sometimes blood does that. It's like that with me and Teresa. She's goofy sometimes, but she's family. Anyway, maybe planning the funeral triggered Bob's emotions. I think he understood Blythe, and knew that the life—the family—she was born into didn't give her much of a start in life."

"Danny said something similar," Nell said. "Bob appeared a little cavalier when we first met him, but once he realized our intent wasn't to shed a bad light on Blythe but only to find out who did this horrible thing, he warmed up a little."

Mary agreed. "He mentioned Danny—he's meeting him for dinner tonight, I think. Danny got him thinking about Blythe's murder in a different way, he said. A more personal way. To look at ordinary things that might not have been ordinary beneath the surface. Appointments, meetings. Anything. Bob said it was good advice. He was up all night thinking about it and things were coming together. The dots were starting to connect."

"That's curious," Nell said. "Do you have any idea what he meant?"

"No." Mary sat thoughtfully, her feet barely touching the rungs on the stool. She held the string of her tea bag with her fingertips, dipping it in and out of the cup. "Blythe wasn't *evil*, he told me. And even if it was painful and unfair to someone else, she did what she had to do for herself."

"I wonder what it was he was referring to," Nell said, echoing what each of them was thinking. He didn't seem to be talking about relationships ending or an attempt to have a headmistress or teacher fired. They were pieces that didn't fit smoothly into the puzzle, their edges too big or too small. She'd done something for herself, something that was painful—maybe unbearable?—to someone else.

Mary thought about the conversation more carefully. "Bob agreed that she treated people carelessly sometimes—much the way she'd been treated growing up. People didn't like her because of that. But he also indicated she'd done something recently, something that would have been hard for someone to forgive. He seemed to fumble with the words, as if his own thoughts weren't clear about it."

"Someone who lives here in Sea Harbor?"

"I think so. And then he got up and said he needed to settle it. He shouldn't be sitting around. He was resolute, determined. Not just a man going out for a sandwich. I reminded him to take his key—"

Birdie and Nell smiled. Mary's thick gold rings with the name of her bed-and-breakfast on them, along with the room number, were not always welcomed by her guests. They were heavy and bulky—and created lumps in men's back pockets. But hard to lose, was Mary's rationale.

"I heard him leave a little while later," Mary said.

"So he was meeting someone?"

"Yes, he was going to meet with someone. And though I nudged, he didn't mention who."

She reached for a beat-up brown folder, tied with a cloth string, and pushed it across the shiny surface to Nell. "This was in his room. Danny and Ben's names are scribbled on it. Along with a couple of meeting times."

"He was having dinner with Danny tonight. And meeting with Ben tomorrow," Nell said. And both men had encouraged him to bring some of Blythe's personal papers with him.

"I thought there might be something in it to tell me where he went yesterday and when he was coming back. The inn is getting booked up with leaf peepers and he forgot to tell me how long he was staying this time. But it wasn't helpful. It's mostly a packet of bills, financial mishmash, papers."

Nell held back her surprise that Mary had gone through the papers—but then, maybe she'd have done the same thing if a guest in an inn she owned had disappeared and she had no idea if and when he was coming back—and if he was going to pay his bill. She picked up the envelope. "It's some papers needed to finish up the will business. Bills, mortgages, that sort of thing. I'll take it to them."

Mary looked at the packet. "Good. But I think it's more than bills. Maybe you can make some sense out of it."

The crowd at the Gull was large, noisy, and sent even Pete's most devoted fans to the roof of the popular bar. Because of an unexpected north wind, it was chilly and they had the wide space with the view of the harbor to themselves, for a while, anyway.

Ben and Nell settled in next to Birdie at the round rooftop table next to a large heater. Izzy and Sam sat across from them. They had invited Elizabeth, but she was staying close to home. Nell wondered if perhaps Jerry was checking in after hours, ignoring the boundaries Elizabeth had set.

She hoped so.

"Cass and Harry are downstairs," Izzy said. "They're listening to the band up close for a while."

"Making sure Pete knows they're there," Ben said.

"Probably. But Harry hadn't heard the band before, and he wanted to get the full effect," Sam said.

"And you don't have to talk down there. It's so dang noisy," Izzy added. "Harry isn't much of a talker. And Cass seemed to have something on her mind."

Harry wasn't much of a talker, that was true, but he had shared personal feelings with Nell, and she was nearly a stranger. She knew people often did that, shared things with strangers. Had he shared the same thoughts with Cass? Nell imagined her response, probably pulling away at the intimate conversation. Or would she have? None of them were sure of how she felt about the relationship. She'd been to his house, Nell knew. Even helped him fix some walls. But were they to the "do you want children?" stage?

Deep down, she hoped not, but it was Cass's business, Cass's heart. Not hers.

"He may not talk much," Ben said. "But he sails."

"Which covers a multitude of sins, I guess?" Izzy asked.

"Yep," said Sam.

They tried to keep up the banter, to act as if life were normal, but in an hour it had grown old.

And beneath the words ran a silent river of thought of Bob Chadwick.

He hadn't checked in with anyone. He seemed to have disappeared, leaving his car, his room, and a concerned innkeeper behind. Ben had called the chief but tried to act as though it was a personal inquiry—not a police matter.

But Jerry sensed his concern—and shared it. Bob was the only one with direct family connections to Blythe, and hopes still hinged on what he could tell them about his cousin. They weren't finished talking with him. He understood why Ben didn't want to exaggerate the man's absence—there had been enough exaggeration and innuendo in Sea Harbor in the last few days to last several years.

They agreed it wasn't unusual for a man to go AWOL for a couple of days, especially considering what was on Bob's plate.

If only the Subaru had left with him, it would be so much easier to believe their own reasoning.

The conversation ended with a promise to keep in touch, and Jerry's promise to do a little poking around on his own.

Danny had begged off the Gull gathering. He was still hopeful he'd get a call that Bob was just running late for dinner. They were going to meet at the yacht club. He was going to hang out there for a while and see if Bob showed up.

From the large speakers in each corner of the rooftop, the Fractured Fish—Pete, Merry, and Andy—entertained the crowd, encouraging sing-alongs with an array of tunes that hit every age group in the entire town. The hat was passed around several times, upstairs and down, and was full with each go-round. The Big Brothers sailing club would thrive.

Cass and Harry had come up to the roof, but sat at the end of the table, separated from the others by Harry's quiet manner.

Nell moved down on the bench until she was just across from Cass. But it was to Harry she spoke. "How is the cottage coming?"

Harry rubbed his mustache with one finger. "It's getting there," he said. "I'm heading back to Boston soon." He looked at Cass. "But I'll be back often, you can bet on that," he said.

"Well, good. I'm sorry you weren't here at a better time, Harry. Fall is usually one of our favorite seasons. Filled with color and a sense of peace. This week hasn't been like that at all. It's been rough."

He nodded. "Rough. Yes." He glanced at Cass. She was actively attacking a Gull double burger—and winning. He looked back at Nell.

Nell held his gaze and in the silence she saw something she hadn't noticed in the time Harry Winthrop had been in Sea Harbor, sharing their days. The man who had moved into Cass's life and seemed to be staying there.

What she saw surprised her.

She saw a profound sadness.

Chapter 32

B en was working on understanding, but he didn't see the significance in what Nell had seen in Harry Winthrop's eyes. He pulled on a shirt and jeans and gave his hair a quick brush.

"I'm not sure, either," Nell admitted, watching him from their bed. Ben had his mind on other things, she knew. A will with one of its benefactors missing, a friend who happened to be the police chief who was under great stress to find a murderer. And she knew he harbored hidden concern about her, hoping she'd stay safe. Everyone was on edge.

She thought back to the night, to the week, all the way back to a party at a lovely school—a party that had ended in murder.

Dots. All sorts of them. Enough to fill a canvas. With a myriad of lines connecting them.

"I'm worried about Bob," Ben called from the bathroom, where he stood at the mirror, a razor in one hand and his chin white and frothy. "Danny is, too. He texted that he'd tried to reach him all night, even drove around a little, checking a couple restaurants and bars." He was trying to convince himself that their worry was foolish. They really didn't know the guy that well. "Maybe the whole mess got to him and he went drinking."

But neither of them believed that to be the case.

By the time Nell took a quick shower, dressed, and walked into the kitchen, Ben had the coffee on and was rechecking his messages.

"Anything?" Nell asked.

He shook his head. "I need to go over to the club." He checked his watch. "Liz thinks someone's been messing with the keys and they want people to check their boats. I'm picking Sam up on the way."

"She mentioned that to us." Nell repeated what she knew and that Liz pretended she wasn't concerned, but she was. The club was small, the members friendly—something she and Ben had always appreciated. People treated each other—and each other's property—with respect.

"Liz seems to think there might be a need to initiate some security, new protocols. Members won't be happy about it. They like the trust factor."

Ben grabbed his keys and kissed her on the cheek. He waved a hand toward the papers. "What's all that?"

Nell explained.

"Good, glad he remembered. I asked him to bring bills and financial papers so I can figure the will out. Danny and I also thought, who knows, there might be something there that will give us a better look at who Blythe was when she wasn't arguing at a school board meeting or dictating relationships. If you get a chance, maybe you can sort through them and pull out what I might need."

Ben left, then stuck his head back into the kitchen. "Almost forgot. Birdie's on her way over. She was skipping Annabelle's today and bringing coffee cakes and knitting."

Nell frowned. She knew Birdie. Sudden changes to rituals meant more than buttery coffee cake. Which was why she wasn't at all surprised when Izzy, Abby, and Birdie showed up at the same time.

Abby had been up for hours already, Izzy said, and she settled her down upstairs for a morning nap.

"Is Cass coming?"

"Yes," Cass called from the front hall, and walked in with a bag of apples. She wore jeans and an old paint-spattered sweatshirt.

"Apple picking?"

"Yesterday. It helps me think."

"About?" Nell brought mugs and a coffeepot to the table in front of the fireplace.

Cass followed her but didn't answer. Her expression said whatever it was was still being processed.

It was about Harry Winthrop, Nell suspected. But it might have little to do with her affection for him. Cass was perceptive, and Nell wondered exactly what it was she had perceived.

Cass dropped a set of keys on the table. "My car wouldn't start. Harry loaned me his BMW."

"Nice of him," Nell said.

"No, not really. He owed me. I plastered a hallway full of cracks. It's payback, I suppose."

"You don't look like you're enjoying it," Nell said. The *it* was undefined and Cass's face showed that she knew Nell was throwing her a wide-open question.

She looked at the car keys, then back to Nell. And then she changed the subject. "Did you see Josh Babson at the Gull last night?" She scratched at a spot on her jeans, flaking off plaster residue.

Nell and Birdie hadn't seen him, but Izzy had, and she had talked with him.

"We talked about his painting that the Mansfields bought. Although he had painted the same spot where Blythe was murdered, it was painted before that. But I wondered about the Mansfields buying it, because they didn't know that. Josh was convinced they bought it because they liked it and they loved the school. Barrett told him the last thing he saw in the painting was murder—which was exactly what I thought."

"Hmm. Well, I guess that's one person's perspective," Cass said.

"I think it means they didn't see a murder there. If either of the Mansfields had been involved in Blythe's murder, I don't think they'd have bought a painting to remind them of it."

It was only an opinion, but it made sense to all of them.

Birdie spoke up. "I think another thing Barrett Mansfield is saying is that the sooner we stop seeing murder on that beautiful campus, the better."

Nell looked at her. Something was clearly on Birdie's mind. It resonated in the tone of her voice.

"There are too many casualties of this unsolved murder," she continued.

Izzy and Cass turned toward Birdie. Her voice was stern now, advocating a serious cause.

Birdie looked around at each of them. "It has to stop. For the sake of the town. For the sake of our friends whose lives have been turned on their heads. And especially . . ." Birdie's breathing became audible and her face grew so severe that Nell hurried to her side with a glass of water.

"Birdie, take a deep breath."

"Especially?" Izzy sat on Nell's slipcovered couch, pulling her legs up beneath her.

"Especially for the sake of the children." Once the words were out, Birdie's face relaxed. She took a drink of water and sat down next to Izzy. "Gabby and Daisy found the rest of Elizabeth's scarf yesterday."

Izzy's eyes widened. Nell put down her coffee mug.

Cass forked her fingers through her hair. "Where?" she finally asked.

"At the school. They were rehearsing for the fall festival and when their part was over, they wandered down to the boathouse, doing exploring or some such thing. The kids all play on those rocks."

Birdie reached into her knitting basket and pulled out a plastic bag. Inside was an exquisite, bright turquoise scarf. "I'm dropping it at the police station on my way home."

Birdie wanted them to see it first, something Ben would have raised the roof over. Nell held back an opinion. At least Birdie wasn't letting them touch it.

"Two things," Birdie said. Her voice was matter-of-fact but heavy with authority, as if she were chairman of the board, making a decision for all. "First, having children—*children*—exposed to this murder in any way is awful. We need it solved and all traces of it gone from our lives. *Now.* And I think we can. I think we have so many things rattling around in our heads that we're not seeing the forest for the trees. It's all here. Right in front of us."

Nell walked over to the kitchen island, listening, and came back with napkins and coffee cake, sliced in thin pie-shaped pieces—one thing in her life, at least, that was neat and easily managed.

"That's the first thing. Here's the second—" Birdie's voice mellowed slightly. "I know it isn't quite kosher to run off with something that might factor into a police investigation. I'll get it to them. But in truth, this scarf proves something. It was the actions of some frightened individual determined to put the blame for a murder on someone else. He's trying to speed up the investigation, too. But in the wrong direction."

They all looked at the scarf, partially smeared with mud, one edge frayed and torn.

"It's a foolish attempt. Clearly we're not working with a hardened criminal here. It's amateurish."

"It may be amateurish, but he or she *did* kill someone," Izzy reminded her.

"Yes, of course." Birdie's white cap of hair moved slightly. "And being an amateur doesn't mean this person isn't dangerous. My point is if the person is this sloppy, there's no reason he can't be found. Immediately."

She paused for effect, and then continued. "The scarf was probably tossed into the ocean with hopes that the tide would miraculously land it near the scene. And somehow it did that. But the scarf is in decent condition. Muddy, but not something that's been out there in choppy salt water for a week. And it has no further tears or rips. It's dirty. And it's soiled, but probably not from the ocean." She smoothed out the large plastic bag on the coffee table, the scarf becoming visible through it. "See that?"

They all leaned closer, looking at Elizabeth's beautiful knit scarf and remembering the way it had transformed her from a schoolmarm to an elegant sensual woman.

"What are we looking at?" Cass said. "I see mud."

"Look closer. Right there—" Birdie pointed with the tip of her finger to a spot near one corner. "I think sugar or baking soda or paint—something from sitting in a house or car, not floating in the ocean. Elizabeth wouldn't have worn it with a stain that night—so it has happened since Blythe died."

They squinted at the scarf until they were all seeing an off-white smudge, garish against the silky turquoise yarn.

"A workman at the school?" Izzy whispered. "Surely not Angelo."

Nell's thoughts turned immediately to an artist with messy, paint-stained jeans.

But the thought didn't settle comfortably this time. Josh Babson was slowly but effectively becoming more to her than a brooding artist. She was beginning to like him.

Birdie removed the plastic bag from the table and slid it into her purse, her face registering resolve. But more concerning to her friends were the deep worry lines that filled her face.

Nell moved over to the couch. Birdie's emotions were intensified because of Gabby, of course. The worry, the urgency. The thought that a murderer walked so close to where the girls played and painted and laughed. The worry wasn't healthy. And it wouldn't go away, not until they made it.

They took out their knitting—a small Abby-sized sweater in a finely knit wool, long winter socks, and the poncho Gabby was making in class that required a little frogging and fixing. The sound of the needles, the rhythm of the stitches, knitting and purling and yarn overs helped them think.

Angelo's words returned again, as they had so many times. A

hurt so great that someone would kill to dull the pain—or punish the person who inflicted it. Or struck out in anguish and took a life.

The mental list of people was becoming ragged and worn, so often had they returned to it. They all had motive. They all had opportunity. But none of them seemed likely suspects any longer, no matter how they fared on paper.

Nell, Izzy, Birdie, and Cass were all unconvinced, and without a connection that knit Blythe with one of the people on the list so tightly that the stitches would refuse to come loose, the four women forced themselves to think outside the box, to make themselves invisible, like ghosts, tracing Blythe's footsteps through her days and nights, listening to what she said, to whom she spoke.

"We're missing something," Cass said. "We've boxed ourselves in and can't see beyond it."

They all agreed. They needed to step back and look beyond the narrow prism they were looking through. They needed to dig into the shadows where they'd tucked aside things they'd seen, facts they'd recorded. Suspicions that caused them sadness.

Nell moved back to the kitchen counter and put on another pot of coffee. She rinsed off a bunch of grapes and put them in a basket. And all the while she listened to the conversation humming in the distance.

Then in her head she heard Chelsey Mansfield threatening Blythe.

Elizabeth Hartley shouting at her in the middle of Harbor Road.

And dear Angelo, his face beet red, his anger and dislike almost palpable.

But it was the party itself, the night Blythe was killed, that came back with the most clarity. Nell followed Blythe as closely as a shadow. Every step she took that Nell could remember. Every word she said.

The thought brought a quick, uncomfortable thump in her chest. The critical moment had been there all along, but inconsequential, hidden in the banter and warm lights of the evening. Hidden among good friends and food and music.

She repeated each word in her head, then turned her memory to the look on Blythe's face as she had said them. Nell looked over at Izzy and Birdie, talking in hushed tones, as they picked their way, inch by inch, to a murderer. Did Izzy hear Blythe that night?

Surely Cass did. And ignored it, thinking Blythe was talking to her.

But she wasn't.

They needed more. An expression, a look, wasn't enough. It needed a paved road in front of it so it wouldn't slide off the cliff.

Nell carried Bob's brown envelope back with the grapes and set both on the table.

Birdie took the envelope and emptied it as Nell explained where it came from.

"There may be nothing of use here," she said. "But Ben asked me to sort through the contents. Maybe seeing this side of Blythe's life will help us look at her from a different angle, one that will help us figure out what she *did*. Mary Pisano said Bob used that word. And it meant more than casting a boyfriend aside."

"Something she did . . . ," Izzy repeated, giving it a larger space in their thoughts.

"Something she did that brought about her death."

"And when Bob comes back, he can answer any questions we have," Birdie said.

The phone rang—Nell's landline—and they all looked up, somehow thinking Birdie's words had reached Bob himself.

And he was calling to say he'd be over in a few minutes to help them finish up the puzzle. They were that close.

But it was Ben. He was calling from the hospital.

Chapter 33

They had found Bob Chadwick early that morning. The coast guard was doing a routine patrol out near Sunrise Island. Bob was washed up on the shore, still breathing, but unconscious. He'd been beached there for a while—it could have been a day or so—with a severe blow to his head. He must have fallen off a boat. It was a miracle he hadn't drowned.

"We're going to stick around here for a while," Ben said. "Danny and Sam are with me, and Father Northcutt is on his way to see if he can help. But there's not much anyone can do. He's in pretty bad shape."

"Danny?" Nell asked. Ben had been at the meeting with Sam.

"The coast guard called Danny because he was the one who had reported Bob missing," Ben said. "He came to the yacht club and got Sam and me."

Ben paused. Then said, "It's odd. Bob had fallen off a boat—it's the only way he could have ended up on the island. It probably happened Friday night, because that's when he went missing. That was the same night the keys were messed up at the yacht club and one of the boats went out without being signed out."

"I thought they got the keys straightened out."

"They did. The missing set belonged to an owner who has been out of town for a few weeks. The police are checking, but they think that was the boat that was taken out Friday night. They'll know for sure once they examine it, since it hadn't been used for a few weeks. The security guard keeps track as best he can, though owners can come and go as they please—but they always do a morning check. And all slips were filled Saturday morning."

Ben talked for a few more minutes, then promised to call back soon and hung up.

They sat in silence, absorbing the news and trying to make sense of it.

"It wasn't an accident, Ben said. Someone wanted Bob Chadwick dead."

The word *why* screamed unsaid in the room. And an avalanche of loose pieces of yarn seemed to float around as if to strangle it.

"Why was he on a boat?" Cass said.

"He likes to sail," Ben had said the other day. But it certainly didn't fit his schedule for Friday. At least as far as they knew.

"Mary Pisano said Bob was disturbed about something, someone. Danny sensed that, too. He thought Bob was onto something regarding Blythe's death," Birdie said.

"He was meeting someone," Nell said. She knew they were close. The pieces were scattered, but there. Had Bob Chadwick followed the same trail? A person hurt so badly by something his cousin did that he killed her?

In a short few days, Bob had met nearly all their friends. Casual hellos. He'd gone out with Pete and the others. The person he went to meet Friday night was not a new friend who wanted to have a friendly beer. They were sure of that.

Their thoughts pulled painfully together. They were filled with people and conversations and facts and dates, and narrow lines moving from one to the other, examining the connection. Throwing it aside. Hanging on to it.

Nell stared at the pile of papers. They needed to do something, to keep their minds working, to keep connecting the dots until the picture emerged clear and flawless.

"Let's see what these tell us," she said.

They took turns laying the bills and papers out in neat rows. Many were financial statements, mortgage reports, renovation bills for the condo in Sea Harbor. It looked as though Blythe was using her Boston townhome more as an office for the last few months.

More interesting to the women were the receipts and checks and credit card statements—a day-to-day record of where Blythe bought groceries and took her dry cleaning and shopped for clothes. In addition, there was a spiral-bound desktop calendar that surprised them. Nell picked up the calendar and leafed through it.

Izzy looked over. "I'm surprised Blythe wasn't more high tech. I haven't used one of those for years."

The cardboard cover of the calendar was decorated with flowers and birds.

"Who knows?" Nell said. "She was one of the only people on the board whose phone didn't ring during meetings." She glanced back at the large wall calendar she and Ben both scribbled things on. "There's a certain security in paper."

Izzy laughed. "You'd be lost without that calendar, Aunt Nell."

"Let's hope Blythe felt the same way," she said, slipping on her glasses, her eyes smiling over the top of them. She went back to reading.

"There's not much here for the last month. Board meetings. Those are in big letters and that's fitting. She took them very seriously."

Nell turned back to the summer months. There were plenty of Sea Harbor events. Yacht club parties, meetings with architects, dinners. Tennis lessons both in Boston and Sea Harbor. And scribbled here and there were dates with names of recognizable men.

"They were ever-changing," Nell said. "She certainly had an array of men at her beck and call."

"They were probably using Blythe as much as she was using them," Birdie said. "I don't think most of them are probably important to us."

Birdie continued flipping through a stack of bills, some paid, some still needing to be paid. She stopped at one, frowned, then checked several others. She looked at the calendar. "Nell, check the calendar for August."

Nell went forward a couple of pages. In one week there were several tennis matches, but they were all crossed out. There was also a line through a dinner event. A charity event at the Boston Mandarin Oriental Hotel was canceled.

Nell looked up. "She seemed to have put her socializing on hold for a week or so in August."

"Maybe she was sick?" Cass said.

"Maybe." Nell looked at the beginning of the crossed-off week. There was an appointment at a clinic. This one was not crossed off. And another a week later.

Nell read out loud: "Massachusetts Women's Health Clinic. Arrange with Bob." Each item had a phone number, one presumably for the clinic and another for her cousin's cell phone.

Birdie pulled out several checks and set them aside. "These are made out to the same clinic." She frowned. "That's odd," she said.

"What?"

"These checks are for more than a throat culture or cold. Wouldn't you think Blythe would have insurance to cover medical expenses? It looks like none was applied."

Nell shuffled through until she found the receipt. It looked as though Blythe had paid the clinic the day she went in. Nell lined up all the papers next to one another and looked carefully at the dates of the checks, the dates of the appointments. And a computerized receipt that indicated treatment. And a checkup a week later.

They all realized it at the same time, surprise showing on each face. Of course. It made sense now.

Nell looked up. "Her insurance probably wouldn't have covered the procedure," she said slowly, pointing to the medical abbreviation on the receipt.

Izzy nodded. "Blythe was pregnant."

They all knew how Blythe felt about having children. She would never have them, nor husbands. Never, she'd said many times. Another scar afflicted on her by the Westerland men.

Nell looked over at the bills again, then the calendar. The brief hiatus that her social life took.

August.

Liz's conversation about Blythe and the guest cottages came back to her in a rush. A dam burst as the dates lined up.

Nell repeated the conversation they'd had with Liz the day before.

"So Liz said she'd been there a couple times with this guy?" Izzy said.

"Yes. The timing would fit. That was probably when she got pregnant."

"And Bob took her to the clinic in August. Not unusual, since they depended on each other for that sort of thing. But it was Bob, not someone else, who took her, and perhaps that is significant. He clearly wasn't the man who got her pregnant," Birdie said.

"I wonder who else besides Bob knew about the pregnancy," Izzy said.

"Or cared."

"Or maybe cared a lot?" Nell's comment brought an eerie, uncomfortable quiet. She looked around the table, and then her gaze came back and settled on Cass. She sat in one of the large slipcovered chairs, scratching absently at the stiff spot on her jeans. Then she stared more closely at it. She looked up and saw Nell watching her. "Plaster," she said. "Just like on the scarf."

Cass turned her attention back to the bills and the calendar and checks, into Blythe Westerland's personal life, now laid out on the Endicotts' coffee table for all to see. It seemed a violation of sorts.

Nell watched her as she scanned the checks that had been set aside, the calendar, then picked up the clinic report and read it again. Then put it down and looked off into space.

In that moment Nell knew she wasn't the only one who had heard the story that had haunted her for the last couple of days.

Cass had heard it, too.

Sweet sounds came through the baby intercom announcing that Abby was awake, a welcome break to the ponderous silence in the room. Izzy hurried up the stairs while Nell stacked the coffee cake plates and carried them into the kitchen.

Cass followed her. She stood at the kitchen window, staring out into the gray day.

"Are you all right, Cass?" Nell asked.

"I'm not sure," she said.

"None of us are."

"Do you remember Blythe coming over to our table at the party?"

Nell's memory was crystal clear.

Cass's was, too.

Izzy and Abby appeared, and attention turned immediately toward a baby who woke up from her naps smiling, nearly every time. Her blond curls were slightly matted, pressed against her head, her cheeks rosy. Nell kissed her on the cheek, but Cass got the first hug. "Godmother prerogative," she said to Nell, scooping the cheerful baby into her arms.

Nell watched the power of a child. In an instant, terrible thoughts could be pushed aside by a toddler's joy.

She watched them for a minute, seeing Cass's lovely face transformed for the moment.

"Take care of her, Abby," she said to the baby. She turned to Izzy and Birdie. "I'm going to check back with Ben and see if there's a change in Bob's condition."

Izzy and Birdie looked at her, Izzy's clear lawyerly look in place. They both knew she wasn't calling Ben. Izzy and Birdie knew exactly what information Nell would be trying to attain. Almost all the stitches were cast on.

Nell stepped into the den and quickly looked up a number in her contact list.

She punched in the numbers, hoping Liz Santos wouldn't mind being disturbed on a Sunday.

Of course the yacht club manager didn't mind. Her memory hadn't served her well, but she had checked the guest cottage log. She was going to call Nell later that day. There were several reservations for the same couple. Or for the gentleman, at least. It was one of those lifetime memberships that the club didn't do anymore. In the case of this family, there was only one family member left.

Nell scribbled down the name of the family, then stood silently in the den, the dots connecting so loudly it was deafening.

She walked into the kitchen and looked around. "Where's Cass?" she asked.

Birdie was jiggling the baby on her knee, singing an old nursery rhyme.

Izzy was rinsing the dishes. "Her ma texted her," she said.

"Mary Halloran texts?" Birdie asked.

"Incessantly," Izzy said.

"Did she need Cass?" Nell asked.

"She wanted to be sure Cass had her prescription card. She needs to pick up some medicine for Mary later today."

"So she went home?"

"No. She couldn't find the card in her purse and thought maybe she'd stuck it somewhere in the car. She's looking for it."

Nell walked to the front door and looked out. She saw the backside of Cass in the open driver's door, digging around.

She walked back into the family room. "Izzy . . . ," she began.

Izzy nodded before Nell had a chance to say anything. "It fits, Aunt Nell. It's awful, but it fits."

Birdie looked over the baby's head. Her face said that everything they needed sat on the coffee table or in things they'd observed in just one short week—a week that seemed like a lifetime. Maybe they didn't have proof, but in their minds they had certainty. And the scarf that Daisy and Gabby had found might well provide whatever else the police would want.

Nell walked back to the front door. The car door was still open, but Cass was standing beside it now, staring at something in her hand.

Nell pushed open the screen door. "Cass," she called out.

Cass looked up. Her face was filled with anger. She held up what she had found. It wasn't Mary Halloran's prescription drug card.

It was a large gold ring holding a Ravenswood B&B key—with Bob Chadwick's room number on it.

Chapter 34

"**C**ome inside, Cass," Nell said, one hand reaching out as if to protect her, to pull her back from a busy street.

But Cass had already climbed into the small, fast car—too far away to feel Nell's touch. And before Nell could do anything, she backed out of the driveway and headed down Sandswept Lane, the BMW tires squealing,

Nell hurried back into the house, dialing Ben on the way. The call went directly to voice mail.

Izzy was standing by the counter with her car keys in her hand.

"I'm driving," she said. "Birdie is staying here to wait for Sam and Ben and play with Abby." She kissed the top of the baby's head. "I know Cass's anger better than anyone. We need to get to her."

Nell pulled out her phone and dialed Ben again, then sent a text.

In minutes they were driving along the beach road, headed toward the lighthouse and the oceanside cottage that was being brought back to its pristine glory.

"It's a good thing Red isn't with us," Izzy murmured. "She'd never let us stop at that house."

"It's a lot scarier now than when it frightened sweet Red," Nell said.

A minute before they reached the cottage, Nell's phone beeped. It was a text from Birdie. *Ben and Sam on way. Police called. Bob Chadwick is awake.*

Where is Danny? Nell texted back. If they needed someone to keep Cass calm, Danny would be the one. Probably the only one.

He was the first out of the parking lot, driving like a madman, Birdie replied.

They reached the cottage and slowed to a stop. Nell looked over at the main driveway. Cass had pulled right up to the cottage door, scraping Harry's BMW against a bush.

On a side drive, hidden in a thicket of bushes, was Danny's car.

Both cars were empty.

Nell and Izzy parked and walked up to the open door cautiously. Inside, the smell of fresh wood and paint greeted them. Through the screened door they saw a narrow hallway that led from the front door into a light-colored room that ran across the back of the house. Paint cans, plaster buckets, and new windows with stickers on them were visible.

But they couldn't see Cass.

There was a figure in the shadowy hallway that they hadn't noticed at first. He turned and looked toward them. It was Danny, with a finger pressed to his lips. With the other hand he motioned them closer.

They moved toward him and stopped at the end of the hallway, Danny's broad shoulders shielding them from whatever was ahead of them.

And then they heard Cass's voice. Angry and threatening. Her voice grew louder, almost as if she knew they were there.

"You took a life, Harry. A life!"

His angry answer equaled hers. *"She* took a life. My life. Stripped it away, without even letting me know there *was* a life. She took away my progeny!" He was screaming now. A frightening sound, as if he couldn't control the volume—or the words. There was a shuffling of shoes. Then Harry went on talking.

"We had been good together. We came up here, went on a couple trips, fooled around. Then it broke up, just like her cousin Bob warned me it would. I didn't see her around Boston, she didn't answer my calls, and Bob—he introduced us, you know—told me she was up here most of the time now. I thought, just maybe, we could put it back together again. I loved her. Maybe the first time I loved anyone. So I came up to just get the lay of the land, go slow. I called her a couple times, but she didn't want to see me. I knew she'd be at that party, though. And somehow I thought if she saw me there, maybe it'd be a start anyway. And sure enough, she recognized me, even with the beard. And she didn't turn away."

No, Nell thought. She didn't. *"Later,"* Blythe had said to Harry.

"I looked back and saw her point to the boathouse." His voice rose and fell as if he was unsure of his own emotions. "She wanted to meet me there. It was going to work out after all."

"So you went, you foolish man."

"You'd gone home. I went down. I thought this was it, sure, we'd get together again. There she was, behind the boathouse, looking gorgeous. I was going to play it cool, but seeing her waiting there for me, it took my breath away. I blurted out that I loved her. I wanted to marry her.

"At first she was in shock. And then she began to laugh. 'Marry me?' she said. 'Do you have any idea how *over* we are?' Her words were filled with laughter. She was meeting me there to tell me never to contact her again or she'd call the police.

"And then . . . then she told me what she'd done."

" 'That's how *over* we are,' she screamed at me."

There was silence. Even those in the hallway felt the anguish Harry Winthrop had felt. *A pain so great.*

They waited while the quiet grew, not knowing if Harry had a weapon. They tried to assess where Cass was in the room, if she was bound, how close she was to Harry—and what Harry's next move might be. Above all, what was the safest way to get Cass out of that house?

"I didn't mean to kill her," Harry finally said. "I don't kill people. She laughed at me, said I was just another foolish man. She took something away from me that was mine, that was a part of me. Can you understand that?"

But Cass wouldn't let go. She pushed and nudged—and scolded. "All those casualties—the whole town suffered at your hands. Especially Elizabeth Hartley. You tried to destroy her, too. What a cowardly thing to do. You stole her scarf and planted it. You didn't care who you hurt."

Cass sounded like a schoolteacher, reprimanding a wayward student. Nell restrained herself from telling her to be quiet, to remind her that the man she was scolding had killed someone—and tried to kill another.

But Cass was angry. Injustice did that to her.

"You're selfish and hateful and destroyed a life. Nothing justifies that. Not your pain or your suffering. Nothing."

"I didn't plan to hurt the headmistress," he said, so quietly that those in the hallway could barely hear. "I had no choice. Everyone would have kept looking if they couldn't arrest someone."

Nell remembered the look Harry had given Elizabeth when he biked by them in Canary Cove. As if an idea had come to him suddenly, out of the blue. The headmistress wasn't going to be home. How easy to find her house, to find something of hers.

It was also clear Harry Winthrop didn't plan. Perhaps Cass's approach to him was correct. Harry was a child, foolish and selfish—and that was how she was treating him.

"And that nice Bob Chadwick?" Cass said, her voice rising again. "Did you lose it there, too?"

Harry seemed to have regained his anger. His voice was louder. "Nice? Sure. For the ten minutes it took him to introduce me to her. That was nice.

"If you and your friends had left him alone, it would have been okay. He'd have buried his cousin and gone back to Boston. But you swarmed around him, comforting him, talking about finding her killer. He got religion. Started to feel bad, became determined to find out who was responsible. You made him realize Blythe meant something to him.

"So he started thinking about Blythe's life and piecing it together. And he succeeded. He even found e-mails about how I wanted her to have our baby. He took Blythe to the clinic that day. Did you know that? At first he didn't know who the father was and he didn't care. It was when he cared that it fell apart—and that's when he became dangerous. When he knew the father might have wanted a say. And he began to piece it together."

The steely edge came back into his voice. "I thought I could reason with him. So when he wanted to talk I said I had to check out a boat that night. We could talk there. He loved sailboats—I thought I might make him see reason, out there on the water. Private, nothing but the sea around us. So I grabbed a key from the club board and took him out. I could make him see what Blythe had done to me, what she had destroyed in me. I wanted to make him see. But he was beyond seeing. We argued, and he tried to grab the controls. The boat rolled to port, then starboard. Then back. He screamed at me, just seconds before the boom swung across the cockpit and pitched him over the side."

"And you left him there in the water?"

Harry was silent.

"And me?" Cass asked, her voice suddenly pleasant and ordinary, as if she were asking him for a ride home. "Do you want to kill me, too? And then who? Who's next, Harry?"

Those in the hall froze.

Harry's voice disappeared, replaced by a shuffle of boots, and then they heard an echoing, sickening click.

Cass's shout was all that was needed to send Danny Brandley racing around the corner. He skidded on the hardwood floor at the exact moment Cass broke free of Harry Winthrop's grasp and flew directly into Danny, with enough force to send him fly-

ing back against the wall. His head hit the plaster with a re-
sounding thud.

And then silence, and Danny Brandley's long body slid in slow
motion to the floor.

Before anyone could move, police sirens traveled up the hill
and through the neighborhood, and in an instant the cottage was
crowded with boots and uniformed men. Ben and Sam came in on
their heels, pushing their way through to find Izzy and Nell.

They found them standing behind Cass, their faces pinched
with worry.

On the other side of the room, on a police command, Harry
Winthrop dropped the gun, which turned out to be a blunt plaster-
ing tool he had shoved into Cass's side.

He hung his head while Tommy Porter read him his rights.

Before walking Harry out, Tommy told them—and Harry—
that Bob Chadwick was going to make it. The guy was a true sailor.
They were having him flown to a hospital in Boston, but he'd be as
good as new in no time.

And ready to testify.

An ambulance was called for Danny. Cass crouched at his side,
cradling his head in her lap. He was perfectly still, his face as pale
as the plaster that had tarnished Elizabeth Hartley's shawl.

And whether he heard Cass or not, she didn't know for sure.
But it didn't stop her from leaning her head low and whispering
into his ear, over and over, that she had never stopped loving him,
not for one single minute. She needed to straighten herself out. To
be the kind of woman who could handle love in a way deserving of
someone like Danny Brandley.

Harry Winthrop was a foolish diversion—almost a deadly one.
A sad man whom she could make smile while she sorted through
her own life. A selfish diversion.

But her life needed no more diversions.

It only needed Danny.

. . .

Cass wouldn't leave the hospital, but she promised to keep Nell, Izzy, and Birdie updated on Danny's progress—provided, that is, that they vowed not to tease him forever for his heroic attempt to rescue her. He had a concussion, a broken shoulder, and a broken pair of glasses.

But Danny Brandley was going to be fine, and no one on earth was quite as happy about that fact as Cass Halloran.

Chapter 35

No one had known quite what to call the evening, not even the faculty and staff. A fall festival conjured up thoughts of pumpkins and bobbing for apples—and Sea Harbor Community Day School's evening event was not that.

But it was a festival of sorts. It was fall. And it was going to be a beautiful night.

"Celebrating Autumn" was the name used for the event on the colorful posters Josh Babson had painted and spread all over town. The description fit the spirit of the evening.

But every single person who gathered on the lawn that autumn evening knew that the real celebration was one of life—a season of life. The life of Sea Harbor, life of friends and neighbors and artists, of the people who owned the shops and restaurants and bistros.

Laura Danvers had agreed to help pull it all together in a scant three weeks after Harry Winthrop's arrest—and a town's collective sigh of relief.

"It's glorious," Birdie said, leading her parade of friends down the first row of white chairs. The seats—row after row—were broken in the middle by a path and faced a terrace that was now a stage.

The pathway through the middle of the seats was marked by gold and burnt orange and yellow mums. And there were pumpkins, too, scattered in between the tiny stage lights. Teresa Pisano, her hair pulled back into a ponytail, walked up and down the aisle, straightening flowerpots and helping people to their seats.

Her cousin Mary, sitting in the second row, leaned forward. "Teresa volunteered to help tonight. And she apologized to Elizabeth as best she could. But I suggested she work full-time at the bed-and-breakfast for a while. And maybe I can get her some counseling."

They looked over at Teresa. Her smile had a sadness to it, but there was hope there. With Mary's help, Teresa would be fine.

It was a perfect evening.

"Gabby couldn't sleep all night," Birdie said, settling down next to Izzy and Sam. Nell and Ben were on her other side. "You'd think this was Broadway."

"Better than Broadway," Nell said. She wrapped her lacy shawl around her shoulders, a sea silk shawl Izzy had knit her long ago.

She looked over and smiled at Elizabeth Hartley, standing at the edge of the terrace. She was watching the crowds gather, a peaceful look on her face. She wore a shawl, too, finely knit of silky yarn in the colors of the sea. It floated over her shoulders, as if not touching her skin. Chelsey Mansfield had put in long nights, but finished the shawl in time. And Elizabeth wore it with gratitude.

A lone bench, made of iron and teak, sat at the side of the stage. Elizabeth walked past it now, up to the microphone.

She tapped the microphone and brought the crowd on the lawn to attention. There was standing room only, with people lined up behind the last row, just happy to be there.

At first Elizabeth's voice was faint, even with the microphone in front of her. But when Chief Jerry Thompson stood and started clapping, the need for words disappeared. In minutes the applause rippled through the crowd, and then became a roar as what seemed like the entire town of Sea Harbor embraced the headmistress.

When the applause finally died down, Elizabeth uttered her thanks, her face flushed. Then she collected herself and welcomed the town to their school. "I want us to touch each one of you," she said. "Through programs and caring and opportunity, no matter where your children go to school." The programs would be expanded, she said, the scholarships increased greatly.

She pointed over to the bench at the side and explained why it was there.

Blythe Westerland. Her generous gift to the school would benefit everyone in Sea Harbor through the school. The board would make sure of that. "Her name will be engraved on the plaque and it will be set alongside the flagpole, a spot that was once important to her. It will be a reminder of the good she did here through her gift."

They would be tearing down the boathouse, Elizabeth told everyone. A small studio would sit in its place—"A place to make beautiful art," she said, and looked over at Josh Babson, sitting with Ham and Jane and the rest of the Canary Cove contingent. He nodded slightly.

Josh would design the studio, she said, and teach student classes there now and then, but most of his time would be back in a studio on Canary Cove. Josh Babson had found his home.

When she had exhausted her thank-yous—although she said it would take a lifetime to really do that—she looked over to the side where the choir director was waiting. "I think it's time for the real evening to begin. The reason you have all come. Let the show begin."

And it did, with a bang.

Daisy Danvers came out and spoke loudly and clearly into the microphone. She smiled out at the audience, waved at her parents and sisters, and asked for a rousing welcome to their opening act. True to their word, she and Gabby had talked the director into having the Fractured Fish open the show. And open it they did, accompanying a cast of munchkins, a ballerina lullaby league, and a lollipop guild that welcomed the audience, filling the terraced stage with fluffs of color and joyful dancing—all while Merry and Pete and Andy played in the background.

Cass and Danny, sitting next to Ben, had trouble holding back laughs, though even that slight motion caused Danny to wince, his hand instinctively touching his shoulder sling.

Esther Gibson's guitar-playing granddaughter was next, accompanying Anna Mansfield, who was dressed entirely in green and singing with every bit of Kermit's pathos. She held the audience spellbound as she sang "It's Not Easy being Green." Behind her, Nell felt the soft rustle of tissue as the singer's proud mother wiped away a tear.

Gabby and Daisy led a group in a medley of songs—happy songs—about rainbows and sunshine.

But it was the finale that brought it all together. The terrace stage was empty, darkened. Quiet. The audience shifted in their seats, talking softly, waiting. Shuffling. Wondering if it was over.

But it wasn't.

And then the finale began.

The Fractured Fish appeared on the darkened stage. And with nothing but small spotlights aimed at their sheet music, they began playing so softly that the audience wasn't sure what they were hearing. A soft, rhythmic strumming.

Next, a spotlight fixed high in a tree turned on.

But it didn't shine on the stage musicians. Instead its beam moved back to the very last row of white chairs, behind the standing room only crowd who shifted now to the side.

Angelo Garozzo appeared first, a fedora on his round head, a bow tie beneath his chin.

He began slowly, moving up the aisle, his finger shaking in the air and pointing to those in the crowd. To the right. The left. His fingers moving to the tempo of a familiar Pharrell Williams soul song.

Slowly the familiar strains filled the air as the lawn came alive with the Sea Harbor Community Day School's very own rendition of the "Happy" video shown round the world.

" 'Because I'm happy. . . ,' " Angelo sang, his voice so rich and full no microphones were needed to pick it up. His head moved from side to side, and then his shoulders and his whole body began to bounce as he sang on.

Daisy and Gabby followed right behind him, their bodies shaking and moving, their hands stretched high in the air, clapping along to the rhythm.

" 'Because I'm happy,' " Daisy and Gabby repeated, belting out the refrain, their hands in the air, hips moving and legs spinning.

" 'Clap along . . .' " Angelo sang, his head thrown back and his eyes closed, the words filling the air all the way to the moon.

And the crowd did.

The entire school paraded up the aisle, in groups and pairs and alone: a joyful parade of students and teachers and lunch ladies. Maintenance men and nurses, counselors and administrators. Hands high. The rhythm of their clapping moving their bodies.

The "Happy" refrain repeated over and over, clap by clap.

They waved their hands in the air and followed Angelo toward the stage, their refrain so full and rich it began to pull the audience from their seats, first a few in the back, and then the entire yard filled with people who moved back and forth, arms reaching into the air, hands clapping in perfect time.

" 'Because I'm happy . . .' "

Elizabeth Hartley appeared in the line, her narrow shoulders moving, her head high, her hands free and moving above her head.

The refrain grew louder and louder as happy tears were wiped away and the parade moved onto the stage, with Angelo, Daisy, and Gabby in the front, clapping and moving and grinning at the audience, who they had pulled to their feet.

" 'Because I'm happy . . .' "

Finally, they bowed as one, the wild cheering of the audience forcing another and another and another bow.

And then they spilled out into the audience for hugs and apple cider and to continue their celebration.

Birdie and Nell found Cass and Izzy sitting on a flagstone step, their arms looped together. They sat down beside them.

"Group hug," Izzy said, and they complied, humming the catchy tune as their bodies leaned into one another.

They sang the refrain softly, the words almost tangible now in the evening air, their arms around one another, their words as one.

" 'I'll be just fine . . .' "

And even without clapping, they knew it to be true.

Gabby's Fingerless Mittens

Materials

Yarn: Sport weight; 1,2 balls; 130 yards-160/50g
Needles: US #4 or #5 DPNs or #4 or #5 circular needle 32" or longer, or size needed to obtain gauge; markers and stitch holder (or waste yarn)
Gauge: 24 st = 4" on US #3 needles, st stitches

Abbreviations:

CO=cast on
BO=bind off
pm=place marker
sm=slip marker
st=stitch
St st= Stockinette stitch
sl=slip
k=knit
p=purl
KFB=knit into the front and back of stitch
K2tog=knit two stitches together

Directions

(Knit two of the following; right and left mittens are the same.)

CO 42 (46, 48) stitches, pm for beginning of the round, and join to work in the round.

Work k2, p2 rib for 2 inches.

Work St st for 3 more inches (5 inches from beginning).

Shape thumb gusset

Set-up round: k1, pm, k to 1 stitch before the end of the round, pm, k1.

First round: k to 1 st before 1st marker, KFB, sm, k to next marker, sm, KFB, k to end of round. You will now have 46 (52,56) st.

Second round: k all stitches.

Repeat first and second rounds 4 (5, 6) times.

Set thumb aside.

K to second marker, remove marker, k1, sl 5 (6, 7) st to holder or waste yarn (these stitches will be worked later).

Remove marker at beginning of round.

Sl 5 (6,7) stitches to holder or waste yarn (these stitches will be worked later).

PM at beginning of new round. Join to work in the round.

Work 1 inch (1.5", 2") in St st.

Work 1-inch rounds in k2, p2 rib.

BO loosely.

Finishing thumb gusset

Join yarn and pick up and knit 10 (12, 14) thumb stitches from
holder or waste yarn.

Pick up and knit 4 st from join at side of mitt.

PM and join to work in the round.

Next round: k to last 4 stitches, k2tog, k2tog.

Work a half inch (.75", 1") in St st.

Work 3 rounds in k2, p2 rib.

BO loosely.

Finishing

Weave in all ends.

Grilled Shrimp Salad

Serves six

Ingredients

18–20 medium shrimp, peeled and deveined
½ cup minced red onion
½ cup minced celery
¾ cup fresh lime juice
3 large garlic cloves, minced (1 tablespoon)
¼ cup chopped cilantro leaves
½ cup olive oil
2 T soy sauce
2 avocados
2 cups fresh snow peas
1 bunch arugula
Salt and pepper to taste

Directions

Grill shrimp on soaked wooden skewers over medium coals, brushing lightly with olive oil, about 2–3 minutes on each side.

Wisk together lime juice, garlic, cilantro, soy sauce, and olive oil.

Blend in celery, snow peas, and onion.

Add shrimp to dressing; toss until shrimp is coated.

Before serving, toss shrimp and dressing once more, add sliced avocados, toss with arugula, and season with salt and pepper.

Nell usually serves this to the Thursday-night knitters with warm crusty rolls and an assortment of cheeses, gherkins, olives, and mild peppers.

(Nell also keeps a bottle of hot sauce handy for those who like an extra kick.)